# Life is Good
# and Other Lies

**Magdalena di Sotru**     **Sophia Soames**

ISBN: 9798354797721

ASIN: B0B9192JCH

Beta reading by Karen Meeus Editing

Editing by Debbie McGowan

Proofreading by Suki Fleet

Linguistic advisors Mary Vitrano (Italian) and Dieter Moitzi (German)

Sensitivity reader Vin George

*When we no longer have the kids to keep us glued together,*
*will there be enough left to make us stick?*

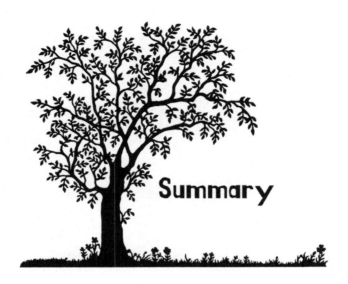

# Summary

This is not a romance. This is what happens when life goes on, when people grow and fall out of sync. Not out of love; some people are just meant to be.

Thomas at least hopes that is the case, even though he sometimes feels like he's clinging to his marriage by a brittle thread.

Frank clutches to the scraps that are left, knowing he's the root cause of Thomas's grey hairs, their kids being hormonal monsters and his own sanity being questionable at the best of times.

Gabriel needs to stop worrying and take control of his life, but with young kids and a body that refuses to do what it's supposed to do—to sustain and nourish and build muscle to keep bones in place—his feels like a traitor, laughing in his face when he struggles to keep it together. He knows he is loved. His kids are everything. But his marriage feels like a distant memory, and he's tumbling from one disaster into another. It's just...life.

Bruno thought this holiday would bring them closer together as a family. Isn't that what a trip abroad is supposed to do? Four weeks in the Swedish mosquito-infested countryside, sharing a farm with strangers. He should have known better.

Life is good. But the rest? Lies. All lies.

Trigger Warnings

This book contains the following possible triggers:

- some graphic descriptions of childbirth—a near-fatal experience for one of the main characters;
- a graphic fishing scene that some may find upsetting;
- discussions around menstruation.
- a brief flashback to a suicide attempt, and thoughts surrounding this.
- content warning for a rather large and clumsy misgendering comment.

We are authors, not medical professionals, and any flaws in our descriptions in this novel are our own mistakes. We prefer not to diagnose our characters, but they have the following traits graphically described:

- body dysmorphic disorder (BDD), or body dysmorphia;
- postpartum depression;
- depression;
- bipolar disorder.

Life is Good
and Other Lies

## Prologue
## THOMAS

*Private 3-bedroom lakeside cabin in the Swedish forest, far away from city life. Enjoy a peaceful vacation with your family, friends and pets. No Wi-Fi or cable TV.*

*The perfect place for relaxing and embracing a simpler life.*

*Vintage-style interior with original pieces of furniture, a cosy step back in time. The cabin has everything you and your family need. Three bedrooms sleeping a total of six guests, bathroom and living room. The fully equipped kitchen includes an oven, stove, fridge, coffee machine, utensils and cutlery.*

*Large garden around the house with sun traps all day, equipped with garden furniture, playground area and BBQ equipment. Several bikes as well as water toys, sandpit and fishing equipment are available on the premises. We have a sauna on site.*

*Rich, untouched nature with fairy-tale woods, swamps, a lake suitable for swimming and a wide night sky filled with stars. Unforgettable hiking tracks for true nature lovers, where a wide selection of birds and wild animals can be seen. It's a birdwatchers' and photographers' paradise.*

*Henriksvik village (40 minutes away) offers some small shops for basic groceries.*

*Pets allowed; no smoking.*

*Family friendly, gay friendly.*

THOMAS SIGHED AND read the text again. This was as good as it would get. He might have borrowed some bits and pieces here and there, some cheeky copy and pasting from other, more detailed postings on Airbnb, stolen in frustration after he found out he'd accidentally deleted the old presentation of the cabin. The draft he'd started out with had been somewhat different, less polished. Maybe he should have stuck closer to the truth, but it wasn't himself he was letting. It was the run-down former workers' cabin that sat neglected in their garden.

The house had once belonged to Frank's aunt but was now their responsibility and second home...slash financial burden. It was also almost four hours away from their home in Oslo, across the Norwegian/Swedish border and never an easy drive. It was one thing managing property in Norway, but doing that in a different country was more stress than he was willing to deal with. It would have been easier if Frank was here, but tonight his husband was drowning in another work project, and they really need to get this listed now. Yesterday. Last week. He should have done this ages ago.

He'd considered asking his colleague to have a look at the text but had decided against it in the end. She would probably have made a lot of suggestions and unnecessary changes and then complained about the photos they'd taken and suggested a trip to Sweden for a glamorous, more professional-looking reshoot. The pictures were nice, of course, but they weren't styled enough; they didn't tell the story of a unique cabin experience. Rather they told of someone desperate to get the damned cabin listed and not wanting to waste time fluffing pillows and putting all the cups the same way on the shelf.

*Fuck it.* He sighed and clicked publish. They only had a few weeks until their own well-needed break, and having someone occupy the cabin would bring in money while also ensuring the old shack got some TLC. Perhaps, if the weather stayed good, they'd manage to give the outside a lick of paint this summer.

"Dad! Can you drive me to football practice?" There it was, the inevitable crashing and banging, the sound of shoes being dropped and bags being flung against floorboards as their sixteen-year-old son Fredrik came running into the office. He and his twin sister Maria were supposed to ride their bikes to football practice down at the local youth club. It wasn't far away, but Fredrik was always late, and Thomas almost always ended up driving him, especially when it was raining, and the sound of droplets hitting the leaves of the tree outside his office told him it was. No surprise there. Oslo was supposed to be basking in the glorious Norwegian spring weather, but the downpour had been constant for weeks, and his pale skin hadn't seen sunshine since last year.

Maria would already be on the pitch. She loved football, at least the practice sessions. Having inherited his perfectionist traits, she was always on time, lined up and changed alongside her friends. Fredrik, on the other hand, was much more like Frank, laidback and disorganised to the point that Thomas wanted to scream. Their personality traits made no sense since they were the product of a surrogate and had come from the same batch of sperm. Nature or nurture? He preferred not to think about it.

*** 

*Dear Thomas,*

*We are a family of five and would like to rent your cabin for the entire four weeks. You have no idea how hard it was to find a property vacant for that amount of time. I'm not sure what kind of information you need, but feel free to ask if you want to know more about us. It's me, my husband and three kids. Is there enough room for us there? One of us can sleep on a sofa in the living room if necessary.*

Yeah, yeah, whatever. They seemed legitimate. Established profile, previous positive feedback, standard payment before arrival and an extra deposit to cover damage. Thomas and Frank would be staying in the main house for the entire period, so any potential damage would be limited to the cabin, which was a small risk to take. Thomas scratched his head, clicking through the prospective renters' details. A German couple, looking normal enough in their profile photo.

He accepted the request, sent back a standard reply with all the practical information and marked the cabin as occupied. Another job ticked off the list. It was only for a few weeks, and God knew, they all needed a break.

# One

# BRUNO

"SHUT THE FUCK UP!!" Andreas shouted and stuck his earphones back over his ears.

Bruno didn't bother to answer, and Gabriel just sighed as he tightened Lilly's seat belt, securing her in the car seat. She was grumpy and tired and sweaty and her legs ached, and Bruno knew.

Like most things in his life, this month-long holiday in a foreign country had been booked on a whim without considering that their car was an old wreck and the drive would take over twenty-four hours, by which point the kids would have thrown up all over the ferry, and who would have known that eating an entire bag of Haribo in one go could make a kid projectile vomit all the colours of the rainbow? Not him. But things never really went how Bruno imagined.

He'd known it would be a long journey with hours and hours of driving, of course, and they'd spent a ludicrous amount of money on educational colouring books, sticker books with glitter unicorns, damned expensive iPad chargers and holsters to hang them up over the seat backs. Yes, they knew Lottie got carsick easily and that Lilly couldn't cope with being strapped in a car seat for too long. They were *all* overtired, and it probably *was* Bruno's fault for letting them buy *all those* sweets on the ferry over the sound, and the Swedish motorway was driving them *all* insane. They'd already exhausted the joy of reading the foreign words on the road signs and looking for stray moose. There were no moose to be seen, and Bruno felt like throwing a tantrum himself, kicking his feet into the footwell and hurling abuse at the never-ending road in front of them.

"We should have booked the train. Done the Interrail thing," Gabriel said from the back as he leaned forward to grab the packet of tissues next to Bruno's leg. Bruno leaned in, hoping for a touch, perhaps a soft stroke, but knew it wouldn't happen. Not even a little caress of his neck.

He loved his family. Loved them to the point that sometimes he wanted to cry into his pillow and pick Gabriel up and shake him and scream that this was all he'd ever dreamt of and *please, please, please don't leave me.*

Not that Gabriel had ever even hinted at leaving. There was nothing wrong with their marriage. There was nothing wrong. And yet...*everything* was wrong. Things changed when you'd been together for as long as they had. They'd met at school, and then they'd messed about for a year or two before that night they'd got stupidly drunk and had too much sex and not left their bed for days.

That was maybe a slight misrepresentation of the truth. Bruno had fallen in love with Gabriel, then he'd found out a few things he hadn't known and acted like a jerk and broken Gabriel's heart. It had taken him another year to put that right—something that still overwhelmed him with sadness and guilt when he thought back to his younger, stupid self. But things had worked out in the end and...yes. Sex. Lots of sex.

It had been his fault; he knew that. It had been his responsibility to put a condom on his dick as much as it was Gabriel's to ensure he checked his levels and took his T. They'd both known all of this, and then they'd panicked and screamed at each other, and there had been tears.

So many fucking tears.

He remembered very little from that year when Gabriel had to come off the T and their lives had been filled with anger, resentment and fear. Looking back, they'd been a couple of messed-up kids, and they'd been so fucking scared, both of them. Then suddenly, they were supposed to be all grown up, responsible parents to this tiny thing they'd named Andreas.

Despite the nightmare of it all, Bruno wouldn't change a thing. He reached out and stroked his son's blond mop of hair, laughing to himself as he always did. They did that. He and Gabs somehow created the human being next to him, although there seemed to not actually have been a single strand of DNA from Gabriel present in their joining of genes because seventeen-year-old Andreas was a carbon copy of a younger Bruno. He still gasped for breath sometimes when his son stared at him; all he could see was himself. Where the Bruno he was now was all thinning hair and eyes lined by crows' feet, and he needed the dentist because he'd probably cracked another filling—another bill to pay—Andreas was perfection, a vision of youth and beauty.

And it still made no sense in his head. Bruno Moretti had a family. Who would have thought?

"I love you," he said to the rear-view mirror. Gabriel looked up for a second, and Bruno heard a sigh, but there was a small twinkle in Gabriel's eye.

"Love you too, Boo," he said, still trying to wipe Lilly's face with a wet wipe to cool her down. "We should probably stop in a bit, let the girls run around for a while. It's roasting back here."

Bruno nodded, mouthed "OK" in the mirror and winked, which made Gabriel smile.

Gabriel. His gorgeous, dreamy boy.

He was still the same. Still that irresistible smile that lit up his face. Still all that messy hair, regularly subjected to a buzz cut only for it to grow back within days into an unruly mane. He had a full, neatly trimmed beard, and his broad shoulders barely fitted between the two girls.

"You OK?" Bruno asked quietly, noticing that the front of Gabriel's T-shirt was soaked in sweat.

Gabriel nodded but reached under the fabric and scratched, a gesture so familiar it made Bruno ache. It was more a habit than a need now, but it had been a horrible couple of years.

Gabriel had gone through his first top surgery many years ago, and it had never fully healed—not the simple procedure the surgeons had proclaimed it would be. Infection after infection hadn't helped his already unbearable stress levels, and his hormones being all over the place had created complications. More corrective surgery, more infections and scarring that just wouldn't heal. On top of that, they had been broke and miserable. Gabriel had started a new job; Bruno had been trying to complete his degree. They had moved homes, and managing parenthood had been a constant nightmare, but Andreas had still somehow managed to grow into the beautiful human being he was today. No thanks to Bruno: he still felt like the worst father in the world. He had no idea what he was doing, and he'd probably failed as a husband too. He would always be a disaster.

While Gabriel had fought and struggled and given birth and then retreated into depression and tried to push everyone away, Bruno had been riddled with guilt over having caused most of the mess. It had taken him far too long to realise that his sexuality had nothing to do with body parts. All that mattered in the end was that two people needed and loved each other. No matter what.

Things were better now. They had to be because the last couple of years was something Bruno never wanted to live through again. No more. It stopped now. They were going to have a month's holiday and get to know each other again, love each other, have sex.

Bruno wanted sex, more than anything. But he also wanted hugs and strokes and hands on his neck and all those little signs of love that he'd missed out on for so long. He wanted his Gabriel back. He wanted his life back.

It had been another of their impulsive decisions, high on some misguided idea that Andreas needed a sibling. Gabriel had come off the T, and they had sought advice and seen a fertility specialist. All those things that had once almost destroyed them had suddenly seemed insignificant and distant.

Lottie and Lilly had come into the world seven years ago, and Bruno had cried. Buckets.

They'd survived, of course they had. But it hadn't been easy. Gabriel had been bedridden for the first year after having the girls and struggled to bounce back. The girls still wouldn't sleep in their own beds; Andreas had withdrawn into teenage angst. Bruno worked until he collapsed into bed every night, pressing an exhausted kiss on Gabriel's forehead as the girls thrashed around and kicked him in the balls.

Something had to give. Something had to change.

"I'll pull over here." Bruno turned the car into a small, wooden clearing overlooking a lake—one of those typically Swedish places with bins and toilets and a couple of rickety tables for public use.

"Good," Gabriel said, sounding defeated. "About time. My legs are all cramped up."

"Can we talk?" Bruno asked quietly. "When the kids are out of earshot?"

Gabriel shot him a worried glance.

The girls paddled in the shallow water without fighting for attention, and Andreas lay on the ground, the band of his headphones shielding his eyes as wind shifted the tree branches above him and the sun drew leafy patterns over his pale face.

"Isn't he the most handsome thing ever?" Gabriel said softly, settling next to Bruno on top of a rickety, moss-covered picnic table no longer suitable for anything other than sitting on. Despite the occasional car passing at speed, the forest behind them was peaceful, just the gentle whoosh of the wind and the pleasant warmth of the summer sun.

It was always safe, talking about the kids, complimenting the weather, discussing dinner.

"We need to stop this," Bruno whispered, looking straight at his husband. His Gabriel. His beautiful, gorgeous Gabs. Even dressed in a plain T-shirt and threadbare shorts, he was like one of those Greek statues in a museum or perhaps a fitness model—all olive skin and dark hairs down those muscular legs that made Bruno's throat constrict.

"I know," Gabriel whispered back. "I don't feel like me anymore. It's like I've lost myself in being a parent and not working and being sick all the time."

"You're doing so well. Don't put more pressure on yourself, but this holiday, I need us to talk, babe."

It was hard just getting those words out, but if he didn't, nothing would ever change. Gabriel hid and ran away from their problems, pushed them conveniently under the carpet and pretended they didn't exist, while Bruno chased those very same problems all over the place, beating himself up with guilt.

"I want to get back to normal," Gabriel said in a rare confession of truth. "I want to take Andreas running in the mornings, and I want to spend time with him. I want to play football with the girls. I want to sit topless in the sun and not feel so damn conscious about all the scars on my body and my stupid wonky nipple."

"Your nipple is not wonky, and nobody gives a fuck about some scars. You are beautiful. Despite all this shit, you are still the most stunningly handsome man I have ever met."

He meant every word. Those razor-sharp cheekbones. That cheeky smile. Those dark eyes so deep he could drown in them. There had never been anyone else. Nobody had ever caught his eye or turned his head. He'd always known this was it—that the man sitting beside him, playing nervously with his fingers, was the only one that had ever mattered.

"I don't know how you've stuck with me. I know this hasn't been easy for you," Gabriel said quietly.

"And I would do it all over again. I'd make the same choices and the same mistakes, and I would always choose you."

"Then give me some time to find peace with myself. Help me get my head back on straight. I don't know what I'm supposed to do right now."

It broke Bruno's heart to hear Gabriel talk like that, but at the same time, he understood. He knew how hard this had all been, how battered Gabriel's body was. This wasn't the future they had planned.

"I love that we made it. I love that you stood by me too, with my crazy swings in career choices and stupid study plans. You supported me when I was so broke I couldn't even buy you a bread roll for breakfast. You still loved me and fed me and hugged me when I cried."

"I can't believe you pulled it off and graduated. My little gynaecologist."

"On paper. In real life, I stitch people up and assist on the occasional C-section. I'm the most junior gynae surgeon, and I'll be doing the shit jobs for years before I get near something juicy."

"You pervert." Gabriel laughed, and Bruno's stomach gave a little jolt of joy.

"I only did it so I could get my kicks," he joked. He could barely believe it himself. Dr Bruno Moretti, consultant gynaecologist. Okay, he was getting ahead of himself there, as he was still a junior surgeon, but one day, he would have a specialist title in gender reassignment procedures and corrective aftercare.

"I know, despite all your shit lies, you only did it for me," Gabriel said. "All you ever wanted was to learn more so you could help me achieve the impossible. And don't put yourself down. You help people every day. The support clinic you run, the hours you put in on the trans helpline, the overtime for your charity work..."

"I do it for you, and for the kids. I don't want them to ever worry about being themselves. They need to have someone to talk to. If not to us, then someone else. Someone to listen."

He sounded like one of his own corny taglines. He barely talked to his son as it was. Whenever he tried, his efforts were met with grunts and foul language, and his daughters were little shits. He wasn't always sure his husband still loved him, but he hoped he still did. At times like this, Bruno tended to sink into dark thoughts, doubting everything despite the sunshine and the trees and his daughters laughing down by the water.

"I love you," Gabriel said, "and this was, however stupid, a good idea of yours. You were right. We needed this. A change of scenery and to get out of our rut. The fresh air..." He slapped his thigh and grimaced. "Getting eaten alive by mosquitoes—are you sure there were no cheap deals to the Maldives? Bahamas? The Cayman Islands perhaps?"

"One day, babes. But we're going to have the best holiday." Bruno grinned into the sun and let his sunglasses drop down to shield his eyes. "Because I always have the best ideas."

# Two
# THOMAS

MARIA WAS AS grumpy as ever, having been woken up too early and then forced to sit around for ages before they'd finally set off. Waiting on the front porch with her while Frank and Fredrik scrambled around trying to get themselves ready, Thomas could see more and more of himself in her, recognising the frustration over wasted time and the need to follow clearly set plans. Even his work colleague had commented on it, after overhearing a particularly heated conversation with his daughter during lunch.

"She's inherited your heart and soul, Tommy," she'd laughed. "I bet you were just the same at that age, and don't fight me on that."

Thomas had made a face at her. His younger self would probably have snarled and given her the middle finger, but he was older now. Smarter, wiser, more mature. Right.

Still, they had survived the journey, taking turns behind the wheel with whoever wasn't driving checking the satnav, placating the kids and wondering how people had made it through long trips before iPhones, headphones, Netflix and downloadable content. Thomas had even managed to flick through a couple of chapters on his Kindle before his stomach protested, but at least he hadn't been sick this time. That didn't stop Frank teasing or the kids making unsupportive gagging noises in the back.

Now they were here and already arguing like feral cats, and they hadn't even left the car yet.

"Maria, please tidy up before you get out."

She rolled her eyes, making a big show of dropping another chewing gum wrapper on the floor that was hidden under all the rubbish she'd accumulated since they'd left home. He took it all back. She was *nothing* like him, nothing at all, despite her dark-blonde hair and slim build almost identical to his own.

"Maria! You've been sitting on my hoodie! Oh my god, that's disgusting!" Fredrik chimed in. They were exactly the same age—well, he was a few minutes younger—but at times they seemed years apart in mind. In body, poor Fredrik had taken on those early, awkward features of adulthood but could still be childish.

"Fuck you," Maria muttered as she rolled stiffly out of the car and slammed the door.

"Language, Maria! And will you *please* pick up your goddamn rubbish?" Thomas glared at her with what he hoped was determination. She stared back at him with her usual steely defiance.

"I need to pee. Do you want me to pee my pants?"

"Fine. Go. Then come back here and clean up this crap."

She rolled her eyes again and ran off. Fredrik sighed deeply and watched his sister leave.

This would be their fourth summer in this house. They'd inherited it from Frank's aunt Bella, an old woman whose entire life was spent here. She'd run it as a farm until taking care of cattle had become too much, and for the last twenty years of her life, most of the land had been rented out to neighbouring farms, leaving Bella to tend to the gardens and keep a few cows and chickens. The animals were long gone now, and Bella would have turned in her grave if she could see the state of her garden, all overgrown, the once-pristine paths hidden under wildflowers and long grass.

Frank had told Thomas he'd never spent time here as a kid or been on any kind of terms with Bella, so when she'd died suddenly and he'd inherited it, it had come as a surprise to them both. In a moment of what Thomas could only put down to weird, sentimental grief, he'd agreed that they should keep it, but the glorious dreams of summers in the countryside, wholesome fresh air and Instagram-worthy holiday snaps had quickly been overshadowed by paperwork, essential repairs and the sheer cost of a second home inconveniently located way over the border in the neighbouring country.

The main house was a picture-perfect postcard: a rustic, red-and-white-painted two-storey with three bedrooms and a modern bathroom upstairs, a huge kitchen with a proper dining area and a living room downstairs, and a big patio and roofed deck facing the evening sun over the nearby lake. The garden surrounded it all: once filled with well-pruned fruit trees and a manicured lawn, it was now a wild meadow of anything and everything and in the summer was quite beautiful.

"Found the first surprise." Frank huffed, coming back outside, carrying a sealed bag with gloved hands. "Must have come in through the fireplace. It stinks in there."

Thomas didn't want to know. Leaving a house abandoned for most of the year yielded all kinds of problems. It wasn't an ideal situation. Never would be.

"There's something else! Dad! Come back!" Maria was leaning out of the upstairs window, looking flustered. "Tell him to bring more gloves, will you?" She disappeared back inside. With a weary sigh, Frank dropped the bag in the bin and trudged back along the path.

So that was the main house. Then there was the smaller house, which had been home to the many farmhands' who had worked in the surrounding fields. Aunt Bella had seen the possibilities and potential years ago and refurbished the house with what had once been all mod cons. Thomas and Frank had spent their first summer here trying to bring the interior kicking and screaming into the current century so they could get their pipe dream of a rental empire off the ground.

As with most things, it hadn't been an easy road to riches—at least, not as easy as the rental websites proclaimed—but the small house now had three bedrooms all decorated in light grey and blue, old creaky bed frames with quilts and white linen, bathrooms, a small living room and a vintage-looking but fairly modern farmhouse kitchen facing the garden. It had all been surface patching, though, and any small scratch would easily show their shoddy craftsmanship and Frank's questionable plumbing skills.

The house was perfectly placed at the end of a road in the middle of nowhere in the Swedish forests, turning what looked like a simple three-hour drive on the maps into an almost four-hour expedition due to the lack of signs and badly maintained roads. Their little piece of costly heaven being some forty kilometres from the village of Henriksvik and a couple of kilometres from the nearest neighbours, it was not only very quiet there—not a sound beyond the bees and wind blowing from the lake—it was also eerie and dark, full of imposing trees and rocks that could have been randomly dropped by ancient giants.

For all of that, the stars were brighter than anything they'd ever seen at night, being so used to the Oslo lights and city environment, and the lake shore was about two hundred metres from the front door, along a narrow, winding path. A small beach was visible from the edge of the patio, and they could now let the kids go alone, the lake being shallow and safe, the water clear above the sandy bottom. Further out, the lake held secrets, the dark waters full of magic and myths. Thomas often thought of it as a small piece of paradise. An errant, problematic, terrifying paradise at times, but still.

And there he went, just as expected. Fredrik, disappearing down towards the lake, bouncing a football against his knees as he made his escape.

"Hey!" Thomas shouted after him. "We still have to empty the car!"

His son didn't even turn around.

Frank returned, empty-handed this time.

"How bad is it?" Thomas asked.

"Not too bad. A good airing and a bit of a clean-up job. It'll be fine." Still empty-handed, Frank headed back inside. He seemed surprisingly unbothered, but this was the part Thomas dreaded and made him want to run away himself—the cleaning, making up beds, trying to get rid of the stale air and whatever other odours lurked in there. Finding their feet once again.

Down by the lake was a tiny wood-fired sauna, built with thick walls, a stove and a couple of benches. It was incredibly dangerous by today's standards, but they had kept it as a memento of old traditions, although they hadn't had time to use it properly. It took too much time to heat, and they never seemed to have those hours alone because although this was supposed to be a holiday, the work was endless.

There were other places, too, enchanted corners of a world long forgotten: a small waterfall where the river passed the hills to the north of the farm, with deep pools and dark stones that served as perfect benches in the lukewarm water after a sunny day; the field that magically opened up between the dark trees when you chose the other, almost-hidden path;

the cave in the hills whose walls told myths of creatures from another world. Thomas could imagine being a kid here during long-gone summers, exploring the terrain, finding his own places to hide, seeking out hidden treasures.

He was too old for that kind of magic now, of course, and Frank had never done anything like that, being a total city kid, but Thomas hoped Maria and Fredrik would find their summer paradise, their secret hideaways, and build memories they would carry through life. All parents wanted their kids to look back at their childhood with happiness. Thomas tried to hold on to that wish as he once again growled at the thought of the weeks ahead.

He had never been convinced of the place's ability to bring peace and joy. It felt like they failed epically at everything here, every year somehow overshadowing the last in catastrophic events. The first summer, they'd all played around, forced the kids to go out exploring, initiated activity, cheered when the kids wanted to do something on their own. In the evenings, they'd asked if they could watch TV, but there was no signal, no internet. They'd coped, though, going outside when the weather was good, reading books and playing old board games they'd found in the living room. Or so Thomas and Frank had thought, but at the end of that magical summer, the kids had decreed it a disaster and the most boring holiday ever.

The year after, they were better prepared. The piles of books were bigger; they'd brought their game consoles and more stuff for drawing. The kids had helped with renovations, made a fort in the garden, swum in the lake, enjoyed the small shop in the village on their twice-weekly trips to get fresh food and entertainment in the form of other humans. The main house had been transformed, with light-coloured paint now covering every wall. The furniture had been updated, and Maria had found a snake in the laundry room. Better prepared, yes, but they had argued more than ever and had all taken a sigh of relief as they locked the front door behind them to return home.

The third year had been a total nightmare from the start. The spring had been awful: too much stress and work and colliding school and work events, they'd all ended up with a cold before they went. Then a stomach bug had felled them, one by one, so they spent almost two weeks with someone being sick in one way or the other. The weather was horrible with loads of rain, and the roof started leaking, so they had to make emergency repairs themselves. Thomas remembered vividly the arguments that ensued—he might even, at one very low point, have yelled at Frank something along the lines of "Why didn't you climb up on the roof instead of running around naked?" In the end, they'd called out an emergency roofing service at a price that could have fed a small country.

Now it was their fourth year, and Thomas was once again questioning everything. They should have sold up and counted their blessings, rid themselves of this burden that had them in a financial stranglehold. The place caused more stress than joy, and the kids had been complaining about coming here again, ruining their precious time off school, whining about lack of internet and threatening to boycott the holidays once and for all. Maria had wanted to go work at a summer camp in France, and Fredrik had begged to go to an unbelievably expensive football camp in the States. Neither option was viable. The repairs ahead of them, just to ensure the house was still standing next year, would again no doubt cost them a small fortune and would inevitably become Thomas's weapon in any future arguments with his husband. He knew because he'd spent the past half hour in the car moaning about the cost of installing the mobile router Frank had read up on, a technical monstrosity they could fit on the roof and which might, on a good day, bring them a smattering of 3G.

Thomas sighed in frustration at his own bloody-mindedness when he discovered they only had crappy EDGE connectivity he didn't dare measure the speed of. He didn't know what had happened, as 4G used to work in the garden and even sometimes in the kitchen if all the windows were open. Maybe the holidays were a mirror of their lives, which somehow had become worse over the past months with more stress, more chaos, more stuff to do, more complications—sometimes it felt like the world was spinning so fast he could barely manage to hold on to it.

One positive: Frank hadn't had a bad episode for a few years now, and in theory, he'd survive this holiday with his mental health still intact, but he was stable because the projects that used to swamp him had stopped coming in. This spring, he'd only signed a couple of small campaigns for a grocery store chain, a far cry from his previous high-profile clients. Frank blamed the industry for moving on from the handcrafted designs he'd built his company around, leaving the likes of him way behind where the computerised industry had taken over. However, Thomas feared that wasn't the whole truth. Frank was exhausted, and Thomas was dreading the decline in his husband's health that the coming weeks would bring. The signs were all there, staring them both in the face. The tiredness and insomnia, the apathy, the way Frank had stopped taking the initiative to do anything and refused to take responsibility, the lack of affection...

The constant worry whether this was the day when their well-established fine line of sanity would finally snap.

Unfortunately, they were both as stubborn as ever and as bad at communicating as they had been when Thomas was twenty-three and Frank was twenty-one and life had been much simpler. In fact, the only substantial thing they had talked about over the past months was money. With Frank's income drying up, they had to rely on Thomas's, and as a university professor, he didn't make more than a standard civil servant wage. A fancy title meant nothing anymore, not when you were employed by a shitty university with no funding. He was supposed to take a research sabbatical next semester but had a feeling he would once again need emergency leave, and soon. He'd started to dread every meeting at work, every snide email from his team and the constant threat of redundancies in the science department. He'd have taken voluntary redundancy in a heartbeat, but they needed more money not less, if only to have a small buffer of extra cash, and he would work his ass off if that was what it took to avoid the shallow breathing when yet another bill dropped in his inbox. It wasn't that they were poor. They could pay their bills and buy clothes. The kids could comfortably do soccer and karate and arts and piano lessons and whatever, but their savings were gone, and it was stressing him out. Keeping Bella's farm had been a massive mistake, they both knew that, but it was a mistake neither of them wanted to address.

All of that was why, when his darling husband had suggested they let the cabin during their entire holiday this time, Thomas had been fully on board. Frank insisted it was his excellent photographic skills that had seen the place booked within minutes. More likely, they'd set the price too low because the renters didn't even question the lack of internet connection or cable TV, and while the cabin itself was, ahem, fairly modern, the surroundings were not. And now they were going to share their space with strangers for a month.

Two grumpy fathers, two grumpy teens, no internet. And strangers. It would be hell.

"We don't have to be social," Frank had said as they'd crossed the border into Sweden. "The patio and the veranda face away from the cabin. we can spend our time there. Alone. In privacy."

"There won't be *any* privacy. They have kids. Kids get in everywhere."

"Who are they? Do you know?"

Thomas had shrugged. "Not really. An Italian family, I think, from the name. Probably loud."

"Weren't they from Germany?"

"Yes, but their name is Moretti. Isn't that Italian?"

"No idea. Maybe they just live in Germany."

"Maybe."

After that, the silence in the car had been thick with Maria and Fredrik oblivious behind their earphones in the backseat. Thomas no longer knew their tastes. Maria might have his mood, but she certainly didn't have his taste in music, with the K-pop clones whining from her Spotify. Fredrik was different, easier, less grumpy, more stable, go with the flow. He was content with whatever he got, unless he wasn't, and then it was usually a matter of food, which he needed a lot of. He could easily eat five slices of toast for breakfast, then ask for more two hours later. As long as they had plenty of bread, he'd be happy. Bread and cheese and jam. And Nutella. Easy. Or he had been.

"I have no network connection, Dad!"

Fredrik was back from the lake, his face grumpier than before as he paced aimlessly through the long grass in front of the house and shook his phone in frustration.

"There is no coverage here, you know that." It was the second time in as many minutes Thomas had said it, but he tried to stay calm. "This is what holidays are all about. Getting off the grid. No internet. Enjoying the peace and quiet."

"But I need to go online!"

"I told you to download whatever you needed before we left."

"I know! But—"

"Enough!" Frank shouted, walking back from the house. His whole body was tense already and they hadn't even been here ten minutes. "Can you please just be quiet, all of you? Thomas, do we have bottled water left? It's too hot in there!"

He wasn't wrong. It was one of those sticky, warm days, the thermometer in the car having taunted them for most of their journey. The sweat from Frank's forehead dripped from his chin, and his T-shirt was wet under his arms. Even so, he was a handsome man, tall and willowy with a face that could once have graced magazine covers. It probably still could. A little more weathered and mature, Frank always turned heads.

"Can you guys please help carry the stuff inside? And before you unpack anything, we need to vacuum up all the mouse droppings downstairs. It looks like we've had a rodent rave in the living room. Not sure if the sofa's made it, but someone needs to fucking hoover."

Having made his demands, Frank shrugged and sat on the ground, then lay back in the grass, letting the hot sun soothe his temper. His breathing was laboured as he struggled to control himself. Thomas was struggling too. If he'd had a choice, he'd have gone upstairs to bed in the hope of waking up in the morning to a perfectly clean house and a hot cup of coffee. But like with everything, if that was what he wanted to wake up to, he'd have to do it himself.

"Come on, Frank," he goaded, then he grabbed the first of the boxes from the car and made his way towards the house.

The air was somehow thinner here, fresher, crisper, and it smelled different. It wasn't the lack of car exhaust and human smells; nor was it the scent of trees, flowers and soil. It was so different it felt like another world. Thomas breathed in and out, in and out, and it calmed his frazzled nerves, if only for a second. Perhaps with the air and the views and the smell of grass, they could manage after all. This place was supposed to be their slice of paradise, after all, not a prison sentence. He shook his head and, with a resigned sigh, kicked the front door open.

***

Thomas slept late next morning. He'd carried almost everything inside when they arrived, with some reluctant help from the kids. It had taken a bit of coddling, but they'd achieved a civilised family swim in the lake, after which they'd whipped up some pasta and sauce from a jar and had a few beers, and with hardly any arguing, they'd all gone to bed and fallen asleep.

Now he was alone in bed, and the sun was shining through the windows. It was probably that and the lack of blackout blinds that had woken him up. Or maybe it was the noise. There were voices, more than three clinking glasses, clattering plates, the sound of something falling and breaking, giggling and laughter. He tried to separate the sounds and made out Frank's laughter, but he didn't recognise the others.

Grabbing his shorts and T-shirt from yesterday, he sniffed and, deciding they were passable, put them on. He hadn't unpacked his bag yet, and they'd do until he'd had a shower.

As he slowly walked down the stairs, the voices became louder, the smell of fresh bread stronger. There was at least one other adult male voice, someone who laughed and talked a lot, and another, muffled by a bout of low laughter. There were smaller kids too, giving him flashbacks to when Maria and Fredrik were younger; happy, carefree sounds. Maria and Fredrik's voices now also blended into the strange symphony, along with another teen—a boy, he thought.

Thomas's mouth was watering. He craved coffee and fresh bread, the essentials of holiday mornings here. It always made Frank happy, getting up early to make a quick dough—he might even have started before they went to bed—his big hands kneading that dough into loaves, usually a couple of them, and rolls, loads of rolls. It warmed Thomas's heart and reminded him how much he loved his husband, those small gestures that had always been so much part of their life together.

Thomas peeked through the door opening, finding the kitchen full of people. The six chairs around the table, plus two more from the deck were occupied by two men and three kids in addition to his family. Two bread baskets sat on the table, still with rolls and slices left, along with cheese, ham and something that strongly resembled the mouth-watering salami he'd tried at a conference in Rome a few years ago. And there was Nutella, of course. He shook his head when he saw that the jar was already half empty.

Cosy as the scene was, it was too early for this kind of social interaction. Thomas quietly tried to attract Frank's attention and find out what this impromptu breakfast gathering was all about, but Frank was preoccupied, listening to the darker of the two adults, a smiling man with a frizzy mop of hair, the two of them clearly engrossed in a phone, probably looking at pictures. It stung Thomas that once again Frank was putting others' needs first before even saying good morning to the person who should have mattered most. He once had. Now he felt like he didn't matter at all. He was halfway to the table before anyone noticed him, and even then it wasn't Frank.

"Good Morning!" The man who appeared in front of him was ash-blond with a receding hair line and dark circles under his eyes that spoke of a sleepless night, but he still reached out to shake Thomas's hand and introduced himself, his gravelly voice exaggerated by his thick accent. Thomas missed the name and didn't offer his own in return, instead standing there like an idiot while the man smiled at him like he'd said something amusing.

The idyllic view from the doorway was a straight-up nightmare at close quarters. Frank barely acknowledged Thomas before returning his attention to the phone in his companion's hand. Maria and Fredrik were sharing earbuds with the oldest of the stranger-kids, oblivious to everything else. Then there were the two small girls smearing either shit or Nutella across their faces while making a doughnut from a slice of bread. It was like walking into a stranger's home, and now Thomas had to pretend he enjoyed the company of others before breakfast.

"Coffee?" The ash-blond man who had greeted him handed him a steaming cup of espresso.

Thomas knew he should say thank you and introduce himself, but this was too much to take in. He accepted the cup with a grateful nod and for a second thought about fleeing to the silence of the garden. He didn't, though. Just presented a polite, awkward smile and took a sip of his coffee.

This was not what he'd agreed to. And fuck this holiday already.

# Three
# BRUNO

"GOOD COFFEE," THE man said. He was stupidly tall, strong and muscular with days' worth of scruff around his face. He looked like he should be wearing a helmet with horns and body armour and appearing in a *Game of Thrones* action sequence. Bruno knew better, though. He was your typical overworked professional, anxious and tired, and now he'd woken up to an impromptu breakfast party that his husband, this Frank dude, had decided to throw at nine on a Sunday morning.

The guy needed a Valium and a week's worth of sleep, and if Bruno'd had one of those coveted pills in his pocket, he'd have happily shared it with him and dragged them both out to the big hammock for two in the garden that looked so inviting that Bruno could cry.

They had been on the road most of the night. First, they'd gotten delayed in the traffic jam of the century, then missed the ferry, and the motel Gabriel had looked up had closed down ten years ago and reopened as a pizzeria. Bruno had kept driving while Gabriel and the kids had slept, not that Gabriel had slept much, as he'd kept offering to take over the driving, suggesting they stop, pleading with Bruno to think of himself, but Bruno pulled all-nighters at work all the time, and he knew his limits. He was still alive and awake, so they continued.

It was worth it to see Gabriel now, laughing at something Frank had said, and Frank... Wow. Tall AF, handsome as they came and bloody charming, but he was totally wired, talking animatedly with his hands, his mind flipping backwards and forwards between subjects to the point that Bruno had trouble following him. By the look on Thomas's face—Bruno assumed the other man was Thomas—this was nothing new. He just rolled his eyes at the chaos and gratefully accepted the cup of coffee Bruno handed him.

They'd brought their own coffee beans, since Bruno—despite being the world's worst specimen of a gay man and much to Gabriel's constant delight—had in his old age become a total coffee snob. He might not have been able to dress himself to save his life, had never figured out how to work an iron, his gaydar had never been wired correctly, and he had so far refused to watch a single episode of *Say Yay to the Gay* or *Queer as Folk* or whatever the current must-see show was, and his idea of high-class interior design came from the IKEA catalogue—Gabriel very deservedly called him a disaster-gay—but he liked good coffee. His Italian genes would have revolted with retching and disgust at anything less than the overpriced espresso beans he ordered online. Then he would complain about the bill, stomp the delivery box flat and hurl it into the recycling while Gabriel laughed and stroked his cheek. Yeah, coffee was his vice.

"Bruno Moretti." He reached out to shake the man's hand.

"Strand. Thomas," the guy replied with a stiff shake only to then relax as he kind of swooned. "This isn't that Gevalia shite, what is it?"

"Caffè Diamante, L'Espresso Cremoso Italiano," Bruno said in his best Italian accent, gesticulating to emphasise the need for such extravagant coffee in the morning.

Thomas laughed, throwing back his head full of thick, unruly hair. He gave the impression of being a kind man, and from the smile he shot at his husband, he loved as passionately as he drank his coffee. Downing it in one go, he held out the cup to Bruno.

"I'll need a lot more of that to wake me up, and what the hell have you done to my children?"

Bruno glanced over at the two Norwegian teenagers sat at the table. The girl was helping Lilly with her sticker book, and the boy engrossed in something on Andreas's phone.

"I see you've met Fredrik and Maria." Thomas gestured to his kids.

"Yeah, and that's Andreas," Bruno said. Not surprisingly, Andreas didn't even look up. "And that's Lilly and Lottie. Lilly has the longer hair, and Lottie has a freckle on her cheek. That's the best way of telling them apart. To be honest, the hair thing is for us as much as everyone else. I sometimes struggle to figure them out. When they were babies, we put nail varnish on their toes so we wouldn't feed one twice and the other not at all. We were totally unprepared for parenthood the first time around, and the second time...twins."

"Twins," Thomas echoed, looking distant for a moment. "I feel your pain."

"Maria, and Fredrik? How old?" Bruno asked. His English was good, but he still didn't feel comfortable with casual chitchat, wasn't much of a social person, and thank fuck Gabriel wasn't either. They didn't entertain or do big dinner parties or go out much.

"They're both sixteen, turning seventeen this autumn," Thomas replied and raised his hand, fist-bumping Bruno. "Twins. Welcome to hell."

It was nice to laugh for once. Maybe it wouldn't be so bad, however awkward this impromptu breakfast date was, although Bruno just wanted the key to their cabin so he could tie the twins to their bed so they wouldn't escape or find some full-on death trap, read Andreas the riot act and then faceplant a pillow. He'd have loved to drag Gabriel into bed with him and made sure he slept for a few hours too. He looked so tired, despite his laughter.

"This is my husband, Gabriel," he said instead, waving towards the table.

"And the idiot burning the scrambled eggs is my husband, Frank," Thomas added.

On hearing his name, Frank turned and winked at Thomas. That one small action instantly calmed Thomas and filled the room with warmth and so much love, and Bruno felt a sting of jealousy. They used to be like that, him and Gabe. He remembered how the room would grow warmer when Gabriel looked at him, and his stomach would jolt when Gabriel smiled. It still did, just subtly. Calmer. More distant.

Bruno was jolted out his thoughts by a shriek from Lottie, and the eggs were definitely burning. Frank swore, and Andreas howled with laughter— at the strong language or something on his phone, it was hard to tell—while the boy, Fredrik's cackle was evil incarnate. There was no hope for the future, should those two become friends.

"Shall I show you the cabin?" Thomas sighed, like he was defeated. Like this was just how things were going to be from now on. Chaotic. Weird. Too many people.

"I'll just grab more coffee," Bruno said. He needed a lot more caffeine to deal with today. Preferably intravenously. Buckets of it.

He filled their two cups and slid into the hallway, quietly following Thomas onto the veranda.

"You Italian?" Thomas asked, grabbing a set of keys from a peg on the wall.

"Half Italian. Dad's from Rome, Mum's German. Always lived in Berlin, but Dad made sure we could speak the lingo. He lives there now. New family, new kids. We don't see them enough."

"Bummer." Thomas's voice sounded strained. "I spent years struggling to have a relationship with my parents. It wasn't good. Now, it's better. I can deal with it, but when I was in my twenties, things were God damn hard."

"Because you're gay?" Bruno should just shut up with the words because this was not how to socialise. He knew better than to be insensitive and ask intrusive questions. It was even part of his job to know this shit, but he was too tired to figure out how to politely converse with strangers and too worn out to care. He just needed to sleep.

"Nah, they were fine with that," Thomas answered anyway. "And they've always loved Frank like another son. He's easy to love, my Frank, entertaining and all over the place and charms the hell out of everyone. No, it was more me. I'm a grumpy, stubborn fucker."

"Tell me about it." Bruno's laugh was hollow. "I've been up for twenty-four hours and I can barely function. Thank God for coffee."

"Good start to the holidays." Thomas reached out and clinked his cup against Bruno's. "I should have offered you a beer."

"Beer would've been good, but I need to hit the sack for a few hours at some point or I will be the grumpiest man you've ever met."

"I'll save the beer for later then," Thomas said with a wink.

The cabin was great. Beds. Kitchen. Bathroom. Essentials. A small veranda with chairs. Sunshine. It was all good, and Bruno took a deep breath. They could do this. They could stay here and eat and sleep and live. They could even scream at each other in peace. He had a place to rest his head and should be able to sleep. *Please let me sleep.*

"I'll leave you to chill," Thomas said, placing the keys on the table.

"I need to go get some food later, if you wouldn't mind giving me directions."

"It's a Sunday, man. Nothing's open close by. There's a petrol station about forty minutes away, but they barely sell more than milk and sweets. Sometimes bread, but it's never fresh."

"Fuck." Bruno rubbed his forehead. "Is there a pizza place? McDonald's?"

"We're in the mosquito-infested Wild West out here. Nothing for miles worth eating unless you're a moose, and we tried the bark. Not tasty."

Thomas was a dork. Bruno liked him already.

"Chill," Thomas continued. "There are meatballs, bread and stuff in your fridge, and Frank never lets anyone go hungry. I have no doubt that he and that husband of yours are already plotting some kind of obscene over-the-top dinner party, grilling hot dogs by the lake and all kinds of shit that you and I will be the last ones to know about. That's the way things usually go around here."

*Meatballs? Here around this small kitchen table, overlooking the lake in the distance?* That, Bruno could do. The socialising with strangers bit, though, too many kids and far too little sleep...

"Sounds good," he said.

It sounded like hell, but whatever.

## Four

## FRANK

FRANK STRAND WAS exhausted. Every bone in his body ached, and his mind was whirring out of control.

There wasn't a single reason he could pin down; instead it was all of it. All the stress. The mess with work. Projects that had failed, were delayed, were snapped by someone else. His pathetic anxiety and the urge to hide ideas and thoughts from his competitors for fear that they would steal them from him. Decreased income, no time for producing perfection, too much time to think about work, clients, family, Thomas, the world, life, everything. Some days, his head was spun, or maybe the brain was spinning while his skull was still because when he looked in the mirror, he seemed normal. His dull face, dull hair, dull smile, dull clothes, washed-out blue eyes—he wasn't sure what he saw in them anymore.

He didn't know if this was just tiredness or if he was sliding into something bigger. He couldn't find the energy to sit down and feel it, which he kind of knew was a sign, if only he could wrap his mind around systemising it. He'd relied too much on Thomas lately, letting him take over so many of the controls in Frank's life by simply being a step ahead. It had been a comfortable way to live; he wasn't complaining. Thomas had never tried to control him, never tried to force him into anything, except for maybe a few stays with his parents when the kids were babies and Thomas couldn't cope with them all. God, the kids, he loved them, they were his lighthouses, light fountains, sparkles, glitter, he loved them so much. They'd truly transformed his life, their lives, everybody's lives with their smiles, their laughter, the small victories when they learned new skills. Sometimes it was something new every day.

But sometimes they were a burden, and he was an even bigger burden for feeling that way because it was his fault. If he'd been a well-functioning, mentally healthy dad, it wouldn't be like this. If he could have been a better parent, one that had adjusted his life to them, like they always adjusted to him, then perhaps they wouldn't...*he* wouldn't be so tired all the time.

The trip yesterday had been exhausting. He'd ended up driving because that seemed the only thing he could contribute and then tried to block it all out and concentrate on simply existing. The constant noise. Thomas's worried glances in the car and his heavy sigh when he'd asked him to *please pull over and stop because we need air—can't you feel that?* The too-loud music blasting from the radio that nobody cared to turn down. The fighting in the back seat, he didn't know about what. The bang of the doors as the kids climbed out. The silence that filled the car. The pressure of the steering wheel against his forehead, the calm...he had to find it. The bubble had burst when he'd leaned too heavily on the horn.

But he loved this place. It had been love at first sight, the feeling of coming home, when they first got here after Aunt Bella's last will and testament had so generously gifted it to them. He'd packed and cleaned out some of her stuff, but there was still a ton of it in an old barn. She'd been the weird aunt he'd heard distant tales about, whispering voices when any of the youngsters came too close at a family reunion. She'd sent a Christmas card now and then from her farm in the middle of nowhere, yet they'd never planned or discussed visiting her, and the kids had never met her. He was quite sure now that she had been as sane as anyone, just wildly eccentric and full of unusual quirks. Frank thought he would have liked her had she still been around.

When Thomas had suggested they rent out the cabin to guests, they'd both been equally reluctant. No, Frank was more than reluctant; he felt an intense resistance to letting anyone else into his place. Their place. Nobody else should be allowed to climb their rocks, explore the tracks he used to walk, swim in their lake, stand under the waterfall—not that Thomas ever did that either; he was lazy as fuck and didn't want to fight the mosquitoes to get there—or look into the old barn full of Bella's stuff.

While he wasn't sure about having guests in general, he liked Gabriel, to the point that he wondered if this was how real friendships formed. They'd clicked immediately, and he'd seen something in Gabriel's eyes that reminded him of himself. He couldn't really put a name on it, but it was vibing between them, a burst of colour in his vision, similar but different.

The guests had arrived in the early hours. He'd heard the car come to a halt, the crackling of tyres against gravel, and checked his watch. He'd known they would arrive today, but he'd expected them to come in the afternoon, since they were driving from Italy. Or Germany, as it turned out. Next came the steps on the driveway, a face peeking in through the small window next to the door to check if anyone was at home, then a soft knock at the door. Frank had startled the guy outside by opening it as he knocked, and the guy had taken a step back and said something in German that Frank didn't understand.

"Good morning. We...we have rented a cabin here?" he'd then asked in perfect English, maybe wondering if they were in the right place.

"Yeah, yeah, come in. I'll get the key," Frank had answered, feeling strange swapping to yet another language, but at least English flowed in his head, not like the thickly accented Swedish they spoke locally.

He'd waved the man inside and turned to go get the key, wherever he'd put it, and was suddenly uncertain. He'd planned to organise everything before the guests arrived—print maps of the area, download booklets from the tourist website, leave the key somewhere he could find it. It was probably on the kitchen counter where he was baking. *Oh. Behind the flour, perhaps? Or under a baking bowl.* He had to bake the rolls, cool them, pack them, clean up this mess, put away the leftover flour and oats, check what they needed to restock. He wanted fresh yeast for the next batch, even if some dry yeast was useful to have, and more grains and seeds for baking. Everybody loved a crunchy muesli bread. *Dried fruit. I must remember that as well. A list. I should write a list. Shit.* His brain had raced off ahead again, while the guy stood there with a pleading look on his face.

"Thanks. Uhm. My daughter. She needs to pee. Do you think she could use the bathroom first before we sort the formalities? Shit, I don't know what kind of formalities you do. I forgot to print the contract and the stuff from Airbnb, but I have my passport in the car. I can get it."

Frank saw the little girl at the man's side, tugging frantically at his grey hooded jacket. "Ja, Schatz, einen Moment, bitte."

Frank smiled at her. "Sure. The bathroom is just over there." He'd pointed to the door at the other side of the kitchen, chuckling to himself with embarrassing memories on loop in his head of trying to get his kids to a toilet when there was none to be found. They'd ended up borrowing facilities from a fire station once, something the kids still remembered fondly.

Filling his mug with an extra-large espresso topped off with milk foam, he'd listened to father and daughter's low chatter from behind the door. They'd come out as Frank was about to take a sip.

"OK, so..." The man spotted the mug. "Shit. Sorry. I am so close to falling asleep. You think I could have a cup of coffee? We have coffee beans in the car. You can have some later—"

Frank interrupted him. "What would you like? Espresso? Milk?"

"A double espresso?"

"Sure thing." Frank quickly and efficiently made the drink and noticed the guy's lightly shaking hands as he took the cup from him, the relief as he lifted it. He closed his eyes and sniffed, a little smile on his lips before the cup touched them.

"Papi! Ich habe Hunger!" The little girl tugged at her father's jacket and gabbled so quickly Frank couldn't follow what she was saying. She glanced past him at the rolls he'd left proving on the countertop when these people had knocked on the door.

"Oh, you're hungry?" He smiled at her. "Eh...bist du hungrig?" He had no idea if that was actually a proper German sentence, but he thought so. Apparently, some of the things Frau Müller had tried to teach them way back at school had stuck. "Do you want to stay for breakfast before you get settled in the cabin? I was just about to bake some more of these rolls." He waved at the four trays behind him.

He saw the man swallow all his embarrassment and pride, the obvious tiredness clouding his judgement. "Ehr, yes, please." He looked down at the little girl. "Wir können zum Frühstück bleiben. Du kannst ein paar Brötchen haben, wenn sie fertig sind."

Frank smiled at them. "We have some bread left from yesterday if she wants some right now. What would she like on it? Or does she prefer it plain? Or toasted, perhaps? We have jam, cheese, liver paté, salami, ham, caviar, Nutella—"

"Nutella!" Her face lit up.

"Oh, she speaks English?"

"No, but I think you gave her a pretty universal offer," the guy said with a chuckle.

"What about the rest of your family?"

"They're in the car. They were still sleeping when we arrived."

"Why don't you go fetch them while I set the table and get out some more food?"

"That sounds terrific. I'll bring in the coffee beans. I'm Bruno, by the way."

Soon after, the kitchen had been full of people and sound and chaos, and it was a surprisingly welcome bliss. The kids seemed to get along well, especially after Bruno dug out an enormous bag of Haribo sweets and melted Kinder chocolates, and Frank had spent half an hour or an hour or two, he really had no idea, talking to Gabriel, Bruno's husband. Looking a little younger than his husband, Gabriel was witty and charming and smiled a lot, and it felt like they'd somehow connected, the conversation flowing effortlessly as the topics jumped from art and drawings and photography and film making to politics and family and loads of stuff he couldn't remember now, except that it had all been interesting and energising to hear about.

Now the guests were back in the cabin. Thomas had taken them there while Frank cleaned the breakfast table, or at least he'd taken Bruno there. Frank wasn't sure where Gabriel and the kids had gone, but it was quiet inside and he couldn't hear any voices from the outside either.

The spreads from the table had migrated to the countertop next to the fridge. Although he couldn't remember moving them there, it made it easier to stack them into the boxes Thomas had bought two years ago. They could do with a second fridge, though: one was not enough when you had to shop for the entire week. They'd brought two shelves' worth of jam and cheese and cold cuts and other spreads, plus dinner for several days, barbecue stuff, condiments, salmon, meatballs, fresh pasta. The last of those made Frank frown. Why did Thomas insist on buying it when Frank had told him more than once that it took a mere half an hour to make fresh pasta, and it was next to free, not to mention being better than the pre-processed, plastic-wrapped shit that was now taking up precious space in the fridge.

They'd been throwing too many insults at each other recently. Not big ones, just small snippets of sarcasm now and then, back and forth, without really meaning to be mean, but it was exhausting. Frank would stiffen whenever they had more than a simple conversation, waiting for the next little poke and knowing that the answers to all their problems were staring them both in the face. They needed to talk. There were things that needed to be said, inevitable things that were bloody hard to even think about, because there was only one way to go from here.

The distance between the countertop and the table suddenly felt like kilometres even though it was five metres at most. He leaned back against the counter and looked at the mess, trying to figure out what to do next. Plates. Glasses. Cutlery. Napkins. Wads of paper soaked with milk and juice. Carry everything between the table and the counter, which would be several trips. Fill the dishwasher. Clean the table. Brush the floor. So many things to do.

He slid down against the cabinet door and sat on the floor. The surfaces were hard against his body, yet when he rested his head against the door, he felt the ache in his neck ease. It had been too long since he properly tried to relax. His heavy eyelids drooped over his eyes, the room getting darker as his shoulders slumped and his nails scraped against his palms as his hands slid down his thigh. Everything felt heavier, softer, limper, like he was about to melt all over the floor, going from his human shape to something flat.

He could see the dirt better from down here, the dirt and the mess. Strange-coloured streaks ran down the cupboard fronts, and there was a nasty-looking, grey layer of smudge around the doorknobs. There was dust under the cabinets along with something grey and sticky, a pile of clothes, shoes, toys and papers behind the door and a bag filled with recycling next to it. It must have been there since last year, which was appalling. They couldn't even keep up with simple household tasks.

The sudden sound from the fridge startled him. It was a really loud, high-pitched hum that felt like it had pierced his head. He pressed his arms against his ears, squeezing his cheekbones. If he pushed any harder, it would hurt, and maybe the pain would remind him of something else, although he wasn't sure what.

# Five
# GABRIEL

Bruno had been right about one thing. Things were truly shit.

Most of it was in his head, Gabriel knew that, but he seemed to be having never-ending, wall-banging unsolvable issues with everything lately. Kind of like a really fucked-up midlife crisis. Not that he was anywhere near a crisis, because God knew, they'd had a few of those, and this was nothing compared to the absolute mayhem of disasters they'd lived through in the past. This? Nada. Zilch. Their doctor had said most of his issues were stress related. Take some vitamins, the woman had said. Cut down the caffeine and get plenty of rest. Drink less wine.

Bullshit.

None of those simple life hacks would even touch the surface of the iceberg of issues swirling around in his head because here he was, standing in front of a mirror in a strange house in a foreign country, looking at himself once again and wondering what the hell had happened.

So yes, he more than 'passed as a man' these days, in every fucking way. He couldn't even remember the last time he'd questioned himself in the mirror. He could pee standing up with his prosthetic—when he could actually be bothered to use it. His body was his own, and he questioned himself more about whether the extra effort he used to put into his appearance had been worth it, even though the fake bulge in his trousers could still sometimes make him smile. Well, it used to make him happy, a small part of him that had once filled him with peace. Now he felt like a constant disappointment.

His fingers traced the scars on his chest. They should have been faint and barely visible, but to him, they would always stand out. Angry red welts where his skin had once been smooth. His muscles created the right shapes, and his shoulders were broad and strong in the bright light from the bathroom cabinet, but he still sighed. No wonder Bruno barely touched him these days.

It wasn't like when they were younger and Bruno's hands had snuck under his top whenever he got the chance, stroking his skin while sucking little marks on his neck. They'd been obsessed with sex when they'd first got together and couldn't keep their hands off each other. They'd tried everything, not only once. No, they had pretty much fucked constantly for months. Gabriel had built muscles in places he didn't know he could, and Bruno had broadened out too. Gabriel had run every morning, worked out, lifted weights, played football. He'd been so bloody fit it scared him now, looking at the remains of his stomach, the skin still a bit wobbly and the stretch marks like pale claw marks across his lower belly, with the C-section scars to remind him that he and Bruno had created three children. Fucking hell.

Those younger, immature versions of Gabriel and Bruno were the ones who had made all those ridiculous plans. Places they would visit. Things they would do. Jobs they would have. None of those plans had included having a child, or three, because they had been children themselves, stuck in a cheap bedsit and barely able to afford to eat. Yet Gabriel had been at peace with himself for the first time in years, thinking everything had finally fallen into place, and then suddenly, everything he'd known and understood had been ripped from him.

Except Bruno. Bruno had stayed and loved him, no matter what. t hadn't always been easy, not with all the impossible secrets Gabriel once had, but they'd made it, and Bruno had been there and kept his promises. He'd held him, fed him when he couldn't even attempt to put food in his mouth, told him he was beautiful when his body turned into something he tried to ignore, shouted at people who called him a freak and protected him from the world when everything had become too much.

He loved his kids, like insanely much. Sometimes his brain couldn't quite comprehend what had happened over the last couple of years—until he stood in front of a mirror and it all came crashing back like a bucket of ice had been chucked over his head.

Hormone therapy was safe and reliable. Contraception worked. He snickered at the fool in the mirror.

Top surgery was supposed to magically fix half of your problems. Fuck that.

Children were supposed to cement the marriage you were in. Lies. Fucking lies.

His torso was a patchwork of proof that you shouldn't mess with what you were given. He cringed even saying that because it was all his insecurities talking again. All the fucked-up thoughts that would creep into his head at night. All the questioning when he knew there was not a single mistake that he wouldn't make again. Bruno kept saying it, and Gabriel knew it too. The two of them would have chosen this path, lived exactly this life, over and over again, in every universe, every time. It was just that nothing in those ten-year plans on the carefully formatted spreadsheets they used to make had ever come to fruition. The trips they were going to take? They'd managed one trip to Paris. Apart from that, there'd just not been room to move in their budget. Not a freaking millimetre.

He couldn't remember the last time they'd had sex, the last time they'd touched without the hidden meaning or shared affectionate kisses without fear of having to give in to more.

Gabriel could hear Bruno some nights, pretending to fall asleep, then rolling almost off the edge of the bed and wanking behind his back, ending in silent cries, trying not to wake him. But Gabriel was usually awake, listening to Bruno's breaths, hearing the sounds become louder, his movements making the bed creak and the mattress jump however hard he tried not to let them.

Gabriel would have helped him, stroked him, smiled against his shoulder when he cried, held him as his body stiffened and his movements became faster and more irregular, his breath stilling before his release, and cuddled him close in the afterglow. He trusted Bruno and knew he wouldn't do anything against Gabriel's will; he could have been there for him, but Bruno wouldn't let him. Instead, he whacked off in secret, as if it was something to be ashamed off, like a teenager trying to not disturb their parents.

He understood Bruno's concerns about sex, though. Another pregnancy would kill them both, and despite everything, Bruno had said no to any more surgery, and thank God for that because Gabriel had agreed. Enough. They were all good as they were. Things needed to be good again.

They needed to not do anything stupid. Think. Stay safe. Keep things stable.

They had never been good at staying safe or stable.

They'd talked about another child, toyed with the idea like it could be an option. Gabriel had come off the T; they'd spoken to a fertility specialist and decided to think long and hard about it. Bruno had left the then seven-year-old Andreas with his mother for the weekend and taken Gabriel to Paris. They'd had the most gorgeous time, walking and exploring, talking— *really* talking—and going back to what mattered. Being them. It was Bruno's fault because he had finally gotten his degree and secured a placement, and things had been going so well. Gabriel had a good school and loved his job as a PE teacher. Loved it. Mr Gabriel Fischer was well respected and liked, and nobody ever questioned his ability to teach or his gender. Ever. He was stable, safe and happy, and the weekend in Paris had been the icing on the cake. They'd loved every minute, and yeah, there'd been sex.

They had fucked each other into oblivion, until they were sated and sweaty and sore, and even then, they had gone for it again. With condoms. He'd remembered the condoms. There had still been a risk of birth defects and complications, and they were not in a million years taking that risk. Even without it, they weren't ready. Besides, it was just another of their idealistic daydreams of perhaps one day having a sibling for their son.

Still. It was Bruno's fault. Or maybe it was Gabriel's. They'd never figured it out. Either way, six months later, Gabriel was asked to step down from his position since a visibly pregnant male teacher should not be teaching physical education, which was bullshit, but even Gabriel had agreed. It had become unbearable for everyone—for himself, his colleagues, the students, the parents—and now, years later, Gabriel couldn't even find the right words.

He pulled a clean T-shirt over his head and smoothed down the front, pulled his fingers through his hair, scratched his beard.

He looked OK. He looked absolutely fine. He wasn't fine. He was a fucking mess, but he still smiled when he walked into the bedroom, where his husband was half asleep, with his arms around Andreas, who was desperately fighting to get out of his father's grip.

"I need cuddles," Bruno grumbled.

"Get off me, you shithead," Andreas hissed in return, trying to bend Bruno's arm away from his body, which only resulted in him getting a kiss on the forehead before Bruno pushed him off the edge of the bed.

"Where are the girls?" Gabriel asked, a pang of anxiety rolling through his veins. *Calm down. Calm the fuck down.*

"With those other kids," Andreas answered. "They've gone off to look at something. That Thomas dude is with them. Why is there no Wi-Fi, Papi? You never said there would be no Wi-Fi. This holiday sucks!"

"With no Wi-Fi, you can use your head. Read a book, Andreas. Go out and enjoy nature."

Gabriel didn't even believe those words himself. He'd have killed for an hour on the net bleaching his brain with nonsense.

"More time for cuddles," Bruno said from under the covers, his voice muffled by a pillow.

"This is like child abuse," Andreas whined and clumsily kicked Bruno's foot that was hanging off the bed. "You can't force us not to have any contact with the outside world. I have friends, you know, and my YouTube channel and my gaming community, and this...sucks! How am I supposed to keep up with my Twitch?"

"Tough," Bruno said. "We're going to be here for a while, so get used it. Now your Vati is going to make us some coffee." Bruno sounded far too sure of himself.

"Fuck that!" Gabriel cut in with an involuntary chuckle. Andreas's language was disgusting at times, and they should be setting a better example, although Bruno still sounded like a disgruntled teenager despite his degree, age and, well, sense. "Get your Papi to get up and make us all coffee. I'm going to go and chill. Enjoy the sunshine."

"Come cuddle first," Bruno begged, holding out his hand.

He was desperate for things to go back to the way they were. Gabriel knew because Bruno was like an open book. Gabriel used to be a complete cuddle slut himself, used to love any little touch. At one time they'd been the butt of everyone's jokes, the two of them joined at the hip, always sitting on each other's laps, their lips practically fused together.

"Please," Bruno tried again.

Now, he felt so far removed from his own body he couldn't bear to touch it himself and definitely recoiled from anyone else touching him. He hurt everyone around him every time he pushed them away, even the kids, and he couldn't quite explain it. It was just the way things had become.

It wasn't all him. Life was nothing like what he'd expected it to be.

"I'm starving," Andreas muttered and shoved Gabriel out of the way with his shoulder. "Is there at least food? Or is this holiday about us starving *and* dying from lack of communication with the outside world? Is there at least a fucking TV?"

"No TV," Gabriel said like a fool reading straight from the handbook of bad parenting. He wasn't helping the situation. Bruno stared at him, gave him *that* look. Disappointment. Hurt. Fear. It made Gabriel want to throw up, hurl regurgitated bread and ham and coffee and shit all over their room. Bruno did this all the time, the guilt trip that floored him emotionally and then killed him off with that look.

"I got a bloody mozzie bite. This place sucks. Look! It bit me twice!" Andreas stormed back into the room, furiously scratching his elbow where two large red bumps glowed angrily on his skin.

"I love you," Bruno said, his voice low, his blue eyes dark. Gabriel felt like he was drowning. Andreas rolled his eyes and snorted, scratching his arm until it bled.

"I know you do." Gabriel couldn't make himself say the words. Not right now. "I'll go make some food. Frank gave us more of those bread rolls from this morning," he replied instead and walked out the door.

"Coffee!!" Bruno shouted at his back.

Gabriel permitted himself a small smile. "Get up and make it yourself, dickhead."

"Fuck you," came the muffled response from behind, where Bruno had no doubt curled back into the foetal position with a pillow over his head.

Gabriel laughed. "Fuck you too."

They were back on safer ground, for now. Keeping it simple. Stable. Safe.

## Six
## THOMAS

"Daddy, I'm bored."

"This holiday is the worst."

"OK, let's go fishing."

Half an hour later, Thomas regretted even suggesting it. After three days of constant whining from the kids and embarrassed greetings across the lawn from their new neighbours, he'd thought it couldn't get any worse, yet here they were, fighting their way through the bushes and trees that had stretched across the path, and the rain, which had been a refreshing relief last night, meant they were pretty much drenched by the dripping trees before they left the clearing. Their shoes squelched and whenever the person walking ahead touched a stray branch, the people behind would be sprayed with water. The kids were now walking at a safe distance behind him, hoping to avoid a wet branch in the face. The mosquitoes had also woken up, and Thomas was constantly swatting and blinking and scratching his face, neck, arms and any other exposed skin.

"Are we going on our own?" Maria asked.

Thomas was surprised by the question. "Yes. Who would you like to bring?"

"Well...the guests?"

"They're not really our guests, Maria. They've rented the cabin, and we shouldn't bother them. They probably want to relax and go for walks and stuff. Enjoy the peace and quiet of the great outdoors."

"Andreas says they just sit inside the cabin doing nothing," she protested, kicking a rock.

"I'm sure they've been outside as well. The twins have certainly been outside." Thomas tried to be encouraging rather than dismissive, and it was the truth. He'd briefly seen them by the sandbox yesterday evening.

"Andreas says it's super boring here," Maria continued in that tone that grated no end.

"Who wouldn't say that?" Fredrik added, sounding frighteningly similar. Bored and fed up.

"Well...nobody?"

"I like it here," Thomas said in a firm voice—one that was starting to reek of desperation.

"You're an adult. Adults like boring things." Maria grimaced at her own words. It was funny seeing her suddenly switch from whingeing like a seven-year-old to acting more like a mature sixteen-year-old.

The truth was, Thomas didn't particularly like it here himself. At least, he liked the house, the cabin, garden, beach, lake and surroundings, but he hated that it was a constant reminder of their collective failure. Every summer, the nice family holiday they dreamed of turned effortlessly into the stuff of nightmares, and this year felt no different, with that creepy anticipation of doom constantly at the back of Thomas's mind.

"Can we bring the boy next time?" Maria whinged on.

"Andreas. His name is Andreas," Fredrik said, scratching his arm.

"I know his name is Andreas!"

Behind Thomas, Fredrik swore. Thomas turned around and glared. Fredrik had a face like furious thunder.

"Maria pinched me!"

"Did not!" Maria looked just as mad.

Thomas's heart was sinking back into that feeling of total failure, and they hadn't even reached the lake shore.

"Did!"

"Maria! Fredrik! Can you stop, please! I am not taking you fishing if you're going to behave like this!"

"He's pissing me off."

"I just asked if she had a crush on Andreas, and she pinched me! Ow! She did it again!"

"Maria! Fredrik! Stop it!"

"Are you blaming me for it?"

"It takes two to tango," Thomas was shouting himself.

Fredrik just stared at him, said, "Fuck this," then set off in the opposite direction.

Thomas wished he could turn his back instead of watching Fredrik's as he set off, bashing branches, towards nowhere. Parenting was supposed to be easy, but action, ultimatums and consequences hadn't worked when these two had been toddlers, so he had no hope of getting his will across here. They were almost adults and had their own minds, and this was a holiday, not that he could find much joy in these critter-infested swamps. He sighed. "OK, are we fishing or not?"

"Fishing," Maria grumbled. "There's nothing else to do here anyway, and I don't want anything to do with HIM."

"So, you like Andreas?" Thomas asked. He was glad the guests had clicked with the kids. Even though they were paying to stay here, hanging out with the newcomers could be a welcome distraction all round. Andreas was probably as bored as Maria and Fredrik, and Gabriel and Bruno were probably as keen as Frank and Thomas to get the grumpy little bastards off their backs for a while.

"I *don't* like him," Maria protested with some effort of fury a mere moment later. "But he is nice. Funny. Easy to talk with." She scuffed self-consciously through the gravel.

"Good. Good." Thomas nodded a little absently. His thoughts had already moved on to other things—worries, ideas, the damned wet forest and who knew what else.

At least Maria helped setting up the rods without too much grumbling. They had no live bait, so the fake ones in the old-fashioned tacklebox would have to do. After a few throws with her rod, Maria had last year's technique nailed and was managing to cast her line further than Thomas. He was clumsy, and his lure kept getting stuck in the bushes.

"How on earth did you learn to fish?" he muttered at his daughter as he tried to free the thin strings from a shrub without catching his finger on the hook.

She shrugged. "Not from you or Daddy, it seems." She turned towards the water and pulled in the lure again. "I think I may have caught something," she huffed, struggling with the reel.

As the line got shorter, the fish came into view. It looked like a decent-sized perch, a bit under a kilo.

"Don't lose it, Maria! Be careful! Pull slowly!" Thomas was stretching out over the water, not even noticing his feet becoming submerged in the excitement of the first catch of the summer.

"Daddy! Stop it! I can do it myself!" Maria shook her head in frustration as she continued rolling in the line.

Finally, with the fish on dry land, Maria grabbed it with her left hand and expertly prepared to kill it with a stone. She was a competent human, and the pride filling Thomas's chest was not because of her hunting skills but because he'd taught her something and taught it well. He'd shown her how to humanely and correctly catch food, and that meant fresh fish for dinner this evening.

His thoughts were abruptly interrupted by noises from the bushes behind them, and a screaming figure storming out of the greenery. "Bist du verrückt? Are you going to kill it?"

Maria stared at Andreas, still holding the fish at arm's length, the stone heavy in her other hand. "Uhm. Yes?"

"You can't fucking kill it you...you...idiot!! It's a living thing, and it's probably got family and lots of baby fish to look after!" Andreas was waving his arms around, and Thomas couldn't help noticing the pattern of insect bites. *Yeah. Welcome to the beautiful Swedish countryside.*

He was a tall boy with an untidy mop of sun-bleached hair covering his eyes and a definite unhinged look as he stomped around in a circle.

Maria glanced from the fish to Andreas and back again. "Uhm...I think they leave their babies once they have hatched?"

"How do you know that?"

"I read about it. In a research journal."

"Bullshit." Andreas looked over his shoulder as if he was expecting a scolding, or perhaps he thought Thomas would back him up. "I mean, researchers don't know shit about fish. How can they know what the fish actually think or do?"

"They observe them?" Maria sounded uncertain. Meanwhile, the fish flapped violently in her grip.

"Maria! Are you going to kill it or not!" Thomas shouted, frustrated with the entire surrealistic situation. The fish was clearly distressed, but she didn't seem to notice, preoccupied by staring at Andreas.

"No, I don't think so," she muttered, a blush of confusion blooming on her skin.

Thomas shook his head, stepping forward to take control. "Let me do it. Don't let the fish suffer."

"You can let it go," Andreas protested, his hand gripping Thomas's arm in despair.

"Yes, we can let it go," Maria agreed, sounding bewildered.

"That's a thing," Andreas continued. "Catch and release, I think it's called. Then you can have the nasty pleasure of catching the fish without killing it, and it can return to its family."

"I don't think there is a family anymore," Maria added weakly, but Andreas wasn't listening.

"Catch and release is really cruel. Jeez, kids." Thomas shook his head angrily. "Look at the hook here. It's all the way through its chin. It's a deep cut. How can you call that unharmed?" He looked at Andreas, who gawped, visibly shaken. "If I release it, it won't be able to eat properly and will probably die of hunger."

Thomas grabbed the fish from Maria, who willingly loosened her grip around it. It wiggled slowly, considerably weaker now. He held it firmly in his left hand, thumb and index finger around its neck, and took his knife from his belt with his other hand. With a quick cut, he slit its throat and neck precisely before turning it around to let it bleed. "This is the quickest and most safe way of killing it," he explained, pointing at the wiggling fish. "It will die almost instantly. The movements you see now are reflexes from the nerves along the spine making the muscles contract."

Andreas and Maria both grimaced, disgusted by the grisly murder scene playing out in front of them. Andreas wasn't buying Thomas's explanation either.

"I have a degree..." Thomas began, but it was pointless trying to argue with these kids.

"I won't eat it," Andreas muttered.

Thomas grunted right back at him. "Him. Look." He pointed at the milt. "Definitely not female."

"It doesn't have to be male," Andreas protested. "Gender is not binary, and gender assigned at birth is not necessarily correct."

"That's true," Thomas replied, feeling like he was in a parallel universe of some sort, "but I don't really think fish care that much about gender. They hatch, catch, mate, repeat." He silently shook his head. Discussing gender assignment of fish with a seventeen-year-old vegetarian felt wrong. "Anyway, this will be dinner for tonight. We will fry it up in butter and serve it with potatoes and sour cream and chives—we have plenty in the garden." His mouth was already watering, while Andreas had turned a pale green. "Do you want to come for dinner, too?"

He didn't expect a yes, not after the scene that had just gone down, and the kid was clearly having some kind of inner boxing match of ideals and standards versus spending another evening locked in the cabin with his family.

"Yes, please," he accepted. "But I won't eat the fish!"

Thomas shrugged. "Whatever."

*** 

When they got back to the house, Frank was gone. He'd left a hastily scribbled note—*gone shopping*. Thomas sighed. There had been a half-completed shopping list on the fridge earlier, and some of the stuff he'd wanted had been on there, but he'd meant to join the upcoming shopping trip to Henriksvik, so he hadn't thought the list through. The nearest town was a good forty minutes away, and it was a highlight to get out of this place, if only for groceries and perhaps even an ice cream. Besides, the mobile network was decent there, so they could read emails and download some new stuff to watch and whatever. Fuck it. He'd wanted to go.

But not this time. He sighed and looked for Fredrik, but he was nowhere to be found either. The kid had probably hidden somewhere, found a secret cave where he could be alone. Thomas didn't blame him; it was bad enough with four people here and several times worse with nine.

The car engine approaching from somewhere between the trees could be heard a mile off, and soon their car came a halt in front of the house.

Frank jumped out, grinning with excitement. "I went shopping!" he happily announced.

"I saw that. Why didn't you wait for us?" Thomas asked trying not to sound too cross. "There was a bunch of stuff I wanted to buy!"

"I got everything on the list," Frank assured him, not picking up any of Thomas's hints of anger.

"Well, I hadn't put everything on the list yet because I had no idea you planned to go there today."

"Oh." Frank's face fell from smiling to shame. "I'm sorry, I should've asked you before I left."

"And I'd have liked to come, too," Thomas added sourly. "It's, you know, there's network there, unlike in this godforsaken place."

Frank tried to hug him, but Thomas shrugged out his arms. "Let's get the stuff you've bought inside," he said, grabbing the bags and peeking at the contents. "So, we'll have homemade pasta sauce and meatballs today, too? Like yesterday?"

"Was it yesterday? I thought it was a few days ago."

"And bread, did you get that?"

"Fuck. I knew there was something I forgot! You see, the supermarket's bread seemed so stale, so I planned to go to the baker's, but then I forgot that there isn't one there! But I can bake, don't worry!" Frank cheered up again, which just made Thomas's anger boil.

"Yes, I know you can bake, Frank. And I also know who'll have to clean the kitchen afterwards, and that's not you!"

"This time I will do it, Thomas, I promise!" Frank put his hands around Thomas's face and tried to kiss him. It wasn't even a kiss of passion, more a desperate attempt to calm him down, but Thomas felt too distant to care, his mind in a loop as he wondered how he was going to fit everything Frank had bought into the fridge and the cabinets. All stuff they didn't need.

Sometimes he wished they just ate crappy, cheap fish fingers and greasy chips, something they could throw in the oven for half an hour and wouldn't have their bank account screaming at them.

"No Nutella either. You know how grumpy the kids get when we don't have Nutella for breakfast."

"No Nutella?" Maria lifted one of the bags out of the boot and shook it violently, displacing its contents. "And no filled pasta? I love cheese-filled pasta! And biscuits! I'm so fed up with your organic sugar-free cookies, I want Oreo cookies or Safari cookies, I told you! Anything but homemade."

"Aren't you the one trying to be health conscious?" Thomas said. "You don't eat meat half of the time because it's bad for you, you say, but then you eat Nutella and crappy cookies?"

"They taste better than the other stuff!" She stomped off towards the house, taking the bag with her. At least she was trying to help.

At the front door she stopped. "And I needed tampons and pads, too, and of course you forgot to buy stuff for me—again! I bet if I had a mum, she'd remember. I have needs too, you know! But all you can think of is bloody organic flour and shit!"

## Seven
## GABRIEL

"I MIGHT HAVE done something stupid yesterday," Gabriel said as he joined Bruno on the porch in the morning sun and swatted away a few lazy mosquitoes. The entire family was covered in bites, and Gabriel had already used the whole tube of itch-relieving cream they'd brought from home. He was now scratching in places he didn't even know he needed to scratch.

"I've got a bite on my arse. I wore boxers, and the little fucker must have bitten through them," Bruno said, scratching desperately. His chair gave a dangerous creak as he tried to position the cushion under his bum, and they looked at each other in alarm then started to laugh.

It was nice when things weren't so tense, which they usually were when they were alone and didn't have the kids to act as a buffer between them.

Still laughing, Bruno asked, "What stupidity have you done now, babe?"

"The guys up at the house had some kind of argument yesterday, and I heard Maria moaning that her dad had forgotten to buy her sanitary products. I didn't want to embarrass her, but I gave Thomas a bag of my stuff. I mean, I only have it in case I have a stray bleed, but I can always get more. I said it was my friend's, but he looked like he didn't buy that. I might have some explaining to do."

"You don't have to explain shit, babe. You know that. People carry sanitary products for all sorts of reasons. They are great fire starters, and tampons are often used to stop nosebleeds—"

"Fuck off," Gabriel said, but he was smiling. "Do you have to turn everything into a joke?"

"Sorry." Bruno immediately sat up straight. "Don't bullshit yourself, babe. You're my husband and our kids' father. You do not owe people any explanation. Ever."

"I know that, but we also know what the girls are like. We'll be sitting at dinner one evening and suddenly Lilly will pipe up with 'Vati used to be a girl, and me and Lottie used to live in his tummy, and it was really tight for space in there, so we kicked and kicked until Papi cut us out with a big knife.'" He mimicked a childish voice and made a graphic stabbing action, loud and animated like Lilly when she was really excited about something.

"My fault, I know." Bruno shook his head. "But we've always been honest with the kids. Admittedly, Andreas was never one to share our private matters at the dinner table. I've no idea where Lilly gets this over dramatic attention-seeking showmanship from."

"From you!" Gabriel accused, keeping his tone light. "You're a repressed clown, and you know it. A few beers and you're dancing on tables and getting naked. I've seen you, remember?"

"That was once, and it was all your fault for making me drink Jägerbombs. I never want to see a Jägerbomb again."

It was weird sitting out here, leaning back in their chairs and laughing together. Gabriel propped his feet against the railings and watched the kids running around screaming; even Andreas had ventured outside and was lazily sunbathing on a towel with his headphones on.

"Is he wearing sunscreen?" Bruno asked leaning forward, the bottle already in his hand. No doubt he would shortly be handing out skin cancer facts like any of his kids actually cared.

"Chill, Papi." Gabriel laughed. "He's got it. Remember when he burnt his chest to a crisp a few weeks back? He won't be doing that again. I saw him with the bottle earlier. He's pretty much slathered in it."

"Good." Bruno sighed. "Fuck, I'm trying so hard to be chill and de-stress, but every so often I just get all wound up. Like food. We need to buy food. Andreas hasn't eaten anything healthy in days. He can't live off pasta and bread for every meal."

"Maybe we should venture out?" Gabriel suggested but was interrupted from saying more by another shriek. The girls were taking turns jumping out of a tree, daring each other to go higher and higher. It should have freaked him out, but...they were having fun. Besides, it wasn't as if the tree was any higher than the playground equipment at their local park in Berlin, *and* they were getting physical exercise and honing their distance-judging skills. "You're the doctor here. You can tell the girls when to stop. I'm going to go and sunbathe with our oldest kid—the one who's not causing me to have a heart attack every thirty seconds."

"They're fine." Bruno picked up their cups. "I'll make more coffee. You go chill."

"We still need food."

"I'll take Andreas out later and find network and food. I promised him. He's asked for chia seeds and that yeast flake shit he pours on his food. I doubt they sell it here in the sticks. Who raised this kid? Yeast flakes? When I was his age, I would happily have lived off paprika crisps. The cheap kind." He disappeared back into the house.

Gabriel took a deep breath before pulling his T-shirt over his head. Filling the palm of his hand with sun cream, he smeared it over his chest first with strong, firm movements, then moved on to his shoulders, neck, behind the ears, face, arms...a little more on the chest.

He self-consciously wanted to cover himself back up, just in case someone walked past. It was stupid, and almost an automatic instinct.

Standing to kick off his pants, he tried to remember the last time he'd been misgendered. His features were unmistakably male, his voice dark and deep. He was OK. He was, well, himself. He liked the shape of his chest under clothes. But naked...it was not quite the perfection his younger self had naively hoped for. The older him was grateful to be alive, yet he still shuddered at the sight of his bare skin. The muscles sat tight in the right places, but the scars would always be there and there were so many; the wedge of soggy skin on his stomach; the welts cradling those red scars. He tried to see the positives, but the negatives were still there reminding him of how things had been and bad times. Some really bad times.

"Let me do your back."

The coffee cups touched down on the table, and a gentle kiss was pressed to Gabriel's neck as Bruno's hands travelled down his back. It felt surprisingly...fine.

"Take your coffee with you, go sit in the sun. Get some colour in your cheeks."

Gabriel had always loved the sound of Bruno's voice. The softness when he spoke to him was like a caress that made him all warm on the inside.

"Love you," he whispered. He meant it. Despite everything they'd been through, the idea of life without this man by his side was unthinkable. Bruno had been an awkward teen with unkempt hair, bad skin and glasses that had never fitted his slim face. He still had all those features, along with crow's feet and a thinning hairline, but he was still his Bruno. He still made Gabriel's head spin.

"I thought, when I was having top surgery all those years ago, it would miraculously solve all my problems, like someone would wave a magic wand over my life and everything would fall into place," he admitted almost absentmindedly, the words spilling out from almost nowhere. Bruno's hands came to a slow rest on his shoulders, tense and tentative like he expected Gabriel to pull away at any second. "Then I thought, if I could just get back on the hormones, things would be fine. Then it changed to if I could just get my T levels stable again, I would feel better. I still don't feel like myself. I don't know what to do."

"I know." Bruno voice was full of nerves. "I thought it would, too. We were young and still naive despite being fathers and having our own home and even managing to budget and pay bills. My dad was really impressed with me—for the first time ever, I think. He liked you too. Remember? He sat down and just stared at you and said, 'You're nothing like I thought you would be, and I'm glad because you're a fine young man and I'm proud to call you my son-in-law.' Or something like that."

"Yeah." Gabriel smiled at the memory. It had been the same for him. The cold, distant father figure he'd imagined was a far cry from the man who had sat at their rickety second-hand kitchen table that day. They had a good relationship with Ludovico and his wife, and that was something that made them both happy.

"Give yourself some time," Bruno said. "The girls are just about sleeping through now, sometimes even in their own beds. You're back working full time, and money-wise, we're fine. We have less stress. Just enjoy it."

Bruno sounded so sure, as if he was sharing definite truths, while Gabriel doubted every single word. It had become a habit, as if his brain couldn't compute anything other than *everything goes wrong all the time*, over and over again.

"I hate this job. I didn't do all that training and three years of uni to be some stupid personal trainer. I want to teach again. I want to be Herr Fischer, the PE teacher, not Gabe the freaking personal trainer. Gabe the trainer is a pompous twat trying to change frumpy housewives into Kim Kardashians, and I can't stand it. I work them over, I tell them what to do, and then they smile and nod and go and drink lattes and eat giant chocolate muffins. Then they come back and blame me for putting on another two kilos. Not my fault."

He was shouting. Bruno stared at him and blew air out of his mouth. Gabriel knew what Bruno was thinking without him having to say it. *Chill. Calm down. I'm here. It's you and me. You and me against the world.*

"You don't have to do anything, babe. If you want to teach, go apply for jobs. If you want to quit the gym job, then resign. We can cope. I know it's not easy."

Bruno's arms were around him before he had a chance to escape, smothering him in warmth while kissing his neck. Gabriel tensed, and Bruno eased off but didn't release him.

"I thought," Bruno said, circling Gabriel's wrist with his fingers, his thumb circling lazily over the sensitive skin. "I thought maybe I should see if I can get a vasectomy."

"We said no more operations, Bruno," Gabriel said sternly. Bruno flinched but turned Gabriel around so they were facing each other. His blue eyes fixed on Gabriel's own, flickering back and forth.

"Not having sex with you is killing me, babe, but I don't want to hurt you. I can't risk fucking losing you again. I can't. I couldn't live with myself."

"I don't want you to risk it either. Surgery is not a good thing in our family. Things always go wrong." Gabriel could barely look up. This was hard. These were all the things he didn't want to discuss or even think about. His breaths were suddenly too heavy, fast and laboured.

"It's a simple procedure. In and out. I'd go to the Uroxx clinic, not the hospital. I don't like the idea of my colleagues handling my dick. That would be...yeah. *Peinlich*. Weird. Wrong. On so many levels." Bruno laughed, and Gabriel knew what he was doing. He was trying to make light. *A simple procedure. In and out.* Not a life-changing, death-defying surgery, as it would inevitably become in Gabriel's head.

"Can we not think about it right now?" Gabriel whispered, lightly resting his forehead against Bruno's cheek, craving a little contact to soothe his racing heart and panicking thoughts.

"We'll talk about it later," Bruno whispered back. "Now go and lie in the sun and catch some rays."

There was nobody around apart from Bruno and the kids, and for once Gabriel didn't feel so damn self-conscious. It was fine, sitting in one of the deckchairs casually placed in the middle of the lawn and letting his neglected, pale skin catch some of the sun's warmth. Hopefully, it would give him a healthy glow instead of the stress-induced grey sheen that city living brought.

Andreas had disappeared, probably gone inside, and the girls left him alone. Having discovered a caterpillar, they had quickly gone from being trapeze artists in that tree to creating a caterpillar farm complete with a McDonald's toy in the grass. He chuckled to himself, listening to their conversations. The only other sound was the wind rustling the leaves, and for a moment, life was soothing, peaceful—

"Can I sit?"

The question startled him, and he'd gestured with his hand before he could think. Frank dropped down onto the grass next to the deck, wrapped in a blanket with a beanie on his head.

"You cold?" Gabriel asked. Frank looked like shit, pale and gaunt and nothing like the man so full of life who had greeted them the other day.

"Yeah. Not a good day. Sorry. I can leave you in peace." Frank moved to get up, but Gabriel urged him to stay, then froze and pulled back, covering his chest with his arms. It was instinctive, and it was fucked up. He knew that. So what if he had a few scars? It wasn't like Frank was even looking at him. The guy had sunk back down to the ground and was rubbing his nose and coughing gently.

"I couldn't get out of bed this morning. Thomas threw me out and told me I'm not allowed back in bed until the room smells better and I've had a walk. Sometimes I hate my husband."

Gabriel laughed gently. Not that Frank's statement was funny.

"I know what you mean. I..." He stopped himself. Sharing was not always caring, but Frank had closed his eyes and was taking deep, noisy breaths, like he was trying to calm himself down, so Gabriel continued softly. "I understand depression, if that's what we're talking about here. I barely left the bed for a year after the girls were born. Complications. They were ill, I was ill..." His face flamed in realisation of what he'd just said. *Fuck.* Caring and sharing could go to hell.

# Eight
## FRANK

The ground underneath him was smooth and cool, despite it being a warm day. His fingers on one hand randomly played in the grass, the other hand clinging to the blanket like it was some kind of lifebuoy. The wool fabric was soft against his skin, which was the only reason he was carrying it around. He tried to focus his thoughts enough to make sense of the overwhelming noise around him, picking out individual sounds to calm his mind—the wind rattling the leaves, the birds, the children. *The damn children.* They weren't his, yet it hurt to hear them. Even the smallest sound seemed to intensify everything, making the world scream in his ears. Silence was soothing.

He drew in air through his nose, then pushed it out through his mouth, just like his yoga teacher had taught him, deep breaths, in, hold, out, calm and relaxed. *His yoga teacher* sounded so pretentious; he hadn't been to a class for ages. The timings had clashed with his schedule, and there hadn't been enough in the budget for something that felt like self-indulgence. Maybe he should have made space, but the kids had to come first.

His mind felt sluggish. When he was well, his mind was firing quick and sharp, in control of everything, and he felt competent. When he was confused like this, walking into the garden with no idea why he was even outside, the sluggishness of his thought process was a sure sign. That feeling of the earth rotating too fast, of not handling his commitments and struggling to hold on to the smallest things when everybody else seemed to be coping just fine—yeah. He was depressed.

He opened his eyes and stared into the mass of trees, gazed blankly at leaves and bushes and stems and grass and the redcurrant shrubs between the garden and the forest. It was a mix of greens, but still not the same. Green was not only green but all the shades and gradients and structures. At least he could still see the green, he thought. His mind hadn't gone grey yet. He pinched a blade of grass between his thumb and index finger and pulled it free. Maybe if he could physically keep hold of the greenness, it would never turn grey, not even when he closed his eyes.

Gabriel was talking next to him, his words swirling around somewhere in the back of his brain, slowly translating from sounds to meaning.

He seemed to be just another sad man, like most of the population. His words made no sense, claiming to 'understand depression'. *No one* could understand depression. Frank couldn't even understand it himself. If he did, he wouldn't get himself into these low moods, having already spent the stupid amounts of time in this very state. Too many weeks, months, years, missing from his children's lives when he should have been present, not hiding under a blanket like it was some old-fashioned, stripy, woollen invisibility cloak because nobody should have to deal with the pathetic human underneath.

What else was Gabriel saying? Frank frowned, trying to process the words, which seemed to have stopped swirling but seemed to be missing here and there, like each sentence had skipped every second word. Something about birth, about the girls, his twins.

He looked at Gabriel, trying to take it all in. Brown eyes, long lashes, a slender, strong body covered in skin darker than his own. Tense arms, shaped torso, light-pink horizontal scars just below the pecs. Something Gabriel had said must have drawn Frank's attention to them; he probably wouldn't have noticed them otherwise.

He nodded slowly as he tried to think of something to say—something someone else might have said to him at some point—but nothing occurred to him.

"I also had postpartum depression. But it was different, I guess."

He wasn't sure who was speaking. Perhaps it was him.

Gabriel looked at him, confused. "Are you...did you..."

Frank shook his head. "No, it was paternal postnatal depression. My doctor mixed it up with my regular depression at first and increased my medication, but it didn't help. I just felt like a drug zombie on top of the sleepless nights."

"But why?" Gabriel asked. "No, sorry, it's not my place to ask," he excused himself, embarrassed.

Frank shrugged, tightening the blanket around him. He needed it tight. Keeping everything together. "It's OK. It was the usual stuff. Lack of sleep. Changes in life. The stress. The feeling of distance between me and the babies. Then Thomas took on most of the responsibility to protect me, and I felt even more separated from everything." It was the first time he'd spoken to anybody about that hellish period of their lives, well, beyond his psychologist and, after a while, Thomas.

"What about you?" he asked Gabriel. "If you want to tell me," he added. This was still not a comfortable conversation or one Frank was sure he wanted to have.

"I lost a lot of blood, more than two litres. They couldn't stop the bleeding, and my heart stopped twice. I had at least ten bags of blood, and they wouldn't even remove my uterus afterwards," he added bitterly. "Shit's still in there apparently keeping my insides together. Scar tissue. Stuff like that."

Frank felt overwhelmed by all the information slowly reaching his tired thoughts. He had to close his eyes and take a few deep breaths to stay focused. When he opened his eyes again, Gabriel was still there, quiet and steady, watching him.

"Sorry, I didn't mean to dump all that on you." Gabriel moved in, leaning closer. Too close. In his space. "Shit, are you OK?" He squatted down on the grass next to Frank and gently touched his arm through the blanket. "You're very pale."

Frank nodded. "Blood and gore aren't really my thing. I even faint when the nurses take my vitals. But it'll pass." He drew air again. Deep breaths. In. Out.

"Can I get you something to drink?" Gabriel offered

Options were no good to Frank. Thomas never made him choose anything when he was like this. He made all the decisions for him because that helped. Anything else was too much work for his brain, and it took a minute for his head to gear up to answering. All the while, Gabriel sat there, patiently waiting.

"Coffee, perhaps?" He sounded weak. "You got that capsule machine to work?"

Gabriel laughed, seemingly relieved at the change of subject. "As if. Apparently, we're only allowed to drink expensive Italian brews in this family." He smiled at Frank. "But it takes too long to make. Lungo good for you?"

"Yes, please."

Gabriel left.

Frank leant back, losing his balance, and gladly let the grass catch his inevitable fall. He lay there like a broken ragdoll, turning his face towards the sun. Sunglasses would have been nice, but closing his eyes was good enough. It changed the sunlight to a darker shade of orange, much to his pupils' relief.

Gabriel returned a few minutes later with two cups and some biscotti on a plate. Frank managed to sit up again, finding a reasonably comfortable position with his legs folded under his body. *Yoga pose. Pompous twat.* He almost laughed at the thought. Thomas would never have gone to yoga, yet Frank had kind of liked it. Perhaps he should try going again. Maybe that Hot Yoga place in town. Hot like this coffee. He wished he could put words to the flavour, but the colours were fading. His taste buds had packed up and left, and now everything tasted bland.

They slowly sipped their drinks in a surprisingly comfortable silence. Frank dipped the biscotti into the black liquid, gnawing at the hard edges, letting the crumbs sit on his tongue until they turned into wet cardboard in his mouth. Textureless and tasteless.

"When I was expecting Andreas, I didn't even drink coffee," Gabriel said. "I was just a baby myself. Then, when I was expecting the girls..." He laughed. "Well, I was addicted to the stuff by then, and giving it up was the worst thing ever. I had the shakes for weeks."

Frank smiled, but it probably came out as a grimace.

Gabriel took another sip of coffee, his expression becoming serious. "How did the depression affect your and Thomas's relationship?"

It was a surprisingly honest question, perhaps a little bit invasive, but Frank's mouth seemed keen to answer, even if his brain thought he should change the subject.

"First it felt like my normal lows, textbook depression, then the doctors connected it to the birth and the postpartum period. Thomas had been like this strong cliff through all of it, taking care of the twins and then me as well, organising everything, dealing with all the medical appointments and feeding schedules, weighing the babies and getting up through the night. I couldn't figure out how to help because I slept through the days and struggled at night, and...I don't know. It came to a point where Thomas put me in the car and shipped me off to stay with my parents for a while."

It had been the darkest time of his life, yet it was still the clearest memory from that period, one of the few moments he remembered well, probably because it was so obvious. They had been exhausted; the babies had never slept or given them a moment's peace, and Frank had been, even to himself, obviously sick and behaving like he was some kind of zombie guest in his own home, so caught up in his guilt to notice the chaos building around him. When Thomas had finally realised he couldn't do all of it, he'd done the only sensible thing: asked for help. That help had included Frank leaving.

It had been a horrific wake-up call, even if it had only been temporary and Thomas and the babies had visited him almost every day. He'd always thought, no, he'd been absolutely convinced, that Thomas would be the one to leave, the one to give up on them.

They had spent a long time rebuilding their relationship after that. It hadn't helped that for every step forward, they had both felt like they'd taken one back. Every time there was a hint of him getting low, Frank feared Thomas asking him to leave again, even though they'd talked about it and Thomas kept reassuring him that it had been an extreme situation, a one-off, so Frank could get the help he needed.

His thoughts had stalled, lingering on that feeling of walking on eggshells around his family, hoping he could mask anything negative from his husband, pretending everything was fine when it clearly wasn't. The scars were still there. They always would be.

"It didn't really affect us, not in the long run," he lied. His throat felt choked up, like he suddenly couldn't breathe. "You know," he continued, trying to sound normal, "Thomas really loves to touch me." It was another cop-out, avoiding the truth. All the while, the stupid thoughts were on loop in his head, and he couldn't stop them. "Sometimes he can't keep his hands off me." He giggled and felt his cheeks flame at his absurd outburst. He sometimes came out with crazy shit that made people around him balk, intimate details nobody needed to hear. He took another sip from his cup, trying to shut up. Oversharing was another one of his many traits and would no doubt come back and bite him in the butt later on.

"I may feel all angry with him at times, but those feelings are a blatant lie." He laughed, even though it wasn't funny, and tried to rein all the madness back in, tugging the blanket tighter around his bony shoulders. He looked at Gabriel, hoping he'd say something to rescue the moment, pull them back on track to that easy, friendly conversation that meant nothing and left no trail of scars. "You know that feeling of being so small, when it feels like you can disappear at any moment?"

Gabriel nodded uncertainly. "I think so?"

"Thomas is so good to me when I am that small. It's like he minimises what he does. Instead of big gestures and loud talk, it's all tiny things. Silence, small touches. And he doesn't make me feel like shit when he does it." Frank swallowed the last of his coffee. "I'd better go back." He smiled feebly at Gabriel. "Thanks for listening. Sorry if it was too much." The poor bloke was probably freaked out. Frank tended to have that effect on people. Depression and insanity wrapped up in one fine-tuned messy blanket parcel.

"The pleasure was all mine." Gabriel got up and reached for Frank's hand, helping him to his feet. The blanket slid off his shoulders, uncovering his pale, naked torso, and he erupted in goosebumps at the sudden contact with the air and his distress at baring this version of himself. Nobody walked around in public wearing boxers and a blanket accessorised by a not very fetching woolly hat. He'd only planned to wait outside until Thomas was done changing the linen or airing the room. He thought. It was hard to remember anything these days. Was he supposed to be doing something outside? Fetching something off the washing line? Thomas would no doubt be annoyed with him again for forgetting stuff.

Still, he felt a little bit lighter for some reason, and it occurred to him that he was missing Thomas. He wanted to see him, give him a long hug. Maybe they should do something together tonight, go for a walk or something, if he was still up to it. He never knew how he would feel later; that familiar sense of doom and darkness could creep back in at the edges of his vision at any time without notice.

The house was silent on his return. Sunshine peeked through the trees outside the windows hitting the kitchen counter, highlighting the dust, fingerprints, crumbs, a pile of dirty plates and grease-spotted glasses. The shoes, clothes, toys, paper and rubbish from earlier today—no, earlier this week—were still there too, like they had become stuck there and were now a permanent installation.

In a haze, he walked through the kitchen into the living room, picking up stray stuff as he passed—clothes, a magazine, the used batteries from the smoke detector. He'd remembered to change them on the day they'd arrived but forgotten to recycle them afterwards. He sighed and left everything except the batteries on the dining table to deal with later. The batteries made it as far as the counter, where he noticed a jar full of useless odds and ends—weird-looking bolts and screws and ties for bags that would never be full long enough to need sealing. Why did they keep shit like that?

The silence and emptiness closed in around him. His body and mind were exhausted, drained, but he couldn't tell if those feelings came from within or if his surroundings were trying to crush him. He kept going, finding a hint of calm and what he thought might be relief as he opened the bedroom door. The blind was down, just the way he liked it, creating darkness with a hint of light. A movement in the bed startled him partly out of his stupor, and he moved closer, inspecting the bump under the duvet, the familiar shape of a body rolling over. With a smile, Frank let the blanket slide from his shoulders and hit the floor with a comforting dull thud before he eagerly climbed into bed. The linen smelled fresh, of flowers and summer, the Swedish detergent they used here strong in the air. He tugged at the duvet and curled up behind Thomas, sneaking an arm around him.

Thomas shivered and rolled away until he was belly down on the far edge of the bed. His breath was slow and steady like he was sleeping, but Frank wasn't sure he really was and felt a pang of sadness. Thomas's skin was so warm and vital under Frank's now outstretched arm and palm, and he circled his fingertips over Thomas's shoulder blade, then brushed them down Thomas's spine, each vertebra greeting him like an old friend. He counted them, one by one, until he reached the waistband of Thomas's boxers. For a second, he lingered at the elastic before backing up again, every millimetre of skin offering comfort as his hand came to a rest on Thomas's flank.

When Frank woke up a few hours later, he could feel the familiar panic setting in even before he opened his eyes. The sounds were too loud, the chirping of the birds outside piercing his head, the light too strong, the smell of detergent too heavy—he almost retched when the perfume hit his nose. He rolled over and pushed his face into the pillow, trying to find some comfort in those well-known smells buried deep inside it, but the artificial scent was overwhelming. In desperation, he pulled at the pillowcase, but it tangled and the pillow got stuck in the fold. He pulled harder, hearing the seam rip, but he didn't stop until the pillow was free. The white fabric inside was stained, brownish clouds with darker edges. It should have made him cringe in disgust and throw it away, but instead he clung to it, shoved his face in it, trying to find something, anything other than the dreaded *spring breeze* scent that lingered up his nose.

He found it, a faint smell of Thomas's shampoo and sweat, a hint of him behind the cleanliness, and breathed it in as if his life depended on it. Maybe it did to some extent because he didn't know how he could ever live without Thomas.

"Aren't you getting up?" Thomas's voice sounded muffled, even though he was standing right next to the bed.

Frank stilled and tried to find something to say. "No."

Thomas held his breath for a while; Frank could hear it. Anxiety fluttered in his chest. He hoped Thomas wasn't mad. Hoped he was rested, not too stressed. Frank knew he was a handful, not just now. Even on a good day, he wasn't an easy person to live with.

For a moment, Thomas stood there staring down at Frank, who was still trying to give the pillow some kind of messed-up mouth-to-mouth, then he sighed and muttered, "Fuck."

Frank didn't answer. He couldn't really think of anything to say or do other than lie there with his eyes shut and keep taking in tiny puffs of air through his mouth so he didn't lose the scent. His lungs felt too heavy to breathe with his entire chest, so only the upper part heaved with every strained breath.

"Did you manage to get anything sorted before you came back to bed?" Thomas asked. His voice was soft, calming.

"Like what?"

"I don't know. Anything. Cleaning, laundry, cooking?"

"No."

Thomas's silence was his answer. There had been so much to do. Too many choices in where to start.

"I went outside, like you told me to," Frank said weakly.

"You could have done something inside, too. There was a load of laundry ready to hang."

"I'm sorry."

"It's OK." It didn't sound like Thomas meant it.

"I was exhausted."

"Of course."

Frank felt so feeble. His limbs were too heavy, and his eyelids were sore. He could hear Thomas's frustration without him saying anything. The air was thick with it, his heavy breaths, his fingers scratching at his head. He'd have his hand over his eyes now; Frank didn't need to see. He knew what a frustrated Thomas looked like.

"It's just that somebody has to do it!" And now Thomas was shouting. "The cleaning, the laundry, the cooking—it's not going to do itself. The kids can't be raised like this. They need support, love, adult role models in their life. And when none of us can manage, everything goes to shit."

Frank swallowed, knowing he would start crying the second he opened his mouth.

"You're lying there, under that blanket, being sick, and sometimes it's completely unpredictable. You'll just wake up one morning and you won't get up, and then I have to do everything, no matter how crap I feel. Sometimes it's too much for me too."

Frank wanted to protest, to say he'd felt it coming for days, maybe even weeks, but before, years ago, they'd talked about it, checking in with each other, asking how they felt. Back then, Frank would have told Thomas about the gradual feeling of dread, his mind fogging up and how everything seemed slower yet everything spun faster but different from when it was spinning up.

"I can't do this!" Thomas shouted, and Frank opened one eye. Thomas stomped around in a circle, tugging at his hair. "We said we'd paint the house, and we haven't even found a paintbrush yet. The windows are falling out, and there's cracks in the floorboards to fill so we don't have to deal with the fucking mice every summer. I just... Ahhhrghghgh! You need to figure this out too. Not just leave it to me."

"I know," Frank whispered.

"Then please! Fucking please, Frank!"

Things had changed after the kids. They'd once made time for it, created a safe space for Frank's illness, but that space had gradually diminished until there wasn't even room left to breathe. Now they just shouted, cried in frustration and anger. There were only stray moments left between arguments when they both had the time and energy to talk about it before other more pressing matters inevitably took over. The kids, food, their crappy economy, work. It was hardly ever themselves and never enough to acknowledge that Frank wasn't getting better, that this would always be the way things were, despite new, groundbreaking medications and bloody mind-bending yoga.

Hushed voices outside the bedroom door startled them both. The kids hated it when they fought. The harshness of their voices made them sound angrier than they were, so it was no surprise to hear doors slamming, followed by feet running down the stairs and another door getting slammed before the house was once more filled silence.

"I'm sorry," Frank whispered so quietly he could hardly hear his own voice.

"It's OK." Thomas sighed and knelt down next to the bed, his breath warm on Frank's cheek. "It's not your fault you get sick. It's not often I get a chance to have a nap. Did me good earlier, but I can't cope with this. I can't do everything."

"I'll fix it," Frank promised with no idea how he could and lifted his arms, preparing to get out of bed. Everything was so heavy. His brain was shouting instructions, but he couldn't get his body to follow them, and it seemed like a century passed before he was sitting upright with his feet on the floor. Resting his elbows on his knees, he pushed the heels of his hands into his eye sockets until he saw white spots. His legs felt like jelly.

Apparently, he was going to attempt to stand up but had no idea how he was supposed to find the balance or manage to walk.

"Daddy, we're going with the Germans to find food and network. Bye!" Fredrik bellowed from the bottom of the stairs. Frank wanted to tell him to please use his indoor voice and come upstairs to ask them before going anywhere. Also, could Fredrik pick up some good orange juice? Not the cheap variety; the thick one in a bottle. And salted liquorice, the kind they had loads of in Sweden and Finland. But Fredrik was gone before Frank could command his voice to utter any of those things.

The duvet rustled behind him as Thomas tucked it around his shoulders. More heavy breathing of the Thomas variety, followed by creaking steps across the ancient wooden floor, each one sending a metal spike through Frank's brain. The door carefully opened then caught in the wind and banged shut, leaving the blind flapping at the open window.

# Nine
# BRUNO

Bruno liked Frank and Thomas. He got good vibes off them, even though he'd heard them earlier, arguing loudly. He'd only walked up to their house to ask for directions to the shop and found Fredrik and Maria sitting quietly on the front step while their house pretty much shook with tension and anger.

"Want to come?" he asked, eyeing the Norwegian teens with sympathy. He'd been where they were, when his father had screamed at his mother and his mother's sobs had resonated through the thin walls.

Fredrik and Maria had stared at him like he was an axe murderer, which was good. They'd obviously been brought up well.

"I need directions to get to the shops, and Andreas needs to find a network for his phone. Unless you have other plans?"

The two of them had nodded like puppets, and Fredrik had bolted inside, shouting to his parents that he was leaving with the German dude to find network and food. *Real food. Stuff you can eat.* There was so much passive aggression in his voice that it had radiated off him as he jumped down the steps and landed on the grass next to Bruno, phone and headphones in his hand, while Maria swept her hair into a messy ponytail.

"Sorry." Thomas's voice came from the doorway. "I assume you heard all that. It's...you know. Years of marriage does that sometimes."

Poor Thomas looked exhausted—like Bruno felt most of the time except worse, and Bruno knew exactly what Thomas was *not* saying. He'd been through it with Gabriel, shouting and pleading and trying so hard to understand, virtually carrying him out of bed some days, wrapping him up on the sofa, forcing him to have a shower... Trying. Trying so damn hard.

He'd even been there himself. There had been a few weeks before his initial surgical exams when he'd thought about giving up, when walking away had seemed a better option than to go in and knowingly fail. He remembered the panic, the sheer fear, the cloud of hopelessness, the sleeping tablets and the sound of Gabriel crying. It had been bad, fucked up, but it had happened. He looked after himself better these days; he had to. He had Gabriel and the kids, and they would get through the bad times together, taking nice holidays, making memories with the children and raising them into fully functioning adults. Grow old gracefully.

He looked over at his son moping by the car, his head hunched over his phone, feet stomping around in those damn trainers Bruno paid half a month's wages for and look at them now. Rubbish. Junk. Shredded to bits with felt tip marker all over the laces.

"We need food. And directions. Translators perhaps. OK if I take your kids with me?" He was going for light-hearted.

Thomas nodded. There was relief hanging in the air, along with gratitude and a myriad other emotions Bruno didn't need a dictionary to define. Thomas closed the door, and the two Norwegian teens climbed into the back of the car, carelessly throwing the twins' car seats out on the grass.

Bruno drove in silence. There were headphones on ears. Eyes closed. Andreas, in the front, bobbed along to the beat, and almost startled Bruno out of his seat when he spoke.

"Papi?"

"Yeah?"

"We still doing the Pride thing? When we get back?"

"Yes, of course. We always do. You know you don't have to join us if you don't feel up to it, right? I don't want you to feel forced, but Vati and I would love for you to be there with us."

"I know." Bruno could almost hear Andreas's eyes roll.

"It's fine, Andreas. Really—"

"Don't lecture me, Papi."

"I'm not."

"I only asked because you know you were saying the hospital stand is doing the *Free Mum and Dad Hugs* again, and that you were having those T-shirts printed with *Free Dad Hugs?*"

"Vati wants *Free Trans-Dad Hugs* on his. I don't know if he's serious or not."

"You do know Vati's depressed again, don't you?" Andreas said calmly like it was nothing.

"You talking about depression? It's the same word in Norwegian I think. My dad's always depressed," Fredrik piped up from the back. "And he's not even the one who's bipolar."

Bruno hadn't noticed his earphones coming off. "Depression is not easy to live with," he said, trying to get his brain into gear in English. This was hard, and he was in uncharted territory with a stranger's kids. At the same time, he was so immensely proud of Andreas, bringing it up and talking about difficult subjects openly like a grown-up. It was almost like...wow. An eye-opening parenting moment.

"Tell me about it," Fredrik muttered. "I hate when they shout at each other. I mean, it's almost easier when they both mope around and shut the hell up."

"My parents fight. A lot," Andreas said.

Bruno wanted to defend himself, say, *no, of course we don't fight.* Well, that was a lie. They bickered and shouted and slammed doors. Gabriel would huff and puff and send him passive-aggressive texts, and Bruno would spend the day walking around with a thundercloud hanging over his head, and sometimes things would just explode. Then he would kick stuff, throw kitchen utensils. He wasn't proud of his temper. Not proud at all.

"You talking about Daddy?" Maria chimed in, suddenly hanging over Bruno's backrest. "He's not too bad this time. At least he's talking and getting out of bed. We've had worse."

"Which daddy?" Fredrik asked, leaning forward in his seat.

"Frank, of course!"

"Frank's fine, he's just depressed," Fredrik countered. "It's Thomas who's a disaster. He can't even get dressed. His T-shirt was inside out this morning, and his socks don't match. He has this thing about socks. I can't be arsed to find ones that match, and it drives him crazy."

"Frank is actually much more chill than Thomas." Maria's English was surprisingly confident, her voice strong like she was stating an everyday fact. "He's even more chilled when he's sick. He takes us out and does weird things, and we kind of have to look after him like we're the adults and he's the kid. It's quite funny. One day, he bought all the ice-cream flavours at the Co-Op, one of each, because we couldn't decide which one we wanted. We had like *soooo* much ice cream. Thomas was furious and shouted, then he sat on the sofa until midnight eating ice cream because he didn't want to throw away the stuff that didn't fit in the freezer."

Fredrik laughed, obviously remembering that incident well. "We still have some of it in the bottom of the freezer. Like some ginger caramel shit that was just rank. Nobody eats it, and Thomas won't throw it away. He's so bloody stubborn."

Bruno chuckled quietly, embarrassed on Frank and Thomas's behalf, yet it was comforting to hear that other adults were just as irresponsible as he was.

"Do you always call your dads by their first names then?" he asked.

"Nah, they're both Daddy. *Pappa* in Norwegian. They always seem to know which one we're calling, and if they don't, we just say their names. We always have. Too complicated otherwise." Maria smiled. "You have different names for yours, and that would be confusing to me. I mean, they're both your dads, aren't they?"

"You're weird," Andreas said, but he was laughing too. "And that sounds far too complicated. It's like naming all your kids the same thing."

"What were you saying about the T-shirts, Andreas?" Bruno asked. He needed to move this into safer territory. He hadn't realised the Norwegians had been listening in, and he should bloody know better than to out Gabe to these kids, and he sure as hell wasn't ready to counsel them in front of Andreas. He knew very little about bipolar disorder, which apparently was what Frank was struggling with, and it didn't take a degree in psychology to see that Thomas was a mess. It was all falling into place in his head, little pieces of a puzzle. He should have asked Thomas if they needed supplies. He could try to take some of the pressure off; it was the least they could do after coming here and invading their personal space when this family needed peace and quiet. He could imagine the strain Thomas was under right now, not only dealing with his husband and two bored teenagers but also having a strange family roaming around. If Frank was unwell on top of that, things would be unbelievably hard.

"My Vati, he's depressed a lot," Andreas said, completely ignoring the T-shirt question. "He's not bipolar, though. Just really anxious. He gets really overprotective about us all and freaks out over tiny things. It freaks me out too, to be honest."

Bruno took it all back.

"Vati is overprotective because he loves you. It changes a person when you realise how fragile life is and how easy it is to lose the people you love." He hoped he wasn't being too aggressive, but he would instinctively protect Gabriel till his last dying breath.

"I know he almost died, and that the twins were sick," Andreas muttered.

*Also. Note to self. Your kid's hurting.* That realisation was fucking difficult to stomach.

"I don't want to have twins," Maria said cheerfully. "I don't think I want kids at all. It seems hard work, having to look after people all the time. I want to have fun when I grow up. Travel. See things."

"That's good." Bruno nodded a little too enthusiastically. Anything to talk about something easier.

"I want kids," Andreas said. "They're fun. I'm just scared that they'll turn out as ugly as me. I mean, I look like my dad, and he's got a face like a... what do you call it?" He was on a roll, much to Fredrik's delight.

"Shut up. I'm handsome," Bruno protested, laughing.

"You're an old man. Your hair is thin on top, and at least Vati has muscles. He should make you go running again."

*Yeah. Right.* The last time the three of them had gone for a jog, Bruno had ended up hurling in the bushes. Maria and Fredrik laughed in the back as Andreas enthusiastically re-enacted his not so finest moment. Bruno was no athlete, unlike Gabriel, who loved anything that made you sweat, and Andreas, who was sportier than the two of them together. Genes were funny like that.

"What were you saying about Pride?" Fredrik asked. "We just had ours. It's kind of fun. Lots of weird stuff, but a bunch of our friends are always there too."

"Papi and Vati are involved with the Berlin Hospital Pride Trust," Andreas explained, "so we usually man their stand. Last year, they did this thing called *Free Mum and Dad Hugs*, you know, for people who don't have supportive parents and stuff? They can come and get a mum hug or a dad hug. It was pretty good. A few people cried. Emo, you know. That was what

I was going to ask—can you make me a *Free Bro Hugs* T-shirt? I thought that might be cool."

Bruno gave a small nod. It wasn't that he wasn't emotional or proud of his son. He was both of those things, and these were moments when he should enthusiastically support his son's frankly excellent ideas. But it was different hearing it out loud, in front of other people. His son was freaking awesome, almost an adult, and he cared.

"Of course," he stuttered out. "Brilliant."

"I'm not gay, Papi. I'm perfectly clear on who I am, and I'm almost eighteen," Andreas said in German, like he knew exactly what Bruno was thinking.

"I know. You told me."

"And Vati needs a fucking hug," Andreas continued in a voice that sounded unmistakably like Bruno's when he told his kids off, which made him blush and smile at the same time.

"Look! Strawberries!" he said, spotting the stand on the side of the road. Things like this were so very Scandinavian. Strawberries for sale at the roadside, ridiculously expensive but warm from the sun, and they tasted like heaven.

He freely passed strange-looking money to Andreas and Maria to buy as many as they could carry, smiling as Maria sighed and reminded him that cash was for old people and that he needed a card or a phone. Whatever. The kids always made him feel old and outdated, but Andreas was on the case and fished the card out of Bruno's wallet.

Bruno watched from the car, following the kids' conversation with the salesperson despite not being able to hear a thing. Maria whacked Andreas on the arm for something he'd said. Fredrik laughed and asked the teenager selling the berries a question. The teenager nodded and took off his earphones.

Bruno's thoughts ran on a loop.

Gabriel confused him. He'd tried so hard earlier, but Gabriel had dismissed him as usual. Then an hour later, Gabriel had stood next to him in the kitchen and reached for his hand, gripped his fingers until he could barely breathe. It had been a step forward. Or maybe a step back. He wasn't sure.

*Small steps. Small touches.* Gabriel had whispered the words. *Small. Right now, I feel really small, and I need you to treat me like that. Like I'm tiny. Can you do that? Just start small.*

He quickly swiped away his tears before the kids came back to the car.

Andreas shoved a massive strawberry in his mouth. "Fucking gorgeous," he grunted, juice dripping down his chin, while Fredrik laughed and Maria yapped away in Norwegian.

"So, left at the next crossing, and what was the village called that has the shop?" Bruno asked, sounding more enthusiastic than he felt. But it would be fine. He would have to figure this out. Small. He just needed to start small.

"Henriksvik," Fredrik said, shaking his phone. "I've got 4G! Fuck, yeah! Network!"

The car stayed silent after that.

***

The kids finally agreed to come back to the car after everything in town had closed.

Bruno had left them at the small parking lot while he went to the grocery store and returned to find all three with their faces scrunched in concentration above their small, blue-lit screens. He'd suggested a visit to the café, but they'd wanted to stay in the car where the 4G was stable, so he'd gone in on his own, gotten an expensive espresso and a delicious chocolate mud cake and ignored the few locals glancing over at him from time to time.

He drove back to the farm in silence, having tried several times to start a conversation, but the kids clung to their tiny means of communications as long as possible, and when they finally lost connection cast sour looks out the windows.

# Ten
# THOMAS

Thomas wasn't sure if this was a joke or not. He was standing in front of what looked like a homemade wooden stage, seemingly placed at random in the middle of the village square in Henriksvik. The clouds were low, and rain was steadily dripping from them, darkening the dusty gravel beneath his feet, and drenching his thin T-shirt—a perfectly appropriate choice when he'd left home. Rain wasn't forecast the last time he'd looked, but they'd had no network; clearly that forecast had been out of date. Hence he was now being punished for his earlier optimism by getting a sour drenching and cold, stiff jeans.

It had been a weird week, and to be honest he was thrilled to escape the house, even though Frank had been a little bit brighter over the last couple of days, spending less time in bed and even attempting to make coffee for himself. Thomas had given up believing in miracles but still hoped that they'd turned a corner. Frank's moods were not always a predictable cycle, and he had more than once seemed headed for better days, only to tumble back down to that dreaded dark baseline again.

At least there had been no major drama. Their guests were decent and polite, the kids pleasantly loud, their laughter cutting the normally thick air into something that seemed easier to breathe.

Fredrik, Maria and Andreas had disappeared from sight before Thomas had even parked the car and were probably in the café spending all his money or, worse, in the famous Henriksvik science fiction bookstore—

odd for a little town with not much else. There were two rival grocery stores, which even combined hardly counted as a supermarket, and a Salvation Army second-hand store carrying extremely unwearable clothes, according to Maria, who'd taken one look before declaring it awful. There was also a pizza place, a kebab place and, of course, the café, which the kids said was 'surprisingly cool'. It was likely run by some newcomer in search of the good life who'd stumbled across this godforsaken town and thought, optimistically, it would make a decent place to live. Thomas's optimism had fled the first summer he'd spent here. These days, it was a draining exercise in extreme parenting and a failed attempt to rest. It felt more like a prison sentence, this year more than ever.

They'd driven into town for the annual Henriksvik Summer Festival. Bruno and the kids had seen posters about it, showing a Ferris wheel full of happy kids and listing various concerts and events. The kids had insisted it would make a great family outing, but the Ferris wheel turned out to be an inflatable bouncy castle adorned with large signs screaming about age restrictions and occupancy, and even the people running it seemed to have got up and left. All that remained were a bored-looking clown showing off his mediocre juggling and the local musical 'talent'.

There were a few other drenched people hanging out in the square. A group of older men hunched around a plastic table outside the pizza place, having found a dry spot under a colourful umbrella advertising a brand he was sure was long defunct. A middle-aged couple huddled under an awning drinking coffee from paper cups. A half-size smiling plastic clown showing the Wall's ice cream logo wobbled back and forth in the cold breeze. A woman with two heavy shopping bags stood bravely in the middle of the road, watching the struggling artist singing away on the wooden stage.

Thomas looked around, at a loss what to do with himself. There was clearly none of the summer party mood advertised, and he suddenly longed for the familiar summery streets of Oslo, their favourite café in the park, sunshine on his face. This place was nothing but dark and unsettling.

The artist, who called himself Barry Styles and wore a chequered shirt, scarf and dirty jeans, was playing once-popular covers that consisted of strumming the same three chords over and over. His voice might, in a parallel universe have been decent, but in this universe he couldn't hit a single note, and his guitar and the recorded backing track were way too loud for Thomas to actually hear the words. At least the noise swallowed some of the out-of-tune half-tones.

"Hello! Thomas, isn't it?" A middle-aged woman stepped in front of him and smiled uncertainly. She wore tight jeans and a too-small jacket that left a ring of fat around her midriff uncovered. Thomas must have looked as confused as he felt because she kept talking and waving her hands excitedly in his face.

"Maybe you don't remember me! I've mostly talked to your partner," she said in the strong Swedish dialect they spoke around here. "I'm Anita, your neighbour." She gave an embarrassed laugh. "I live on the farm on the other side of the lake. It's nice to see you back at the house again this summer. And you have visitors, too?" she asked, digging for gossip.

"Uhm, yes, we've let the small cabin," Thomas confirmed.

"So, they live in the cabin, not...OK." Thomas saw a glimpse of confusion on her face. "Some lovely friends. Are they like you?"

"Like me?"

"Like you and your...partner?"

"Well, I don't know if..."

"And they have kids too?"

"Uhm."

The woman continued, clearly frustrated by his vagueness, and Thomas wondered how she knew so much about them. There was only one farm, on the other side of the lake, with its own road a kilometre further along the main road from their own. There were also a hill and a rift in the terrain between them, making crossing the lake from her farm to the cabin almost impossible unless you followed the right path around the lake and then through the rift. He was starting to worry that she was stalking them, but then he caught what she said about seeing "that other man and the older kids" in town the other day.

So that must be how she knew they were back this summer and had guests. Still, it was a little intrusive coming from a Swede. The Scandinavians prided themselves on their privacy, and a polite nod was usually as neighbourly as people got around here. Thomas preferred to avoid the neighbours, not interested in forming any kind of relationships. This was their holiday time. Family time. Not *getting to know the weird people who lived nearby* time. Even so, he mumbled a polite but hasty goodbye before escaping the interrogation and crappy concert. He needed to find the kids, go grocery shopping and head back home before he went slightly mad. It seemed everyone else in this town was already lost to delusion, and it was infectious, he realised with a grim chuckle. The only thing they had achieved during this holiday was getting to know total strangers...who no longer felt like strangers. More like...extended family. *See? Delusional.*

The main street was a little busier than the square, although 'main' was redundant since it was the only road through the town, and the square was little more than a bump in the road, a fenced-off parking lot next to another parking lot. The café was a little further along the street, between the second-hand store and a church house.

The rain had intensified, and Thomas was squeezing the water from his hair when he stopped in his tracks outside the entrance to the café. *Closed for the holidays!* the bright sign screamed in his face. *See you in September!* He almost cackled. The only event this town put on, the only time there was anyone visiting this godforsaken place, and the café shut for the holidays. Well, that was typically Swedish.

"It's shut," Maria's voice came from behind. We went and got pizza instead."

The smell of greasy pizza hit him like a welcome return to sanity. The boys dug out slices of cheesy gunk dripping in garlic sauce from the cardboard box they were carrying.

"You Scandies have weird taste in pizza, and I say that as a half-blood Italian," Andreas mumbled, chewing furiously, "but this kebab pizza is bloody epic."

Maria giggled. "You made all those barfing sounds at the prawn, banana and curry pizza, and then you ate half of Fredrik's!"

"It was good! Come on. I need to try new things."

"I thought you were vegetarian, Andreas," Thomas said, laughing. Andreas's face was a picture.

"Shit. I totally blame these two. They keep roping me into trying all these things I would never eat at home. I didn't even think to check. You're evil!"

"Seriously, 'Dreas, did you really believe it was vegan kebab meat?"

"Well, you said it was, and I don't bloody understand Swedish! It had a green thing next to it."

"That, was a chilli, mate," Fredrik heckled. "Chilli. Heat. God, where did you grow up? Deepest darkest space, or what?"

"I hate you!" Andreas said and gave Fredrik a friendly shove, which Fredrik promptly returned and sent the pizza box flying down the street.

"Can we go home now?" Maria asked, scowling at the sky. "It's raining."

"We only just got here!" Thomas said. "I still need to eat something, and we need to shop."

"Boring." Fredrik huffed, fishing his phone out of his pocket.

"We'd better go with him," Andreas said. "Make sure he buys the right sweets this time. Those pick-and-mix things were awesome, the ones we got last time. What were they, Freddie?"

Thomas zoned out from the kids' chatter and relaxed as they followed him through the drizzle towards the closest of the shops, then ran ahead of him because their phones were getting wet. Their laughter filled his chest with hope. As long as the kids were having a good time, he could cope, despite the screeching from the musician on stage that pierced the rainy gloom with his terrible eighties metal covers. There were only so many ways you could butcher 'The Final Countdown', and Barry Styles should certainly have won all the awards for his rendition. And what was it with the Swedes and their obsession with Bruce Springsteen? Thomas shook his head, glad to reach the sanctuary of the grocery store, pausing to read a poster in the window announcing the event of the year with an all-inclusive bus ride to a forthcoming Bruce Springsteen concert in Gothenburg...which had happened over a month ago.

He knew the layout of the shelves here now so took the opportunity to check his voicemails while aimlessly throwing things into the trolley in front of him. The kids' new football kits were ready for collection. A book he'd borrowed from the library was overdue. *Shit.* It was probably still sitting by the door at home, another job he'd completely forgotten about. No point worrying now. *Next message.* He froze as the familiar voice of his head of department filled his ear.

*Thomas, hello. Hope you're having a good break. Just to give you a heads-up with regards to the reorganisation for next term. If you could give me a call, we have some exciting news, and it would be good if you could check in before you return so we can connect and sort out the practicalities. Uhm. Yes. Speak soon.*

Thomas stood there, letting the words sink in. Work had become a distant memory over the last weeks, and the shock of hearing those seemingly innocent sentences made his blood run cold. It was funny how easily words could be twisted. He knew full well that positive-sounding message was anything but, and it made him want to run back to the car, drive home and crawl under a duvet and disappear. He was a middle-aged man, for God's sake, and the truth was unavoidable. The last few years' subtle threats were finally coming to fruition. He closed his eyes for a few minutes and took deep breaths. He would be fine. The world would be fine. His life legacy of research was worth nothing in the end, and if that meant he was out of a job...fine.

*FINE!!* the voice in his head screamed, yet his lips still smiled as Fredrik dumped what must have been hundreds of Kronors' worth of pick-and-mix in the trolley.

"You're going to eat all that? I hope that's your combined sharing bag," he teased, his head spinning at the potential sugar and E-number overload. He'd stopped eating sweets a few years ago, when he'd started suffering migraines regularly. He'd never known for sure it was the sweets, but the migraines had gone away. Still, the bag in the trolley made his mouth water.

Fredrik smirked. "It's the holidays. We can go back to all the healthy eating when we get home. I mean, Frank hasn't cooked at all this time."

"He'll get back to it," Thomas said, suppressing a sigh at the family packs of ready meals he'd selected. Back when they'd just moved in together, Frank used to make a delicious lasagne. Thomas missed it. "When we were younger, he cooked all the time. Huge, elaborate meals that took days to clear up after."

"Yeah, you keep telling us. There used to be tomato stains on the ceiling and pasta stuck to the walls. You hate when Frank makes a mess." Fredrik wasn't being mean. He just told it like it was. But things were different now. Back then, time had still been plentiful and Frank would start cooking lasagne when normal people had dinner and serve it three hours later, insisting that the sauce had to cook for at least two hours before baking it. They had usually been too drunk to care, too sexed out to notice the lack of food in their stomachs. Later in life, when Maria and Fredrik had started on solids, Frank had insisted on making organic lasagne from scratch before mashing the food in the blender to feed them. Thomas had laughed and pointed out they'd have been happy with the fresh sauce mixed with macaroni, which would have been a lot faster and cheaper.

"He enjoys it. It makes him happy," he tried, but Fredrik shook his head.

"It's just one of his obsessions. Remember last year? He got into candle making and was making those horrible wax melts that stank like rotten potatoes. He almost set the house on fire! At least we don't have to put up with that anymore."

"You get obsessed as well, Fredrik. Remember when you and Maria got that fabric dye kit for Christmas and tie-dyed all my work shirts?"

Fredrik grinned. "It was epic. Have you still got them?"

Thomas nodded. They were at the back of his wardrobe, reminding him of better days when Frank hadn't been unwell. It also reminded him that the kids sometimes took on more responsibility than they should have to.

"I remember when he tried to teach me to make ratatouille." Fredrik walked next to him, frowning like he was trying to figure out if the memory was a good one or one he should keep to himself. "I just wanted to make dinner, and we ended up spending five hours slicing vegetables, cooking sauce and baking bread, and proudly served dinner at midnight. It was so much fun, but you were so mad. It was way past everyone's bedtime, and Maria had fallen asleep at the table."

Thomas had to laugh at the memory. "That was just before he ended up in hospital," he said and immediately wished he hadn't, but Fredrik didn't miss a beat.

"He was much better after that. For a long time, things were really, really good. I don't know what happened this time around."

"Nobody knows." Thomas pulled his son in for a quick shoulder squeeze. "It's nothing any of us can control. He's just who he is."

"Then stop shouting and arguing with him. It's horrible when you do."

Trust Fredrik to gut punch him when he was already halfway to losing his own mind.

"Sometimes I don't know what to do. How to cope."

"Everything doesn't have to be perfect, all the time. Sometimes you could just leave him to do his thing. Because afterwards things get better."

"Yeah." Fredrik was right. Things usually did. "We just have to love him."

"We do," his son whispered. "We all do."

*When did things change?* He wished Frank was there to answer. Thomas didn't know when he'd started to see things differently. At some point, he'd been happy, and he'd honestly thought Frank had been happy too. Then life had crept up on them, and now he mostly felt trapped in a corner with no way out.

"I was kind of pissed about missing out on that football camp," Fredrik said, walking alongside the trolley. "I'll be too old to go next year, and Maria and I will be off to uni, so this will probably be the last summer we come here. I mean, things will change after we graduate. We won't even be living at home anymore."

More things Thomas didn't want to think about. The guilt. The future. Things that right now seemed too big to even grasp.

"Sorry." He could at least say that. "I know how much you guys wanted to go. But three weeks of residential camp for the two of you? In America? Maria wanted to go to France too."

"I know. Money," Fredrik muttered. "It doesn't matter. It's much better here with the Germans around. It's fun. Well, not *fun*, but it's bearable."

Thomas laughed. "Thanks for that. We take you on holiday, and it's *bearable*."

"It's not like we're going to move out here. I mean, nobody wants to live this far into nowhere. I'd go mad if I had to be here, like all the time. What do people do in winter? Just veg out in their houses? Take up crochet?"

Fredrik was joking, but Thomas had a feeling he wasn't far off.

"Or candle making," he said, and they both laughed.

"I chatted with Petter earlier, by the way," Fredrik continued as they moved into the next aisle. "He said the camp is lame, too many kids. He spends most of his time tying up shoelaces and being some kind of junior coach."

"I bet he wishes you were there too."

"Nah. He's just pissed off with his parents. They decided to get divorced and didn't tell him until he was off to camp. His mum's moved out, and his dad's selling the house and...I mean, doing all that behind his back, *and* they've packed up all his stuff. That, Dad, is disrespectful."

"It must be hard for him." Thomas didn't know what to think. All he knew about Petter's parents what they were polite people who sometimes greeted him when they attended the same school events.

"Don't ever do that. Just give up on Frank and move out. That's a seriously dickish move. Promise you won't."

"I'd never do that," Thomas said with conviction but shuddered at the thought. There were times it had crossed his mind, when arguments had gotten out of hand, frightening episodes when he'd thought there was no way forward. But they had always found one.

"If you left, he wouldn't make it. You know that, right? He'd just sink and…" Fredrik seemed to shudder too.

"Fredrik, I love Frank. More than anything in the world—except you and Maria, of course. I'm never in a million years leaving him."

"What if you have an affair? Petter said he thinks his dad's been messing around behind his mum's back. Why the hell do adults do that? It makes no sense."

"Humans sometimes do strange things."

"Tell me about it." Fredrik sighed and threw a packet of crisps in the trolley. "I'd never do that to someone. Ever. Let's talk about something else."

"You know you can always…" Thomas started, but Fredrik had already walked off.

***

The steady wall of drizzle became a sturdy shower as they packed up the car with another week's worth of food and drove out of the village. The wipers couldn't keep up, and Thomas considered taking a break at the side of the road, but the humidity inside the car made him carry on. The fan was slightly more effective against four bodies in wet clothes when the engine was running. Not that he could do anything to lift the damp mood, as the kids had gone back to their usual grumpy selves. He glanced at Andreas in the back; he'd put his phone down and was leaning heavily on the door.

"You OK, kiddo?" he asked, trying to remember which turn-off would take them in the direction of home.

"I don't think my stomach liked that bloody pizza," Andreas grumbled.

"You should have had the Margherita. I told you so."

*Yeah. Maria, that's not really helpful.*

"You also told me the kebab was vegan. I'll never trust a word coming out of your mouth, ever again."

"You said you were the expert on all things pizza, being Italian and all?" Maria—sitting in the front—laughed and leaned over into the back. "And if you barf in the car, I'll truly kill you."

That remark set off some serious retching, and Thomas almost lost the car to the ditch before he managed to safely stop in a small clearing where an oncoming car would see them and not smash them to dust. These small roads were lethal. The kids driving tractors had no sense, and neither did the timber lorries that sometimes came out of nowhere. Which was a lesser worry now that Andreas was emptying the contents of his stomach into a wildflower field. Fredrik stood supportively next to him, stroking his back. Both of them were soaked to the skin.

"I'm not getting out." Maria huffed. "Well...perhaps Andreas should sit in the front."

"Good idea," Thomas said, having spotted the bag of sweets on the back seat. They were almost adults, these kids, yet still had no idea how much their stomachs could handle.

Amid the quickfire arguing between Maria and Fredrik with regards to the chances of vomit and never ever riding in this car again, Andreas crawled into the back seat and slumped, his head falling heavily into Fredrik's lap. Fredrik strapped them both in. Safety first.

"Are we good?" Thomas asked, hoping that would be the end of that little episode.

"No!" Andreas shouted and scrambled back out of the car, disappearing into the field.

"We're never having pizza there again," Fredrik said. "The place was rank."

"Then why did you eat it?" Thomas despaired. He'd taught them better.

"We were hungry!" Maria went on the defence. "There was, like, no breakfast this morning. And it looked OK."

"You just wanted to trick Andreas," Fredrik accused.

"Because he's so much fun to wind up." Maria laughed. "You OK, 'Dreas?"

"Just drive," Andreas murmured, once again lying with his head in Fredrik's lap. "Just bloody drive."

The rain stopped as unpredictably as it had started. The clouds split and the sunrays suddenly hit them, like opening the curtains in the morning. The light was almost blinding after the dim greyness of the dark, wet forest and the gravel road. Thousands of tiny water droplets made the trees sparkle, reflecting the light in all directions.

The kids disappeared inside once he stopped outside the house, doors slamming without a word of gratitude or relief. Maria and Fredrik rushed inside yelling about who'd get to shower first, while Andreas walked slowly towards the smaller house, not caring that the muddy driveway was dirtying his trainers. Thomas stumbled out, his body tired and worn, and grabbed the heavy shopping bags, clenching an economy pack of toilet paper under his arm.

The smell of hot cinnamon buns met him as he entered the kitchen and dumped the bags on the floor. More surprising still, Frank was sitting at the kitchen table with the twins. Thomas couldn't remember how to tell them apart—something about one of them having longer hair than the other. *Hopefully, the kid won't cut it themself,* he thought, like Maria had done one catastrophic autumn afternoon when she'd envied Fredrik's buzzcut. They'd skipped the photo on the Christmas card that year. Thomas remembered Frank being happy back then, too, like he was now, smiling and not caring that he had icing sugar in his hair.

Thomas kicked off his wet shoes. For a second, he considered mopping up the puddles between the door and the fridge, but he needed to sit down so went over to the table instead and flopped onto the closest chair. He was exhausted but managed to smile as he asked, "Backt ihr?" in the best German he could muster.

"Ja, wir haben Zimtschnecken mit Frank gemacht!" one of the girls answered in German. He scrunched his forehead and tried to figure out what she'd said, but all he could grasp was something about pink decorations. He looked at Frank, his mind suddenly slowing down, all the stress and anxiety seeping away like air. It always did. Things may not have been great between them, but they were still...who they were. Thomas belonged here, right next to Frank, whatever the weather, whatever state his husband was in. Whatever happened in their future.

"So. Baking?" he said, trying to gauge Frank's mood.

Frank was deep in concentration, meticulously placing pink and lilac glitter pearls on an over-enthusiastically iced bun. The girls seemed less obsessed with patterns and were smearing liberal amounts of frosting and violently shaking the box of silver stars and glitter, sprinkling the contents over the table as well as the buns.

"Yeah. Gabe asked me to look after Lilly and Lottie. He wanted to talk to Bruno, I think. They never get to talk with the kids around all the time. He wanted to make...like a date night and asked if the girls could stay here. Andreas as well. He can stay with Fredrik in his room. I bet we won't see them anyway."

"Why not with Maria?" Thomas asked out of curiosity. Despite Andreas crashing out in Fredrik's lap, he and Maria seemed closer. And Gabriel was *Gabe* now?

Frank put the bun down and looked at him, his eyes sparkling. "Thomas, *think*."

A second later, Thomas realised what Frank had meant. "Ohhh!" He grimaced, and Frank laughed, sending Thomas's stomach into a flutter. It was an unfamiliar feeling these days. He composed himself and said mock sternly, "And what if Fredrik and Andreas are gay?"

"Then they won't get pregnant," Frank said and returned to decorating his bun. "But I suppose we should protect his virtue. We could put a mattress in the office."

"I guess it's OK if he stays with Fredrik. He's got condoms, hasn't he? He probably hasn't used the ones we gave him last year," Thomas continued, swallowing his amusement. It didn't matter that the girls could hear. They didn't speak a word of Norwegian anyway.

Frank laughed again—one of those belly laughs that made the table shake and warmed Thomas right through. These were the kind of ridiculous discussions they used to have, coming out with silly things just to make each other laugh.

"Thomas, they're still only sixteen. Do you really expect them to have sex? Even if they do, what's the risk? They're still kids, not rampant twenty-year-olds."

Thomas shrieked internally and held up his hands to stop Frank going into any more detail. He could absolutely imagine the kids having sex. He remembered his own hidden fantasies at that age, and just the thought of them not being held in check by the same enormous internal fear of his youth terrified him. "OK, let's not talk about this now." *Let's build a prison tower for them. One each. Keep them safe forever.*

"You know I love you, don't you?" Frank said softly. "And that we'll be OK. We always will be, whatever happens."

With those words, the stress from the day ran off him like water, and all he could see were the sunrays playing in his husband's hair. He didn't know how to answer, but of course he knew. They would survive this and everything else that came with life.

"We *will* be fine," he said, almost whispering. "And I love you too. Always have, always will."

"Good." Frank smiled. "Because this place would be kind of shitty without you."

"Even when I shout at you?" Thomas was going for apologetic humour, but his voice still wobbled.

"Even when you shout at me. Sometimes I deserve it. I'm not easy to live with, especially when I'm a dick."

"You're never a dick."

Frank smiled and pushed the over-decorated bun to the centre of the table. "Where is Andreas, by the way?"

"Shit. He went back to their cabin."

One of the girls started crying, *Lottie*, Thomas thought, *or is Lilly the one with the longest hair?* She'd dropped her bun in the spilled sprinkles and was sobbing for her dad. She rubbed her eyes, and Thomas checked the time: the oven clock said 17:03. She was probably hungry. That would be typical Frank—to keep them occupied and not even think of giving them proper food. "Please tell me you fed them."

Frank looked hurt and, underneath the lights, as drained as Thomas felt. "Yes, I fed them. We had that leftover potato salad, and they had a bath earlier after getting soaked in the rain, so Gabe said to just put them to bed later on. Chill. Well, perhaps you could try to get Andreas first? I'd hate for Gabe and Bruno to have him walk in on them...you know."

Almost tipping the chair over, Thomas got up and put his wet trainers back on, then he ran. No child should have to walk in on their parents like that.

In a way, he was glad of the kids being there. He didn't think he had the strength to handle his family on their own. There were discussions to be had, subtle warnings to be delivered, confessions to make. Not tonight, though. With visitors in the house, they would all have to be on their best behaviour.

# Eleven
# GABRIEL

GABRIEL DIDN'T KNOW what had changed. Well, nothing had changed, but he thought that Bruno was trying to. Or maybe it was simply because Gabriel was trying to be more receptive and figure out how to give a little bit back. Either way, everything was different somehow.

Gabriel had felt a little better since he'd talked to Frank, and God damn, it was good to be able to talk. Frank was all up and down still, good days blending with the bad, but he listened and didn't judge. Gabriel had been seeing a therapist for years, a young dude with zero understanding of what Gabriel was going through. He should have asked to change to a different therapist the very first time he set foot in that clinic, but with every visit, week after week, year after year, it had become more difficult to bring it up.

In a way, it was a small comfort to sit in that chair every Thursday and breathe and do stupid relaxation exercises and listen to the dull voice of the guy who must have been at least ten years younger. He was more interested in asking about Gabriel's 'complex gender issues' than the fact that he'd completely gone off sex and was terrified of dying and hated that he couldn't behave like a normal grown-up. And he had zero complex gender issues, thank you very much, as he kept telling the guy. He knew exactly where he stood on his gender. His body may have been a mess, but his husband's was kind of godlike, yet Gabriel still had zero interest in sex. The whole thing had become absurd. All he needed was to figure out how to be a dad and a husband and get everything back under control—including remembering to buy more Anthisan cream for their mosquito bites and asking Frank to fix the netting on the kitchen window. Fuck, he could probably fix it himself if he could find some nails and a hammer. One more night with a damn mozzie hissing out-of-tune heavy-metal classics in his ear would probably drive him to drink. Lots.

He'd made more progress talking to Frank over the past few days than in all those years of paid-for therapy. Each day, they made time to sit down and level the field, talk about where they were at in their heads. While the cotton-like dull cloud in Gabriel's brain had lifted a little over the last week, Frank said he still felt numb, tired, exhausted generally but was having the occasional kick of energy, and that made life a little easier. He also talked about Thomas, like constantly. How much he loved him. How much effort Thomas put into making Frank's life easier. How he couldn't manage without him. How Thomas made his life worth living. How sometimes when he felt like he couldn't even put one foot in front of the other, Thomas might grumble or even rant and scream and sulk, but he would always step in and take his hand, kiss his fingertips, stroke his hair. Call him every name under the sun. Gabriel had added a few new cuss words to his repertoire of English that he was sure would come in handy when Bruno was being especially twatty.

"He's the sunshine in my life. The compass on my ship. Hell. He's my fucking speedboat to sanity." That was how Frank had described Thomas, who at the time had been dealing with some stubborn bushes he'd decided needed a trim. Gabriel had watched with one eye shut. Thomas wasn't a born gardener and should never have gone near those bushes, and now the disaster formerly known as *the hedge* made Gabriel laugh every time he walked outside.

"He makes me feel like it's OK to be me," Frank had said. "Even when I'm an absolute arsehole to him. When I'm unwell. When I come across like the laziest wanker in the universe, leaving him to do everything while I'm too lost in my head to realise he's struggling too. He still loves me. That's what I cling to when I feel bad. At least I have him and the kids. Everything else is irrelevant. As long as you have your tribe, your people, you will always be fine."

It had seemed so simple, and Gabriel had looked out at his own little tribe. His gorgeous darling husband who'd been sporting a pink sheen all over his pale torso, despite being slathered in sun cream. Bruno's Italian genes were clearly not playing ball with the Scandinavian summer sun. Even though they loved having daylight late into the night, the kids struggled to settle down and go to sleep when the sun was still out and there was fun to be had.

The girls had had a blast over the last week, loving the newfound freedom of running wild around the gardens. There were no real dangers here, except the lake, but the girls could swim, and he had drilled into them never to go near the water unsupervised.

Yet here he was, stood in the doorway clinging to the doorhandle like a fool. Gabriel was on the verge of a full-scale panic attack. His chest was tight, and he kept looking up towards the main house with an irrational longing mixed with absolute fear. He felt like he'd been pushed into deep water again, roped into something he had no control over, forced to agree to this bloody holiday when the safer option would have been to stay at home and relax in the safety of their little flat. But then all five of them stuck indoors for a month would have ended in World War Three and full-on carnage. They'd needed to get out. Do something. Make memories with the kids.

"The kids are fine," Bruno said as if reading his mind. "Frank and Thomas are great with them, and they've raised twins and done a fine job of it. Besides, it's important for the girls to experience independence from us. And they love Maria. You should have seen their faces when I told them they were having a sleepover. They were so excited! She's their idol." Bruno looked just as thrilled, with a bag slung over his shoulder and a blanket in his arms, raring to go.

*"We can go sit down by the lake, just the two of us. Have a drink. Relax,"* he'd said, and Gabriel had agreed because he knew they need to sit down and talk, bond a little, no pressure, but he'd meant for an hour or two, and it definitely didn't involve sleepovers or trips down to the lake or coming home to an empty house where they might have a drink or two and his defences would be down and he might not be sensible. He still found Bruno attractive, and a blow job was up there at the top of the things he had thought about. Giving one, that is. He might be into that, on his terms, given a little time to adjust, not getting dragged down to a deserted beach where there was no one around to interfere. They hadn't actually seen another human being anywhere, apart from the Norwegians.

"It's raining," Gabriel protested, taking a small step back through the cabin's front door and hoping the ground would swallow him up. It was a poor excuse and he knew it.

"It stopped several hours ago," Bruno pointed out, "and the blanket has a waterproof underside. Anyway, we can eat inside the sauna."

"We're going to get bitten to death by mosquitoes," he tried, knowing he was being a dick.

"Yup!" Bruno said and grabbed his hand. Then he let it go and stepped closer until he was right there in Gabriel's face. He reached up and trailed his fingertip along Gabriel's cheek. "Small steps. No pressure, babe. I promise you. Let's just sit by the lake and have a drink. I have a bottle of that Prosecco we brought and two glasses—an incredibly romantic picnic."

It seemed natural, instinctive, the way Gabriel leant in and kissed his husband. His darling, darling boy.

"I dread to think what's in the romantic picnic," Gabriel murmured, and Bruno blushed. He'd meant it as a joke, although Bruno wasn't exactly a skilled cook, nor was he good with planning picnics. There had been more than one occasion when he'd forgotten the ice blocks and none of it had been edible and once he'd even forgotten the food. Then there was the time Andreas had cried over the chicken drumsticks and all the little dead chickens lying on his plate.

"Frank made it for us," Bruno admitted, clearly embarrassed. "I promise you, it's safe and looks rather yummy. Pizza rolls, cherry tomatoes, Scandinavian gourmet crisps and homemade dip. You'll like it."

"Sorry," Gabriel whispered, trying to calm the panic still rising in his chest. He reached out and carefully tangled his fingers with Bruno's. "I love you. Do you know that?"

"I do. It's you and me, babe. You and me against the world. Always."

"I'm sorry I'm such a mess. I just need time, and it's good being here. It's just when the kids are not with us, I get shitty, and then all these bloody worries crop up..."

"I know, but you know as well as I do that the kids are safe here, safer than they are at school—you don't worry about them every day they're at school, do you? And Andreas could probably outrun anything around here, even the rabid moose Fredrik keeps going on about. They're fine, and to be honest, they would probably rather be without us than with us right now." He winked, and Gabriel's stomach churned.

"I can't do sex," he blurted and pulled his hand from Bruno's grip.

"I'm not having sex with you down on that beach, babe. The mozzies would have a field day with my dick, and the sand would get into all kinds of places where we don't want it. More importantly, Gabe, darling gorgeous love of my life, there is nothing I would like more than to bend you over that log over there and fuck you into oblivion, but I understand. I know where you're at in your head, so please don't make this into anything bigger than it is. One drink. Two maybe. Pizza rolls. Crisps. And I would love it if I could hold your hand and kiss you a little. Just a tiny, you know, kiss. Perhaps have a swim. That's all I'm asking for. That would make me happy."

Gabriel was smiling. He'd started somewhere in the middle of Bruno's monologue because he always knew the right things to say. Even if they sounded all wrong in Gabriel's head, Bruno made things better, a little calmer, a little lighter.

"I could do kisses," Gabriel said and stole one. Bruno reached for him but held off.

"Can I hold your hand?" he asked. "No, scrap that. Hang on." He cleared his throat and put on that damn silly voice he did—the one where he sounded like a posh Italian twat with a suspect accent. "Mr Fischer, would you do me the very large honour of taking a walk down to the lake with me? I promise that your virtue will be intact by the end of this fine evening stroll."

"Wanker." Gabriel giggled, and Bruno smiled that shy smile he could still get away with from under his fringe. He needed a haircut. He needed to smile more. He needed a lot of things that Gabriel wished he could give him.

"Can I tell you something without you shouting at me?" Bruno asked as they started walking slowly down the path towards the lake.

"I suppose so. I'll try not to shout."

"You never wear your packer anymore."

"Too much hassle." That was the truth. "The harness doesn't sit right anymore, and it just seems a lot of extra work and clean-up for something nobody notices anyway."

"I notice," Bruno said softly. "Not that it matters. You look amazing whatever you wear, but it used to give you confidence, and you always said it made you happy."

"Not happy, more...like everything looked perfect when it's not. It stopped making a difference a long time ago."

"I know, but maybe you should wear it. Just to kind of, you know. Maybe."

"I didn't bring it." Gabriel sighed. Maybe he should have done. It hadn't seemed important. Far from it. It was just another thing to pack and forget and leave behind. Because that was always fun.

"Remember in Paris when you left it at the Airbnb?"

Yeah. He remembered, all right. They couldn't afford a new one so he'd emailed their hosts and asked if it was possible to post it back.

"We were both cringing so hard when the parcel arrived and they'd wrapped Mr Limpy in clingfilm." Bruno smiled softly at him.

"Good times." Young, innocent times when things hadn't been so damn hard. "I don't even know what happened to Mr Limpy," Gabriel said. Another solid truth. He couldn't remember where he'd last seen it, but it was probably hidden away at the back of the wardrobe among clothes he never wore anymore.

"I brought him with us," Bruno admitted quietly. "Don't shout at me. I just thought you might want to...perhaps, like a special occasion."

"It's not an accessory, you know." Gabriel couldn't help being snarky.

"No, Gabe, it's a rubber prosthetic dick. And it looks bloody sexy on you, harness or not. So suck it up and just tell me to fuck off, or I can get Mr Limpy out and he can have a swim in the lake with us."

*Oh, fuck off, Bruno,* he thought as he shoved him into the brush, making sure he fell over in a place covered in pinecones. Served him right. He would have bruises up his bum to match the myriad of mosquito bites he already sported. Gabriel had seen them because Bruno had proudly shown them off.

"I'm not getting naked," Gabriel said. Bruno just laughed and rolled around in the goddamn pinecones.

"I am. There's nobody around for miles, babe, just humour me. Get naked and for once, let go. There will be no sex involved. Apart from kissing. Promise."

This was stupid. He shouldn't have felt so self-conscious, but Bruno always was a stubborn shit.

A few minutes later, he was watching a stark-naked Bruno wade into the freezing water, splashing and promising not to look. Promising all sorts of things if he just got his ass in the water, clothes on or clothes off.

"It's cold," Gabriel complained.

"I might have to come and pick you up then and drag you out here and dump you in this shitty lake. Because you *are* swimming with me. In the water. Now. Or no pizza rolls for you, and Mr Limpy will die a horrible death in that sauna over there."

"You're so cruel!" Gabriel yanked his shirt over his head.

"Would you let Mr Limpy succumb to such a devastating fate?"

"Fuck you."

"I think you should keep him safe. He's in the outside pocket, with the harness," Bruno directed, then promptly dived under the water, out of sight.

It was that feeling of half panic, half relief. He'd never liked being watched, but there. Yup. There he was. Mr Limpy. In a Ziplock bag alongside the harness that he hadn't worn for years. And...

"You brought a butt plug?" he almost shrieked as Bruno's head breached the water.

"Yeah? So what? I'm always a frustrated bottom, you know that. If you ever feel like sticking that thing up my arse, feel free. But I promised no sex, so it will stay in the bag, with the crisps and pizza rolls. Scouts honour."

"Fucking hell, Bruno. I mean, the pizza rolls look fantastic, but you brought a butt plug to a picnic? I think that's one for the history books."

"Best picnic of all times?" Bruno smirked, and then he was full-on laughing, which made Gabriel laugh as well because talk about being ridiculous. Absurd. Everything he loved about Bruno Moretti.

"You win!" he spluttered with laughter. "I haven't even had a drink and you fucking win. Turn around while I get this harness sorted."

"Yes, sir," Bruno shouted and disappeared under the water again.

It was the weirdest thing, frolicking around naked in the lake. Freeing in some ways. There was nothing to distract them here, no mobile phones waiting to deliver messages of doom. Lilly was probably raising hell and Lottie would be eating her weight in cinnamon rolls or whatever they were baking. Andreas would be fine, lost in his own world of music and whatever occupied that brain of his. Gabriel started to relax a little, sitting on a blanket, stark naked and being fed cherry tomatoes by Bruno, who looked like all his Christmases had come at once.

"You look amazing," he said softly. "You still make me feel all kinds of lucky that you chose me. That you're still with me after all this time."

"I never stood a chance. You kind of bludgeoned me with feelings from the day we finally got together. Shouting at me for being selfish and stupid because I had you to consider now and it wasn't just down to me what happened in the future. I loved that. I loved that you knew we belonged together, despite all the shit that came with me being me."

"You being you is no shit. You're mine. You always were. Even when I couldn't see it myself."

"I know, babe."

Bruno lay back, swatting away another insistent mosquito buzzing around over his flat stomach.

"You really want to have that vasectomy?"

"Yeah. It's truly just a minor op. Risks are minimal. Worst case, I'll be pissing with a catheter for the rest of my life or my dick will be fucked and I will have to borrow Mr Limpy's friend Mr Stiffy to fuck you, but hey. We can deal with that, can't we?"

"Don't make jokes about Mr Stiffy. He gets very upset."

It was almost like they were young and stupid again. Well, who were they kidding? They were still stupid.

"Do you want to head back?" Bruno asked, leaning on his elbow. "We've finished the drinks, and there are..." He shook the last of the crisp crumbs out of the bag. "No crisps left. Zero."

"You didn't save me your last crisp?" Gabriel accused and leaned over so he could kiss the stupid, stupid boy he called his husband.

"You might have to punish me." Bruno sighed happily.

"What did you have in mind? You promised no sex. So that leaves... spanking, removal of Wi-Fi rights—oh, damn. We have no Wi-Fi in the first place."

"Just shut up and kiss me, Gabe."

He did more than that. They'd said no sex, so they wouldn't have sex. But he did trail his mouth down over Bruno's chest. He sucked on those little nipples that were hard and erect from the chill in the evening air.

He swatted a mosquito away, pretending there were a few more around Bruno's legs, just to catch his breath before he kissed the soft fuzz on that gorgeous stomach, breathed in the musky scent around his husband's groin. His Bruno. His lovely, gorgeous Bruno.

*No sex.* Which was a fucking shame when Bruno had been hard as a bloody rock the minute Gabriel's hand started to stroke up and down his length. He didn't mean to. It was just like, instinct? A habit? Perhaps a little need for some kind of intimacy; something safer than lying tangled in a bed.

"Turn around, babe," he murmured, his stomach birthing little butterflies. Perhaps this he could do. It was kind of safe. Consensual. Easy. Pleasurable without him having to think.

Bruno moaned softly as his dick hit the course blanket. His hips were already arching up, humping the ground underneath them, hoping for some friction, some kind of relief.

"Fuck," he whimpered as Gabriel gave his arse cheek a little swat, a soothing soft one with a tiny sting of pain to show who was in charge here.

"Stay still. No humping. No touching yourself."

"Please," Bruno said so softly it was barely audible.

There was lube in the bag. Of course there was. A brand-new sealed bottle that Gabriel made short work of, removing the Cellophane with his teeth as he checked the plug. It was one they'd played a lot with in the past, and not too big, so Bruno shouldn't need much prep.

"Spread..." Gabriel said, feeling strangely comfortable as he slipped into what had once been familiar territory and Bruno did exactly what Gabriel needed him to. They moved in a well-rehearsed dance, with Gabriel's lube-covered fingers stroking gently down Bruno's crack, making him shiver, little tingles and tics rumbling down his spread legs as Gabriel's fingers danced over his skin.

It was a strange thing, sex. He'd never needed much to get off himself. Just the fantasy or the dirty talk used to dial him up on the inside until his front hole was a wobbly knot of need and his libido was screaming for anything. Touch. Penetration. Kissing. Release.

But it was still there, the warmth of arousal deep in his groin as his fingers pushed and tapped gently at Bruno's hole, the ring of muscle clenching in needy anticipation.

"You want this?" he asked, hoping he still knew what to do because it had been years. Centuries, it felt like.

"Do it." Bruno grunted, his face to the side, his eyes closed against the evening sun.

"Fingers or plug?"

"Both."

He hissed as Gabriel's finger breached the tightness of his arse. Softness and warmth and clenching and Bruno holding his breath—all the little things that made Gabriel clench himself. Humping his packer, he let the straps of the harness give him a little friction of his own.

He used to love this and apparently still did. It was sexy, arousing and a little dangerous, doing this out here in the open with the sunshine kissing their skin, and the mosquitoes buzzing around them.

"Two?"

Bruno didn't respond, just arched his hips higher, making the second finger slide in easily with a drizzle of added lube.

"Please tell me Mr Stiffy is in the bottom of the bag," his mouth blurted without his permission because he sure as hell didn't say that. Did he?

Bruno's hand shot out and unzipped the side pocket, revealing the harder cousin of Mr Limpy, nestled carefully in its pouch.

"Fucking hell."

"Please."

"You're going to kill me."

"Just shut up and fuck me, babe."

"No sex."

"You're one to talk. I was just lying here all innocently, and then you start fingering my arse."

"Your fault for having a cute arse."

"I do have a cute arse."

"Shut up."

"Auuughhhghgggg."

Yeah, that bit always made him shut up. It was a bit mean, shoving a lube-slathered plug straight up his hole, but Bruno could take it. He'd always needed it a bit hard. Rough play. Sexy as fuck, whatever it was.

Bruno was humping the sand, the plug glistening in the flickering light from the evening sun, his voice a low hum as Gabriel slowly pulled the plug from its hole, only to shove it back in again.

"Fuck, babe, don't tease. Just yank it out and fuck me."

"So bloody impatient."

"Need it. I fucking need to come like a bloody fountain. Too much pent-up spunk in my balls."

The spluttering giggle that came from Gabriel's mouth was almost orgasmic. It felt strangely safe here, being naked like this. A cool breeze caressed his body as he swapped the packers out and lubed up Mr Stiffy. He hadn't done it for years, but the movements were familiar, letting Mr Stiffy slide up his front hole, anchoring it firmly in place with the straps, as his knees found comfortable spaces in the sand. The wind blew gently as he sank on top of the warm body beneath him.

"You ready, babe?"

"Fuck me."

"You got it."

He reached down and teased the plug out, sucking a bruise into Bruno's shoulder as he did so. And another. And one more for good measure as the plug came out and landed in the sand with a dull thud.

He didn't want to stop to think, just lined up and plunged in. Bruno moaned with pleasure and no doubt a fair bit of pain, but he fucking loved it. Adored it. He humped the sand, desperate jerks on top of the blanket, as Gabriel slowly pulled out and slammed back in.

"FUCK, YEAH!" Bruno's voice was raspy and perhaps a little shouty.

"More?" Gabriel teased. They used to do this all the time. Fuck. Tease. Make love.

"Hard and fast. I need it. Want to come, so badly."

"I'll make you come. Hang on, babe, here we go."

His reached underneath them both and gripped Bruno's dick, which was already making a mess on the blanket. His hand was drenched in lube, and Bruno didn't waste a second fucking into his slick fingers, trapping Gabriel's arm with his weight as Gabriel started a slow, steady pounding into Bruno's tight arse.

It was hot, sexy, unbelievably arousing. Maybe it was the fact that for once Gabriel had managed to switch off from his thoughts, get out of his head for a few minutes. Or maybe it was the sun, the water, the breeze, the low hum of silence.

"Fuuuuuuuuuuckkkkkkk." It wasn't even a voice, the low screech that came from Bruno's mouth. It was carnal, primal, awesome.

Gabriel orgasmed, all his points of contact rubbing deliciously against the harness and the prosthetic anchoring itself into his front hole with every thrust as his body shivered and shook in surprise.

It was all-consuming, deafening, draining, and he collapsed on top of Bruno, his limbs inoperable. Nothing worked, not even his brain. Just thoughts churning through quicksand trying to make sense.

"Papi!"

The voice came from a fair distance.

"Vati!!"

"Oh, *fuck*," Bruno muttered, pushing up.

"PAAAAAPPPIIIIII!"

"Damn," Gabriel hissed, trying to unstrap the harness.

"Here!" Bruno shouted, throwing a T-shirt towards Gabriel. "By the lake!"

"I love you," Gabriel whispered, trying to catch the last seconds of a moment he knew was already gone. He did love Bruno, so, so much. If only they could have stayed in this little haze of bliss one second longer.

"Thank you," Bruno whispered back and kissed him as he pulled his swimming trunks up over his now sand-covered arse. "I needed that. *We* needed that."

"We did," Gabriel agreed as the three girls came running out of the clearing.

# Twelve
# FRANK

"Sorry, sorry, sorry." Maria was still trying to catch up with the two smaller girls, but by now, Lilly was plastered to Bruno's front. Maria stumbled to a stop, clearly flustered, her shoulder-length hair tangled around her forehead and flopping over her green eyes, everything wet from the rain still dripping from the shrubbery they'd chased the twins through. "I tried to make them stay in the garden. Dad told me to do that, but they just ran. I think they wanted to say goodnight to you."

She looked truly apologetic.

Frank, also soaked from the dripping trees and more than a little embarrassed by his rubbish babysitting skills, stood in the clearing trying to take in the chaos in front of him.

"Maria! Lilly! Lottie!" Andreas called.

"We're here. By the lake. Both the girls and me!" Maria shouted back. She looked at the girls in frustration. "Kommt mit, Mädchen!" she tried. "Sorry, I don't speak much German. I don't know if they understand me." She looked at Bruno like she was hoping for backup.

Gabriel had already run off to catch Lottie, who'd kicked off her shoes and was tugging at her pyjama top, clearly planning to go for a swim. Gabriel, Frank couldn't help noticing, was only wearing his shorts, and his legs were covered in mud and sand.

The air was thick with embarrassment, and it didn't take much to figure out what had been going on before the four of them had so rudely interrupted. Bruno was still trying to fasten his belt.

"They understand more English than you think," Bruno told Maria with a smile. "I'm sure they understand perfectly well what you mean. They're just...not always in the mood."

Maria grimaced back at him. "I guess that's how it is. I sometimes babysit for a child at home. She's also like that. She's five, and Dad says I should ask for double payment if I have to put her to bed."

Bruno laughed. "You'd be worth every euro. The girls like you, and you're very good with them."

Maria smiled proudly, basking in the praise. "I better go get them. Dad said they're staying at our place tonight."

"If that's still OK? But we can, of course, take them home, no problem." Bruno stood up and pulled a hoodie over his head. He had sand...everywhere. Dampness and brown stains showed through on his wet T-shirt. There was also sand all over his forehead and his hands, like he'd tried to bury himself on the gravelly beach.

"No, it's fine. We've already made the bed for them. They got to choose their bed...clothes, or whatever it is in English, themselves." Maria waved her hands to draw a bed in the air. "Lottie chose my old dinosaur stuff and Lilly a pink flowery one from Auntie Bella."

"Sorry about that. It was really not our intention to disturb you." Frank was speaking before thinking again, and now he was looking, there was something sticking out from under the messy blanket. Bruno seemed to read his thoughts and quickly moved the picnic bag to cover it. He winked and nodded discreetly at Bruno a second after he spotted the unmistakable bottle of lube lying in the sand next to a discarded pair of boxers. Well. It wouldn't have been the first time; Thomas and Frank escaped in the evenings for some alone time down here away from the kids. Not this year, though. Nor the year before, from what he could remember.

He was happy knowing Gabriel and Bruno had got some time to themselves. It wasn't his business to ask or even take an interest—or to even think about what had just been happening on the beach—but considering the bright mood and broad smiles of both Bruno and Gabriel, after the conversations he'd had with Gabriel over the past week, this was most definitely a step forward. And he really needed to get the kids back inside the house, get them to bed so Bruno and Gabriel could continue with their evening, resume what they'd been doing before being invaded by the shrieking girls and their crazy hosts.

Gabriel was lying back in the sand, getting tickled by the twins and faking defeat before suddenly roaring to life and making them clamber to get away from him. Frank missed that age, when life was simpler, when every sentence to his kids didn't need to be meticulously planned so as to not cause massive offence or irrational tantrums.

"Geht mit ihr mit, Mädchen. Geht mit Maria mit!" Gabriel urged before hugging the twins again, laughing as Lilly, or Lottie—Frank still couldn't remember how to tell them apart—planted wet kisses all over his face. "Ich habe euch lieb," he added in a low voice loud enough for Frank to hear.

"Come over here and give me a cuddle too, you terrible little monsters!" Bruno said, catching one of the girls in his arms as the other one made a beeline for the picnic bag. Frank couldn't help but laugh as Bruno made a clumsy swan dive, covering the bag with his body and spraying sand everywhere. There were probably things in that bag that children should not see. Frank snorted at Bruno's attempts at zipping up an outside pocket and quickly signalled to his daughter.

"Maria, let's get the girls to bed!" he said, then burst into another fit of laughter as Bruno tried to get up, fell over and tumbled head first into a bush.

Frank grabbed one of the girls' hands while Maria took the other, calling, "Don't do anything I wouldn't do!" over his shoulder. He stopped and turned around to catch Bruno and Gabriel in hysterics, having once again fallen over next to each other by the blanket. "We'll make sure they stay inside all night! No more surprise interruptions. Promise."

"Thanks!" Gabriel said with a wink, while Bruno looked down at their entangled hands and tried to pull out of Gabriel's obviously tight hold. They were play-fighting about who had the hardest fist crunch, it seemed, and Frank smiled, remembering. He and Thomas had been careless and playful once, or maybe they'd just pretended to be. They'd lost that during the past couple of years as he'd tried to stay sane, pretending to be a fully-fledged adult.

Thomas *was* an adult, though, and was waiting for them at the kitchen table with cut-up fruit for the kids' evening snack. Frank would have offered popcorn and sweets or even ice cream sundaes, but Thomas was always the sensible one. Something sweet would have been comfort food, as it was for most kids, and sleepovers should be full of fun and treats, but it would also wind them up. Thomas was thinking ahead, and a few slices of apple and a glass of milk might settle them for the night, or at least make them feel safe here. Not that the girls paid any attention to Thomas's fruit platter, and they flat-out ignored Frank's attempt at getting them to wash their hands. He didn't even know what 'wash your hands' would be in German. The sentences he'd been taught and memorised in his high school German classes had been far more complicated and, he realised now, totally useless. He may have known his German *Geschichte* and *Literatur,* but he had no idea how to talk about everyday things like garden work or what tools and ingredients you would need to make scrambled eggs. Knowing how to inform people that *Mr Bauer lived in Berlin* wasn't much use when trying to have a conversation with children.

The girls had disappeared with Maria, and he didn't know where the boys had gone and had only now noticed the roll Thomas had made for him, carefully lined with folded slices of ham, the way he liked it. Just the sight of the damn roll made his stomach churn with anxious butterflies again. He loved Thomas so much it hurt. Loved all those little touches, the gestures, the way he always thought of him and his needs, even when he wouldn't speak and refused to look at him. Then, when all the feelings were swirling around in Frank's head and the words were all stacking on his tongue, Thomas was suddenly nowhere to be found.

Frank felt unimaginably drained again, but the sounds of laughter from upstairs called for him, and he ended up on the floor reading to the girls way past their bedtime. He was surprised none of them were ridiculing him or laughing or getting bored by his meagre attempts at reading a book he hardly understood, but apparently, it sounded German enough for them. When the story was over, he tucked their duvets in under their chins and said good night, and that was enough, as the girls whispered good night and stayed quiet. He left Maria to read in bed and stood in the doorway taking everything in.

Back downstairs, he found Thomas sitting in a chair in the living room. He was probably tired of fighting the mosquitoes; usually he'd sit on the deck and watch the lake in silence.

"Do you want a beer?" Frank asked on his way to the kitchen.

"No, thanks, I'm fine."

Frank paused, expecting more. A question, perhaps, about how things were.

The remains of the evening meal were still scattered around the sink. He sighed, exasperated, and opened the dishwasher that hadn't been emptied since breakfast.

"Just leave it, Frank. Fredrik and Andreas haven't eaten yet," Thomas called.

"OK. What are they doing? Why haven't they eaten?"

"They're upstairs. Didn't you check on them?"

"I'll do it now."

"I'll do it," Thomas said and got up without waiting for a response.

Frank shrugged and grabbed an almost-empty bottle of wine from the fridge. It was one they'd opened on their first night, and it wasn't a very good one, having been left here since last summer. Perhaps they should plan a venture further afield to one of the larger cities and stock up on a few nice bottles. And proper beer. Although he shouldn't really drink on the medication he was on, but he was usually sensible. And he liked a nice glass of wine. He didn't realise he'd said it all out loud until Thomas entered the room behind him.

"We bought plenty of alcohol-free stuff from the supermarket. Isn't that good enough? We can't really afford to buy posh stuff all the time!"

Frank looked at him, wondering what he'd done wrong this time. There was clearly something in the air; he didn't understand what.

"Sure," he muttered. "How were the boys?"

"Andreas was playing some shooting game, and Fredrik was reading a comic. As usual."

"Will they come downstairs to eat?"

"I don't know. Probably not yet. Said they weren't hungry."

"Should I put away the food then?"

"Can't you just leave it out? They'll eat when they come down."

"But it's quite warm tonight. The food will be better off in the fridge. Too many flies about."

"Leave it," Thomas insisted, his voice like angry wasps buzzing with every word. He pulled out a chair and sat. Frank did the same on the opposite side of the table.

The view was slightly different from this side. He could see more of the endless forest and less of the lake. Pretending to admire the view wasn't cutting any of the tension, thought, and Thomas looked like he was about to erupt.

"What's wrong, babe?"

Thomas didn't even blink. "Nothing."

"Sure?"

"Yes."

"Have you heard more from work? I know you were really worried before we left. All the redundancy rumours?"

"No." Thomas wouldn't even look at him, instead gazing out the window.

"You've just been so...different lately." He tried to read him, taking in his usually sharp haircut that was now growing too long, his chiselled jaw hiding under the messy start of a beard, his finely shaped lips, skin full of lines and stories of a life lived in the city rather than tanned and weathered by the sun. All the while, Thomas sat in silence. Frank didn't say anything either but put down his glass hard on the table.

Thomas gave him an ice-cold stare. "Have I? *I've* been different? Huh! What about you?" His voice raised at the end of his sentence, and there was a definite tremble in his hands. Things were wrong. So, fucking wrong.

Frank frowned. "Huh?"

Thomas was quiet for a minute. "Where did you find the girls earlier?"

"They were by the lake."

"By the lake." Thomas's eyes flickered again. Window. Table. Hands.

"Yeah, by the lake." He was silent for a second, then added, "Let's say we all should be relieved that the girls hadn't run off three minutes earlier. Things would probably have ended very differently tonight, with some uncomfortable discussions not suitable for innocent ears." He was trying desperately to bring some humour into the conversation. A little light. Anything to break the thundercloud in the room.

"That close?"

"*That* close."

"You wanted to join in?"

Frank twitched. "What?"

"Nothing." Thomas got up. "I'm going to bed. Can you lock the door when you're done with your wine or whatever?"

"Thomas, what's the matter?"

"Nothing."

"Right. It's not *nothing*," Frank stated, his voice raising to a more confident tone.

Thomas stalled by the door and turned towards him. "OK, it's not *nothing*. It's Gabriel. Gabe this. Gabe that. Gabe said. And that's all the time. You've been hanging out with Gabriel all day every day, more than you ever do with me. You made him and Bruno a..." Thomas was almost stuttering with anger, waving his arms in the air. "You made them a romantic picnic. Now you claim you didn't know they were having sex on the beach just before you arrived? You're full of shit."

Frank really didn't get what Thomas meant. He wasn't used to Thomas being this blunt and opened his mouth to answer, but nothing came out.

"Good night," Thomas said, and before Frank could answer, left the room. He heard that familiar, annoyed sigh accompanied by heavy footsteps as Thomas walked up the stairs.

Something was very wrong, and Frank couldn't figure it out. Well, he could. He just didn't know how to bring it up without setting off another war in the house. As the rain started to hammer against the windows and the first rumble of thunder rolled through the air, he lay on the sofa and pulled a blanket over his head, hoping everything would be clearer in the morning. Perhaps even forgotten.

\*\*\*

The next morning, the air was warm and sunny again, the grass still damp from the night's rain, but everything seemed to quickly dry out as the sun rose. A thin layer of mist resided over the forest, slightly obscuring the view of the lake.

Frank had stayed in bed, trying to calm his weary head with all his regular tricks. Thinking about sleep. Listening to white noise. He'd gone to bed sometime after midnight, having fallen asleep on the sofa, and then detoured to the bathroom to try to jerk off when he couldn't settle down, but his brain wasn't with him. For a while, he considered trying to wake Thomas and begging him to just...whatever. Cuddle for a bit, maybe. He needed his breath, his heat, the so familiar warm skin against his own. But something in him made him hold back, not just Thomas's mood last night; his own reluctance to talk about things.

He remembered tossing and turning for what could have been hours but was probably less. He didn't remember seeing the dawning sky outside.

Still, his brain felt foggy this morning. His thoughts were slow, like everything, mind, body, heart, was stuck in slow motion while the world around him spun at normal speed.

The girls had woken up early and disappeared to the cabin but were now back eating breakfast, watching cartoons and having drawing lessons from Maria. Frank went in to get some coffee and suggested a morning play on the beach, but the girls threw a tantrum. "Nicht ohne Vati!" they scolded him with angry faces and waggling fingers.

Frank took them back to the cabin in the end. He needed a little bit of silence to find his head so he could figure out where to go from here.

He made sure to knock extra hard on the cabin door and waited a stupidly long time before letting the kids run inside. Bruno appeared in a dishevelled T-shirt and boxers with ruffled hair and sleepy eyes and thanked them for looking after the kids. He seemed happy. There was something in his steps and his smile that told Frank something had changed or was about to change. Frank just smiled back at him and left quickly, not wanting to intrude on their happiness.

Thomas had taken the boys to the lake to try to repair the old decking down there, and more fishing, Maria briefly informed him with a huff before disappearing back to her room. Frank was glad to have the house to himself. A few hours of comfortable peace, not heavy silence.

But Frank was Frank, and his head was too busy spinning, and somehow he ended up in the rickety old barn, staring at boxes full of paintbrushes. The house needed a new layer of paint; it had been a good couple of years since its last paint job, and a refresh was long overdue. Frank had promised to do it for a while, well, since at least last summer. Sometimes it felt like they weren't really made for this continuous state of work and repairs that owning an old farm apparently entailed. Who was he kidding? Thomas had never set foot on a farm before they'd owned this place, and Frank had grown up in a top-floor flat. The closest he'd ever come to wildlife had been the fruit flies on their shop-bought bananas.

Frank sighed as he inspected the chipped paint and clearly rotting windowsills. The old paint was flaking everywhere, and he suddenly longed for simple things like a Google search. He remembered something about a steel brush and removing the old layers, then applying some kind of primer before new paint.

The farmhouse was painted in classic Swedish Dalecarlian red, and Frank had been trying to imagine it in another colour. Not a bright one; that would have been too harsh against these surroundings, unless they continued with the traditional colour scheme, but he didn't like red, so he sat down for a while, going back to what must have once been the chicken coop to look for more paint. White was always good. That was the colour their block of flats had been when he was a kid, a safe, unoffensive choice, but adding a more vivid colour would be nicer, perhaps light yellow or sky blue, bordering the greyness of the cloud layer on a rainless day?

He frowned, wading through bucket after bucket of old paints. Most of them were the same dreary red colour. If only he'd bought some paint in Oslo, the right kind from one of those hypermarkets with aisles full of rainbow-themed paints. Maybe he could try a few combinations, perhaps attempt to mix his own paint with what he had, but the mix available here was red and white, which meant the house would forever be pink. He put down the tin in his hand and laughed to himself. Thomas would kill him.

Half an hour later, he finally started painting. He'd found an unopened can of green paint in the back, and it had been like the universe had thrown him a subtle hint. Aunt Bella must have bought it one of her last summers here, probably with the intent to repaint the house bright green. It was a fabulous colour choice and would be perfect. He could already imagine the green against the grass and trees, like the beach houses he had once seen in Denmark, row after row of small, colourful buildings. He smiled widely as he smeared the paint on the wooden boards. A younger Frank wouldn't have hesitated; he would have chosen a solid colour like this from the start, or several of them, not considering what would fit in here, just what he wanted. Maybe he would have actually painted a full-on rainbow house.

He frowned at the wall. The paint looked different up there than it had in the bucket. Lighter, more turquoise. Maybe it was too light. Maybe it would look better after a second coat. Or maybe it would make the house look like a giant blob of vomit. He considered the bucket of green paint again. It was still almost full, and it would be a waste to throw it out. Maybe the colour would be different after drying. He was always like this. He could create a marketing campaign, choosing the exact shade from millions of pixelated icons, but he felt restricted and not fully bonded with this curious shade of green. If nothing else, he could use this as an undercoat, a foundation layer—a mood board perhaps. The house would probably need several layers to cover the red anyway.

"Hallo!"

The voice startled him more than it should have. The silence here did that. People tended to sneak up on you, their footfalls almost undetectable in the grass. When he turned, Gabriel's brown eyes were looking up at him, and he was smiling broadly. Frank instantly relaxed. "Painting today, huh?"

"Yeah. The house desperately needs a new coat of paint." He looked towards the forest and the lake, but he couldn't see the others. "What you up to? Not taking the girls swimming?"

Gabriel shook his head. "Nope. I let Bruno sleep in when the girls came back this morning, and I had a nap after breakfast instead. And then they were all gone when I got up."

Frank nodded. "Lucky escape for you, I think. There are shitloads of mosquitoes near the lake when the weather's like this." He looked up at the clouds, huge, cauliflower-shaped dots gathering in the north. Maybe they would float this way, maybe not. A thin layer lined the rest of the sky, the sun visible as a pale, creamy circle through it. The air felt sticky, though. It was warm today, and humid after days of rain.

"Do you need a hand?" Gabriel asked, looking at the paint. "Nice colour, by the way. Like...green?"

"I thought it would be more like the grass. It kind of looks like a dark mint instead, doesn't it?"

"Maybe it will look different when it dries? Perhaps a bit more... pistachio?"

"Yes, maybe." He wasn't quite sure. It was funny how neither of them had stated the obvious. The colour was awful. Truly so.

"Do you have an extra brush? I could do the other end of the wall. Bruno and I tried to paint above each other once, but that got messy fast. Not recommended. Well, maybe some extra mess had happened too." He blushed slightly and laughed dreamily, his eyes seeming distant above his small smile.

They painted together in comfortable silence after finding another decent brush. Frank listened out for voices in the forest and tried not to feel uneasy about Thomas stumbling upon them, focusing on the brush movements instead. The strokes were calming, the regular back and forth movement of his hand along the panels, the other hand holding tight to the ladder, the bucket hanging on a hook a couple of steps above his feet. The paint was smooth to paint with, liquid enough to spread well but not too runny. The brush made thin stripes in the layer, but they would melt out to an even surface within seconds. Dip, stroke, back and forth, it reminded him of something. An old film perhaps. He smiled at the thought, trying to make the movements identical for each stroke, back and forth, back and forth.

Gabriel chuckled below him. "Lost in thought there, are you?" He smiled up at him.

Frank shrugged. "Yeah. A bit."

"Everything OK?" Gabriel's brown eyes were still following him, watching his every movement.

Normally, he'd just say yes, everything was chill. Normally, he'd say everything was better than the day before, and none of it would have been wrong. He wasn't lying; things *were* better. Today was better than yesterday, much better than the day before and the day before that again. He would probably have more ups and downs next week, as he had yesterday and the day before, but in general, when drawing the average line, today was better than yesterday; he was pretty sure about that.

But this was Gabriel. He was willing to listen, and he was not Thomas, absolutely not Thomas, not in any way. Just the thought of anyone thinking he could replace Thomas with Gabriel made him feel like he couldn't breathe.

Even so, he couldn't deny that they had this comfortable connection. He'd felt it almost immediately after they'd met. Gabriel could listen and talk and listen again, and he never asked about things he couldn't give answers to, but also, if he did ask those difficult questions, he seemed ready to accept the answers. Not everyone was like that. Frank faintly remembered his early adulthood, a time when people had asked him how he was. His answer had usually been something along the lines of wanting to die or oversharing the ways that he had thought about killing himself and how he had already tried, more than once. He'd top it off with having given up for the day and, "We're not yet at lunch, thank you very much." That had usually been the truth, but normal people were not ready to hear truths, and they became so stressed by his answers, even though they had asked the question in the first place, that eventually he stopped answering. Some of them freaked out and ran, some looked nervously around for assistance, like there would immediately be a crew of hospital workers ready to take him back to the madhouse. Some would ask if they should call his parents; most would just call someone else. Anyone really. None of them was ready for the honest answer. He rarely knew the answer himself.

Gabriel wasn't like that. He always seemed ready to listen, no matter what stupid nonsense Frank shared, although Frank didn't get that urge to be scarily honest around him, as Gabriel seemed to recognise his moods. Frank was also older and wiser now, understanding that there was no need to scare other human beings with truths. Instead, he stuck to simple words, describing what he *felt*, not what he wanted to do or thought or did.

"Not really," he finally answered and continued to paint. Back and forth, back and forth.

"OK?" Gabriel sounded hesitant.

"No, nothing." Frank shrugged. He considered telling Gabriel about Thomas's weird behaviour. Frank still didn't understand why Thomas had reacted like that, and he wasn't sure if he could or should tell Gabriel about it. It wasn't Frank's place to share things about Thomas, but on the other hand, it wasn't just Thomas's behaviour either, because mostly it had been Frank's. He should have talked to his therapist about it, of course, but the therapist wasn't here now. It was probably vacation time for her as well, and in any case, he couldn't do an online consultation stuck in this godforsaken place with no Wi-Fi or proper network.

"Tell me about it," Gabriel said. He'd taken a break from painting and was sitting on the grass. He patted the ground next to him. Frank accepted his invitation.

"Thomas is acting really strange." He cringed at his admission. "I think he's...jealous." It felt wrong to say those words.

"Jealous? Of what? Or whom?"

"No idea. You, I guess?" He sighed, already regretting this conversation. "He's been complaining that all I do is hang around with you."

"Oh, jeez." Gabriel laughed. "As if you'd be interested in me when you have Thomas."

He blushed at those words and shifted into a more comfortable cross-legged position.

"He seems perfect for you," Gabriel continued. "You seem to love him so much. You talk fondly about him. Everything you say kind of shouts love, but..."

Frank nodded, hoping he could change the subject. *But what?* "Yes. I have no idea where it comes from." He sighed and lay back. Resting. Rest was always good. "Thomas has always had a jealous streak. He got into a fight once because he thought someone was flirting with me." He let a small huff of dry laughter loose, then sat up again. "We were at some uni party, and there was nothing going on, but Thomas is like that. Overprotective. With a temper."

Gabriel laughed with him. "Wow, he got in a fight for you! That's never happened for me. Kind of romantic, really. But, in another way...Bruno has been fighting for me all the time. Not, like, getting in a physical fight." He laughed as if the thought was ridiculous, a soft laughter, his eyes glittering.

"Yes, but this is kind of...I don't know. Out of the blue? It wasn't just jealousy. Thomas, he seemed angry, as if it's all too real for him."

"Are you two talking?" Gabriel's question was candid. "Not just talking, talking. Really talking."

"Yes..." Frank paused. "I guess?" He was uncertain. "Or...well, of course we're talking. We have kids, so it's always centred around them, around practicalities. Who does what, groceries, driving to sports practice, laundry, money..."

His stomach knotted when he thought about money. The last couple of months had been tough, not because they didn't have enough money. They weren't rich, but they got by, even with Frank's drop in income. But they never talked about it. Thomas had been paying more than his share, Frank knew that. He'd made sure the car was filled with petrol, bought groceries and new shoes for Fredrik when he'd grown out of three pairs at the same time, given the kids money for new summer clothes, filled the fridge with beer, not only the bland lagers he liked himself but with expensive craft beers for Frank, too. Things they didn't really need and which Frank would never buy himself. Then, at other times, Frank would spend money like it was nothing and Thomas would burst into tears. Sometimes he didn't think, just acted, and he was well aware that sometimes he behaved like a total idiot. A selfish, foolish idiot.

"And then it just gets harder to talk," Gabriel stated. "The longer you leave it."

Frank didn't need to answer that one. It was as if Gabriel could see through him, as if each of their lives mirrored the other even if Gabriel's was more perfect.

"You know," Frank began, then he looked up at the wall he'd painted and at the almost-empty can on the ground. "Shall we take a break now? I need to find some more paint. I wonder if Aunt Bella bought more of this colour or if we have to go to the village, or perhaps the town, to get more."

"Aunt Bella bought this paint?" Gabriel's eyes widened. "I thought you were the crazy one in this family. I really love this colour," he added quickly with a smile. "It reminds me of...I dunno. Graffiti, I think."

"Graffiti? Yeah perhaps. Bella was eccentric, and the colour choice was definitely hers." Frank smiled sentimentally. He was sorry he'd never gotten to know Bella, having been gifted her farm and books and notes and everything she'd gathered over the years. Now those things made him feel like she was a lost piece of his past, a part of him he'd never know.

They grabbed some water bottles and took a seat on the bench down under the apple trees. The shade was cool, and for a moment, Frank wondered if he'd remembered to apply sunscreen on his neck and shoulders. His skin felt too warm, but he was pretty sure he had. Still, he couldn't stop himself from trying to trace what he'd done this morning, before he came outside, in the hallway, in front of the mirror, the white bottle on the small table, the icky feeling of sun cream on his hands, the smell... Yes, he was pretty sure that had been today.

Gabriel got up and disappeared into the house with a familiarity that made Frank smile. It was like he'd always been here. The farm felt more homely with more people in it. Gabriel returned from the kitchen, with two cups of dark espresso and cinnamon rolls from yesterday's batch quickly reheated in the microwave as the coffee brewed.

"I found the mocha pot," Gabriel explained.

Frank nodded approvingly. "No capsule machine here."

"I'm married to an Italian. Making coffee is an art form. Bruno wouldn't be seen dead drinking instant. He's a snob. Still can't fry an egg, but he does make a mean cappuccino."

Frank chuckled. "I feel you, really. That excuse of a coffee maker in your kitchen? We got it from Thomas's father a few years ago and just put it in the rental cabin since none of us... Well, since I don't approve of it."

"Coffee snob, are you?" Gabriel joked.

He shrugged. "Environmental injury. I worked as a barista during my many university years. Coffee was never the same after that." Frank took a sip from his cup. The rim was warm against his lips, and the hot liquid filled his mouth with its sharp taste. It was calming and energising at the same time. And apparently a trigger to overshare once again.

"I've been stable for years now. I've taken my meds regularly, adjusted the doses, gone for regular check-ups, therapy, kept journals, written check lists—done all the right things." He looked at spot far away in the middle of a cherry tree. "So, I guess I am doing well." He sighed. "At least, I thought I was, but these episodes are getting more frequent. Perhaps with the kids getting older, Thomas getting older, this worn-out body getting older, the world is moving forward. Maria and Fredrik will be out of here in a year or two."

"Really? You'll let them leave? Ours will be living at home until they're at least thirty. I'm not letting them out of my sight!"

"You've met mine, haven't you? I don't think I could stop them, even if I tried. Maria is apparently moving to New York as soon as she can legally get on a plane."

"I guess you're right. I just worry. I always worry."

Frank went back to silence, his gaze stuck in the trees again. He wondered how far the view here would have reached, had the landscape been different, if there had been no trees or more hills, or if the cabin had been on top of the slope instead of next to the lake. Maybe there would have been fewer mosquitoes, he thought, scratching a bite on his calf.

"But what then?" he said. "We all know children aren't here forever. They're meant to move on. But what happens when they leave? Thomas and I have changed. We're not the people we were when we met. Thank God. The kids are clearly changing too. As they grow, they mature, they shape into their personality. It's kind of predictable how a baby develops through its milestones to toddler and child and teenager and then becomes an adult. But we're already there, we're adults. How is all of this supposed to shape us?" He looked at Gabriel, who took a big breath of air, letting it slowly seep out of his lungs before he spoke.

"It terrifies me, the thought of the kids leaving. It's kind of weird just thinking about it, it being just Bruno and me, bouncing around in a flat that is suddenly far too big for the two of us. What would we do? Would we still have anything to talk about? We've already lost all the things we used to do as a couple. We don't even like the same TV series anymore. All we do is things for the kids, and then we hardly do anything as a couple. We don't even sleep in the same bed most of the time. One of us ends up with the girls, and the other goes and sleeps in the girls' bedroom. It's crazy." He went quiet and gazed into the distance.

"Not much time for sex then," Frank said bluntly.

"No. And that's my fault. I just...I don't know." He sighed, like this was something he didn't really want to talk about. "I'm just not the same person I was when I was eighteen. I was so fierce and fighting for who I wanted to be and wanting to be this perfect boy. There were all these things in my head that were so important. Then once Bruno and I had gotten together, he saw right through me. I could never get away with any crap. He loved me for who I was. All my hang-ups were totally irrelevant to his view of who I was. Then things changed. We had Andreas, and all the rest of the bullshit went out the window because...well, you know. Kids. We had a kid, and all that other stuff suddenly became unimportant and kind of confusing? Is that the right word? Diluted? Sometimes I lose myself completely, and I don't even know why or what I am anymore. I don't know what Bruno sees in me, and that's what scares me. When we no longer have the kids to keep us glued together, will there be enough left to make us stick?"

"When I first met Thomas, I thought that all I was, was my illness. It was all I could think about, my raison d'être that I was shaped around. Thomas chose me despite my illness, then he ended up with something he didn't deserve, or even worse, something he didn't expect or accept." It looked like Gabriel was about to interrupt him, but Frank put up his hand. "Now I know that perception was wrong. He just chose me, period. The disease didn't play a role at all. He fell for me before he knew about it, and he stayed with me even after the major episode I had not long after I met him and through all the ones I've had since."

Gabriel waited patiently while Frank paused to regroup. It was hard enough talking about this in therapy. It was even more debilitating saying it out here, sitting in the sunshine like nothing in the world would ever be wrong again.

"It's been a bumpy road over the years, but we've coped," he continued. "All of us have had to learn to cope. But now I feel like my identity is changing or should change. I've settled into my role of being a dad first and foremost, caretaker for my kids, responsible, caring, but also in my job role. I'm creative and cool and go to a proper job every day like normal people do."

Every breath hurt. He didn't know why until he felt a tear trickle down his cheek.

"But who am I? I sometimes feel like I don't know. Sometimes I wonder if I just put on this mask of sanity and pretend to cope. Then I start thinking too much, about everything, and asking myself if all this is right, if I really have to be this person, the one I've been for so long, or if it's time to let it go. Perhaps I'm just *not* sane, and I need to get away from everything and not ruin my kids' lives."

Gabriel frowned. "Bullshit. You're not ruining anyone's life. Why would you leave? You'll always be their father. If you left, *then* you would ruin their lives. Fact."

"Yes, I guess. But it's...different. Still."

"Are you sure?"

He looked at Gabriel. "What else can I do? I have to somehow change. The kids will be moving on. I can't be some pretend-dad when they go to Copenhagen or Boston or London or wherever they end up."

"But what about being a family? You said as long as you had your tribe, everything would be fine."

Frank frowned. The twisted paths of his brain were both confusing and confused. He wasn't sure which way was right. He was always doing this, warping into his own thoughts. Sometimes the way out was simple; sometimes it wasn't. This time, the solution seemed more complicated than ever, more crumbled, not just about finding his tribe.

"When I graduated from school, the class was doing all these celebrations." Gabriel spoke softly, the words gently seeping out. "Our class motto was 'Always Family', but for me, it was different. I was only there for the last two years. I had to move schools because it wasn't easy to fit in once I started to transition. I needed a clean break of sorts. The people at school—I barely knew them, yet some of them at one point did feel like family. Some of them became good friends, but they were Bruno's friends. And Bruno, of course. I met him there." His eyes were shining, and he smiled a distant, shy smile. "We were such a cliché in the end, high-school sweethearts. But it wasn't always like that. Try telling an out-and-proud gay man that your body parts are...not what they expect. Bruno didn't take it well. Not my story to tell, but for a long time we didn't even speak until we both got our heads sorted. We don't really see anyone from school these days, but there were other people in Bruno's friendship group, the kind that stayed. I chose them and they chose me."

Frank smiled. "Thomas talked about something similar once. About choosing your family. A family can be something you're born into, but you can also choose your own."

"Exactly. And those friends, or family or tribe, are with you for as long as you need them. I suppose the bonds are somehow stronger than with a birth family because you've made a conscious choice about them. They're not something you're born into."

"Do you mean biological family doesn't matter?"

"No, not at all! But a chosen family isn't forced upon you, it's a mutual choice, and I guess that makes it harder to choose to leave as well."

"But, would you want to leave?"

"Nah. I don't think so. Not now. At least, I don't hope so." Gabriel was looking at something far away. "It's a choice I would never want to make," he whispered. Then they stayed silent.

***

They heard the voices long before the boys came into view, eager chattering coming closer through the bushes. Fredrik started to run as he soon as he spotted Frank under the apple trees. "Look what we caught! Andreas got a huge pike. It's, like, fifty centimetres long, and Dad says it's probably five kilograms!" Both boys were beaming, and Andreas could barely hold the pike on his outstretched arms. "What are we gonna do with it?" Fredrik asked. "Can we fry it? Is it true that it's poisonous? Can we make fish cakes? Or can we have fish burgers? Andreas says he's vegetarian, but we can't make vegetarian fish cakes from pike, so he says he may want to eat them anyway since he caught the fish all by himself, but I killed it, Dad!"

"You're such a dork," Maria heckled. "And you're supposed to be a vegetarian, 'Dreas. Not so much now then, Mr Fish-Murderer."

"It's a life skill, fishing. You said so yourself," Andreas muttered, looking embarrassed.

Frank wanted to smile, watching the kids, but he couldn't make his face work. They looked so happy and beautiful, and younger than they really were. He remembered catching his first fish when he was seven or eight, from the pier in the city, with a friend who knew how to fish. He remembered the joy and pride, all the questions about what to do with it. He knew what fish it was, and apparently how to catch it, but the way beyond had been an unknown. He had never cooked at that time, so how the fish would become an edible dinner within a couple of hours had been a massive mystery.

Now he knew, of course. He could still feel the thrill of catching something and of preparing a meal from a fresh fish. But his interest had waned a little lately. There was too much waiting time; he always felt too impatient, despite Thomas's reassurance that the act of fishing had some relaxing quality to it.

In his mind he'd already started cooking the pike. Baking it on the grill would be easiest, but pike wasn't the best fish for baking due to its numerous small bones, so he was considering fish cakes, or probably burgers, as they were both faster due to their size and also something that felt more summery, with good buns, chilli or garlic mayo, some fresh tomatoes, lettuce and radishes.

He glanced at the pike. Thomas was probably spot on with the weight estimate, about five kilos. It was a good size, and he should be able to make one batch in the oven while frying some on the stovetop so it shouldn't take too long. He could even use the recipe he found in Aunt Bella's recipe drawer—someone must've caught pike here before—and they had onions and some bacon. He could add it to some of the mixture, to improve on the taste, and then some herbs. He had loads of them in the kitchen garden—chives, dill, maybe some spearmint and chilli, although he'd never tried it before.

"Frank! What have you done?"

That was Thomas's voice, and not the good voice. He sounded a terrifying mixture of angry and shocked. Well, more like disturbed, furious, afraid, all the bad feelings at the same time.

It didn't take long to understand why, with Thomas standing crestfallen in front of the house, staring at the external wall, then at Frank. Frank following Thomas's gaze, to the bloody green wall that stood out like a giant paintball shot or a massive alien wound.

"Uhm, I painted," Frank said, no idea how to even unravel this conversation.

"Yes, I can see that! What the hell have you done?" Thomas said again, the helpless whine in his voice reminding Frank of an injured animal.

"Das Haus ist grün, das Haus ist grün!" One of the twins was dancing around on the lawn, while the other moved in on the paint bucket, pointing to it. "Ich will malen!" Then she walked towards it and grabbed the brush Frank had left on top.

"Fuck," he muttered. "Gabriel! Your kids wanna paint. Should I let them?" His voice was cheery, but his head was dark.

And there was Bruno, rescuing his daughter from disaster when Frank couldn't even start to rescue himself.

"Ich will malen!" the girl protested. There would be tears shortly. He could hear it in her voice.

"You can't paint with adult paint," Bruno said gently, and all Frank wanted to do was disappear, erase his very existence from this planet.

"Why not?"

"It's hard to wash off and it's harsh on the skin."

"But I won't get it on me," she protested as she wiped her hand on her T-shirt leaving green stripes behind. She looked at them in shock. "It will come off in the wash, won't it?" That was probably what she'd said. Frank couldn't quite make out the words.

"Well, probably not," Bruno replied, a frustrated edge creeping into his voice. "Come on, let's get inside, and we can at least try."

Driven by an instinct he couldn't control, Frank rushed after them. "Fuck. I'm sorry. I think there's some white spirit in the shed, and I have paint-removing wipes somewhere. And wet wipes. They're incredibly effective. Can you imagine a product meant for babies' bums being that efficient at removing permanent paint?" His breath was quicker and more stressed now. Everything was spinning too fast.

"They'll handle it, Frank." Thomas's voice behind him made him jump, and the world just spun. Around and around. "Just let them fix it. They're not morons. Not imbecile newbies. They're probably more practical than you are. They'll manage without you."

Frank stilled, not knowing where to go, how to act. "Yeah, I guess you're right." His eyelids stung, and he blinked to try to make it go away, but it only got worse. Of course they'd manage without him. Everyone did. They didn't need him and his constant drama. All his stupid mistakes.

In a flash, the forest became grey, the grass dull, the flowers lost all their colourful petals, and dead leaves covered the ground all around him, adding to the silent palette emerging like film in developing fluid. The birds stopped singing, and he could no longer hear the wind through the leaves and the branches. No scent of earth and greenery came from the woods, no sun-kissed warm ground or clean summer breezes.

The picture mirrored his mind, infecting his brain, or maybe his mind was his brain, or his brain controlling his mind. It was all a confused, spiralling mass of complicated thoughts.

"Come on, Frank, it's not that bad."

He could barely hear the words, or maybe they weren't words. Maybe they were only whispers in his head.

"Hey, Frank, it'll be OK." Thomas's voice was stronger, no longer a whisper, a voice forcing itself through his ears, his brain, his mind.

He looked around, trying to ground himself. The forest was green, the grass another shade, the flowers were blooming, red and orange poppies, some yellow, blue, pink, he couldn't remember their names, the bees buzzed from flower to flower, the smell of paint strong in his nostrils, mixed with the smell of Thomas, his shampoo, soap, coffee, sweat, fish.

Thomas's thumb stroked his cheek, his other fingers curled around his chin, resting above the artery, as if he needed to check his pulse. Warm breath fanned his face, and warm strong arms circled his back.

"Don't go anywhere. Stay with me." Thomas's voice was barely a whisper, a brush of air along his skin. Frank shivered with panic. He wasn't going anywhere, but he feared Thomas was, so he clutched his fingers around Thomas's arms and clung to him as if everything depended on it. It felt like it did because if Thomas left him now, he didn't know what would happen, if he could cope with it or if he would just wither and turn into brown leaves on the ground.

"I'm not going anywhere," Thomas whispered.

"Neither am I," Frank whispered back.

"It felt like your mind did for a moment." Thomas spoke softly into his hair. "I'm sorry." He pulled Frank in tighter. "I'm just in a weird mood. It's not your fault."

"No, it's OK. The colour looks shit." He laughed. The poor house looked like it had been violated with slime.

"No, not about that." He drew a deep breath. "I'm sorry I was all shitty to you last night. I kind of...got pissed off, you know. With you and Gabriel being friends." He looked down, then met Frank's eyes again. "I overreacted again. Like I used to." He sighed. "It's always just you and me these days. I'm not used to having...competition. I don't want to be like this. I just want to be with you."

Frank clutched at Thomas's back, grasping the fabric with his fingers. It had been too long since they'd held each other like this. "You're right that we've spent too little time together lately," he murmured, moving one hand to fist his hair. The blond strands felt soft between his fingers. "When I first met Gabriel, and Bruno too, it felt like we had so much in common. Or I thought I did." It felt like an excuse. It wasn't his place to tell Thomas what to feel. "They were just so easy to talk to, and yet they were strangers who know nothing about all the shit in the past or luggage that other people we know find strange. We're not like everyone else. I know that."

Thomas nodded. "I know what you mean, Frank. I...you are better than me at talking. You always have been."

"Always?" Frank asked with a grin. "You're one to talk?"

"Well, not always." Thomas smiled, gently stroking Frank's cheek. "But in general, you're the talker. I think. You talk."

"I think too."

"I know you do." Thomas planted a kiss on his nose. "Maybe you should talk a bit more about what you think?"

Frank nodded. "It's just been a bit much recently, with the kids and work and everything..."

A shadow fell over Thomas's face. "We should talk more," he agreed. "Really."

Frank folded his arms around him, snuggling his face into Thomas's chest. His body was comforting, and Frank melted into all that safety, his leg trying to snake around Thomas's calf, his hand sneaking under Thomas's T-shirt. The skin on Thomas's back was warm and slightly sticky, covered by a layer of sweat after the day by the lake. The smell hit his nostrils, following the paths to his brain and making him pull Thomas closer. His hips ground against Thomas's, who smiled down at him and pressed their noses together in a soft Inuit kiss. Then their lips were meeting in a kiss, much gentler than Frank wanted, but Thomas's quiet laughter brought him back to reality, to the voices of the others, the little girl crying in frustration as Bruno took the paint from her, Maria's and Fredrik's laughter, Andreas squealing, Gabriel's deep voice.

Frank felt like he'd been holding his breath for days. As his body relaxed, Thomas held him tighter, warm and heavy against him, a comfortable weight, and there was a smile in his eyes. They were still green, like the forest and the grass.

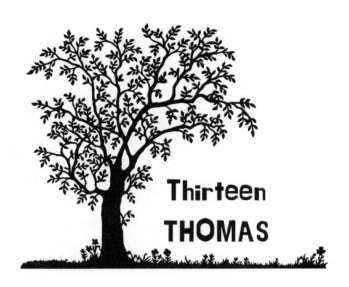

# Thirteen
# THOMAS

THE REST OF the week stayed warm and sunny, with thunderstorms hovering in the evenings, making the nights slightly cooler and more bearable, although the air was thick with humidity even after the rain. They chilled on the patio, swam for a bit, and completed a few small maintenance jobs on the house and the barn. Thomas had found a can of oil in the shed and greased all the doors hinges, so the doors no longer creaked. Hours later, he slipped in one of the pools of rusty oil he'd left behind. His reflex was to be annoyed with Frank for not cleaning up his mess, and he'd been too embarrassed to admit his mistake and apologise. Him and his stupid attempts at adulting.

The truth was that he was desperately worried about Frank, not only because of the dark shadow hanging over his head, but also the mood swings and spontaneous, erratic behaviour. Everything Thomas tried to do to handle the situation made him feel less uncertain—about himself, Frank, their relationship, their family. Frank was spending a lot of time with Gabriel, and Thomas couldn't blame him because he certainly wasn't good company. Recently, he hadn't been good for Frank at all, but seeing Frank and Gabriel in close conversations, talking, smiling, laughing, seeing Frank behave in a way he never did around Thomas made him terribly sad.

It had been with relief, not concern, that he'd left Frank to sleep in this morning. Things seemed so tense, like they'd been tiptoeing around everything for an eternity. The days passed hour by hour, taking care of the kids and the house, working, cooking, cleaning—managing the practicalities—but they still hadn't talked, and the monstrously large ravine between them was becoming more and more obvious every time he looked at his husband. He kept thinking about how things used to be and how they appeared from the outside compared to how they really were because, when he dared to examine it close up, they were falling apart. He wanted to turn in on himself, give in to the paralysing fear for even thinking those thoughts. He'd look at Frank's almost lifeless blue eyes that had once glittered so brightly and barely recognise him. He barely recognised himself.

He felt awful about how he'd tackled it. He should have been more mature, talked to Frank, used some of the skills he'd gained over the years to work with him. They weren't teenagers anymore; they were mature adults who'd been here before and survived. They had gotten through worse crises. For God's sake, they were supposed to be role models to the kids! Yet when it came to it, all he did was yell at Frank, snapping out snarky criticisms and showing him the cold shoulder when what he really needed was a hug.

With every little dig, Thomas felt sadder, but he didn't know how to stop it. The anger would combust, but once it was out, he was left drained. If he could stay in a calmer headspace for another minute, another second, he would throw himself at Frank, hug him, say he was sorry. *Sorry for everything, and could you please just talk to me because you're the mature one here!* Then he would no doubt have burst into tears.

Thomas lay in the hammock, staring at the sky. Small songbirds chirped all around him, and a surprisingly bold magpie cawed from its perch in the cherry tree above his head. Beyond the rattling leaves, the sky was a pristine blue against the vibrant green. The colours mocked him; his life was supposed to be as perfect as this warm summer's day. What he should be doing was heading out in the car to find network and make that dreaded phone call to work. Instead, he was lying here like the coward he was, pretending everything was still fine.

He turned his head towards the barn. The corner beam under the roof looked even more rotten than last year, and they should probably get a carpenter to take a look at it. Aunt Bella's house maintenance had been excellent, but there was a lot she'd neglected too. The weatherboards needed changing, and everything needed painting—at least Frank had made a start on that job, even if the colour he'd found had been...interesting. Thomas couldn't help smiling at the giant green splodge on the side of the house.

His eyes wandered from the house to the garden. The trees needed cutting back, although they should probably leave the fruit trees until after the season, assuming they'd manage to get over here in the autumn. The roses by the fence were out of control. Frank had talked about training them into a picturesque portal around the gate, like he'd seen on some interior blog. Like they could ever turn this into some kind of show home.

Thomas got up from the hammock with all the intentions of making himself useful. There were still a couple of hours before lunchtime, so he could get something done, he thought to himself as he made his way through the long grass towards the creaky old barn door.

The barn smelled of rot and damp, but he welcomed the cooler air inside. He fumbled around cobwebs and dirt until he finally found the old-fashioned switch and flicked it on. Several yellow light bulbs sparked to life, casting their gloomy rays over the large space and the imposing amount of rubbish. The cattle once housed here were long gone, replaced by years of unwanted things, piled high in every direction.

There were probably treasures hidden here as well, but most of what Thomas saw was just old junk: black rubbish bags full of clothes, the old, stained mattresses they'd replaced, an ugly pink velvet sofa with matching even uglier chairs, materials, beams, planks, wallpaper rolls. Paint, loads of paint, tools, garden furniture, a pile of wood, a couple of old bikes. It was truly an overwhelming sight and made him want to turn around and walk back out into the sunshine. An entire lifetime of belongings had been left here to rot because he hadn't figured out how to arrange some kind of collection service. The worst part was that he'd carried most of these things out here himself with the intention of driving everything to the tip. Years later, his inability to finish the job still stung.

"You in here?" Frank's voice came from the outside.

"Yup," he answered, coughing on the dust he'd disturbed and which now swirled in patterns around him, dancing like dull fireflies in flickering glow of the old light bulbs. And there was his husband, coming up and placing his hand at the small of Thomas's back.

"Gosh!" Frank stared in astonishment at the dusty landscape in front of them. "It's worse than I remember. We're a right disaster, aren't we?"

"We're no interior designers, that's for sure. I have no idea where to even start." Thomas couldn't help laughing at the two of them. Two city boys with no clue. "At least we don't have to run the farm. Can you imagine? We'd plant the wrong crops, forget to feed the cattle and probably poison the local community by spraying the wrong organic pesticides or something."

Frank chuckled and wrapped his arms around him. "Thank God we're not farming," he murmured into Thomas's neck. "Remember when we bought that large paddling pool for the kids? We could never figure out how to get the chlorine and the chemicals right. The testing strips were always off, and then the filter-pump thing broke down and we forgot about it for the weekend and the water went green."

The memories made them both laugh.

Frank continued, "Fredrik cried because he wanted to go swimming in the green sludge, and Maria never set foot in the pool again, despite us emptying it out and scrubbing it. Oh, hell, that was a disastrous investment. I think it's still in the garage somewhere."

"Nah, I took it all to the recycling site a few years back. Didn't want to even know what was growing inside of it." Thomas smiled, taking a moment to sneak a small kiss on Frank's temple. It was nice being here like this, just the two of them with nothing to disturb them. "I'm sorry—" he began, because he really was, but Frank interrupted.

"Don't apologise. I'm the one who should be sorry if anyone. This wasn't the best start to our stay here, and I...I didn't plan on this. For all of this to happen." Frank's arms tightened around his back, holding him in place, and for once, Thomas felt like he could breathe, regardless of the shit ton of dust. Something was starting to lift in his chest, a myriad of tiny butterflies coming to life as he reached down and tipped Frank's chin up.

"Remember the first time we had sex?"

"Oh, are we getting sentimental now? That's something old people ask."

"We *are* old!" Thomas pointed out, which always made Frank laugh. It was lovely seeing him smile. He hadn't smiled for a long time.

"Anyway, it was after that first episode you had," Thomas said. "When I had no idea what to do with you, and I ended up just sleeping in your bed, holding you because I didn't know what else to do. I was so terrified I'd done something wrong, and then I spent far too much time googling stuff that scared the living daylights out of me."

"And in the end...it turned out OK. Didn't it?" There was his Frank, a cheeky smile on his face, pouting as their lips met in a familiar softness that made everything seem a little bit brighter.

"It did. You got better, and then you told me you loved me and I got laid, and then I got myself a husband and a bunch of feral kids, and now we have a bloody farm." He chuckled.

"And a barn full of rubbish." Frank kissed him again. And again. "But despite everything—all the shit we have to deal with, never having any money and always arguing and your work being shit and these episodes and the kids being brats—you know what?"

"What?" It felt normal. Like old times.

"When we are really old, like pensioner old, will you promise you'll still love me? That we'll go live in the same old people's home and sit in matching armchairs and play bingo and flirt with the nurses and refuse to take our pills and steal all the biscuits from the coffee trolley?"

"Frank..."

"I'm serious. I don't want to get old without you."

"I promise. Whatever happens, we'll grow old disgracefully. Run naked through the corridors and piss in plant pots. And I'll order paint for you online, and you can paint everything vomit green."

"That's mean. It's a lovely, fresh, sage green."

"Frank?"

"Yeah?"

"I'm sorry I'm not always what you need. I don't always cope well when we get like this." He was choking up on emotion, but the words needed to be said.

Frank sighed and brushed his cheek against Thomas's. "It's not the first time things have become hard, and it won't be the last. It's going to happen again, however much I wish it wouldn't. This is...it's not the life we chose. Not the life you chose. Even when things are good, this will always be in the background. It...it will never go away. I wish it would, but I know it won't."

Thomas hated when Frank spoke like that. Like it was all his fault. They were a unit. A family. And after all these years, they still hadn't discovered any kind of magic formula to deal with it, no medicines to put everything right, no therapy to sort out the messes they inevitably found themselves in.

"I wouldn't change a thing," he said gently but with a conviction that surprised even himself. "Not a single second since the day I met you." However shitty things became, it was the truth.

"You sure?"

"Absolutely. Now what are we going to do with all this rubbish?"

Frank smiled and shrugged. "Let's sort it out another day. I think we should sit in the sun today, pretend we have nothing to do apart from eat junk and drink beer, and let the world spin without us worrying about it. Today is one of those days. A good day. What do you think?"

The suggestion would usually have made Thomas tense up with the stress of all the things on their never-ending to-do list taunting him at the back of his mind. But it sounded perfect, and he couldn't help laughing as he dragged Frank out of the barn and let the wind blow the door shut behind them.

# Fourteen
# BRUNO

THE DAYS SEEMED to blend into one another, each one as lazy as the one before. At least they had been calm. *Well, that's a lie,* he thought, as he once again rolled out of the sun lounger and crawled on all fours through the grass until he could get up. The lounger was old and creaky, and if you tried to stand up the proper way, it folded in on itself and trapped your legs. He'd done that a few times now, much to everyone else's amusement. Not that he minded them laughing at him, but it bloody hurt, and the repeatedly trapped skin on his ankle itched almost as much as the freaking mosquito bites did.

Gabriel said he barely felt them now, his system clearly getting used to the little buggers. Bruno cursed, scratching at another angry red bite swelling on his arm. He wasn't getting used to anything and neither was poor Andreas, who was sitting on the veranda with an electric tennis racket, swatting angrily at the wildlife buzzing around him. They hadn't seen the girls for hours, and Gabriel... Bruno had no idea where Gabriel had gone.

His stomach rumbled. *Must be lunchtime,* he thought and stubbed his toe on the wooden step as he stumbled towards the front door.

"Na?" Andreas called absently, not even looking up from the book he was reading.

*Wait...a book?* Bruno almost choked on his breath but decided against commenting on how unbelievable it was that his son was reading an actual book. By the looks of it, he was almost halfway through. Bruno made a mental note to sneak a look at the title later, find out what he was reading because whatever it was, he would be a good father and order some more similar books. Books were good. His son reading books was awesome. Not that Bruno read himself—apart from medical textbooks, dictionaries and the odd article from a medical journal. Everything was online these days, and what he didn't know, he could always google or ask on the many professional forums he belonged to.

All thoughts of books and reading were forgotten when he reached the fridge and opened the door, staring at the contents in disbelief. He'd stacked the shelves last night, he was sure of it; he'd taken a full pack of those fabulously easy-to-cook meatballs out of the freezer, along with a loaf of bread. He could now see the empty bread bag sticking out from the top of the bin.

"Scheiße," he hissed to himself. Because of course. Breakfast had been eaten, in several sittings it seemed, along with everything else in the fridge.

"Andreas?" he shouted a little angrier than he should have. It wasn't his fault, or not entirely. This was what happened when there were two grown men, a teenager with a bottomless pit for a stomach and two girls who never stopped growing. Or eating.

"What?" his son shouted back accompanied by the buzz of a wasp flitting around in the window.

"Those meatballs were supposed to be for tonight's dinner. Any idea where they went?"

"Meatballs? Hmm. I fucking love those meatballs. Can we get them in Berlin? Do they sell them? Fredrik says you can get them in IKEA. Do we have IKEA?"

"Andreas, did you eat a fucking kilo family pack of meatballs? What the hell, kid?"

"No!!" Andreas shouted back. "I'm a fucking vegetarian, Dad. Are they vegetarian?"

"And I was going to make cheese toasted sandwiches for lunch for us all—" Bruno added as Andreas suddenly appeared next to him.

He stared intently at the contents of the bin for a moment before digging out the meatballs' packaging from underneath the remnants of breakfast.

"*Contents: Svenskt kött från...* What the hell does that mean? Svenskt kött? She tricked me, again. I can't believe it! Damn." Andreas laughed and threw the packet back in the bin with a shrug. "We pulled an all-nighter gaming, and I was starving and couldn't leave my campaign, so Maria made sandwiches with that beetroot thing and tomatoes and those meatballs. I didn't even question it. We had loads. You should make meatball sandwiches for lunch. I've eaten them now, and I ate that fish thing the other day. I might as well continue my hedonistic streak until we can get more vegan food."

"Andreas..." Bruno leant his forehead against the cool shelf of the near-empty fridge.

"I'm starving."

"We are fucking *miles* from a shop, and I'd planned the meals so we had enough food to last until tomorrow. Now you are telling me you want fucking meatball sandwiches? Well, you can walk to the shop and get some meatballs yourself. You ate our bloody dinner! And lunch! What am I supposed to feed the girls? Air and beetroot salad? Oh, hang on, you finished that as well? But wait! There's some mustard left. Wanna feed your sisters cereal and mustard, eh?"

"Chill, Papi. Calmati. Rilassati." The little fucker always knew how to play him, speaking Italian to him like he was fluent, which he kind of was, but Andreas would only ever speak it when he wanted something. Or when he didn't want Gabriel to understand. Or the girls. Bruno had been too lazy with the girls. There just hadn't been time to sit and speak to them the way he had with Andreas when he'd been a kid. There was never enough time, never enough of him to go round.

"We have nothing in the cupboards," he grumbled still with his head stuck in the fridge. At least he could enjoy the cool air, seeing as it was useless for anything else.

"Frank has food," Andreas replied calmly, like it was a given that Frank would just feed them all. "And the girls prefer having dinner there anyway. Frank lets them have dessert. We never have dessert."

"Sugar is evil." Bruno cringed as he said it. They were on holiday, for fuck's sake, and judging by the pile of empty sweet packets in the recycling bin outside, his kids had already stocked up on enough E-numbers and sugar to last them a lifetime.

"It's fucking Sunday as well," he went on, undaunted. "I can't just go up there and ask Frank and Thomas to feed us all, not another night. We had dinner with them on Thursday, and then on Friday we had the BBQ, and it's Sunday. They need a rest and some time away from us."

"Can we make it up to them? Like, take them on a day out? You said we should go to that Moose Safari thing. We could take them too."

"*They* have already done the Moose Safari. They told us about it, remember?"

"Yeah, and Thomas said he wants to go again, and it will be more fun if Maria and Fredrik can come because I'll have company."

"We won't all fit in the car," Bruno pointed out grumpily. A day out actually sounded good, but a day out with his family *alone*. A-fucking-lone.

"Details, Papi. Sono solo dettagli."

Sometimes he hated his son. Sometimes his family drove him crazy. Sometimes he thought about life before Gabriel. Sometimes he wished he didn't think at all because the thought of having a life without Gabriel and the kids crippled him to the point that his hands shook.

He needed to go and find Gabriel. He needed a freaking hug. He needed to scream into a tree somewhere, scoop his gorgeous girls up in his arms and kiss their grubby little faces until they squealed with laughter. After that, he'd see if he had the guts to beg Frank and Thomas for food because the thought of getting in a roasting hot car and driving two hours or whatever to the nearest shop open on a Sunday... Wasn't happening. Andreas didn't deserve the trip, however happy Wi-Fi and a McDonald's milkshake would make him. Right now, he'd happily have killed for a McDonald's milkshake himself.

He left Andreas standing by the still-open fridge door like he was attempting to perform a spell that would make food reappear on the shelves. There was nothing in the freezer compartment, and in the cupboard there was half a packet of dry pasta festering alongside some sugar cubes and a jar of chutney a previous guest must have left behind. He should ask if he could throw it away, since it was years out of date.

Maybe he should just forget about lunch and go and have a nap. It was tempting, but the thought of his girls going hungry stopped him, not to mention that Bruno was grumpy at the best of times, and when his blood sugar plummeted, he was no fun for anyone to deal with.

With no other option, he forced his feet into a determined stride towards the main house, where the front door was open and the mosquito netting was blowing in the breeze.

"Hallo?" he shouted and flinched at the prospect of having disturbed his hosts/neighbours. "Hallo?" he repeated more quietly. "Anyone home?"

"Hey."

Thomas was in the kitchen, on his knees and wearing nothing but a pair of underpants, shuffling a pile of sheets into the washing machine.

It was not like Bruno ever looked at other men. Well, apart from in porn, and he sometimes flicked through Gabriel's fitness magazines since they had a subscription. He had a normal, healthy interest in fine-looking specimens of the human race. He was a bloke, after all and not a dead one, OK? But he had to admit, Thomas was fine. Not only was he ridiculously tall, but he had that Viking-like strong, pale chest and a prominent set of muscles stacked on his stomach, despite his claims that he never worked out, just ran now and then and...well, Frank had laughed and Thomas had blushed, and they had all known what Thomas had been hinting at. A healthy sex drive was beneficial to physical fitness. Bruno instilled that wisdom in his patients too, the people he counselled pre-surgery. Not that he was directly involved in the counselling side, but he'd sat in on a lot of consultations as part of his thesis research, and he liked his colleagues and they worked well together.

"You OK?" Thomas asked, standing up and wiping his hands on a towel, then wiping down his chest and forehead before throwing the towel on the remaining laundry pile on the floor.

"Yeah, uhm," Bruno stuttered, embarrassed. He was thinking of work, for fuck's sake, not anything filthy. He coughed and tugged at his hair, trying to compose himself into a human adult instead of the flustered teenager he suddenly felt like.

"I'm washing the sheets—freshening everything up, hoping I can trick Frank into taking a nap with me," Thomas admitted with a small laugh. "I can barely get him away from the damn paint pots." He sighed and picked up a glass from the kitchen table, looked at it, then put it back. "Bloody kids. They're pretty good at tidying up after themselves at home, but here, it's like they're in constant holiday mode and all the house rules go out the window."

"Tell me about it." Bruno laughed, thankful for the change of topic. Because. Well. The dude was just wearing underpants and Bruno felt like a frump in his threadbare T-shirt and washed-out shorts. He snorted at his own thoughts. No wonder Gabriel didn't want to have sex with him. He didn't even own a pair of underpants like the ones Thomas was wearing. Perhaps he should invest, update his wardrobe. Fuck that, he needed to ask *Gabriel* to help him update his wardrobe and get him some sexy underpants. Tight ones that would hug his arse like that, with that cool-looking writing on the elastic.

"Did you need something?" Thomas asked, jolting Bruno's mind away from the vision of Gabriel wearing said underpants. *Damn. Damn hot.*

"Yeah." He giggled and shook his head, trying to rearrange his thoughts. "Sorry, got all distracted there." He blushed because fuck, this was Thomas, not some random hot dude he could drool over and show Gabriel, and then they could laugh and Gabriel could slap his arse and call him a dirty old man. He wasn't attracted to Thomas. *Not. No. Just no.*

"Lots going on?" Thomas asked with a concerned frown.

"Nah, all good." It was. Things were kind of good. More relaxed, at least. "It's good being here," he continued, shrugging to get the words out right. "Gabriel needed the change of scenery, and Frank's been great for him. Gabriel doesn't make friends easily. I mean, he makes friends, but not people he can really talk to. Sometimes it's good to just be able to talk to someone who understands some of what you've been through."

"Yeah," Thomas agreed with a huff almost like he was irritated. "I mean, I do, kind of, agree. Frank needs friends too. Fuck, he deserves all the friends he can get, it's just...you know." Thomas leaned heavily on the worktop, looking into the distance as he half snorted, half laughed.

"You know, Thomas, there's no need to feel jealous," Bruno said softly.

"I'm not." Thomas laughed again, but it sounded fake. Hollow.

"Well, *I* am," Bruno admitted with a touch of cockiness. "I'm fucking raging that he can talk to Frank, this dude he's just met, about things he struggles to talk to me about. He should be talking to *me*. Shouldn't he?"

"You just said I shouldn't feel jealous!" Thomas almost shrieked, gripping the worktop until the wood creaked under his knuckles.

Bruno grinned. Classic psychology. Worked every time.

"You *are* jealous, and that's the way it should be. You have a very, very handsome husband who loves you to the point that he can barely see through the love haze the two of you have going on. Frank adores you. You just don't always see it, but that doesn't mean he can't talk to other people, have close friends, talk about things that he might not be able to talk to you about. It's healthy and normal."

"Bloody doctors, you're all the same, talking a load of crap." Thomas was smiling underneath the stiff pose he was still holding. Thank God.

"Yup, it's all textbook doctor bullshit, mate." Bruno laughed. "And I wasn't lying about being jealous. But why would Gabriel even look twice at some random Norwegian dude when he has all this prime Italian quality stud at home?" He slapped his chest like some ridiculous alpha male, and Thomas chuckled and shook his head.

"You're such an idiot."

"I know." Bruno smiled, taking a step forward so he could pat Thomas's shoulder. "I wouldn't make it a week without Gabriel. He keeps me going, sorts me out. Puts me to bed at night and gets me up in the morning. Without him, I would probably be dead."

"Did you ever suffer from...you know. Stuff? Do you get it all? Like, do you understand Gabriel?"

"Let me tell you something." He took a deep breath because this wasn't something he'd ever talked about, and he didn't know why he suddenly felt like sharing. "I don't understand much, and let me tell you, I've spent years specialising in the human body and mind. Personally, I've made some horrible mistakes, huge mistakes, and there are things I've done that I will always, always regret. I still struggle to grasp how the human brain works. I learn new stuff every day. But I understand depression. I understand losing control of your mind, and you do too. I bet you've stood at the edge of a cliff in your head and wondered what it would be like to jump. I know I have. I've wobbled and struggled and bloody lost my mind more than once, but the difference between you and me and Frank and Gabriel..."

"Yeah?"

"There is no difference. We're all human. It's just our brains are wired differently. We still live, eat, sleep, fall in love, have families and die when our time is complete. Some of us have to try a little harder. Some of us struggle a little more. Fall a little harder and cry a little longer. Struggle to swim against the undercurrent, while the rest of the world seems to go with the flow. It doesn't make us less human or worth less than anyone else."

It was nice to see Thomas smile, despite his shoulders sagging and the way he shook his head like Bruno was talking nonsense.

"Seriously, dude. Don't be jealous. Don't create drama where there is none. Let Frank and Gabriel have this. They need it. Well, I hardly know Frank, but Gabriel does. We're just a bunch of messed-up gay men on holiday. Take it for what it is. Nothing more."

"Frank is bisexual," Thomas corrected. "He'd just broken up with a girlfriend when I met him."

"Gay, bi, doesn't matter. We're still messed up," Bruno said. "I thought I was bi when I was younger. I tried to have a girlfriend once before I figured everything out. Poor girl. Broke her heart in a million pieces. To this day, she reminds me that I was once a teenaged arsehole with zero morals. Sara, she's called. She's Lilly's godmother, and she *says* she's forgiven me even though she still loves to take a dig at our past. All five minutes of it."

"I had a girlfriend too, when I was around twelve," Thomas said. "And she was also called Sara." He laughed. "Coincidence? She's not Norwegian, by any chance, your Sara, is she?"

"Nah." Bruno smiled. "But you know, despite Sara being lovely, she never did anything for me. Didn't understand shit at the time, but I knew girls weren't my thing. Then I met Gabs, and *bam!* I've never been with anyone else since because he's everything. He's just perfect for me, in every way. Like Frank is for you. I can tell, you just have that vibe. You belong."

"Gabriel loves you too. You know that, don't you?"

"Yeah, and I love him too. More than he will ever know."

"Frank is everything to me. Well, the kids are too, but... But if Frank left me, I don't think I'd survive. Talk about bullshit, but I think my heart would break, and I would just...you know...break."

"Then don't fuck it up over bullshit. Simple. Just love the fuck out of him, and don't fuck it up."

"Solid advice." Thomas smirked. "And same. Don't fuck it up. Not worth it."

They fist-bumped like teenagers, then stared out the window at the girls running around naked in the sun. They'd obviously given up on clothes.

The bloody mozzies were biting through anything anyway, and Bruno *had* brought enough sun cream to last them a year.

"I actually came to ask if you have any supplies," he finally admitted.

Thomas started to say something, stopped, blushed and mumbled in Norwegian. "Yes, we do. I guess..." He straightened up. "Sure. Of course. I need to go upstairs to get them. We don't have them in the kitchen. Not anymore. The kids get into everything."

Bruno stared at him in confusion for a moment until it dawned on him. "Oh. No. No! I didn't mean that! Food. I meant food. Do you have any food?" His face was now boiling, his cheeks on fire and his chest wanting to cave in with embarrassment.

Thomas frowned. "Eh, yes. Food. Of course. I thought you meant..."

Then neither of them could keep it together any longer. They started laughing, unable to look each other in the eye without starting another unstoppable burst of laughter.

"Jeez..." Thomas shook his head and tried to control the hysterical giggles spilling out of his mouth. "But yeah, I probably have extra condoms and lube if you need them."

"Thanks, but I brought my own. Probably enough to last a lifetime the rate we're going."

"Glad to hear it's not just me that fucks up with dinner plans." Thomas laughed again, stretching his arms over his head and running his fingers through his tangled hair. Then he stopped and opened the fridge door. "Just help yourself."

"I will do anything, and I mean *anything*, to make it up to you," Bruno said sincerely.

"Actually..." Thomas slammed the fridge door shut. "Level with me. Would you possibly keep our kids at yours for the night? I kind of have plans involving...those other supplies I mentioned."

Bruno grinned. "Knock yourself out. I'll steal some stuff from your fridge, and I'll be out of here. You won't see any of us until tomorrow morning. Promise." He made a zipping movement over his mouth and winked.

"Let me just grab these sheets." Thomas picked up a pile of folded laundry from the worktop. "Need to make a good impression. Clean sheets and all that. Freshly showered—"

"Too much information," Bruno interrupted and shielded his face. "Just go. Go date-night your guy or whatever, and leave the rest to me. You don't need to know anything else, honestly."

Thomas didn't reply, just seemed to skip all the way out into the hallway, closing the door behind him while Bruno surveyed the kitchen. Then the door opened again, and Thomas's head popped through the opening. "Thanks for the chat. And Bruno?"

"Yeah?"

"Don't fuck it up."

Laughing, Bruno reached into the fridge, grabbed the first thing he found and chucked it across the room as the door slammed and Thomas's answering laughter echoed up the stairs. Bruno retrieved the lid from the butter, taking a moment to look around the room.

It wasn't bad. It was better than the state of their flat at home most of the time, but he recalled when he'd first visited Thomas and Frank's house. At the time, there had been people and cutlery and flour and fresh rolls everywhere, but the kitchen was still clean and there was a sense of organisation underlying the chaos. Now it was just chaos. The kitchen bin was overflowing. Laundry hung over all the chairs. A forgotten packet of butter had melted into a yellow gloopy mess next to the sink among dirty dishes. A dried-out slice of cheese and a half-chewed crust of bread being feasted on by flies. There were crumbs and rubbish everywhere.

Bruno scratched his chin and sighed. Then he got to work putting the kitchen back together, tidying things away, trying to be quiet. Not that there was any sound coming from upstairs. He carefully cleared and wiped down the kitchen table, the worktops, the front of the fridge...

A short while later, with his stomach still grumbling loudly, he finally opened the Norwegians' fridge again and almost cried with happiness. It was a foodie's wet dream come true. So much food, stacked on every shelf. Lots of little boxes of ingredients, all neatly labelled. He remembered now, Thomas's obsession with leftover food waste and Frank's habit of buying random ingredients that nobody knew what to do with. There were sun-blushed tomatoes, boxes of red pesto, a packet of chicken breasts. Well, Bruno knew what to do with them.

"Pasta with Pesto Rosso," he slurred like he was drunk. What were the chances? There were two dishes he knew how to cook, that his family would actually eat. He laughed as he rummaged through the cupboards, collecting a bottle of sweet chilli sauce, some herbs—he almost burst into tears when he spotted a tub of crème fraîche at the back of a shelf, and there were endless packets of dried pasta stacked on the top shelf above the freezer. Every single ingredient he would need was right there.

He found a shopping bag under the sink, loaded all the food into it and surveyed the room one last time. It looked better this way, tidier for the mind, calming, like someone cared, and he did, he realised. He wanted good things for these people, who already felt like friends. He hoped he'd have a chance to talk with Thomas again soon. It was good to talk to someone who had, in a way, walked in his shoes. Or similar shoes, at least. Maybe he needed a friend himself, to get all these messy thoughts in his head straightened out. Everything seemed easier to cope with here in the quiet countryside, where his real life in Berlin seemed so far-fetched it felt almost unreal.

Maybe he should just get back to the cabin and feed his little tribe.

"Where have you been?" Gabriel grunted as he came through the front door and let the shopping bag full of food land heavily on the kitchen table, where the girls were sat sullenly picking at dry cereal in bowls in front of them.

"Milk. Shit, I forgot milk." He looked around and spotted his son. "Andreas, go up to the house, don't knock, just sneak in and grab a litre of milk from the fridge. Don't slam the door. Don't do anything else. In, milk, out."

"Was Thomas angry?" Maria asked, appearing like a ghost from the living room. "I didn't tidy up the kitchen. It was my turn, and I...kind of forgot."

"Nah, he's just stressed out," Fredrik said casually. Bruno hadn't even noticed him sitting at the kitchen table. "He's totally hating on Daddy—Frank, I mean—for the tiniest thing, then screaming and stomping around like he's some kind of demon. Have you seen *Good Omens*, Andreas?"

"Nah. We only have Netflix," Andreas declared with a yawn as Gabriel rolled his eyes.

"*Only* Netflix? Have you got any idea how much it costs to keep you guys in cable TV, Wi-Fi, Spotify and all the other stuff Papi and I pay for?" Gabriel started unloading the ingredients out of the bag. "Wow, where did you find all this?"

"Thomas and Frank's twenty-four-hour supermarket." Bruno grinned. "We owe them, big time. Or should I say, Andreas owes them." He glared at Andreas, who glared back, while Maria just smiled. Obviously, her German wasn't good enough to understand his sarcasm, despite her managing to somehow make herself understood to the girls.

"Papi, Milch!" Lottie whined as Gabriel bent down and gave her a kiss.

"Einen Moment, bitte." He gave Andreas a stern look. "Could you go grab that milk, please?"

Andreas nodded and moved to leave.

"Maria and Fredrik," Bruno said, "you're staying with us tonight, to give your dads some peace and quiet to rest. Is that OK? Thomas needs a good night's sleep, and I'm sure Frank would appreciate some space too."

"Yay!" Maria fist-bumped Andreas as he passed, while Fredrik stood up and started to sort through the ingredients on the table.

"Whatcha cooking?" he asked, poking at the thawing packet of chicken.

"The best pasta you have ever eaten in your life!" Bruno bragged with a grin.

It was a good day. It usually was here in Sweden.

# Fifteen
# THOMAS

THE SHEETS SMELLED of apples. Green apples, the zesty, crisp kind that reminded Thomas of his long-gone university years. He'd lived almost solely on those green apples and cheap noodles, both things he could barely stand these days. The scent still made him smile, though, memories of easier, more carefree times flooding his brain, although at the time he'd been anything but carefree, still struggling with his sexuality, having no idea how to even find a safe space in which to silence the constantly chattering demons in his head. There had never been room for him to explore that side of himself or to come out as anything. As it turned out, all that anxiety had been a total waste of time once he'd met Frank because life became so simple with that messy yet oh-so-beautiful boy in his life.

He adjusted the topper so it covered all four corners of the mattress. They tended to come undone as soon as Frank got into bed, the man always doing at least twenty minutes of wriggling before finally settling down to sleep. He considered putting an extra towel across it but then it would look like a toddler bed. The mattress topper could always be washed. He should have done that, too, he realised, but there was no time for that now. Later. Tomorrow. Before next time.

He smiled at the thought of Frank. His light, his life, his love. Thomas needed to try harder, or perhaps this was enough and he just needed to show it. Show Frank with every piece of himself that he was always loved, that Thomas would stay, no matter what. He somehow needed to get across that nothing had changed even though it felt like everything was different now. Bruno may have churned out a load of doctor's crap, but sometimes doctors were right. After all, they were scientists, too. The laws of physics sometimes blended into the medical field, and he'd always had the utmost respect for those colleagues who dealt with more complex topics than his tiny field of molecules and atoms.

He stretched the sheet tight across the mattress, wishing he'd splurged out on a fitted sheet instead of this a huge flat thing, which, of course, he'd put on the wrong way around. It covered the mattress width-wise but barely reached the foot end, so he rotated it ninety degrees and folded the corners neatly like he'd once seen in some silly housekeeping show. He used to watch things like that when the kids were babies and he'd spent night after night feeding and rocking and shushing. It was strange how he missed those nights, those long lonely hours with just his thoughts for company and Maria and Fredrik in his arms.

He used to walk back and forth in the living room carrying one or both babies, bending his knees to create a wavy movement before they finally fell asleep and he could put them down and collapse on the sofa in front of crappy daytime TV repeats. He couldn't concentrate through an entire movie anymore or even a half-hour episode of a series. Things hadn't gotten any easier, despite the kids growing up. These days, he was usually too exhausted to even read a chapter from a book.

Images of his old uni dorm room popped up in his head as he arranged the pillows, throwing them casually yet systematically against the headboard, wondering how to put the duvet. Should he make the bed properly or just leave it thrown across the mattress? Or perhaps arrange it with all the pillows on top? Or folded down, welcoming them to bed? Or crumpled next to the footboard to signal it being ready for...bed action? He laughed at the last idea; he wanted to make the bed look inviting, like an adult had made it, not like a teenager had just crawled out of it. All he wanted was to make an impression and show he cared. His old uni bed had been a single mattress with a threadbare blanket and a single pillow that he'd bolstered with a sweater. He'd had no idea of interior design or style or making things look alluring back then, but he'd still invited Frank into his bed, and Frank, bless him, had hugged him and stayed, despite the state of his life.

He dug into his sock drawer to find the lube and condoms he'd brought from home. Frank had probably brought his own stash. There were usually supplies in among his toiletries, together with his extra medicines. But Thomas had wanted to be prepared anyway, silently hoping for more action this vacation than he could fit into a small medicine bag with space for a few condoms and matching disposable sachets of lube. Condoms. Yes. Because clean-up was a bitch, although they didn't always use them in the end.

The thought made his dick pulse in his tight briefs, and he stroked his fingers across the bulge, his mind filling with the thought of Frank touching him, his fingers sometimes creating sheer magic. He knew exactly where to touch Thomas to make him feel good; sometimes it was just like when Thomas touched himself; other times, he would stroke him in a new way, with both hands, from a direction he couldn't reach himself, and his body would react in complete surprise, hurtling into that space that was hard to define. Those moments could make him burst into the most powerful orgasms. A moist spot formed under his thumb. *Better get changed*, he thought, giving his dick a final stroke before he went back to his cleaning mission.

Their bedside tables were full of rubbish, as always. On his own was a pile of books, research journals and textbooks for next term. He'd moved them from his bag to the table but had yet to actually open them. He'd also meant to give feedback on a couple of articles, but they were on his laptop. He vaguely remembered the PhD student who'd wanted a response within a week before she'd left for her vacation. He made a mental note to get it done at some point.

Frank's side was more chaotic, probably the same number of items as Thomas but more diverse: drawing pads, pencil, pen, the markers he currently favoured for colouring, a book from the library. Thomas had no idea what his husband read these days, if he had a new area or interest, if it was fiction or facts. There were also notes in Frank's untidy scribble, a wad of tissues and a hairband, wherever that had come from. It had been a few years since they constantly had to carry them around for Maria.

Rather than go full throttle on the bedside tables, Thomas did a quick sweep to make sure his books were stacked neatly and gathered the rubbish off the floor, then put the condoms and lube in his drawer. It felt like a very grown-up thing to do, out of sight, but still in reach. It had been such a different feeling all those years ago. He'd had a condom in his back pocket that night too, not a fancy packet like he'd buy these days, but a freebie from some club. Not that he'd thought he'd have had any chance of using that condom; back then, he'd been so bloody repressed he'd barely known how to open his mouth.

They'd met on a crowded dance floor, although Frank hadn't been dancing. He'd been standing there, mesmerised by the crowd and immersed in the music, and Thomas, who was usually glued to the walls in places like that, had joined that swaying crowd and edged forward until he had an almost direct view of the slim, boyish man with the white shirt soaked in sweat and messy long hair that covered the most intense blue eyes Thomas had ever seen. He'd reached for Thomas, pulled him in and plastered himself all over the bewildered man Thomas had been back then. They'd kissed a few minutes later, and it had seemed the most natural thing in the world. Him and Frank. Frank and him.

Sex had come much later, after a couple of months of constant togetherness, more kissing than his chapped lips could withstand and hours of talking. Because Frank couldn't half talk, and Thomas had come to terms with the fact that it didn't matter that Frank had a dick in his trousers or that Thomas was so deep in his self-inflicted closet he could barely see daylight, or that Frank sometimes became unwell and Thomas could be a jealous twat. Frank had looked at him and said, "What does it matter when all I want to do is lie here in your arms, and I think all you want to do is stay wherever I am. So, what does it matter?" It truly didn't.

The truth had been a lot more complicated than the simple story his memory liked to display. There had been hurt and anger and betrayal and none of the understanding and knowledge he possessed today. He'd known nothing about life back then. Now, at times, he felt he knew too much and envied those who seemed to live simpler lives. Yet, they were still here. Their bed was tidy. The curtains billowed gently in the wind, letting in the fresh air. The room was peaceful. Neutral but pleasing art adorned the walls—sunflowers, poppies, fields, probably by some local artist or perhaps by Aunt Bella. Who knew with all the paint they'd found in the barn? The door to the closet was closed, the clothes neatly folded inside.

Thomas frowned, wondering if it was all too much and 'calming' wasn't the vibe he should be aiming for, even if it did mean fewer distractions. He should have just left it all in a mess and dragged Frank down and let things happen. Things were starting to feel forced in his head, and he didn't like it.

Back downstairs, the last load of laundry lay still in the tumble dryer, and he pushed away the thought of doing something with it. He would put it away tomorrow, but he dug through it to find some clean briefs—the black ones with the red elastic—but he couldn't find them. He shrugged and grabbed another pair that had once been dark blue but now sported a myriad of washed-out shades of colour. Still, they were comfortably tight and hugged both his ass and his bulge. He pulled on a pair of old shorts too, since walking around in only briefs felt a bit too naked, like he was trying too hard.

The kitchen looked surprisingly decent, all tidied up with a bag of empty jars and cans hanging on the hook next to the fridge, newspapers in a box by the wall. It felt like a welcoming place, with the afternoon sun streaming through the windows. Someone had made quite the effort. Maria must for once have remembered to do her chores.

The fridge was emptier, though, and for a few seconds, he cursed the damn kids' stealthy food raiding again, but then he remembered Bruno. It must have been him. He smiled, wondering what to do with all this clean space. And the quiet. God, the silence was almost deafening. There were still tomatoes left on the counter, some onion, salted butter and garlic, and stale bread from the day before yesterday. Frank would tell him off—he was probably planning to make croutons with the bread or something equally useless—but Thomas fancied a simple piece of bread. Frank would have insisted on chopping the tomatoes and crushing the onion and garlic, adding an over-fancy dressing with more ingredients than Thomas had the patience for. His own simple cooking would do: a slice of cheese to go with the tomato. It was his signature dish, such as he had one. Bread, cheese and tomato. Easy, plain and comforting.

It was one of his few vices after the kids were born. There had been an evening when the kids were two and finally fell asleep at the same time, and Thomas had rushed around trying to get them a quick meal, something that could be cooked and eaten before the kids woke up again. After all the rushing around, for the first time ever, the kids had slept through until morning, and he and Frank had got by on a couple of sandwiches for dinner.

He took out the bread, slicing it into thick wedges ready to toast. He could hear Frank moving the ladder outside, a gentle scraping against the wood. Frank had been painting for hours now—it was almost three o'clock, and both of them had missed lunch. No wonder the kids raided the fridge. He sighed. The house had to be pretty much green by now. Perhaps Frank was even working on the second coat. The colour looked surprisingly cool, although he wasn't used to it yet and was still taken aback whenever he saw the bright-green exterior.

He stepped outside, Frank's always out-of-tune humming coming from around the corner. Together with the bees and wind and the other sounds from nature, it was comforting in the silence.

"Frank?" he called, stepping barefoot onto the grass.

Frank sat on an overturned bucket, painting the lower part of the wall.

"Hi. Almost done now. What time is it?" He took off his straw hat and wiped sweat from his forehead, smearing even more paint onto his already painty face.

"It's three. Wanna come inside for some food?"

"Sure. Just need to finish this first." He pointed at the remaining half a metre of the wall.

"Just that?"

"Just that. I promise. I think I've had enough for now."

"For now?" Thomas asked suspiciously. "No third layer or a new colour or a splash of graffiti or anything?"

"Hm. Good ideas!" Frank laughed. "No, just kidding. I'm done. For now. Let me finish here, then I'll clean the brushes and come in."

"OK." Thomas frowned, puzzled. Frank was being unusually reasonable.

"Gimme say, fifteen minutes?"

"Great. I'll have some food ready."

Forty-five minutes later, Thomas was still sitting at the table staring at the cold pieces of toast and sweaty cheese. They'd been perfect earlier. Now his attempts at a snack just looked sad.

"Sorry that took so long," Frank said, entering the kitchen, trailing grass and mud in his wake.

"Only twice as long as you said it would." Thomas couldn't help himself. "As I expected," he added and leaned in for a kiss. Frank smelled of sun and sweat and paint and white spirit.

"I should shower," Frank said against his lips, scratching under the filthy singlet clinging to his chest.

"After." Thomas winked at him. "At least have some lunch first. Or whatever."

"Outside?" Frank suggested, picking up the plates and pointing towards the cool shade on the veranda.

They sat in the old rickety chairs, protected from the hot sun by the roof but with a perfect view over the slight slope towards the lake, the glittering blue water between the trees as calming as always. Thomas brought out a couple of beers, a light lager for himself and some handcrafted stuff for Frank. He'd given up on knowing anything about beers a long time ago. Frank knew it all, whereas Thomas just liked his beers wet and cold.

"Great toast, babe."

"Thanks." He smiled at Frank and raised his beer. "To good simple food."

"Good food." Frank nodded back.

"The colour's pretty cool." Thomas gestured towards the walls. "It stands out."

Frank chuckled. "You don't have to pretend that you don't hate it."

"Well, it was unfamiliar at first, but I'm getting used to it."

"Since we're on our own, is there anything on your mind? I mean, I know there's a lot on your mind. Perhaps if we...you know. Try to air those things?"

It was surprising to hear Frank talk like that. And the air was suddenly thick again.

"No. Nothing that we need to bring up right now. Not here. We're on holiday."

"Still no word from work?"

"No network. I think my phone's dead anyway."

"Sleeping OK? No nightmares about this green monstrosity of a house chasing you into the lake and eating you?"

"That sounds like something the kids would dream. But no. No more nightmares. Just a few dreams about being forced to eat vegetables and having a barn full of rubbish, but that's normal, isn't it?" The jokes were lame, but so was he.

"As long as the house isn't running after you, I think it's unrelated."

"What would Freud say?" Thomas asked with a smile.

"Well, trust me, I have decades of experience with therapists... Where are the kids, by the way? I haven't seen them for a while."

"Oh, I forgot to tell you." Thomas suddenly felt nervous again. "They're staying at Gabriel and Bruno's until tomorrow." He bit his lower lip and hoped he wasn't blushing.

Frank didn't answer, just stared at the forest and the view. He was a little too serious for Thomas's liking. His eyes were distant, and Thomas couldn't quite read him. Maybe Frank didn't want this. Maybe he wanted to keep the distance between them, the forced lack of intimacy that came with kids, the lack of solitude, the constant disturbance and distractions. Maybe this afternoon was as far as he could get from what Frank wanted and needed. Maybe it would trigger something in him, Thomas wasn't sure what, probably not a serious episode, but he suddenly feared rejection.

Thomas's brain was working too fast for a change. Trying to cajole his voice into working, to say it didn't matter, that they could get the kids back home, invite themselves for dinner at Gabriel and Bruno's, they didn't have to be alone, didn't have to do this, whatever 'this' was.

"So, we are alone?" Frank asked.

Thomas nodded.

"For the first time in months?"

"Yeah."

Frank didn't say anything for a while, but then he turned towards Thomas, and his face cracked up in a mischievous smile. He leaned across the table and gently took Thomas's hand. "So, you're mine for the night, then?"

"I am." Thomas stood and dragged Frank up from his seat. "Come on, let's get you showered."

They ran up the stairs two steps at a time, and Thomas was about to enter the bedroom, but Frank dragged him towards the bathroom. "You need to shower too, babe," he said with a cheeky grin.

Thomas stopped mid-step. Part of him wanted to rush into the bedroom, remove all those filthy clothes, jump into bed and fuck like rabbits. He looked Frank up and down for a second, noticing his damp skin, the shades from the dark spots on his singlet, flecks of paint on his skin, and nodded. "Sure. Shower."

Thomas hadn't thought about joining in, but now that he was, it seemed as natural as breathing. The two of them stepped into the small shower, the water heater for once having done its job, and Frank put his arms around Thomas, leaning in for a hug that seemed long overdue.

"Turn around." Thomas's voice was raspy through the running water.

Frank did and leant on the wall with his arms wide and his head resting on the tiles between them. The water ran down his back, making small waterfalls along his spine before disappearing down between his tightly clenched buttocks.

"Spread your legs, dumbass." Thomas laughed and put his foot between Frank's to make him move.

"What if I don't want to?" Frank teased.

"You do. Just spread them."

Thomas would have to wait for the good stuff because there was far too much paint on Frank's skin, and he got to work with lathering with a sponge and soap. It took a while, and Frank's skin was red afterwards, but the paint was gone. Thomas continued stroking, slowly moving his hands over the familiar shape of his husband's body.

"Just relax," he whispered into Frank's ear, alternating his hand movements between small circles and long strokes, and bent down to kiss Frank's shoulder, to taste. It was almost too many sensations to take in at once—clean water, humidity, soap, perfume, smooth skin against his lips— his kisses were more like hungry licks, his usual hesitation and worries gone, rinsed down the drain. Somehow the scents of Frank were gone too, but he was still here, in front of him, between his legs, under his hands and lips.

Frank kept his eyes closed, his chest rising and falling in deep, slow breaths.

"You OK?" Thomas's hand slid between Frank's cheeks, still wet and smooth from water and soap, the tip of his middle finger brushing over the tight opening. Frank tensed, and Thomas laughed quietly. "I'm not even there yet." Frank relaxed again. More deep breaths. Perhaps even a smile. Thomas slid his finger back again, up and down a few times before he slowly poked at the opening and carefully nudged his fingertip inside. A shiver went through Frank as the first knuckle glided in, and Thomas could feel Frank forcing himself to loosen up before the finger went all the way inside. He held on tight to Frank's hip with his left hand, holding him in place as his right finger started probing, in and out in smooth movements.

Frank's breaths were getting faster and shallower, his rim tightening against Thomas's finger. It was a dance they had danced so many times, the movements frighteningly familiar. Thomas was now stroking himself at the same pace, pulling slightly at his dick every time Frank clenched around his finger. He shifted, gifting his left hand to Frank, stroking his husband's shaft, knowing Frank would come from this. His movements were but shivers, and the small, desperate moans were pulling Thomas closer to the edge himself. He loved this. All of this.

"No, wait," Frank panted, pushing Thomas's hand away. "I want to do this in bed." His cock was hard and red and pointing towards his stomach.

Thomas had to agree. He wanted this to last, not just get themselves off in a hurry. He offered a lazy kiss, which should have calmed them down but instead seemed to create an even more frenzied urge to just exist the way they were right here, right now, because they were never like this anymore. They'd once taken all this for granted, but there was no longer time or space to be themselves, not like it had been years ago, when there were fewer cavities in their lives, craters full of obstacles that had somehow dulled the basics of their marriage.

They slowed down a bit as they reached the bed, almost like the apple scent calmed them, giving their bodies a break from the steamy bathroom with their slick skin, the tiles, the memories of what they once used to do almost every day.

Things were still different. Instead of softness, Frank's callused hands cupped Thomas's face. Thomas mirrored the action, pulling him closer, stroking his temples with his thumbs, following the ridge of his eyebrows, kissing him again as they tumbled onto the clean sheets.

"Can you remember when we last did this?" Thomas asked.

"Stuff in the shower, you mean?"

"That too. But I meant in general."

"Yeah." Frank looked up at the ceiling. "I know things have kind of changed."

"They have."

They stayed silent for a while, Frank's hand sliding into Thomas's.

"Do you miss it?" Thomas asked and held his breath, not sure what he wanted the answer to be.

Frank met his gaze, his fingers gently stroking his cheek. "Do you?" His voice was just a whisper.

Thomas shrugged. "Maybe?"

Frank smiled and stole a kiss. "I like what we have now, too. This. Everything. Even if it's different."

"Everything changed when we had Maria and Fredrik."

"Yes. And no. It started to change long before that. It changed soon after we met, and again when we became a couple. Marriage. We bought a house. We evolve all the time, and we can't change that."

"No, we can't." Thomas closed his eyes and moved closer to Frank. Trust his idiot husband to put everything into simple words. Make all the mountains in his head make sense. "And I wouldn't. I wouldn't change a thing. No matter how much shit life throws at us. No matter how much stress everything is, I will never change it."

"But there are perks to being just the two of us too." Frank stroked down Thomas's neck and chest, his thumb lingering around a nipple, playing with the brush of hair, his fingers lightly moving across ribs and abs, reaching the path going down from his navel, downwards and downwards.

Thomas sighed contentedly and turned onto his back. With his arms behind his neck, he let his body stretch and relax, his hips rising up against Frank's roving hands. He was semi-hard, his dick filling and pulsing against his thigh.

Frank was doing all those things Thomas loved, kissing a trail down from his throat, closing his lips around his nipple, lightly biting and tugging. It made his body shiver in anticipation. It had been deprived for too long, waiting for Frank's tongue, which was drawing fast streaks across the hard nipple. He couldn't resist joining in, playing with his other nipple, massaging it lightly between his thumb and index finger.

Then Frank was suddenly between his legs, pushing them apart and arranging them around his hips so he could get into position. Thomas loved this feeling of being exposed, his legs spread wide. Even though he knew what would happen, this feeling in between, the anticipation, the thrill of knowing...

"Do you have lube?" Frank muttered.

"Yes, in the drawer." He nodded towards the bedside table.

Frank chuckled. "Always prepared, like a bloody Boy Scout."

"I didn't want to waste your silly sachets."

"Maybe there's something in my drawers too," he said, reaching over Thomas so he could rummage around in the bedside cabinet.

"Uhum?"

"Yeah?"

"You gonna do me then? That's...unexpected."

"Maybe. Maybe not. Maybe you will find out." Frank let loose a silent laugh. "Can you bend your knees a bit?" he asked, shuffling closer as his fingers flicked open the bottle.

Thomas's body immediately reacted to that snap. He always did, with anticipation, desire, excitement, a hunger for what he knew, wanted and hoped would come. His hips strained, pushing his legs even further apart. His nipples became harder and more sensitive, his breathing faster and deeper. He clung to the sheets with both hands, not wanting to touch himself now. He wanted to let Frank do this. Needed Frank to do this. He thought Frank needed this too, to be in charge, feel in control and remember that despite everything, he was the only one that mattered. The only one who would ever love Thomas like this. The only one who had ever been this close to him. There had only ever been Frank, and the realisation, as always, hit Thomas like a thunderbolt. He didn't ever want to do this with anyone but the man who winked as he hitched Thomas's legs over his shoulders.

The first stroke of Frank's tongue made his brain short circuit, a now rare occurrence that had once been almost a textbook part of their love-making.

"Stay still," Frank warned, his voice merely a hum from down below.

"Can't." He jerked uncontrollably against Frank's strong hold that forced his body to comply with everything he needed. Because this...this was what he needed. These moments when he could just let go and let Frank lead the way. His body slowly relaxed and made space, then tensed up as Frank pushed inside him in a well-rehearsed dance of pleasure and pain, smooth, silky movements with his legs angled just so and his hands gripping the headboard as the bed creaked with every careful thrust.

"You OK?" He heard the words but couldn't reply. Yes. He was OK. He nodded and managed a needy whine, begging for more.

"It's going to get good. Just relax."

It could have been hours with his perception skewed by the touching and kissing and scents and tastes, his body shivering and jerking with every new move, then that familiar push and press and sting and pain that grew and grew until Thomas was practically shouting and pleading and needing. Frank was right, it did get good after that. Really good. Words and movement and moans and more kisses—his throat felt dry as he told Frank to go faster, harder, more, anything to get him where he needed to go. He didn't think any coherent thoughts again until much later, after his body exploded in a haze of stars.

*\*\**

They lay in silence afterwards, enjoying the bliss and the afterglow, their bodies sinking deeper into the mattress with every breath, skin fused to skin. A cool breeze trickled gently through the open windows, mingling with the sound of chirping birds.

Thomas rested his head on Frank's chest, Frank's heartbeat slowing under his cheek as he drew slow circles over Thomas's back and counting his ribs one by one with his fingertips. Their skin was damp, and he was already hoping they would take another lazy shower soon, even though the water would probably be running cold now. He smiled at the thought, remembering when they were younger and their weekends were spent alternating between their tiny shower and their crappy old bed, only breaking off from their routines to lazily fuck on the couch or over the couch or hard against the kitchen counter. He felt a flash of arousal in his crotch again, a comfortable friction forming where his hips met Frank's thigh.

"It's been a while," he murmured. "Since we did this."

"Mm." Frank tangled his fingers in Thomas's hair, a comforting touch that Thomas had missed. He'd thought about a buzzcut in time for summer, even considered shaving it all off because it was practical and convenient, but he was glad he hadn't. He could feel Frank's steady breaths, the satisfying little hums as he combed through Thomas's unkempt tresses, very different from the usual quick finger sketches on his scalp, somehow more sensitive even though the scientist in him knew it should be the opposite as hair didn't have nerve endings.

"We should do this more often," Frank said.

"Yes." Thomas sighed and tilted his head so he could see Frank's face. His gorgeous face. Those eyes that were still as mesmerising as they had been that night on the dancefloor.

"Thomas, can I ask you something? Don't get mad. I just need to know."

"Why would I get mad? I have nothing to hide, and you know you can tell me anything. Always." He pulled Frank in tighter, hoping to settle whatever was playing on his husband's mind so it didn't ruin this moment, when they were just finding their way back to some kind of peace.

"It's...the Gabriel thing. Do you mind? I mean, I know you don't like me hanging around with him so much when I should be spending time with you and the kids. It's just. It's..."

"Me? Jealous? No! No, no!" He shook his head, at first offended, but then he rested it back on Frank's chest with a sigh. He'd had a stupid nightmare last night, one that had shaken him to the core. Disturbing scenes of being tied up, anchored in darkness with a strange man—a man that wasn't Frank. He'd woken up in sheer panic, kicking and screaming and all because he couldn't admit what was bothering him, not even to himself, was his fear of losing Frank to someone else and spending the rest of his life alone because the thought of being with anyone else? That was never going to happen.

He couldn't look at Frank as he mumbled what he knew was a load of crap. "Or, well. Maybe I was. It's just, I thought you would be able to talk to me, that you'd want to spend time with me, but instead you're with Gabriel all the time. Everything is 'Gabriel this, Gabriel that.'"

"You know you are the only one for me?" Frank asked softly, and Thomas sighed. It hurt to talk about this.

"Thomas, look at me."

Frank pushed his chin up, forcing Thomas to look him in the eyes. They seemed softer and lighter now, glittering with something, even though all Thomas felt was shame.

"Darling, I know you worry sometimes. When I talk too much, when I loosen up with strangers, when I travel for work or work too much and we don't see each other properly for long periods. I can see it in your eyes—your entire face closes in fear. And it hurts. It hurts so much that you still, after all these years, doubt us, that you doubt yourself, doubt me. Not because you're not allowed to, because you are, of course you are! But it hurts that you doubt yourself, that you don't believe that I still love you and always will. That's the truth, Thomas. Maybe I will look at other people, talk to them, even flirt, but I will always love you. I once promised you that. I will never leave you, I will always be here, as long as you want me to be. As long as you will have me. I know it's not easy. I know...I'm a lot to handle for you, even now, after all this time."

Thomas's eyes stung, and his cheeks soaked with tears. He couldn't speak, just clung to the man in his arms, wetting him too as he let his kisses say what he couldn't—that he would always love him, even if he was afraid half of the time and didn't trust himself or Frank or the world. He had loved him since the first time he saw him, when that flash of bravery had hit him on the dance floor and forever bolted them together, his anchor, his life, his love.

"Whatever happens, whatever the future brings, it will be fine. OK? You and me. We will be OK, won't we?" Frank whispered.

Thomas hoped so; God, he hoped so. With all the uncertainty of the future and some seriously frightening decisions to be made—the thoughts of work, of his job, all came back, flooding over him like a chilly blanket. The loss of a steady income, the forced changes. Redundancy. His colleagues, his students his team...

*Thump! Thump!*

An angry pounding against the wall, and there were voices too, male voices shouting in another language, then children's voices followed by giggles and panicked laughter.

Frank turned around and sat up, moving the curtains so he could look out. "What on earth is happening out there?"

# Sixteen

## GABRIEL

"Lämmchen!" Lottie shrieked, jumping up and down with excitement as Lilly ran around in circles trying to catch the sheep that were roaming the garden.

"Böse Schafe," Lilly shouted, wagging her finger as Bruno tried to shoo the startled animals, looking more like a confused policeman than a shepherd.

"They're not lambs, stupid," Andreas said, plonking himself on the ground and scratching the stomach on the nearest sheep. "These are adults. Even the smaller ones are pretty grown up. They're sheep." He fell over backwards as one of the animals stepped right over him, trying to get away from his attempts at affection. "Big freaking sheep."

"They're not dogs, 'Dreas." Maria laughed, making some weird whooping sounds as she waved her arms around like a windmill. "They're from the farm to the east. They keep escaping from the field up the road and usually end up in our garden. Our bushes seem to be tasty, and they like the grass." She whooped again, making the sheep scatter all over the place, one making a beeline for Bruno and startling him enough for him to jump in surprise.

"I'm quite sure they're not supposed to eat the roses," Gabriel said, slight panic rising in his chest. He could cope with students. He could make thirty teenagers do press-ups with a swift whistle. He was fucking good at teaching. Sheep? He would make the worst farmer in the world, and by the looks of it, Bruno would be no better. He was terrified and had climbed onto the main house's veranda.

"How do we make them leave?" he shouted, clapping his hands in an attempt to scare off the influx of creatures. Their lives had been surprisingly peaceful over the last couple of weeks, and the noise and all the movement were deafening and surreal by comparison.

"HOP, HOP, HOP, HOP!" Fredrik shouted, his voice strong and steady, his hands clapping as he rounded the rear of what Gabriel hoped was the entire herd.

"Forbanna sauer!" And there was Thomas, bursting out of their front door like a deranged herding superhero in underpants.

Now they'd done it. Bruno had said Thomas and Frank needed alone time. Fucking time. Literally. Bruno had winked. Gabriel had blushed. His stomach was somersaulting just thinking about it. Not again. The other day had been good; he'd felt in control, in charge, and his body had somehow been detached from it all, despite the orgasm that still made his groin tingle. Part of him wanted to do it again, press Bruno down on the bed, restrain his hands as he plunged the prosthetic cock into him, felt the tension grow in his limbs as the straps pulled against his skin, heard Bruno's deep breaths as he adjusted to the intrusion, the heady sounds that always spilled from him, the water gathering in the corners of eyes scrunched shut as he let himself feel. Gabriel could imagine it, then his head would switch their roles, his legs curled around Bruno's shoulders, his arse up in the air as Bruno's cock plunged into him. He liked the idea, could imagine Bruno's hands on him, the way his lips felt on his skin, the slow soft strokes of his fingers, their chests pressed together. Heat. Sweat. Closeness. The pictures in his head aroused him, yet his body tensed and his shoulders shuddered.

"They come in and chew on everything. Eat the bloody roses and destroy the grass, and then they poop everywhere," Frank said, following Thomas out. He shouted and waved his hands the same way Fredrik had, sending the startled sheep running in every direction. They were everywhere.

"Dad! Leave it to me and Thomas!" Fredrik yelled. "We had them all going the right way. Now look at them!"

Gabriel could almost feel it himself, the way Frank tensed up at his son's irritation. Thomas sighed and got on with it, barefoot in the grass, shouting loudly at the sheep running amok with parts of their rose bushes in their mouths.

"Bloody deranged animals. Have you even heard of sheep devouring rose bushes? Only in bloody Sweden," Frank muttered as he stormed back inside the house. Gabriel noticed he looked unusually pale, and the boxers he wore were far too big for his skinny frame. He didn't have Thomas's muscle structure or broadness, which was already forming in Fredrik. Frank was all skin and bones, a pale slimness all hunched up like he was trying to hide. Gabriel's instinct was to follow him, scoop the guy up and give him a hug, make him a tea and tell him to calm the fuck down. They were just kids and sheep. Things happened. Not his fault.

Instead, he stood there watching Bruno clumsily try to follow Thomas's lead until, finally, the sheep headed up the drive towards the field where they belonged.

"I hope they at least got to come," Bruno murmured, coming up behind Gabriel and snaking his arms around him.

"Seriously?" Gabriel laughed. "You're worrying if our Airbnb hosts got laid?"

"It's important. A good orgasm is good for your health. Doctor's advice. You know." Bruno pressed a kiss to his neck just where he liked it.

"We're still having the kids overnight, so maybe we should get them inside, load up another film for them to watch. They haven't watched that other *Nanny McPhee* in a while."

"Gives Lottie nightmares. What else have you got on your laptop that they haven't seen?"

"*Hunger Games*. Oldie but goodie."

"Serial -killing teenagers. Nope. Anything else?"

"Classic nineties films."

"You're such a nerd."

"So are you."

"That's why I love you."

"I have *Aladdin* The live-action version with Will Smith. His abs were hot."

"Your abs are hotter."

"I don't have abs anymore."

"Don't care. Still fancy you. And you have a tight arse. I want in there one of these days."

Gabriel tensed up all over, his body going into automatic fight or flight mode. It was more than he could handle just now.

"Your terms," Bruno added quickly. "You say when, where, what. No pressure, babe. I was just talking bullshit. Flirting. Sorry." He held Gabriel tight, trying to take his words back with his whole body. He had nothing to apologise for.

"OK..." *Here we go again.* He always felt like he was running out of excuses. Out of ideas. Out of time. "Not now," he said instead. "Get the kids inside. We need to sort out dinner." Another load of rubbish excuses.

Bruno walked away, his shoulders hunched like Frank's. Gabriel pushed everyone away. It might not have been intentional, but he was standing in the middle of the lawn watching everyone disappear into the distance.

Things were fine. Of course they were. Bruno magicked up leftovers for dinner. For once, everyone agreed on a film, and the twins fell asleep on the sofa, the soles of their feet black with dirt and the clothes they were wearing doubling up as pyjamas.

"Can we just let them sleep on the sofa?" Bruno whispered, standing in the dusky evening light with that look on his face, the same that Gabriel carried.

Love.

He adored these girls as much as Gabriel did. The most beautiful little creatures, the perfect mix of the two of them. Gabriel's dark skin and Bruno's blond streaks blended into their Mediterranean looks. Perfection.

"They're so beautiful," he said softly as his gaze fell on his husband. The streaks of grey in his scraggly hair. The crow's feet around his eyes. The smile that still made his heart skip a beat.

"They're ours," Bruno said. "Yours and mine. The Moretti-Fischer twins. Most beautiful little girls in the world."

"I know." Gabriel smiled, his head jerking to the side at the sound of laughter coming from Andreas's room. "Should we really let Maria sleep in there?"

"Her brother is sleeping in there too. There's space for two in the bottom bunk, and Maria can take the top."

"So, Andreas and Fredrik will share? One duvet?"

"Don't even go there, babe," Bruno said sternly. "Have you looked at them? Because I do. Maria looks at Andreas with that kind of half-disgusted look, like, *you're a dude and I kind of want to smack your face in, but you make me laugh so I won't.* That's good. She's not in love with him. Doesn't fancy him. Fredrik doesn't seem interested in him either. He barely looks up from his gaming anyway, so I think we're pretty safe to let them sleep there. And I've hidden the rest of the bread so we'll have something for breakfast, because if those kids eat the contents of the fridge at three in the morning again, I will lose my shit."

"Is that so, Dr Moretti?" Gabriel laughed.

"It is my professional opinion," Bruno replied. "If you take Lottie, I'll take Lilly, and we will put them to bed, like this, not even brushing their teeth, and then you and I are going to go lie in bed and have a glass of wine. I have a couple of bottles stashed in the car." He stopped and placed a kiss on Gabriel's nose. "Wine. Bed. Nothing else. Deal?"

"Deal." Gabriel could do that, the nervousness slowly draining from his body. It was weird, but he didn't notice until he relaxed: the intense pain in his back; the way his shoulders ached from being pressed up against his neck. He stretched his shoulders, pulled one arm to either side and then the other, a few simple exercises. Then he smiled. It felt like the first time he had smiled in years.

***

He regretted the wine the next morning when they were all piled in the car heading for some godforsaken place two hours away. At least the kids were quiet as the 4G had kicked in, and Andreas's breathing had slowed down after almost having a panic attack over the amount of missed messages and social media interaction that had escaped him over the last couple of days. He was tapping away furiously, holding the charging lead in place with his teeth, while the girls watched something that sounded annoying as hell, constant screeches seeping through their headphones.

At least it was just them, a welcome chance to breathe with nobody judging, nobody to impress. Frank and Thomas drove ahead of them in their own car, and Andreas was texting with the Norwegian kids, keeping them all on the right roads.

"Where are we going again?" Gabriel asked, searching in the glove compartment and then sighing with relief as he felt the familiar packet of painkillers. "Want one?" he offered Bruno, who stroked his cheek, then changed gear as they turned onto another main road.

"Nah, I'm good." Bruno smiled. "Remind me to show you something when we get home, and for God's sake, don't let me forget to put it back. I borrowed something from next door—if you could help me buy some?"

"Some what?" Gabriel asked then swore when Lottie threw up over herself in the back. Still. It was a good day. As Bruno kept saying, it always was here in Sweden.

The moose farm was actually fun, despite it taking almost three hours to get there with the pitstop to clean out the car and let the kids play in a lake then stopping for ice cream twice. The place was basic, run by an overly jolly woman who took the children under her wing and had them hand feeding a young moose and cutting apples for the 'safari', which turned out to be a beaten-up old tractor with a converted trailer. The whole set-up gave Gabriel heart palpitations and made Maria howl with laughter as the kids took their seats up on the makeshift trailer roof, Andreas with Lottie on his lap and Lilly crying with fear but refusing to come down.

Thomas looked bored stiff and unimpressed with the rickety transport while Bruno and Frank happily chatted away, not the least concerned about the death trap of a trailer their children were currently riding. Gabriel took a seat next to Bruno, letting his hand fall gently in his husband's lap and receiving a quick squeeze before another family climbed on board, their children getting casually thrown up onto the roof as the trailer leaned heavily and the moose woman shouted excitedly in Swedish.

It was kind of fun, he had to admit. Watching the herd from a distance, seeing the majestic animals walk on their long legs across a field just a few metres away was a sight. Then the woman left piles of food at designated places in the forest, and the moose came to eat it right in front of them. Bruno, always making a show, held a raw potato in his hand and got his fingers slurped by a wet moose tongue while Frank scratched the giant animals behind their horns, calling them a good boy like he was dealing with a significantly oversized lapdog.

The gift shop was ridiculous, and the café was beyond expensive, but they had their third ice creams of the day there, and the girls were having the best time playing with their overpriced stuffed moose toys and clinging to Fredrik like he was their new best friend because he had chewing gum and was teaching them to blow bubbles.

"Gabriel?" Maria asked quietly as they walked towards the car. She looked pale and had Frank's hoodie wrapped tight around her waist.

"Yes?" he asked, stopping. She looked upset and kind of scared, and his heart was racing. *If Andreas has done anything...* They'd talked about everything. Andreas knew all about boundaries and consent. If he had fucking done something to this girl, Gabriel would kill him.

"Can...can you help me?" she stuttered, her English sounding tentative like she was trying to find the words.

"What's wrong?" he asked quietly. "Has Andreas done anything? If he has, I will bloody—"

"No, no, no, no." Maria shook her head. "I don't...I have, you know. Blood? I have had it before, but today, it's too much. I have blood everywhere, and I am...scared."

"Period? Monthly period?" Gabriel guessed, exhaling in relief. This he could deal with. "It's not your first one?"

"No. I've had them for a while. But it's too much blood. I have marks on my trousers. I don't want anyone to see. I haven't got anything to change into. Is it OK? So much blood that you leak? I put a tampon in this morning, and now, it's...everywhere."

"Sweetheart," Gabriel said, and he smiled. He couldn't help it. He remembered his own first period well. The disgust with himself. The fear. The shame. Having to tell his mother when all he wanted to do was sink into a hole and disappear.

"What's going on?" Thomas had snuck up on them from behind.

"Go away, Pappa!" Maria shouted, tears filling her eyes.

"No, something is wrong, Maria. What's happened?"

"It's OK. Maria and I have a little secret," Gabriel said, then stopped. That sounded dodgy.

"Secret?" Thomas almost shrieked. "My daughter is sixteen. *Sixteen*. She is a child, and you are a grown man. She's not supposed to have secrets with you!"

"Dad, shut the fuck up!" Maria screamed. Frank and Bruno had stopped further along the road, and Andreas and Fredrik had caught up behind them.

"I'm not letting you have bloody secrets with strangers," Thomas hissed.

"He's not a stranger, Dad. He's the only one who knows about real things, and I need his help, so can you just go away?" Maria was crying now.

Thomas crossed his arms. "Now you've upset her, Gabriel. What the hell?"

"It's...it's not what you think," Gabriel protested. Classic. Now he sounded guilty as fuck. This was just the kind of inane mistake he'd heard about in numerous safeguarding lectures. He was a teacher, for God's sake. He knew better.

"Then why are you making my daughter cry?" Thomas reached for Maria, who shoved him away, wrapping her arms around herself, sobbing quietly.

"She had...questions. I was just answering them," Gabriel spat out, standing up straighter. He'd done nothing wrong, yet Thomas looked like he was about to bite his head off.

"I have my period and I'm scared, and my stomach hurts and I'm bleeding a lot, and I just wanted to talk to someone who knows about things and not have to talk to you because you and Dad know shit about women's things, and I just wanted a bit of privacy! Can you fucking respect that?"

He looked kind of proud of his daughter, Thomas, despite her outburst and choice of language. Gabriel got the gist of that, the words making sense even in Norwegian.

Thomas's reply was soft, his voice calmer. "What the hell does Gabriel know that I can't help you with?" He was clearly hurt. Then he switched to English. "Why does she need you? What can you do that we can't? We're her parents, Gabriel. You of all people should respect that."

He was being unreasonable, yet Gabriel knew where he was coming from. He'd have been shouting and screaming himself if this was Lilly or Lottie, ten years down the line.

"Because he's a woman, Dad!" Maria shouted, then she covered her mouth with her hands and whispered, "Shit. Shit. Shit. I'm so, so sorry. Fuck. Fuck."

Andreas stared at her, while Fredrik's face looked like she'd just dropped a bomb on them all, and Thomas...

Thomas said nothing.

## Seventeen
## FRANK

So THAT'S WHY *Maria wanted to borrow my hoodie,* Frank thought, which rapidly devolved into, *Why did it have to be that one? It's my favourite! I don't want bloodstains on it!*

After that, all he felt was shame.

He wanted to comfort Maria, his little girl, now all grown up. She'd had her first period a year ago and asked for extra money to buy pads, then suggested they could increase her pocket money so she could get whatever she needed when she needed it. He'd shrugged and agreed. It didn't matter either way; they could order stuff with their groceries anyway and stash it in the bathroom cabinet together with extra toothbrushes and condoms, but of course, they'd promptly forgotten all about it. Luckily, Maria was well informed; she'd watched pre-teen TV shows dealing with puberty for ages, and they talked about it in school. Frank suspected Maria's best friend Mariam's mum had done 'the talk' with both girls. At least he hoped she had because he hadn't.

He'd always planned to. He wanted to be a good father who could talk to his daughter about anything, teach her everything she needed. He'd been hellbent on proving that having two fathers didn't mean she missed out on anything. He'd failed spectacularly. All his energy had gone into just existing, working, trying to ensure all the necessities were dealt with. It left no time or mind to keep on top of things like talking about stuff. Important stuff.

He regretted that now. All his priorities had been wrong. His baby girl was scared and ashamed, and it was, once again, his fault.

Bruno's expression was a mixture of shock and terror, his feet seemingly cemented to the ground. Gabriel was bright red yet rested his hand supportively on Maria's shoulder, and Thomas...

Thomas was furious.

The boys were standing behind them, Andreas looking confused, Fredrik shockingly pale. The whole world seemed to have stopped, as if Frank was looking at a photo, or maybe life had continued apart from for him because he could only see this frozen moment.

Finally, Bruno moved, although it was nothing more than a panicked flitting of his eyes between all of them, like he didn't know what to do, who to take down first.

Frank kept shifting his gaze between Thomas and Gabriel. What the heck was this thing about secrets? Frank might not have known shit about what this was really about, but that word had been a low blow. This had nothing to do with 'a secret'. He could see that from Maria's shocked expression, while Gabriel's face cycled between shock, anger and sadness. He looked ready to run away. To where, Frank didn't know.

Then, to top off what was already the most awkward moment in history, Thomas exploded.

"Maria! What did you say?"

She startled and stared at him.

"What did you say?" he demanded again, much calmer and quieter this time.

"What do you mean? That you and Dad don't know anything about women's things?" She seemed to have run out of steam, deflated.

"No, no, no, about Gabriel. Why on earth would you be calling him a woman? What the hell?"

"But he was! He was born a girl, and even if he looks like a man now, he knows what it's like to be a woman! Or a girl, at least," she added in a shaky voice.

"No, he doesn't." Thomas's tone was gentle now. "He's never been a woman. He was perhaps born into a female body, but he's always been who he is. A boy, then a man."

Frank's whole body warmed with pride, hearing Thomas speak like that. His Thomas. The bravest, cleverest person he'd even known. It was like listening to those people giving the Pride lectures they'd attended many years ago. They'd finally found a reliable babysitter, and for their first outing, sans babies, they'd gone to a Pride event, the only safe option at the time. Everything had been new and frail, and even the thought of being away from the kids for more than an hour had sent Thomas into a tailspin. The only session they'd managed to get seats for had been on trans rights, and it had been incredibly enlightening. Thomas had looked at Frank several times during the lively lecture, seeming proud that they were engaging with something they'd believed was totally irrelevant to them, and Frank had whispered, "This is a very adult thing to be doing."

What had struck them the most, Frank remembered, were all the personal stories about the incredible amounts of hate directed at people for wanting to be who they truly were and how others felt they had the right to impose their views. Neither Frank nor Thomas had problems accepting that people could be born in a body that didn't match their true self, although Thomas had sighed a bit at having more boxes to tick on forms, but even if they'd had any problems with it, it would never have occurred to them to impress their opinions on others or deliberately deadname or use the wrong pronoun. It was enlightening and awful to hear how some human minds worked.

"I don't really understand heterosexual marriage," Thomas had said afterwards as they sipped their second beer in a calm corner of a busy gay bar. "But what right have I to decide how other people live their lives? Their marriage doesn't make mine less valid. And besides, if it wasn't real, if people truly didn't feel they knew exactly who they were, why would anyone go through all the struggles to live their true life?"

"Do you ever wish you were straight?" Frank had asked him. He'd regretted those words as soon as he'd uttered them, even if he had wanted to know the answer.

Thomas hadn't delayed for a second. "No." He'd swiped his finger around the rim of his glass and looked at Frank again. "Now I don't, but I did when I was younger. All those times I tried not to think about men, about boys. When I tried to imagine kissing girls. All those nights when my brain was running in circles and I was afraid and angry and frustrated..." He'd shrugged. "But then I met you, and...yeah. I never looked back. You changed everything for me. I went from being someone who was all wrong to a man who was suddenly...I don't know. Not right. But I made sense. Does that make sense to you?" He'd put his hand over Frank's and smiled. "You didn't think I'd ever wish for something different, did you?"

Frank had known it, of course. He'd known Thomas loved him. He'd known there was no reason to doubt it, to fear his answer, but sometimes life felt like balancing on a narrow ledge, and thinking about losing Thomas was one of those things that could start to spin and make him fall off.

He'd stroked Thomas's hand, tickling lightly along a vein, between his knuckles, following his fingers to the tips. "No, I didn't," he had said quietly while studying Thomas's hand.

Then the babysitter had called to say Maria was crying—did they want to come home or stay? Frank had heard Maria wailing in the background as he rose and motioned for Thomas to follow him home...

Frank's head was suddenly back in the forest, the tense standoff still a reality.

"Look, Gabriel, I'm really, really sorry. I..." Thomas straightened up, taking control of this insane situation. "I didn't mean to accuse you of anything. I don't know why that was my gut reaction, and in any case, I understand now that this had nothing to do with that. And..." He looked over at Maria. "And I'm so sorry, Maria. I didn't realise."

"Daddy!" she shouted, her body shaking in anger, before turning to Gabriel and drawing breath. "Gabriel, I am really sorry for calling you a woman. I just... I..." Tears tumbled from her eyes, and she tried to wipe them away with her hand, but the sobs were harder to stop, and her words were difficult to understand. "You're not a woman even if you have been before, but I thought you could help me."

"Of course I will help you, Maria." Gabriel took a tentative step towards her and put an arm around her. Then he seemed to freeze, apologetically looking over at Thomas as he once again stepped back. "If it's OK with you?" he added quickly.

Thomas nodded. "Absolutely, Gabriel! I...*we* are very grateful for your help. We'll help her too, of course, but if she wants to talk to you and it's OK with you, it is absolutely OK with us."

A shriek shattered the awkward tension, and everyone turned towards it. One of the twins was standing next to a large, shallow trough, while the other was lying on her back in the shallow water like an upended bug, waving her hands and wailing as she tried to get a grip on the slick sides.

Andreas and Fredrik were already there, dragging her and several kilos of ground weed out of the murky water. Andreas wrinkled his nose in disgust, shaking his arms after steadying her on the ground. There were spots of green slime and algae on his hands, and Lottie was covered in mud.

"We just wanted to let the moose drink!" Lilly cried in German, pointing at the sad, wet specimen in her sister's hand. "But Lottie dropped it in the water, and then she fell in. We were only trying to give the moosey a drink." Frank got the gist of that, even with the overdramatic tears. He had to admit the moose was a sorry sight. Its fur hung in tufts, and icky green algae was tangled around its antlers. As if she'd suddenly become aware of the wet toy in her hand, Lottie looked down at it and started to cry again, first clenching it to her chest then holding it at arm's length and wailing louder still.

There was nothing else for it. She would have to get a new one from the store. It was the only tactic that had worked for seven-year-olds who'd lost their 'pets' in the drinking trough. Frank had sneakily run off to replace them and bought an extra toy for comfort, an inflatable plastic moose—one each, of course, so it didn't start another war.

Maria cast long glances towards the German car when they finally got into their own. "I want to go with Andreas," she mumbled.

"Me too," her brother said too quickly for Frank's liking.

Frank shook his head. "Their car only has five seats, you know that." A couple of extra seats in the other car would have been a godsend, he thought with a sigh as he watched Gabriel buckle the girls into their seats and slam the back door before getting into the front passenger seat himself. But then, he supposed, they could all do with some peace and quiet to calm everyone's heads.

They drove towards the main road in silence. Fredrik was occupied with his phone, hunched towards in a corner with his huge headphones, while Maria's sour expression reflected in the rear-view mirror. Every time Frank met her gaze, she rolled her eyes and looked away.

Thomas chewed on a thumb nail and stared out the side window at the trees and luxurious green fields with spots of yellow, pink and white flowers. Frank was grateful to be driving, giving his mind a break from having to find words to say.

"I really had no idea," Thomas muttered. "But it makes sense now, that he gave me this bag of pads and stuff for Maria, saying it was something a friend had left in his suitcase when she'd borrowed it."

"He's struggled a lot with his body," Frank said, feeling uncomfortable revealing things he had no right to reveal. "Being called a woman was probably the worst that could happen."

"I didn't mean it like that!" Maria protested. "And I apologised to Gabriel. It just kind of slipped out."

Frank nodded. "It sometimes does, Maria."

She held his gaze for a moment, and Frank saw sadness in her eyes as she processed what he meant before she looked over at Fredrik, sighing loudly and nudging him when he didn't notice. He turned away, and she didn't argue, just leaned back toward her window and watched the rural landscape pass by.

"I had no idea he was a trans man," Thomas said quietly. "I feel so stupid."

"Why? He's as much of a bloke as you and me," Frank said with a shrug. "I was thinking about the Pride lecture we went to, all those stories, all the struggles, just to be themselves."

"Mm. But it is weird to think about Gabriel as a woman." He scrunched his nose.

"Because he's never been a woman. You said so yourself. He was born in a female body, but he's always been a man. Think about how you feel. You were born as a man in a male body, but no matter how much you tried to live as a straight man, falling in love with women, kissing them, all of that, you were still a gay man in that male body of yours. You couldn't change it. And no matter how much you tried to be a straight man, you aren't one, so if someone asked you what it's like to be a straight man, you can't really answer them even though you may have kissed and flirted with women."

"But gay isn't a body," Thomas protested.

"No, it's not, but being born in a female body doesn't mean you're a woman inside, either. Maybe Gabriel is the adult here with most experience of women's bodies, at least on a personal level, but him having had periods and giving birth to three kids still doesn't mean he's a woman. He just has some female body parts."

"But you knew?" Thomas's brows scrunched as he looked over at Frank.

"Gabriel told me a while ago. We've talked a fair bit, you know."

"Why didn't you tell me?"

"It wasn't mine to tell. We talk about a lot of stuff, and I don't break anyone's confidence."

"But we're married! You could've saved me the embarrassment. Now it seems like we don't even talk!" Thomas sounded more and more annoyed, and Frank got what he was saying. He might have had the same thoughts himself if the tables were turned.

"Thomas, do you *really* expect me to break someone's confidence like that? We are not one person, even if we're married."

Thomas sighed and looked back at the kids before dropping his gaze to his hands. Beyond the car, the scenery changed from fields to endless green forests.

"I know," Thomas said eventually. "It just feels so weird...I...I feel excluded. Like I was the very last to know. You knew, the kids knew, at least Maria."

"I knew too," Fredrik admitted from the back seat.

"Well, both the kids knew then. I was the only one. And maybe the twins, but they're too young anyway."

"They know," Fredrik added. "You bet they know," he said with a low giggle.

Frank sighed. "I kind of wish I'd told you now. It never occurred to me to say anything because the thought of sharing something so intimate, that was told to me in confidence, it feels wrong, even saying it now."

"I understand your reasoning," Thomas said. "I do." He blew out air and chuckled quietly. "It's kind of easier when it's my secret you don't share, or when it's about something that doesn't concern me."

Frank smiled and put his hand on Thomas's thigh. "I promise I'll continue to keep your secrets. And anybody else's." He looked at his son in the rear-view mirror, but Fredrik had his eyes closed, once again lost in his music.

"I'm going inside," Maria said the second they stopped outside the house.

"Me too," Fredrik said, following his sister.

Thomas turned in his seat as the back doors slammed. "Jeez, why can't they tidy up their rubbish?"

"Just leave it for next time, and they can sit in their own mess."

"Have you never experienced the foul smell of rancid chips and rotten meat after two days in the sun?" Thomas was tired and irritable. He picked up half a hamburger inside its wrapping, then wiped his fingers on his jeans in disgust as the sour dressing dripped from the greasy paper.

Gabriel and Bruno were parked outside the cabin, unpacking themselves and the twins, while Andreas disappeared around the corner towards the garden, probably heading for the hammock or the swing he found in the shed the other day. Once the twins were free, they also disappeared behind the cabin. Their special place was a grove halfway to the lake, a small area enclosed by lush bushes and small trees with pinecones on the ground, cool grass and plenty of shade—a perfect space in which to imagine whatever they wanted to imagine.

Frank left them all to it and went inside to get dinner on the go. He'd bought moose meatballs for all of them and made a spicy tomato sauce, fresh tagliatelle, a huge bowl of salad and smaller bowls of vegetable sticks for the twins, since Lilly preferred cucumber and Lottie loved tomatoes. With everything that had happened, he'd considered cancelling their offer of dinner, not sure if anyone was in the mood for more socialising, but then he'd thought *fuck it*. He couldn't bear the thought of spending the rest of their time here in some kind of polite truce, so he set the long patio table for the nine of them.

He loved all the bright colours: the cheerful tablecloth covered in large, vivid flowers; the clear blue plates and mismatched glasses—they didn't have enough identical glasses; the cutlery from Aunt Bella's lavish cupboards where he also found a pile of linen napkins; the green of the salad against the orange flowers decorating the bowl; the red tomato sauce; the yellow juice in a jar; a couple of flower bouquets in red, blue and orange.

"It's dinner time!" he shouted into the evening sunshine. "Middag! "Abendessen!"

Thomas came outside, standing next to Frank. "It looks delicious," he said and kissed his neck.

Frank couldn't stop smiling and kissed Thomas softly on his lips. "Thanks."

"Do you need help?"

"No, I'm fine. I'll get the pasta from the kitchen once everyone is here," he said, becoming a little flustered at the continued lack of people.

Thomas leaned in through the door and yelled upstairs, "Maria! Fredrik! Dinner! Now!"

Frank headed out onto the lawn and looked down towards the cabin. "Bruno! Dinner!" he called to the man peeking out of the kitchen window, at the same time as Andreas came running from the garden.

"Thanks! We're coming!" Bruno called before turning to say something in a lower voice to someone behind him in the kitchen. A moment later, he was heading Frank's way. Five minutes later, Gabriel arrived.

"Have you seen Lilly and Lottie?" he asked, looking at the six others already sitting at the table. Bruno was helping himself to pasta and froze with it halfway between the serving bowl and his plate. "Weren't they with... Shit, where are they?"

"I thought they were in the garden."

"No, they weren't," Andreas said. "It was all quiet there."

"Not in our garden either," Frank said. "And not in the sandbox." He looked over to where the sand lay flat in its enclosure, untouched since the heavy rain a couple of nights ago.

They all moved at the same time, a crush of chairs and bodies and screeching sounds. Frank and Thomas sprinted towards the barn, shouting loudly, moving empty boxes and searching behind the infinite amounts of stuff gathered there. Frank made a silent promise to clear up all that crap once and for all. Gabriel had returned the cabin, and they could hear him calling the girls' names, telling them it was time to come out now as if they were playing play hide-and-seek, while Bruno did the same in the garden, his voice loud and desperate. Frank could only imagine the fear going on in their heads.

Andreas, Maria and Fredrik came rushing from the narrow path from the lake. Andreas was pale despite the run, and holding a pair of lilac shoes, his knuckles white from gripping. He was too breathless to speak.

"Maria found these by the lake," Fredrik explained frantically.

Maria panted and finally got out the words. "They were on the beach."

# Eighteen
# BRUNO

*DON'T PANIC. DON'T panic. Think. Think, Goddammit!*

He had trained for this, yet he had no fucking clue how to handle anything right now. It was like some nightmarish flashback to that time when they'd lost Andreas at the park. That horrible day years ago when Gabriel wouldn't answer his phone. *Scheiße.*

His feet flew through the wild grass on the verge of the lake as he scanned every crevice, his voice hoarse from shouting. Maybe he should've run the other way. Maybe he should be in the actual water, looking, treading, feeling the bottom, searching the murky waters for... He couldn't even think the words and desperately screamed his daughters' names. Over and over.

He could hear Gabriel shouting from further up in the forest, Frank shouting somewhere over by the fields. Thomas's voice came from somewhere in the distance. Right now, he didn't care. He just wanted his girls back. Nobody took his kids away, nobody! They could swim, he'd taught them. He and Gabriel had drilled them last summer, taking them to the local pool every morning, where Gabriel had made them do lengths and dive and practise the crawl. They were good, strong swimmers. Not perfect, but fuck, the water was too shallow...

He shuddered and his voice broke again. "Lillyyyyy! LOTTIEEE! Das ist kein Spiel, das ist nicht lustig! Kinder! Papi wird wirklich wütend sein, wenn ihr euch versteckt."

His throat ached from yelling, and his heart felt ready to bolt out of his chest. Fear. So much fucking fear. He needed to stop the world. Fix this shit. Stop everything.

*Scheiße!*

"Papiiii!!!" The crashing footfalls of Andreas breaking through the undergrowth, his body moving fast through the woods behind him, made him freeze in fear. He couldn't breathe. For a second, he couldn't even move. He didn't want to turn around. *Please. Please. Please no.*

"Frank's got them. They were up in the sheep pen playing some fucking stupid game." Andreas stopped next to Bruno by the water's edge, panting heavily, bent over with his hands resting against his thighs. "Fucking little shits."

Bruno didn't even notice his knees buckle, his body go limp with relief as he sank into the sand.

"They were just playing with those damn ugly toys they got. I'm going to burn those shitty things. They've caused nothing but trouble today, and they were probably made by exploited child workers in some underprivileged country anyway."

It must have been the shock because Bruno burst out laughing.

"Did Maria tell you that?"

"Yeah. She's smart. She's told me lots of really interesting things. I'm going to boycott all those unethical brands from now on, and we need to find our nearest zero-packaging shop at home and start to use it."

"Fuck off!" Bruno said with no venom. He felt sick, exhausted, like the worst father in the world.

"Your shorts are getting wet," Andreas said.

"You're a twat."

"Papi..."

"What?" He tried to get up, stumbling and getting his hand stuck in the mud, but he was grateful for Andreas's arm that pulled him up and steadied him as he flicked his hair out of his face. He needed a haircut. He needed to get a fucking grip.

"Do you need a hug?" his son asked quietly.

Bruno didn't reply, just scooped the ridiculous boy up in his arms and squeezed him. Hard. Breathed in his hair. Kissed his sweaty cheek. Tugged at his unruly mop of hair and laughed softly at his embarrassment.

"You like Maria, don't you?" he asked, relieved his voice sounded light, even though he was still trying to recover from the near-heart-attack-inducing trauma of... *Fuck. Dinner.* They were just about to have dinner.

"She's cool and very pretty, but Papi, chill. I'm not crushing on her. I've got a type, and she's not it. OK?"

"Oh? What's your type?" Bruno asked, grabbing another hug while he could and focusing on breathing. In. Out.

"Not telling you because you'll just use the information to your advantage and give me a load of shit."

"I would not! I'd totally respect the privilege of knowing," Bruno replied, trying to look serious while Andreas punched him gently in the chest.

"Bullshit." Andreas laughed and wiped his forehead with the back of his hand. "You have a thing for dark-haired dudes. I mean, you've only had two major crushes in your life, that guy from *The Matrix* and Vati."

"And Will Smith."

"And Will Smith. Embarrassing, dude. He's, like, a hundred years old."

"He was hot when he was younger."

"You have no taste."

"I have great taste. Look at Vati. I mean. He's like the most handsome dude in the world. Then you have me, and you've got all my good genes."

"Yeah, I'm pretty much fucked in the looks department."

"Don't say that. You're handsome as hell. Trust me. I'm gay, and I know my shit. All the dudes and girls swoon over you. You are totally handsome."

"This is such an embarrassing conversation." Andreas crossed his arms, and Bruno held his up in defeat. Yeah. He was *that* dad. The embarrassment was real. But he knew when to tease and when to back off, and now he was backing off with his hands in the air, his shorts soaking wet and his shoes covered in sand and mud. He might have to dump them, as they were soaking wet too.

"Shall we go home?" he suggested.

"Yeah," Andreas smirked. "Frank was so angry. I've never heard him shout before, but he shouted at Lottie and Lilly and made Lilly cry. He tried to do it in German but ended up shouting random words like *unverzogen*— he probably meant *ungezogen*—and then he went on about *Hertzinfarkt* and called them *Gören*. I mean, where has he picked all those words up from? It was quite funny actually, telling them never to hide when people are shouting and looking for them. I don't think they were hiding, though. They were just having fun playing with the sheep."

"He was probably as scared as we were," Bruno said, wishing his feet wouldn't squelch so loudly, but he was desperate to get back to the others. He needed Gabriel. He needed his girls. He needed to eat. Then he would need a crate of beer. And a coffee.

Everyone was gathered on the patio, the girls looking sullen. As soon as Lottie saw him, she ran up and hugged him, while Lilly stayed firmly curled in Gabriel's lap and refused to look at him.

"You must never ever go to the lake on your own. Do you understand?" he scolded. Lottie squirmed in his grip, and Bruno released her.

Thomas came out carrying a large bowl of pasta. "I microwaved it," he said and placed it on the table.

"You killed it!" Frank said.

"Never reheat pasta," Bruno blurted before he could stop himself.

"Don't you start too," Thomas warned, sending a furious glare his way.

"Sit the fuck down!" Gabriel roared. Then he blushed and said in a voice barely louder than a whisper, "Sorry."

"OK." Bruno decided to rein it all in. At the end of the day, he did actually have training for handling these kinds of situations. Trauma training. Crowd control. Emergency psychology. He was on the hospital Catastrophic Emergency Event team, for God's sake. "Thomas. Please sit," he instructed and pushed Andreas down onto a chair next to Fredrik, who was enthusiastically loading his plate with congealed pasta. "Let's talk about this for a second. The girls ran off playing, and we should have kept an eye on them. It was nobody's fault but mine really because I was distracted."

"Distracted?" Andreas's smile was pure evil.

"Yeah, I was getting it on with your Vati? OK?" Bruno snapped defensively and then wanted to sink through the floor with embarrassment while Gabriel was quite blatantly laughing at him.

"Can I say something?" Gabriel said and shuffled his seat closer to the table with Lilly still on his lap.

Thomas sank down in his seat with his shoulders hunched; Frank breathed steadily.

"I've spent my whole life trying to hide stuff, and it's taken me until now to figure out that not being truthful about who you are always ends up coming back to slap you in the face when you least expect it."

Everything was quiet. Not a word was said.

"The job I'm in now, I hate it, but I've told everyone I work with who I am. What I am. And I really don't care what they think. A few of my clients have told me that they feel safe with me because of who I am. Others are standoffish, and I can tell they're uncomfortable, but that's fine. I'm honest. I don't hide, and I don't lie. I think that's what I have to do, to keep sane. And I should have done the same when we arrived here. I should have told you guys so you knew me. Knew who we are as a family. It can make people uncomfortable when they find out, and I'm sorry you didn't know, Thomas. That was on me. I didn't realise Maria knew, or I would have given her a chance to ask questions rather than feeling that she needed to be careful about talking to me."

"I knew from the start," Maria said defiantly and with no tact whatsoever. "We talked about it in the car that first day when we went shopping."

"My fault," Bruno said, his eyes filling with tears as he realised how he'd accidentally outed Gabriel, the man he loved so, so much. "We talked about Pride and your *Trans Dad Hugs* T-shirt. It was a good discussion, and it didn't even cross my mind that, fuck. Yeah. It was wrong. Sorry, babe."

"No, no, no, that's great! Maria, I'm really happy that you and Fredrik knew, and please know you can ask me any question you like because trust me, people have asked me weird questions all my life, and I can take it. I'd rather you asked me, and then I can explain. And if you want to talk to me privately, you're always welcome to come and talk. There are lots of things I don't know, but if it's anything more serious, Bruno is a gynaecological surgeon, and whatever he doesn't know, well, it's probably not worth knowing."

"Good to know," Maria said flatly, but she was smiling under her hair, looking pleased with herself. Fredrik, meanwhile, was silently working his way through the entire bowl of pasta, and Andreas was staring at Gabriel with a look that said *OMG, my parents are so weird.*

"I'm really, really happy we met you," Frank said. "This has been the most interesting summer holiday ever so far. Traumatic, sure, but interesting. I like it. Now let's eat before Thomas faints from hunger."

"Thomas is no fun when his blood sugar is low," Fredrik mumbled through a mouthful of tagliatelle. "He gets really hangry."

"Hangry?" Gabriel questioned, meeting Bruno's eyes to share a knowing smile. Bruno's chest warmed again. Lottie was tucked in his lap, her body flopped against his chest. She'd probably fallen asleep, but she really needed to eat too. Not that it mattered. She was safe.

"Yeah, when you get angry and hungry because you're starving, it's called *hangry*." Fredrik shrugged. "Thomas is always hangry in the evenings, so we have to eat really early."

"I have no idea what you're talking about." Thomas laughed and shook his head. "Sorry about the pasta. It's like this big, congealed lump of carbs now." He hacked away with the serving spoon and dropped a lump of it onto his plate.

"If I could, I'd have treated you all to a greasy takeaway," Frank said with a wistful sigh.

"But you can't because we're stuck in this wasteland in the middle of nowhere with no decent fast food anywhere," Fredrik added, taking a large gulp of water from his glass.

"At least we're all here together," Bruno said as Thomas got up and left. Frank slumped and covered his face with his hands.

"Sorry," Gabriel whispered.

Thomas came back out and dumped four cold beers on the table, fished an opener out of his pocket and skilfully flipped the caps off.

"Here." He reached across to place a beer in Gabriel's hand, another in Bruno's and lastly one in Frank's with a kiss pressed to his forehead. "A toast. To friends, family and fucking drama."

It was beautiful and funny. The perfect toast.

Gabriel laughed and clinked his beer against Thomas's. "To fucking drama."

A wicked grin spread across Thomas's face, and he made a show of looking down to where a bright-red edge of elastic was visible above Gabriel's shorts. "Dude, are you wearing my underpants?"

# Nineteen
# THOMAS

Gabriel frowned at Thomas, making him backtrack.

"Eh, I mean, I have a similar pair. I could be mistaken." He stuttered over the words, his embarrassment growing with every syllable leaving his mouth. "I couldn't find them the other day, but...sorry. Of course I'm not accusing you of stealing my underwear! I'm being silly. Anyway, nice underpants. Cheers!"

He felt like everyone was staring at him. Frank was giving him that familiar look of disappointment, and now it was joined by Gabriel's nervous gaze flickering between Thomas and Bruno, whose face bloomed dark red.

"I'm so sorry." Bruno lowered his eyes. "They must've fallen into the basket when I borrowed the washing machine the other day."

"*When* did you borrow their washing machine?" Gabriel demanded. "You were so relieved we had our own down at the cabin so we didn't have to go somewhere else to do laundry." For Thomas and Frank's benefit, he added, "We were in Prague the other year and had to use a laundromat with all the crud dust puppies, do you remember, babe?" Gabriel scrunched up his nose in disgust.

Bruno nodded, shame-faced. He was so busted, and it made Thomas want to burst out in giggles.

"I...borrowed it the other day. Because...because we were out of detergent."

"You have bought six bottles of the stuff just because you like how Swedish detergent smells! How could we be out of it already?"

"I forgot it," Bruno mumbled into his shirt but peeked up, his eyes pleading with Gabriel to shut up.

"They might not even be mine," Thomas said. "Frank probably left them to rot in the washing machine. He leaves laundry in there all the time, so all our clothes tend to smell."

"I do not! And our clothes don't smell," Frank protested. "Anyway, I haven't done laundry for ages now."

"No, I bet you haven't."

"Thomas, shut up." Frank handed him his own bottle, which he'd barely touched. "Have some more beer and relax." Things were weird and now everyone was once again on edge, so Thomas accepted the beer and drank it quickly so he had an excuse to go back inside for more. Grabbing a bottle of water for good measure, he returned to the table, where conversation was stilted, but everyone grateful accepted another drink.

After that, they kept to easy topics. Andreas, Maria and Fredrik sneaked away with the twins and a promise about putting them to bed, the girls shrieking with happiness when they realised Maria was coming with them.

Four beers turned out to be enough for Thomas to feel a bit more than relaxed, and he sat back listening to Frank and Bruno reminisce about student life while Gabriel laughed at their stories. It was strange but nice. Mellow.

"You know those chocolate bars you bought?" Gabriel asked, leaning close to Thomas so he didn't disturb the other men. "The ones in the yellow and red wrapper? How are you supposed to pronounce the name?"

"Kexchoklad."

"What?"

"Don't even try. It's one of those words nobody except Swedish people can say."

"Sounds like *Sexchoklad*. My kind of chocolate, actually."

"Sex chocolate." Thomas grinned. "Thanks for that. I'll never be able to eat another bar without thinking dirty thoughts now." He tried to get another glimpse of Gabriel's now-covered-up midriff, but he was sitting too close to the table and it was hard to see without staring. In the end, he couldn't resist. "Are those really my underpants you're wearing?"

Gabriel blushed but stood up and grabbed the elastic, pulling it far out of his shorts before looking down. "Uhm, well, I wish I could say no, but..."

Thomas laughed. It felt good after the day they'd had. "Seriously? What the fuck?"

"Bruno wanted to show them to me because they're the hottest thing ever, apparently, and then I got dressed in a panic and just picked up the first pair I found, and—"

"Show them to you?" Thomas's laughter was now directed at Bruno, who thunked his head on the tabletop. Thomas had heard stories about weird Germans, how they perceived nudity as natural at quite a different level from Scandinavians. Was looking at other people's underwear another kink he'd yet to learn of?

Gabriel looked kind of proud as he gestured at Bruno. "He was afraid he couldn't explain properly to me what they were like. He wears all those sloppy wide shorts that don't hug anything and wanted to buy new ones... like these."

Thomas threw his head back, crying with laughter. "So, you're into sharing underwear," he teased, knowing too well the convenience of that.

"Uhm...kind of. Sometimes. I have some..." Gabriel grimaced. "Some special boxers, with room for..." His hand formed a bulge in front of his crotch.

Thomas frowned and waved, questioning the visible front lump.

"Packer," Gabriel explained.

"Ah. Makes sense." And it really did. He smiled to himself, thinking back to stuffing a sock down his boxers when the other boys at school started puberty before he did...and the time he was almost busted when they went swimming in a waterfall. He'd remembered at the last second to remove the sock but was almost caught when another boy held up the single, rolled-up sock that was clearly several sizes too big for Thomas's feet.

"What?" Gabriel asked, tilting his head curiously at Thomas's smiled.

"I just thinking back to when I used to put a sock in my boxers." Thomas giggled, not in the least embarrassed. The beer was good. This was fun.

"No need for that now, huh." Gabriel nodded towards his crotch, right on time for Thomas to choke on his beer.

"Sorry." Gabriel laughed and patted Thomas's back. "I'm a very happily married man. You're completely safe with me. And sorry about your pants too. Really. I'll wash them and return them. No. Scrap that. Buy new ones. Take it out of our deposit or whatever."

"Keep them. As a souvenir."

Laughter and conversation flowed freely now, but they'd drunk too much, all of them. It wasn't that they were too far gone, just slightly too relaxed—a bit beyond the comfortable feeling of a couple of beers but far from being out of control. Still, when Thomas noticed Fredrik by the door, it occurred to him that they were supposed to be the responsible adults here, and for a second, fear fluttered in his stomach. What if Fredrik was here because he needed help? Could any of them actually do anything sensible right now?

Fredrik stared at them from the patio door, unimpressed.

"Everything OK?" Thomas tried not to slur as he got up from the table.

"We need food. The girls ate all the leftover bread before we put them to bed, and now the rest of us are hungry."

Thomas smiled and waved towards the fridge. "Take whatever you want. There's pizza in the freezer, and I can find you some chocolate from my stash as well." He'd hidden some extras from the others, knowing that between Frank's midnight cravings and the kids' bottomless pits for stomachs, they could completely decimate their rations for the holiday. Himself too. Cravings and hunger—or should that be *hanger*?—seemed to go hand in hand with the country air.

"Does it bother you that we're drinking?" he asked. "Do you want us to stop? You know we would, don't you?" He tried to look straight at Fredrik but couldn't, and he was also steadying himself on the table. *OK, the drinking needs to stop now.*

"Huh? No, it's not that. That's no problem, really no problem, Dad. Just drink as much as you want. Or maybe stop before you get sick, OK? Because that will stink, like it did when Petter puked in your car when you picked us up from that Christmas party."

Thomas shuddered at the memory. "Ugh, no, won't do that. You didn't drink then, did you?"

Fredrik rolled his eyes. "I already told you, Dad, neither I nor Maria drank at that party. You promised me new headphones if I didn't."

"Yes, and you got them," Thomas agreed.

"Yes." Fredrik stood up a little straighter and folded his arms.

"But...is anything wrong, Fredrik?" He hated going on, but something was clearly bothering his son.

Fredrik shrugged and shook his head. "No..."

"Is it Maria? And Andreas?"

Fredrik tensed up, then relaxed again. "She just hangs out with Andreas all the time."

"You're two individuals. She's allowed to have her own friends."

"Yes, but there's nobody else here."

"That's a good point. Have you spoken to her about it?"

Fredrik shook his head. "Nothing is the way it used to be. Things are different with the Fischers here."

"But you used to be so close," Thomas said softly and put his arm around Fredrik's shoulders, only for his son to move away.

"We're not now." There was both soreness and sourness in that statement.

Thomas rubbed his chin and considered for a few seconds. "Yeah, but it's going to be OK. She's always going to be there for you."

"She's always hanging with Andreas. *It's Andreas this* and *Andreas that*."

"They have this effect on us, this Fischer family," Thomas muttered so the men at the table wouldn't hear.

"What?" Fredrik frowned.

"Never mind. What about a camping trip?" Thomas suggested. "There's a tent in the barn. It didn't look that vintage either, and we have sleeping bags and mats. The three of you could go camping in the forest. Take fishing rods, make a campfire, talk all night, eat chocolates and Haribo and crisps..." He smiled as he looked into the distance. "Wouldn't that be cool?" He tried to sound enthusiastic about the idea, but he was already regretting suggesting it.

"Maybe," Fredrik said. "We're shopping tomorrow, aren't we?"

"Probably." Thomas shrugged. They would no doubt be out of food by the morning.

"So we can get stuff for the camping trip too. Snacks and drinks and hotdogs."

"Yup. And more mosquito repellent." Thomas swatted at his arm. "Little bastard suckers." He gave Fredrik a quick hug before his son slunk away carrying an armful of goodies.

"It's not a bad idea sending the kids away camping, you know," Frank said. Thomas hadn't even noticed him coming over.

"No, but they haven't been camping on their own before, God knows what they could get up to."

Frank smiled. "How old were you when you went camping alone for the first time?"

Thomas had to think for a minute, the pleasant buzz of alcohol still clouding his brain. "Not sure. Maybe twelve?"

"Maria and Fredrik are sixteen. Andreas is almost seventeen. Cutting those apron strings is long overdue."

"Mhm." He huffed. "Things are a bit different now. We're more afraid."

"Even more afraid than our parents' generation. Do you remember they were called helicopter parents? We're like fortress parents."

"Well, I somehow doubt my parents would have been considered helicopter parents," Thomas said dryly. "I honestly don't think they gave a damn where I went, as long as they had peace and quiet."

Frank stroked his thumb in circles over the back of Thomas's hand, his touch soft and smooth and reassuring. Thomas interlocked their fingers, holding on to the one thing he knew he could count on.

"Peace and quiet is good sometimes," Frank said.

Thomas studied their entwined hands. "I do think they cared. They just weren't able to act upon it. My mother was working these long hard shifts while my father was busy building the façade of middle-class riches, and taking care of the son he thought everybody expected his wife to take care of was not high on his list. They should have asked for help because I was always on my own." Saying those words, a lump formed in his chest taking up all his breathing space.

"Yes, they probably should have," Frank answered slowly. "You know, Thomas, sometimes it feels like everything is bad and sad and difficult. The horizon is so close, all you can see is what's right in front of you. It's overwhelming and scary, and it may seem almost impossible to tackle it. Nothing helps, and it feels like what's just in front of you will destroy everything and everyone, like a black hole."

Thomas nodded. The black hole was certainly an accurate description of the memories that sometimes popped up from wherever he'd so desperately stashed them away. He opened his mouth to say as much, but Frank continued.

"Our kids are strong. They understand much more than you and I did as kids. And we understand more, so we can be strong for them when they can't. We're not our parents, darling. We never will be."

"The thing is, my childhood... Ugh. This beer has made me all emotional." Thomas had to stop and wipe his eyes. "My childhood wasn't that bad, but sometimes I look at us, and I think, what the hell were my parents playing at? They didn't parent, they just left me to it. Makes me wonder how I would have turned out if I'd had half the support our kids have. Half the exposure, the acceptance, experiences, the money..."

"You would have turned out exactly the same. The best person I know."

The tears stung his eyes, and he closed them when he felt Frank's hand on his face, leaning in to the safety against his cheek.

*\*\**

Two days later, Maria and Fredrik stumbled down the stairs, their bags dragging heavily behind them, and Thomas was once again wiping tears from his eyes—tears of laughter as he looked at them.

"What the heck have you packed? Are you moving out forever?"

"Stuff," they muttered in unison.

"Clothes and sleeping bags and—" Maria began.

"We don't really have much room for the food, though," Fredrik said, already raiding the fridge.

"How long are you planning to stay anyway?" Frank asked, laughing too as he poked his nose into one of their bags.

"Shut up," Fredrik grunted. "Maria, we'll never be able to carry all this."

Maria shot him a sharp glance and went over, loading food from the fridge into her backpack.

"Hey, don't smash my crisps!" Fredrik shoved her, stopping her from dumping soda bottles on top of the crisp bags.

"They take less space then," she argued.

"Daddy, do we have more crisps? I can't eat the smashed-up ones!"

"Have a look in the cupboard next to the fridge. Top shelf, by the wall," Thomas said then sighed loudly. "Shit, you were not meant to know that! Now I need to find a new place for my secret stash."

"Great!" Fredrik shouted. "This's the good brand too! And chocolate. There's a lot of chocolate here. Mind if I take a few bars?" Thomas rolled his eyes in frustration as he listened to the telltale crinkling of the wrappers—signs of his treasure trove disappearing.

"Maria, wait a second," he shouted, stopping his daughter on her way across the room. "Uhm, Maria. When you're camping with the boys...eh... this is kind of awkward. I know you're going with your brother and Andreas, but this is a conversation we should have had ages ago, and since you're not on any contraceptive, if you and Andreas, well...hook up..."

Damn if he wasn't blushing. He'd never discussed this with Maria, or not with a specific name involved. She opened her mouth to speak, but he stopped her.

"No wait, please. So, if you and Andreas end up...having sexual contact in any way, please make sure you use condoms. I guess you don't need lube, but in case you do, there are some sachets of that here as well. And condoms. Do you know how to roll them on? It's a bit hard the first time, but you can practise on a dil—on a banana or a cucumber. A small cucumber, or it can be a bit intimidating. Scary." He needed to shut up. And fast.

Maria was staring at him in shock and something that looked a lot like horror, so he shoved the Ziplock bag he'd prepared towards her. He'd filled it with condoms, way more than she'd need, but better safe than sorry. He was still in a bit of a state of shock himself, having suddenly realised all the horrific things that could happen. Frank would go nuts at him for this. Because yes, Frank had sternly told him not to. As for his daughter...

"Dad!" she hissed. "You...you...*absolute* moron!" She walked towards the door, her movements too slow for his liking, before she stopped and turned around. "I have my own stuff, Dad, but I am NOT in a million years having sex with Andreas." She rested her hands on her hips and narrowed her gaze. "But have you talked to Fredrik? Maybe *he's* the one who needs these?"

A chill trickled down along Thomas's spine. *Fuck. Fuck. Fuckety fuck.* Right now, he hated Frank, who'd insisted it wasn't necessary to talk to Fredrik either. The kids didn't need condoms or embarrassing lectures from their fathers. But there was no way he could let Fredrik go camping without condoms. No way either of them were going anywhere, he decided.

"Maria, take this stuff and stash it in your bag. If any of you need them at any time, just use them. I won't ask. I won't count them. I haven't counted them. Not any of the ten lube sachets in there either—"

"Dad!" she practically growled. "Stop. Just stop. Right now. Please."

There were tears in her eyes, and for a second he regretted all of it, from start to finish. Still, she grabbed the bag—admittedly between two fingertips like it was excrement of some kind—before marching off.

\*\*\*

"So. They left."

"Yes. We're alone. Again," Frank said with a wink.

They were supposed to be mending floorboards in the living room, but instead they were both relaxing on the patio. It was a warm night, just a light, cooling wind, the sun sitting low above the lake. Soothing jazz music played in the background, the old vinyl discs adding a smooth vibe to the summer night.

"I can't just sit here," Thomas muttered, and Frank laughed.

"I can't believe you did that. Seriously. Maria was fuming, but it'll all be forgotten by now. That was an epic parenting fail, and that's all I will say on the matter."

The kids had left a couple of hours ago. They'd agreed to follow the path by the beach along the lake, wide and safe and impossible to fall into the lake from, Frank had insisted, trying to quell Thomas's fears. The kids had replaced half their clothes with food and sweets and decided to carry the tent between them. Their luggage was ridiculous for a camping trip so close to home, but it was a learning experience. Thomas had a sneaky suspicion he'd been just as bad, packing all kinds of things he hadn't needed for a trip he should never have been allowed to take. He remembered asking his father's permission to go, only to be waved off with a dismissive huff. He'd been a child, for God's sake, but nobody had even realised he'd left, although when he'd returned two days later, his mother had called the police, and rightly so.

Not that he wanted to remind himself that his own offspring were now out there in the wild all alone.

"This area is considered safe, isn't it?" he asked.

Frank nodded, letting a finger trail down the green wall behind him. "Very green. And yes, this is a safe area. Unless you run into wild boar. Or wolves. Lynx...rabid moose..."

"Shut up, and don't you complain. That colour choice is all on you."

"I could repaint it. What about yellow? Or blue. Or red again?"

"No." Thomas squinted at him. "Maybe I should throw away the paint and the brushes. And confiscate your car keys so you can't buy more paint on your own."

Frank pouted and took a sip of his beer. "I could hitchhike, then," he teased. "I bet Gabe would give me a lift. We could make it a boys' day out."

"I will lock you in the house and refuse let you out," Thomas threatened with a wink. "*And* hide Gabe's car keys if I have to."

Frank's hand was warm against his arm as he bumped into him.

"Apropos..." Thomas said, then paused.

"Apropos locking me up? Sounds like some kind of horror movie. 'Distraught husband locks up his insane partner in the attic for years. The legend lives on...'" Frank gasped at him with a fake shocked expression.

"No, idiot. I was thinking. Maybe we should clean out the barn while we have the chance. We could hire a skip and just empty it."

"Empty it?"

"There's loads of crap in there, Frank. Broken furniture, rubbish bags, old carpet. It's full of trash. And no doubt rats. To be honest, we have no idea what's actually in there."

"I know what's in there. Paintings, antique furniture. Books, her ledgers, letters..." His voice was stiff. "It's not all rubbish."

OK. Thomas sighed and let out a breath. They were, as usual, not on the same page.

"It's just too much," Thomas tried, keeping a peaceable tone. "The house in Oslo and this large farm—so many houses to maintain, paint, repair. And yes, we could let it, but that's a lot of hassle, too, because we'd have to completely clear out the house. And..." He let himself take another breath. "You've kind of been worse recently. The summers haven't been the good season after all, and I'm too tired to manage all this for another year. I'm just afraid it's too much for us, Frank."

"What do you mean? Cleaning the barn would just be the tip of the iceberg. Would it really help? Sounds more like an excuse than anything."

*Fuck*. His mouth had been a step ahead of his brain again. He swallowed, trying to gather his thoughts. His bravery. Well, the tiny bit of it that was left.

"Maybe we could sell it," he suggested quietly.

"What?"

"We could sell it. Get rid of the work and the mess, invest the money in something else... I don't know. Renovate the house in Oslo. Buy a modern, smaller summer house closer to home, one we could use at the weekends."

Frank remained silent, staring into the distance. His jaw was tense. Thomas knew that expression and half wished he hadn't said anything, but they needed to be honest about this.

Frank turned to him with red eyes, blinking back tears. "Do you have any idea what this farm means to me?"

Thomas shrugged. "Not really. Tell me."

"It's the first time someone gave me something like this, just out of the blue. It's the first time I've owned something that's truly mine. Well, ours, of course, but it's like a treasure to me. A precious, unshaped diamond, the only thing I have left from my past, a place that doesn't carry any bad memories. It's just new and brilliant and good. And I have...or had...so many plans for this place." He looked around. "I wanted to refurbish it. Rent it out more. Spend time here. Maybe make a film studio—the barn could be rebuilt as an indoor location for movie shooting with equipment and power and machinery. Or a music studio—lots of artists want to work in peace and solitude, and God knows this place gives you that." He threw out a hand. "I would also like to keep the farm as a mindful, easy place, in the spirit of Bella. But everything is so much harder than I imagined."

"You don't tell me anything," Thomas said. "You never talk about things like that. All this place does is cause arguments."

"I wanted to make the plans properly first. For once, I wanted to come to you with a real plan, not just throw a bunch of ideas at you without really knowing if they were possible. But if you want to sell it..." He sounded so small when he said it, as if he had already completely failed. "You're probably right. Maybe it is too much. I have all these wild dreams, but I know we can't afford it. I'm not totally irresponsible."

Thomas sighed. "Sorry, darling. I wish I could say this was a brilliant idea and that I fully support you, but I need to think a bit first. It...it's not as simple as saying 'we'll make it'. I agree, it feels overwhelming. I need to sleep on it." He got up and walked inside. "Come to bed soon, yeah?"

Frank was still sitting in the same position when Thomas looked down from the bedroom window a few minutes later. His eyes seemed to be fixed on something on the horizon, his head resting in his hands, his elbows on his knees. The sunrays turned him into a golden sculpture. Only his hair was moving, caught by the light evening breeze, or maybe even by the smooth saxophone sounds coming from the speakers.

Thomas had been a coward to leave him like that, but the conversation hurt. This was always the way things went, and he felt like he was drowning, weighed down by things he couldn't control, tied up in a life he wasn't sure he could handle. Frank had dreams, and Thomas and his big head and big mouth inevitably crushed them.

## Twenty
## BRUNO

THE KIDS HAD been gone less than a day, but Bruno wasn't worried. Not only had he made Andreas attend the Scouts when he was younger, he'd also paid a ridiculous amount of money to have his son go to survival skills camp, and as he kept reminding Gabriel, the kid took Thai boxing classes at school. And played football. Andreas had muscles in places Bruno knew all the names of, and he had no doubt he would come out on top in a fight with anyone unlucky enough to encounter those three kids out there in the wild. Not that there was anyone out there; they'd only ever come across the lady who ran the farm on the other side of the lake, and there weren't any other homes around for miles. Apart from sheep. And moose, apparently.

Still, Gabriel had that aura of worry about him, and it made Bruno tense.

"Babe," he started and planted a loud kiss on Gabriel's head. "Do you remember that road trip? When we hitchhiked all around Europe and ate dodgy food and rode with weird truckers watching porn while driving?"

"Yeah." Gabriel did that low belly laugh that made Bruno all warm on the inside. "We were so bloody naïve and stupid. Anything could have happened," Gabriel admitted with a tentative smile. He reached out to stroke Bruno's arm as he dumped his skinny arse on the sofa next to him. The girls were fast asleep, sprawled out on a mattress on the floor. They'd played pretend camping, dragging all their bedding with them to create a tent with blankets draped over dining room chairs. Gabriel had made a camp picnic, and Bruno had put a firm end to their brilliant idea of creating a campfire on the floor. There was an actual fireplace in one of the rooms, but he had no idea how to use one, and he doubted the flue had even been cleared. Knowing their luck, they'd have ended up setting the house on fire, had they tried.

At least the girls were asleep. Lilly snored quietly with her arm over her face, and Lottie had her teddies in a tight grip against her chest.

"Andreas is safe out there. Maria and Fredrik are sensible, and if anything was wrong, they would just come home. Once they are out of food, they'll be straight back here anyway."

"It's just weird not having Andreas home. I know I worry too much." Gabriel sighed and shot Bruno a weak smile. "I'm being stupid, I know."

"Not stupid. He's our kid. It's our job to worry about him, but we have to learn to give him some space. Let him have the opportunity to grow. I mean, I hated having to move out of home, but I'm glad I was pushed into doing it because I learned a lot of good skills from having to look after myself."

"You were a disaster. Luckily, you found me and let me take care of you."

Normally, Bruno would have fought back at that comment, gone for a playfight, trying to wrestle Gabriel off the sofa, all while pretending to be deeply offended. He would usually turn Gabriel's worries into a joke. Instead, he leant over and laid his head on his husband's shoulder.

"You always look after me," he whispered. "I don't know what I'd do without you."

"I'm right here. You don't have to worry about not having me around. You're stuck with me now," Gabriel replied softly. "Even if I'm always a mess, I do love you. And I'm not going anywhere."

"I love that I am stuck with you."

"Wanna go to bed?"

It was funny the face Gabriel made, like he was grimacing in embarrassment coupled with a flash of fear. Bruno knew it well because it was always there, the underlying, unsaid words. *Please just let me sleep. Nothing else.*

"Yeah. Sleep. Want a shower? You can go first. Just leave me a tiny bit of hot water?"

"Sounds good," Gabriel whispered, visibly relieved.

They left the girls where they were, knowing that both of them would end up in their bed the minute they realised the house had fallen dark and quiet. But for now, it was a treat tumbling into an empty bed with wet hair framing his face and crisp, white sheets surrounding his skin.

"You changed the sheets?" Bruno squealed, burying his face in the pillowcase. Clean. Fresh. Smelling of that laundry detergent he liked. He had to be getting old when the smell of detergent made him all silly-happy.

"Yeah. Frank said it's something Thomas does sometimes when he wants to get in Frank's good books. He changes the sheets and tidies up and makes him a cup of herbal tea. That's when Thomas let's him fuck him."

"What?" Bruno giggled, hoping he wouldn't wake the girls. This was a conversation he was keen to continue. "So, Thomas bottoms? I kind of thought it was the other way around."

"So prejudiced." Gabriel laughed and tapped his nose. "If you really must know, they're both verse and do whatever comes to them. A bit like us."

"I like when you fuck me," Bruno said, leaning up to steal a kiss. His voice was barely a whisper, and he couldn't quite put a finger on why he was pleading like this.

"I like it when you fuck me too," Gabriel admitted. Blushing, he threw himself on the sheets, water droplets glistening on his chest.

"It's nice having you naked." They needed to talk about things like this, otherwise Gabriel would clam up and Bruno would do something wrong and they would end up...well, like they always did. Lying in uncomfortable silence.

"It's too hot." Gabriel moved his legs so he was sprawled like a starfish on his side of the bed, while Bruno was on his front, his legs hanging off the edge.

"We're going to get eaten alive by the mozzies if we don't get under the covers."

*See? I can be sensible.* All he wanted was to lie there and stare at Gabriel's body. His hips. The dark hair trailing down his legs. Muscles. Thighs good enough to eat. His arms, those biceps. He could have just leant over and taken a bite into Gabriel's arms. He loved them. He loved him.

"Can we just...cuddle? For a while," Gabriel asked.

Bruno didn't reply in words. He shifted over, keeping his movements slow and steady, and plastered himself against Gabriel, head nuzzling into neck, arms tight around his body, legs knitting with legs until they were tangled like an octopus. The sigh he released was embarrassingly loud, but he couldn't help it. Bruno Moretti was a total cuddle slut. Always.

"Frank said..." Gabriel started. "Sorry. I'm constantly talking about Frank. It's like I've got some teenaged bro-crush on the guy."

"You do." Bruno snuggled in closer. "And it's fine. I like that you have a friend in him. Talking is good. Friends are good. And maybe when we go home, you and Frank can FaceTime and chat and text, keep up this little daily therapy thing you have going. It's nice."

"It's good for me," Gabriel said and pressed his lips to Bruno's forehead. "I'm sorting out some things in my head, dealing with stuff and realising how to work on my emotions. Frank said touch is really important to him, that cuddling is like a vitamin injection. When he's too ill to even think about sex, he still needs the skin on skin. He sometimes asks Thomas to sleep next to him, naked, because it helps him focus, having Thomas all curled around him. Maybe I need that too." He blew air. Sighed. Held his breath waiting for Bruno to reply.

"I think Frank is very wise. Thomas is lucky to have him. Skin contact is proven to be therapeutic. We talk about it with some of our patients who don't have a partner. We sometimes recommend a massage, go to a spa for the day, just have some beauty treatments to get used to having another person touch your body. It's true, human touch can be magical. And yet it can be frightening and over-stimulating. I understand that."

"I think I just need to figure out who I used to be. I want my life back. I used to love sex, and now I lie here and wonder why? Why don't I crave it? I mean you're right here!"

"I am right here, babe. If you want anything, and I mean anything, I will give it to you."

He meant that, and fuck him. Fuck everything because now his dick was thickening up, and it wasn't like he could hide it, the traitorous thing bouncing erratically against Gabriel's leg.

"Could..."

"Anything." Bruno groaned, sounding like a horny teenager. It was just... Fuck. It was Gabriel, and Bruno's dick craved a wet, warm hole to bury itself in and hump the shit out of until he exploded into orgasmic bliss.

"Get a fucking condom on and fuck me." Gabriel laughed as Bruno's hips jerked uncontrollably. He couldn't have stopped it if he'd tried.

"Really?" He was almost drooling on Gabriel's collarbone.

"Really. The sheets are clean, and you're going to make a mess all over my leg in a second."

"Are you sure, sweetheart?" Bruno whispered, still not quite believing that Gabriel was asking for it. "You never ask. I mean, I know you don't...but..."

"We can discuss the children's schooling or new washing machines if you prefer, babe?" Gabriel chuckled, although his face had turned red. "I want us to somehow get back to normal. Not like we were before the kids, but we need to have sex now and then. Get back in the saddle. Can we try? Please? Just use a condom...and don't split it."

"So bloody domesticated." Bruno laughed and clumsily lent across to the bedside table. He'd stashed stuff there. He was pretty sure he had, along with the cleaned-up Mr Stiffy and a few other toys. And his plug.

*Condoms. Right. Find one. Use it.*

"Extra strong!" he declared, twirling the packet between his fingers. His brain had already short-circuited as Gabriel shuffled down the bed, wrapping his legs around Bruno's hips while he fought clumsily with the condom wrapper. He'd done this a million times, yet it still felt alien.

"Remember the first time we did this?" Gabriel whispered as Bruno finally got the condom rolled onto his uncooperative dick that was leaking and twitching and threatening to release before he even got anywhere near that heavenly place between Gabriel's legs.

"I thought I was going to die, I was so bloody nervous. I thought I would mess up and hurt you, and at the same time I just knew I would come in my pants the minute you took your clothes off."

"I hardly took any clothes off." Gabriel giggled.

"Didn't matter. I came in the condom inside of you, and it felt like the biggest thing ever. I loved it. Couldn't wait to do it again."

"If I remember correctly, we did. Do it again. A lot."

"We did indeed." Bruno stole a kiss and lined his cock up against Gabriel's front hole. "Is this OK?"

"Yeah," Gabriel panted.

"Need me to rub you off a little first? Suck you?" Foreplay was a thing, and here Bruno was, diving in like a selfish teen.

"Nah. You'll make me come like this. Just do it," Gabriel told him as Bruno let himself sink inside.

It was so much better without condoms. But no. Not happening. Still. It was... *Tight. Hot. Lovely.* His hips were doing their own thing, and Gabriel's legs were clamped around him like a vice. Bruno wasn't quiet. No. He was a vocal human being; he always had been. He couldn't control it when it came to Gabriel. When his body reacted like this, his lips sucking bruises into his gorgeous husband's neck, Gabriel's coarsely stubbled chin scuffing Bruno's cheek, hot breath and whispers he could barely make out, and fuck, yeah, hands on his own arse egging him on, faster, harder, please...

"Babe," Gabriel moaned a little too seriously for Bruno's liking. He stopped and panted heavily. He couldn't really speak right now. "I want you in my arse, babe. Properly. No bloody condom. I can't feel you."

Yeah, Bruno knew he was bloody lucky. Sex wasn't quantity but quality right now, and his head was spinning trying to make sense of what Gabriel had said.

"You want me to fuck your arse," he stated, just checking because...wow. He'd almost come saying the words, and that would have been disastrous. However horny he was, he only had one orgasm in him these days. He'd tested that theory: one wank usually put him in a coma because he wasn't seventeen anymore.

"Yeah," Gabriel whispered. His eyes were closed, and Bruno slid out, almost whining at the loss of warmth. Ripping the damn condom off, he sat back on his haunches. He needed to give his cock a few strokes, but he didn't trust himself right now. Fuck. He'd probably come anyway.

"Think of your granny," Gabriel suggested like he could read Bruno's thoughts, as he turned onto his front, arse up in the air.

"My *granny*?" Bruno giggled.

"Yeah." Gabriel was clearly losing it, giggling into the pillow, and God, Bruno liked that. He liked everything about this. "You want this?" he asked as his brain finally snapped back into gear.

"Yeah," came from somewhere in the pillows.

Bruno rummaged through the bedside drawer and came up trumps with the lube—the good stuff that covered Bruno's fingers with silky liquid. He dripped it into Gabriel's crack, and Gabriel flinched at the cold. Self-warming lube was a joke; despite the heat, this shit was still bloody cold.

He started to slowly rub it over Gabriel's skin with firm movements. This part he knew. He knew exactly how to make it good, how to tease and make Gabriel all relaxed and turned on and desperate and fucking slutty, begging for it. Well, he used to, and for a second, he doubted himself and his bloody ego and attitude of knowing exactly what to do. He lubed up his fingers and gently slid them over Gabriel's hole, lightly pressing as he passed the opening, drawing lazy stripes up and down.

"Don't tease," Gabriel warned.

"Behave," Bruno replied.

"Just...ohhh." Gabriel moaned.

That was good, and Bruno's ego relished the boost.

"Let me do what I do best, and I will make you come so hard you'll see stars, babe."

"Promises, promises," Gabriel panted as Bruno smiled, probing gently with his fingers as Gabriel clenched around him.

"Spread," he demanded and pushed Gabriel's thighs further apart with his knees. "Need to see you." *And note to self. Don't bloody come.* Because now he was leaking, and his dick was ridiculously hard. He could feel it all hot and wet bouncing against his wrist at the thrill of realising that this was happening.

Gabriel started to relax, making needy little noises. Personally, Bruno preferred when Gabriel just plunged straight in, the shock and delicious stretch and the pain that made all his senses stand on alert. He loved that part. Craved it. But Gabriel needed a bit more before he truly started to enjoy it.

"You good?" he checked in, and Gabriel nodded enthusiastically, following up with a moan that made Bruno grin.

"Do it," Gabriel hissed.

"Not yet." Bruno pushed two fingers all the way in and twisted his wrist just so he could get a reaction. Gabriel responded beautifully, arching his hips and drooling into the pillow.

"Ahhhrhghgh!"

"Just a bit more, babe."

"Need it. Just get inside of me. Now."

"So bloody bossy." Bruno pulled out his fingers and generously covered his desperate cock with lube, the cold doing its job of buying him a few more seconds before he'd explode.

He panted and lined up, pushing gently, keeping his eyes closed as he sank into the ridiculously tight heat. It took a little effort, a few loud moans. Gabriel's body writhed beneath him. Beads of sweat ran down Bruno's forehead, dripping onto Gabriel's back.

"I need you to pound me good. Make me feel you."

Then Gabriel's body froze up, and Bruno's eyes sprang open in shock.

*Fuck!* his brain screamed as Lottie stumbled through the door, covering her eyes against the bright light before tumbling into the bed and burying herself under the duvet.

"Off," Gabriel whispered.

"Damn."

"Fucking kids."

"You don't mean that," Bruno chuckled. "Don't wake her."

*"What if she saw us?"*

"She saw nothing. She was pretty much sleepwalking." Her breaths were already calm and light under the duvet, and she looked completely relaxed as if she didn't have a worry in the world.

"Damn it."

"Bathroom?" Bruno suggested.

They rolled out of bed, Bruno's cock having gone limp, while Gabriel was all flushed, his nipples tight and erect as he tripped on the bedside rug, making the bedside table wobble precariously and the plug roll out of the open drawer. It hit the floor with a thump.

"We are the worst parents ever."

"We are the most normal parents ever. Fuck what anyone says. Everyone catches their parents fucking at some point, and at least she won't remember a thing tomorrow morning."

"She will need so much therapy."

"Shut up." Bruno slammed Gabriel into the bathroom sink, plundering his mouth with a filthy kiss. He surprised himself with the moan that came out of his mouth as Gabriel humped against his front and they both fought frantically for space before Bruno managed to turn Gabriel around and line up his cock, pressing into that delicious hole that...*fuck.* His brain went blank, like all the blood in had rushed to his cock in a gallant emergency effort to save what was left of his flagging erection. Well, it was flagging no more. It was jerking and pulsing inside its tight home while Bruno roared with the release that tore through him.

"Fuck," Gabriel hissed.

Bruno was gone. Couldn't speak.

"Move," Gabriel pleaded.

He would if he'd been able to. But fuck, he just wanted to stay right here for the rest of his life, buried deep inside his man with a ridiculous grin on his face. He'd just come like a bloody express train, and his body felt all strange and tingly, and his brain was drugged up on hormones, and all he could do was drool and smile.

"I didn't get to come, you bloody useless bastard," Gabriel snarled.

"Love you," Bruno slurred while Gabriel desperately humped against him.

"Then fucking make me come!" Gabriel pleaded as Bruno once again grabbed his face and kissed the living daylights out of him. This man. This fucking man.

"Turn around," Bruno hissed, having suddenly regained control of his senses and rediscovered the use of his mouth. Sinking to his knees, he buried his face between Gabriel's legs, letting his tongue delve in and do its job. *This right here is stuff I'm fucking good at*, he thought as Gabriel jackknifed and roared into the bathroom wall, his hands grasping at the slick tiles and his legs giving way as Bruno's fingers pushed up into his arse.

He made Gabriel fucking come. He made him come until they were both wedged in a heap of sweat and bodily fluids and embarrassed giggles on the bathroom floor.

They were not twenty anymore, and they would both be sore and embarrassed in the morning, but right now? Right now, everything was good. Life was good. And for once, that was no lie.

# Twenty one
# FRANK

"Maria! Hi!" Frank greeted loudly, ridiculously excited—and relieved—to see his daughter emerge from the forest and head towards their garden. Her face and hair were wet from sweat, and she was breathing heavily. A backpack hung low on her back, and she threw it on the ground when she finally reached the patio.

"Fucking boys. They could have actually helped." She grabbed Thomas's empty water glass from the table and filled it with the lukewarm fruit squash from the jug before draining the glass in one go.

Frank wanted to hug her and squeeze her and never let her go even though she was filthy and the smell coming off her was kind of disgusting, so he just smiled and said, "Let me get you some more. Do you want anything to eat? We have fresh bread."

She nodded and plonked herself on a deckchair, and he went inside. They were almost out of squash *again*: he made a mental note as he mixed the remains of the bottle with water and added a handful of ice cubes. He grabbed three glasses from the shelf and put them on a tray with the squash and a basket full of cinnamon buns, realising they weren't that fresh anymore. For a moment, he considered heating them in the microwave, but catching up with Maria was more important than fresh buns, and he had the impression she was too hungry to care anyway.

"So how was the camping?" he asked as he wrangled the tray out the door and looked around in confusion. "Where are the boys?" He'd expected them to have arrived by now.

Maria reached for the jug and refilled her glass. "They're still camping."

"Where?"

"On the other side of the lake. We followed the shore like you said, and when we got to the other side, Fredrik had 4G on his phone!"

"I thought he'd turned that off to save the battery."

"No, we'd thought we'd see if we could find network."

"Ah. OK." Sure. Whatever. "But where are the others? Is anything wrong?"

"No, no. I lost the draw. They got to stay and I had to come back for supplies. I'm just gonna pick up some more food, then I'm going straight back. We have food, don't we? Please don't say we're out of food again, Dad."

"Sure, we have food. Thomas went shopping yesterday. Well, he forgot squash—you have the last of it in your glass there, unless the Fischers have some—but there's plenty of bread, cheese, jam, snacks, hamburgers, salad, you name it. Did you manage to light a fire? You had enough matches and dry paper and firelighters? And you found wood in the forest?"

"Yeah, yeah." She rolled her eyes as she ripped large pieces off the bun and packed them into her mouth. "We had all the hotdogs yesterday and tried to make toast this morning but we burnt it, so we went to the farm and got breakfast there."

"The farm?"

"They have milk straight from the cows. It's icky. They just pulled at their udders and filled the jar before breakfast. It wasn't even cold, and the taste was funny. Fredrik liked it. Andreas spat it out, but I swallowed."

"You swallowed? I mean, what farm?"

"The farm on the other side of the lake, Dad. Are you stupid?" She shook her head and pointed in that direction.

"You walked all the way there?"

"We followed the shore, like you told us to, but the beach was so narrow and there were trees all along and lots of insects, so we kept walking because Andreas said there'd be a stream somewhere and the terrain would probably be easier. We found the stream and there was a great spot there for camping—soft grass and a nice beach, and 4G!" She tugged free another piece of the bun. "But we're all on the farm's Wi-Fi now, so it doesn't matter."

"But isn't that far? *Too* far?" Frank tried to gauge how large the lake was. It probably wasn't any further than they used to walk when the kids were much younger and they'd taken them hiking on Sundays. It was a long-gone tradition. He couldn't remember the last time they'd all gone hiking.

"Na. Just a few kilometres." Maria touched her watch and swiped through the screens. "Five point three kilometres." She shrugged. "Fredrik complained that his trainers were worn out, but he found a stone under the sole, so it was his own fault."

"But the farm? Wi-Fi?" Frank was still confused.

"The farm at the other side of the lake," Maria said again. "Jeez, are you not listening to what I am saying? We've driven past their road lots of times!"

"Yeah, I know where it is, but why did you go there?"

"I already told you! Because they had Wi-Fi!"

"But how did you know?"

"Because Fredrik's phone picked it up."

"And then you just...went there and connected?"

"Yeah."

"So you went to a strange farm in the middle of the forest and just asked them for the Wi-Fi code? What if they were murderers? Child molesters? Robbers?"

"Daddy!" She looked straight at him. "You've watched too many scary movies."

"They could've been criminals!"

"So what? Lots of people are criminals. Weed was a crime once, too," she said dryly.

Frank really didn't want to repeat that discussion now and still regretted confessing to the kids that he'd had a bit of a habit in his twenties. Thomas had thankfully put an end to all that. At the time, it had felt like a useful, pre-emptive discussion. He should have known one day the kids would turn his past into a weapon.

"Yeah, OK. But anyway, you still shouldn't talk to strangers! You never know who they are."

"They're hardly strangers. We've seen them in the village, and Anita knows Dad. And they had Wi-Fi. Do you want us to suffer without Wi-Fi when we're camped right outside?"

He opened his mouth to answer when he heard the crunch of gravel behind them.

"Hi Frank, have you heard anything from the kids— Oh! Hi, Maria!" Gabriel rounded the corner, smiling, but that smile soon faltered. "Where are the others?"

Maria sighed. "They're still at the farm. We got Wi-Fi there, so we're staying for a few days. I just came back for food."

"For a few days?" Frank raised an eyebrow.

"Yes!"

"No."

"Daddy! We can't leave now. We're gaming, and Andreas is livestreaming it all on Twitch. Have you any idea how many followers he has?! And I'm here while the boys are still there. It's not fair if they get to stay!"

"You can't stay for a whole week, Maria."

Maria pondered a moment. "What about three days?"

Frank shook his head. "Nope."

"Two?"

"Tomorrow."

"When tomorrow?"

"Come back before it gets dark."

"But it gets dark so early!"

"Ten at night is not early!"

"OK," Maria accepted reluctantly. "I'll go get the food. Can I take some beers? Just one for each of us?"

"Are you serious?" His voice seemed to go up an octave. "You're sixteen!"

"It was just a question!"

Gabriel's laughter wasn't helpful, and Frank glared at him. Gabriel cleared his throat and propped himself against the table.

"Have the boys sent you back on your own? I hope they've been behaving."

Frank leant over, trying to smell her breath. "Have you been drinking already? Did you steal beer for the trip?" He tried to remember how many beers they'd had in the fridge, but he had no idea, not after dinner the other night. They'd drunk quite a lot, and then Gabriel and Bruno had replenished the fridge yesterday.

Gabriel was looking between them, not fully following their discussion. "You're letting them take beer?"

"No!" Frank shouted. "There is no way. They're what, sixteen and seventeen? The legal age for beer in Norway is eighteen. I won't make myself a criminal by giving them beer before that."

"A bit late to worry about that, isn't it?" Maria muttered sourly.

"What did you say?"

"Nothing."

Frank stared at her. "You won't have beer on this trip or any other occasion before you're at least eighteen." Maria opened her mouth to protest, but Frank held up his hand. "One word and I'll revoke all your privileges for months. Immediately."

Maria let out a frustrated breath and turned around to walk into the kitchen. "I'll grab some *food* then and go back," she said with extra-heavy emphasis on *food*.

"So, what's the deal now?" Gabriel asked, clearly confused by their heated conversation in Norwegian.

"She wanted to go camping for a week. We agreed on until tomorrow night."

"Are the boys still out there?"

"Yes, they're camping by the farm on the opposite end of the lake. Apparently, they have Wi-Fi there and some live-steam gaming thing going on."

"Wi-Fi? Here?"

"No, over at the farm. It's about a five-kilometre trek along the lake, I think. A bit more when you walk along the road."

"I see." Both Gabriel and Frank looked towards the lake. The small point next to their beach was blocking the view, but they would've been able to see the boundary fence from the window upstairs.

"Who are those people on the farm?"

"Some locals. We don't really know them, but I've chatted with Anita. She's lovely. Thomas met up with her last time he was in the village."

"You don't really know them but you trust your kids to stay there?"

"Yes, they are probably OK."

"Probably?"

"As far as I know, but you can never be certain, can you?"

"But you're still letting them go there?" Gabriel's voice had an edge of panic.

"Yes. The probability of anything going wrong is very low, and if you don't let them try, they won't fly either."

"But what if something does go wrong?"

Frank shrugged. "I guess we just need to believe it will end well. Or we'll go crazy."

"That sounds incredibly irresponsible!" Gabriel said with a disbelieving laugh.

"Huh?"

"We're all in a foreign country and they're hanging out with strangers on a remote farm?"

"Well, no. But yes, Maria did make it sound like something straight out of a horror movie."

"I don't like it. I don't like it at all." Gabriel wrung his hands anxiously.

"Look," Frank said quietly. "Thomas and I are no experts, but we have camped with the kids. They've camped with school, and with their friends back home. They're not clueless and neither is Andreas. If you really don't like it, then we'll jump in the car and go check on them. It's fifteen minutes away—ten if we break the speed limit."

"Fuck no! Andreas will think we don't trust him, and Bruno is really big on this trust thing. Says we need to let him be an adult and let him come to us when he needs us."

"But they're not adults. They're kids." Now Frank was contradicting himself and shook his head vigorously as he started to laugh. "We are shit parents."

"Yeah." Gabriel smiled. "We are worse. I'm a city kid. I wouldn't survive out here for more than twenty-four hours. I never went camping or shit like that until Bruno forced me to go hitchhiking for a month and almost got us killed. Never again. I like a real bed at night and a solid roof over my head. And I would prefer Andreas to be at home with us, but..." He sighed deeply. "You two are such cool, trusting parents, and your kids are pretty awesome. It's good for Andreas to spend time with them. He likes them, and he's loved this holiday as much as we have."

"Sometimes I think there are magical things in the air here," Frank said wistfully. "Like...problems come and go, but they don't seem so big and overwhelming out here." He chuckled. "Says the mentally unwell freak who couldn't get out of bed the first week you were here."

"But you're getting out of bed now, and you look fine. You sound fine. *Are* you fine?"

Gabriel's question warmed Frank's insides. "I think so. Really. Right now, I'm kind of OK." He paused as Maria came back out. From the heavy bulkiness of her backpack, she'd completely emptied the fridge. The bread he'd just made was sticking out the top, a bag of cinnamon buns dangled from one of the straps, and she'd cleverly strung bags of crisps to the other strap, taking more care with them than last time.

"I'm leaving now," she said, leaning forward with the poorly distributed load on her back.

"Your backpack looks really heavy," Thomas said, having followed her out.

"Can I take a look?" Frank asked, although it sounded like an order.

"Why? Don't you trust me?"

"Of course, we do?" Thomas said.

"Daddy doesn't," Maria accused, letting the pack slide from her shoulders. "Have a good rummage," she said, crossing her arms. "Since you don't trust me."

Thomas lifted an eyebrow at Frank. "What's going on here?"

"Just a little parenting—around the issue of beer."

"Beer?" Thomas looked at her, surprised.

"It was a joke!"

"Well, I can help you pack this shit a bit better anyway," Frank said, pulling stuff from her pack and lining it on the deck. In addition to the burgers, buns and bread, she had several bottles of soda, a whole block of cheese, a pack of hotdogs, leftover salad from yesterday, some sweets, peanuts and crisps. So much for stocking up the snack cupboard. "Healthy eating," he muttered dryly.

"And no beer!" She looked down at him in grim satisfaction.

"No, no beer." Frank looked up at her. "I do trust you, Maria. *We* trust you."

"Do you think we'd let you go camping alone if we didn't?" Thomas added.

Frank sagged with relief that Thomas was backing him up and he wasn't being a total dick.

Maria shrugged, and Thomas smiled. "Well, if we didn't trust you but still let you go, it would be quite irresponsible, wouldn't it?"

"Yeah. Guess so." Her face lightened slightly. "Can I go now?" She looked down at the food on the deck, then at Frank. "Please will you pack it for me, Dad?"

Frank nodded. "Sure. That's why I unloaded it in the first place, wasn't it?"

\*\*\*

"Wi-Fi, you say?" Bruno scratched his chin, having caught up with them as Maria left. "Do they have better mobile coverage over there?"

"I don't think so," Frank said. "The mobile antenna covering us is in the opposite direction, and there aren't any obstacles between us and the antenna that they don't have. I guess they must have managed to get the cable company to deliver the internet to them. They wouldn't do it for us here since this property is just a summer home."

"Oh." Bruno looked confused. "I didn't know you had such rules here. I don't think we do in Germany."

"Maybe because Germany is less sparsely populated? We're not in an urban area here."

"I guess you're right." Bruno laughed. "I might go camping myself. Or take a long walk on my own with my phone."

"Don't you dare!" Gabriel warned. "You're on dinner duty."

"Oh, yes." Bruno grinned. "Frank has already made the bread, so that's half of it done."

"That bread is halfway around the lake by now," Frank said. "So scrap that for dinner."

"Ah, I'm fucked then." Bruno laughed.

"You know," Thomas said, "if we had Wi-Fi here, this place could be worth a fortune. Imagine using this place for a seminar or a workshop for a company, Frank."

"Yes, that would be über-cool!" Gabriel said. "You could make more bedrooms in the barn. It has two floors, so you can easily fit maybe fifteen people in there."

"Twin rooms, then it will be twice as many," Bruno added.

"And bathrooms."

"Definitely bathrooms."

"Maybe the girl in the café could come cook here," Thomas joked. "She bakes wicked cakes, even though her cooking skills seem a little limited."

"Cakes are not enough," Bruno said. "Whoever runs this has to be able to impress with the food as well."

Gabriel nodded. "And I'm sure there are people in the village who would happily care for the house when you two were away."

"A caretaker, yes."

Frank sprang to his feet. He heard his chair hit the deck as he fled across the yard, then Thomas's confused voice and the calmer voices of Gabriel and Bruno. He wanted to be alone right now, yet for an instant he hoped Thomas would follow him.

The barn loomed in front of him, seeming gigantic; he felt like a minion as he approached the door. The lock was cold to the touch, and the hinges creaked, a long squeak screeching against his ear drums as the door inched open.

The dim light inside calmed his frazzled nerves. Shadows crept from the corners, building a landscape of different shades of darkness, black peaks against grey gradients, punctuated by a few thin rays of sunlight through the old planks.

He followed the wall to the right of the door until he found the light switch at about the same time as his eyes adjusted and he started seeing details.

The shelves were grim; Thomas was right about that. Dust covered every surface other than spots where someone had touched it, probably Thomas, maybe Maria and Fredrik. Frank remembered Thomas saying something about putting the camping gear next to the door, and he could see marks left behind by larger items having been dragged across the shelves.

He walked through the space, past the old-fashioned sofa, table, bookshelf and an old tractor. Boxes were stacked on the antique desk. He stroked his hand along the sleek, dark wood; he wasn't sure what kind it was, maybe teak, he thought, being a dark, reddish-brown. The finish was scratched and worn, and there were watermarks all over the top, a grey half circle in front of the logical place to sit.

He had to try. He had to give it a chance, even if it was more and more unbearable the more he thought about it. Maybe Thomas was right about this being too much for them to handle and that they should sell it. All the ideas, the opportunities, the dreams—the money would always be lacking, and if they failed, they would have nothing left. Maybe Bruno and Gabriel were right about the place having potential and they could transform it into...something. No matter the outcome, he needed to sort this stuff out. Clean the dirt, clear out the rubbish. Rent a skip, fill it, rinse, repeat. Bruno had assured him that they were happy to help, and Gabriel had talked to him about not holding on to stuff that had no value and brought nothing but stress.

The largest of the boxes was open, and Frank tentatively peeked inside. There were papers. Lots of papers. He sighed and looked over at the dusty pile of books next to the desk. Science and engineering topics with strange graphs on the covers mixed with arrows and formulae that made no sense to him. Mathematics for engineers, physics, engines, fluid mechanics. He flicked through them, not understanding anything, until his eyes fell on the first page. *Erik N. Albrektson.* The writing was neat, blue pen, even letters.

He frowned. There was something familiar about the name, he just couldn't remember what. A story his mother or grandmother had told him about Bella maybe?

Bella wasn't his real aunt. She was from a more remote part of the family, a third cousin of his grandmother; there was a generation skew, as she'd been his grandmother's age despite being a generation older. But Aunt Bella had never made contact, even back then. She'd never been part of their immediate family. When she'd died and Frank had inherited her farm, her history had been lost because he'd known nothing about her and truly didn't think she'd known more about him than his name.

Next to the cardboard box was another box containing a pile of yellowing newspapers with colourful pictures and bold headlines despite their age. They were full of politicians he barely remembered from history books shouting opinions, stars of sport he'd never heard of, football scores, events, wars, accidents, murders—page after page of repeating events from a lifetime ago. The papers weren't even in order, and there were editions missing. He didn't understand why they were still here, why the pile had been kept in a cardboard box that looked new compared to the newspapers. The box had none of the dodgy corners age would have brought after decades in semi-humid conditions, nor the half-ripped tape marks from when the box was moved.

He dug deeper into the box and found another bunch of newspapers under to the first, then underneath those some clippings along with printed certificates—a general diploma and one in craftsmanship, Bachelor's degrees from the Royal School of Engineering—the name matching that in the books.

The last piece of paper was a death certificate, dated 1988 and signed by the local parish, along with a photo of the small wooden church in the village. He'd passed that church many times. It looked idyllic, the churchyard more like a park with white fence, benches, birch trees, lawns and, of course, headstones. It was a place for serenity, no stress, no noise. Returning to the death certificate, he read it and frowned. *Erik N. Albrektson, born on 19 September 1941, died on 24 December 1988, buried on 6 January 1989. Holy Three Kings' Day. Epiphany.*

It didn't feel like an epiphany. He was just getting more and more confused. He still had no idea who this Erik was or why there was a pile of his papers here, a collection of bits and pieces spanning over almost thirty years. The most recent paper was dated only ten years before Frank was born, yet nobody had ever mentioned him.

He froze when he read the death certificate more carefully.

*Dödsårsak: självmord.*
Cause of death: suicide.

It felt like experiencing it again, from above, from below, from inside, outside.

The rush of clarity, the actions, the feelings, the lights, the sounds. The ice-cold shock of air hitting the stinking wet spots running down his neck, the smells that still paralysed him whenever he had to sit in a doctor's office, the atmosphere he could suddenly sense in a random corridor at work. The beeping in his ears, increasing to a loud, shrill hum that brought with it a memory of someone rushing towards him, a white-clad figure holding him, lifting him, pinching him, shouting, more noise, unfriendly touches, then silence.

The pain when he did it. The pain when he didn't.

The questions: the spoken, all the whys—why you, why me, why us— and the unspoken—the tears, the looks, the faces, the lips about to open, go from unspoken to spoken, the lips that stayed closed and that he hated for not speaking, the lips he hated for speaking.

The answers he'd never had.

The moment he'd done it, he'd known why. Afterwards, he had no idea, couldn't explain it. The pain, the guilt, the feeling of dread, of not making it; of making it but still not making it.

But still. He didn't do it, and sometimes he wasn't sure if that had been the right outcome.

Erik *had* done it, but had he wanted to? Frank had wanted to. In a selfish moment, he'd known he wasn't happy or himself. Not doing it meant more questions he would never get an answer to; more whys, more, more, more. He'd never come to terms with a lot of things in his past, despite spending too much time and money and effort on damn therapists and...*fuck*.

*Fuck.*

He tried to calm down, concentrating on the old air reaching his lungs, looking around at the things accumulated over many years, dust, traces in dust, spiderwebs. It was old, but it was here, and he was here. He was still here.

He tried to see it through Thomas's eyes. Through a stranger's eyes, someone not affiliated with this place, even though he wasn't quite sure what his affiliation was other than a financial one.

All that was left here was broken furniture, outdated, battered and unwanted. The creaky sofa, moth-eaten mattresses, piles of boxes, tools from the garden, wood, buckets of paint, chemicals, loads of stuff that nobody loved anymore. He wondered if any of these things had a history; if they could speak, would they tell interesting stories? Maybe not the oil can or the paint bucket, but the mattress, the sofa, the papers... He had no idea what they were all trying to tell him here.

He managed to get to his feet and wandered around, sliding his finger across the grime and dirt, trying to centre his thoughts on something.

The desk with its boxes drew him in, and suddenly he was determined to search through every last one. He rifled through the papers, continuing the sorting someone, probably Thomas, had already started. More diplomas and certificates for short courses, books, newspapers, clippings. All of it was printed matter.

Then, as he grabbed the last pile, a small, thin piece of paper slipped from his hands and tumbled, like a falling leaf in the autumn, side to side through the air. It landed face up on the desk; with trembling fingers, he picked it up.

> *Min kära Erik. Alltid min. Alltid din. B.*
> "My dear Erik. Always mine. Always yours. B."

He stared at the words.

It was the closest he had come to something personal of Bella's. There were no letters, nothing personal, no notes, hardly anything written in the margins of the books.

He peeked back into the box again. Under the bottom flap, he could see something else. A black-and-white photo of a man and a woman standing next to each other in front of a barn, presumably this barn, although the other buildings and woods were not present in the image. The man had his arm slung around the woman's shoulder, and they were smiling at the camera, him raising his chin a bit, while she leaned towards his side. Their clothes were typical for the sixties, not the hip urban modern clothing of the era but traditional countryside style. A knitted vest over his shirt; a floral dress for her.

Frank turned the picture over. There were no names on the back, only some small initials in the lower-left corner, just below his thumb. *H.A.* The writing style was of a certain age, like the picture, with slightly crooked letters, the pencil lines blurred by touch, as if written by a loving great-grandmother.

Frank sighed. This was just getting more and more complicated. He had no idea who H.A. might have been and didn't remember anyone with a name matching those initials. Was it the photographer, the person who kept the photo until Aunt Bella got it? Or perhaps it had never belonged to Aunt Bella at all.

\*\*\*

He heard Maria and Fredrik long before they came into sight, returning late in the evening the next day. Frank was sitting on the patio, trying to read a book and instead looking mindlessly at his unconnected phone. Thomas was doing something in the garden, while Bruno and Gabriel had taken the girls to a newly opened trampoline park.

Their laughter was infectious—Maria's loud shrills, Fredrik's deeper snickers, and Andreas's even deeper chuckles. Frank could imagine how they were walking, with Andreas in the middle, the banter, the jokes. He wondered if Maria's pack was still as full as when she'd left yesterday, who was carrying the tent, were they carrying a sleeping bag each or had they split the load in a more creative way?

"Hi, Dad!" Fredrik waved as they crossed the lawn towards the patio. He wrangled his pack off and dropped it on the deck; Maria followed suit. "Do you have anything to drink?" they both asked, their voices blending into one as they had always done as children.

"Sure. Go get..." He changed his mind; he'd get it for them. "You sit. I'll get the drinks." He rose from his chair and headed for the kitchen. "Is Andreas coming too?"

Maria shook her head. "He went back home."

A few minutes later, Frank was back with a tray holding water, glasses and sandwiches. "So how was your trip?" he asked.

"Good." Fredrik grabbed a thick sandwich and stuffed half of it into his mouth.

"Fredrik, manners, please."

"Sowwy. Am hungwy." He chewed.

"We saw some tracks, Dad," Maria said.

"Tracks?"

"Yes, look." She handed him her phone and pointed at some faint tracks in the mud.

Frank frowned. "They're not very clear," he said.

Maria glanced at her phone. "Oh." She swiped a few times and passed it back to him. "This one's better. Could it be badger? It stole rubbish from the bag we left outside the tent."

Frank looked up at her. "You left litter outside the tent?"

"It stank. None of us wanted it inside the tent!"

"Well, it's not a badger," he decided.

"Are you sure?"

"Absolutely. Look." He pointed at the screen. "Badgers have claws that leave marks, but their feet resemble human feet, so their tracks look like ours but with claw marks in front of the toes. This..." He looked down again. "It's more like a deer?"

Maria shook her head. "Nope, it wasn't a deer. It made sniffing noises, like it was digging in the dirt with its nose."

"Could've been wild boar, then," he said, suppressing a shudder of fear.

"Wild boar?" Maria repeated, shocked. Fredrik's jaw dropped, still with a mouthful of sandwich. "But they are dangerous!"

"Yeah, they've been known to kill people, maul them with their fangs. Turn into werewolves in the middle of the night."

"You are so full of shit, Daddy."

"There have been sightings around here. And wolves."

"Like the ones who are human during the day but when the moon rises they turn into wild boar?"

"You've read too many dodgy romance novels, Maria," Fredrik muttered.

"You read them too. I know because I found one in the bathroom at home and you'd bent back the pages. I never deface books."

"I don't deface books. That was Frank."

"What?" Frank crossed his arms defensively.

"You read my Shifter series? The one with the werewolves in Canada?" Maria glared at him.

"Well, I..." He grimaced, trying to defend himself. "I needed some entertainment on the toilet, and it was just there. It was kind of...weird. I mean I didn't like all the bone breaking when they shifted. It was...kind of gross..."

"Daddy..." Maria sighed and rolled her eyes.

It felt good, laughing together. Even after the moment had passed and Maria was squabbling with her brother for the last sandwich, Frank was still smiling at his family. It was funny how the little things made him feel, despite the demons of his past, that his life might sometimes be bloody perfect.

# Twenty two
## BRUNO

"PAPI!" ANDREAS SAID, dragging the overflowing kitchen bin over to the car while Bruno tried to reach the back of the boot with the vacuum cleaner. The car had somehow birthed a massive pile of rubbish that now festered on the grass, and it had twice as many stains and double the dirt than when they'd arrived. They'd brought a lot of stuff with them—basic food items like wine, beer, coffee—all of which was now gone and should've left plenty of space in the car for the journey back. Yet he had no idea how he was going to fit everything back in.

"What?" he snapped, wiping his forehead with the back of his hand. They weren't due to leave until Saturday morning, but he liked to be prepared, and they needed to clean the house, put the sheets through the wash and sort out the towels. It would've helped to know where Gabriel was. Bruno hadn't seen him since this morning despite him promising that he would vacuum the bedrooms and dust down the windowsills that looked more and more like spooky graveyards of doom with piles of dead flies and mosquitoes. It was summer, they were in the countryside, and he was sweating like a boiled crab in the heat that had suddenly engulfed the Nordics, causing everyone to seek out the shade, and the girls had pretty much lived in the lake for the last two days. They were still there now, carefully supervised by Maria. He hoped.

"Can we, like, you know..." Andreas started, looking a little flustered as he leant against the car, then jumped away, rubbing his arm.

"You OK?"

"Yeah. Just. Hot, you know."

He panted. Bruno panted.

"Want a drink?" Bruno asked. Andreas clearly had something on his mind, and Bruno knew him well enough to know what to do. If he didn't prise it out of him now, it would never get said.

"We only have tap water. I'm kind of sick of tap water. Why don't we have any Sprite?"

"Because Sprite is shit." Bruno laughed. "Come sit down and talk to me."

"Papi, dobbiamo fare un discorso serio, parlare da uomo a uomo." Andreas did little quotation marks with his hands as they took their seats on the veranda, looking desperately pained. "Can we do that *Man-to-Man* thing, where what I say never gets mentioned again?"

It was fucking hard to talk about the kind of shit they'd talked about in the past, *Man to Man*. "Of course. Cross my heart."

"I'm not gay," Andreas said and shot a shit-eating grin at his father.

"Noted." Bruno laughed and leaned over so he could bury his face in his hands for a second.

Deep breath.

"I've..." Andreas started, then chickened out. "I've liked it here."

"Me too," Bruno confessed. "It's been good for Vati. He's been more relaxed."

"He's still depressed. You can see that, can't you?" Andreas lectured a touch aggressively.

"Yes, I know he is. It's not something that will go away overnight. He needs to get back to teaching and feeling useful again. That's something I think will help, establishing a good routine and...I don't know. To be honest, Andreas, a lot of the time, I don't know if he will ever be the person he was a few years back. We've all changed in the last couple of years. I mean, look at you. You're not the same kid as you were when you were ten. Or eleven or twelve for that matter. Last year, you were still playing Pokémon."

"I still play Pokémon sometimes. It relaxes me. Kind of like feeling like a kid again, not being so grown up."

"You feel grown up?"

"Sometimes I feel like I don't really fit in my skin anymore. And other times, I feel tiny and stupid, like when Maria talks about stuff

I don't understand or stuff I never even thought of. I constantly feel stupid around her."

"What about Fredrik? Do you feel stupid around him too? Girls are way ahead of boys at your age, so don't worry about it. You'll catch up, and you're definitely not stupid."

Andreas went quiet again, looking out into the trees, his posture uneasy.

"Is there something you want to talk to me about?"

"I fucked up, I think. I did something stupid."

"We all do stupid things. The trick is to apologise for what you've done and offer to make things better. Sometimes just acknowledging that something you did was stupid can fix a lot of aggro. You know? Just admitting you're an idiot?"

"You do that a lot with Vati. Telling him you're an idiot."

"I *am* an idiot most of the time. He knows that. But see? He still loves me, despite all the shit I do."

"You do some stupid shit." Andreas shook his head.

"And unfortunately, you are my kid, and you know—genetics and all that." Bruno laughed and leaned back in his chair. "Sorry, kid. You're destined to fuck up at times. It's just the way it is."

"It's just..." Andreas started. "Fuck. It's hard to talk about, but I don't know what to do. I didn't mean for it to turn out like this. It was just a stupid idea and... Fuck."

"Language," Bruno said softly. "Man-to-Man talk. Nothing you say will come back to haunt you. Promise. It stays here." He thumped his chest, quietly fearing whatever Andreas was going to come out with because right now he didn't have a clue. Nothing. The kids were fine. Maria and Fredrik had been behaving normally. Nothing was broken or missing that he knew of.

"You have to promise. I mean, don't tell Vati. Don't talk about it, and don't try to talk to...*him*."

"OK? Who's *him*?"

"Fredrik."

"*What* about Fredrik?" He tried to keep his voice calm, but he was starting to worry. What was it? Drugs? Did they smoke while camping? Get drunk? *Fuck.*

It took a while until Andreas spoke again, and his voice was painfully strained, like he was about to burst into tears.

"We talked a lot when we were camping, at least until we found Wi-Fi, which, by the way, was bloody awesome. Anyway, we were talking about kissing, and love and sex and boys and girls and all that shit. You know, normal stuff."

"Yes," Bruno said tightly. *Fuck. Fuck, fuck, fuck.*

"Then Maria went to get more food because we were kind of out of stuff to eat, and Fredrik and I kind of got deep, talking about really personal stuff. It was, you know, interesting. He's a lot like me, and we agreed that we kind of thought that the other person was awesome. You know. Bro-awesome. Friends. That we would miss each other when we leave here and that we need to stay in contact. All the normal stuff."

Bruno just nodded. Normal stuff. *Then they took drugs.*

"You look like you're about to yell at me."

"What did you take?"

"We did not take drugs, Papi. Where the hell would we get drugs from?"

"I don't know. The farm? Do they deal?"

"The lady there grows organic wheat and milks cows. They have crazy ass sheep, but she's no bloody gangster. What have you been smoking, Papi? You're behaving all crazy."

Bruno breathed. Deep, deep breaths. "You're sure? No drugs?"

"Have I ever, *ever* taken drugs? Got drunk and got into trouble? Papi? Really?"

"No?" Bruno's voice sounded small.

"We kissed, OK?" Andreas said quickly, defensively. "We kissed, and then we made out, and it was kind of really good and then we promised that we would never do that again, and it was just experimenting, and we were both good with that, and now he's hiding and won't speak to me, and it's fucking awkward, and I think Maria wants to kill me."

"But you're not gay," Bruno repeated, then froze up. Yeah. He was an idiot. But at least the drug thing had worked. Classic psychology. Accuse him of doing something way worse than the thing he'd actually done, soften the blow. At least Andreas was talking now.

"I'm *not* gay," Andreas said sternly. "It's very normal to experiment and try things, and anyway it's no different from kissing a girl. We just had fun and laughed about it and what the hell anyway? I'm not apologising for shit. I just need him to talk to me and be all normal so we can play *GTA* again and be all cool and shit."

"Awkward." Bruno sighed. He was still an idiot. There was no cure for how much of an idiot he could be.

"Yeah, and Maria says she thinks he's in love with me."

"She shouldn't say things like that. That's wrong. And you need to speak to him and not go gossiping with his sister. So, she knows?" Thank God the words were coming out right.

"Yeah. I told her, and before you shout at me, I know that was wrong. I don't know if she hates me because I told her or because I made out with her brother. Who is straight, by the way. We agreed on that. It doesn't make you gay because you like kissing. Kissing is awesome."

"Yeah, kisses are good," Bruno said and shook his head to try to get his brain back into gear.

"So, you know, we're going home tomorrow and I can't leave like this. I feel like shit and everyone hates me, and don't... Don't go telling his dads because they'll kill me. Thomas is scary. He'll probably beat me up and poison me with something, and I'll die a terrible death on the ferry back, and there will be nothing you can do to save me."

"Thomas would never do anything like that."

"Fredrik says he studies deadly poisons and biological warfare. He could kill me. Just like that, and I wouldn't know what hit me."

"Really? Bullshit."

"OK, not really, but it's what happens in the book I'm reading. This guy gets slowly poisoned by something in his clothes, and before he realises, he's, like, stone cold dead."

"OK." Bruno laughed. "He wouldn't kill you. I mean, what the fuck? Thomas is a professor in astrophysics or some shit. Why would he kill you? Because you and his son are friends and shared some kissing when you were camping? He's not insane."

"No, but the rest of us are. Sometimes I think that maybe you're the only sane person here."

"I've been clinically depressed, several times. Nobody is *sane* here, Andreas. We're just totally normal human beings who don't always make the best choices for ourselves. I'm not saying you made a bad choice. I don't think you did. As long as you were both into it and enjoyed it then it's just a choice you need to talk about and kind of, you know, laugh about?"

"No. It wasn't funny."

"But you had his consent? He agreed to the kissing?"

"He was into it. We both were. I mean, I'm not stupid. If he'd said no, I wouldn't have kissed him, but anyway, he kissed me first so..."

"OK. I don't know what to say."

"We can't go home yet."

"We need to go home."

"But you don't go back to work for another two weeks, and Vati is freelance, and school isn't back yet."

"Did Maria put you up to this?"

"No! I know my own mind, Papi. I just need some time to figure this shit out. It's bloody annoying."

"We need to go home," Bruno repeated sternly. "We've only paid until tomorrow, and anyway, the cottage is probably rented out to someone else from tomorrow."

"It's not. I asked."

"We've packed."

"I'm not going. Not yet. I need to get Fredrik to talk to me."

"That's good. A good strategy. But what if Fredrik doesn't want to talk to you?"

"That's the problem. You're not helping, Papi."

"Hi!"

*Shit.* Andreas stiffened up like he'd been shot, and Bruno shuffled awkwardly.

"You didn't hear any of that, I assume?" he asked, hoping Thomas hadn't heard a thing and that he didn't really work with biological warfare because Bruno was a stern pacifist and that shit was scary. And why the fuck had he not asked him more about what he did for a living apart from that it was something to do with astrophysics?

"Hear what?" Thomas smiled, confused. "You yapping away in Italian like some Hollywood mafiosos? Didn't understand a word. Look, I'm here because I have a favour to ask. If you want to, that is. No pressure, and I certainly wouldn't want you to feel like you have to because I know you have lives at home and all that. But..."

"Dude, what are you asking?" Bruno was relieved. Scared perhaps. Shit, he knew fuck all right now.

"Frank is really doing well, and he's talking a lot with Gabriel, and the kids are having the best time, and the cottage is free, and I heard Gabriel saying that you don't have to go back to work for another two weeks, and well... What I'm really saying is if you want to stay for a few more days, then you can. Don't just fuck off because we booked a certain day on Airbnb."

"We can't stay." Bruno was standing firm. "We only paid until tomorrow, and you need your income and it's not fair. Anyway, we've eaten all your food and overstayed our welcome in so many ways. I bet you can't wait to see the back of us so you can have some peace and quiet."

Thomas pouted. "You haven't taught me to cook that pasta thing you made the other night yet, and I have a moose roast in the freezer we haven't cooked."

"Sorry?" Bruno flexed his shoulders and then laughed at Thomas acting like a disappointed child.

"It's been fun having you here," he said, doing a half twist from side to side. "Sorry. I'm worse than the kids. Your girls have me wrapped around their little fingers. They asked me to come talk to you. At least, I think that's what they said. Gabriel wants to stay. Maria burst into tears last night when we talked about you leaving, and Fredrik hasn't left his room since yesterday. He kind of does that, grieves in advance when things are going to change. He's a sensitive kid, and I think he's enjoyed having company here."

"Our twins like your kids," Bruno said quietly. "They think Fredrik is way cooler than Andreas." He winked at his son, who was sitting statue-still.

"My kids adore your kids too," Thomas said. "Maria keeps asking if we can have a new baby."

"What?" Bruno laughed.

"Yeah. She says she's not having kids, but that she would help if we had another one. Fucking madness. It would kill us."

"You're not seriously thinking about it?"

"No." Thomas laughed. "But we have been talking about the future, and we need to make some changes. You know, make us happier." He sat on a chair next to them and picked at the peeling paint on the table. "You really are leaving on Saturday morning?"

"That's the plan," Bruno confirmed.

"Plans are made for changing," Andreas tried and shot Bruno a little smile.

Bruno turned, trying to read his son's face. Worry, with a pinch of relief shone through in that little smile stuck to his lips. Andreas obviously liked the kissing a bit too much and wanted to do it again. That could become shitty, so yeah. They should really go. The kid could go up and talk and sort things out with Fredrik, and they would leave Saturday morning as planned. Experimenting was good. Kissing was good. Heartbreak, on the other hand was shit. Better to cut the strings now before Andreas fell in love and his life became a mess. This whole conversation had just got messy in his head, and in the process, Andreas had found a quiet opening to skulk off leaving Thomas mumbling something Bruno didn't catch.

"What do you say?"

"Moose roast tomorrow night and then you can help me clear out the barn and we can have a few beers and shoot the shit over dirty old furniture and stuff we should burn. Make a big bonfire and grill hotdogs over Aunt Bella's junk. Am I selling this staying stuff to you yet?"

"Sounds tempting," Bruno admitted, "but I think we really should go. We need to get the kids sorted for school and a few jobs done. You know. Get the car serviced…"

"Excuses," Thomas said. "You know you want to."

Bruno sighed. "In a way, I don't want this holiday to end. It's been almost like a…a bubble, where the outside world doesn't exist and I can pretend there's nothing wrong."

"I know what you mean." Thomas frowned in thought. "And to be honest, I have a massive shitstorm to face when we leave. I had a message from my head of department weeks ago. One of those full of subtle threats and well-chosen words. He asked me to call him back ASAP, but it's a phone call I really don't want to make because I know I don't want to hear what he'll tell me."

"And like the normal human you are, you've put off returning that call—for weeks. Am I right?"

"You're not wrong," Thomas admitted, letting his head drop until it thunked against the tabletop.

"Have you told Frank?" Bruno asked, hoping it came out as a gentle opening rather than an accusation.

"No. It's too much for me to deal with, and I don't want to push it all on him. Not right now. Not when I might be out of a job and have no idea what our future will bring. I don't want to even think about it."

"Are you sure that's what's happening?"

The look on Thomas face said it all. Nobody was safe in their positions these days. Bruno had been made to reapply for his job twice already, even in his short career as a professional.

"I'm trying to plan for the worst-case scenario, but even the least-horrible outcome of that phone call—I'm not even sure that's the future I want. It's all a bit overwhelming."

"No wonder you're a mess, mate."

Thomas laughed, and it was a laugh of relief. "I'm an idiot not talking to Frank, I admit that. It's become one of those stupid things that just grows and grows."

Now Bruno laughed. "You sound like me."

"You're just good at this stuff." Thomas scratched his chin, one that was now sporting an almost-full beard.

"OK. Before you beat yourself up over being a secretive dick here, I'm going to confess something. Something that will make you see yourself in a different light. OK? And I'm not after sympathy. Just hear me out, OK?"

"OK." Thomas didn't look convinced, but Bruno sat up straighter in his chair and braced himself. It had been a long time since he'd talked about it, and even finding the right words to start made him choke up.

"I met Gabe when I was seventeen. Same age as Andreas is now. And I was a fully out-and-proud gay man with all that invincible conviction of youth. I'd always known I was different and somehow had an easy ride figuring it out. So, with all that cockiness and stupidity, and knowing that *dick and even more dick* was the answer to my every question?"

"I can see where this one is going," Thomas said with a smile. "Carry on."

"I met Gabe, and I fell in love. I mean, he was just the most handsome guy I'd ever seen, and we got on like a house on fire, and it was just, you know? Everything was so easy. All the angst you see in films, the worries in your chest? None of that. It was just Gabe and me and me and Gabe, and everything was just brilliant. So, so good."

He took a deep breath. Blew air out in a huge huff of disappointment. Because it would always be there. The shame. The regret. The bloody words he'd spent a lifetime wishing he'd been able to retract.

"When Gabe finally told me what he was hiding under all those clothes, under the messy fringe and secretive manners and the subtle lies and the fucking stubborn streak he had going on? By the time we finally talked? Everything had become such a massive lie. The mountain of words we hadn't said had become so huge that we couldn't even talk to each other. I screamed at him and called him some godawful names. I said some really, really horrible things. I ranted and raved and the anger—I'd never felt anything like it before. Carnal raw and brutal betrayal. I think that's what I called it."

He had to stop again. Breathe out. In and out. Thomas sat there, waiting quietly for him to continue, and Bruno laughed—at his own stupidity. He needed to listen to his own advice. Talk more, not build mountains of hurdles.

"I was a gay man and Gabe had all the wrong body parts. How fucking stupid did that make seventeen-year-old me look? I had no sense and a vile temper, and I didn't even think about what I was doing. It took months. *Months!* I didn't see him and I didn't talk, and I festered in my own stupidity until I was going insane. You can see it, can't you? Imagine leaving Frank and being alone with your crazy thoughts on loop in your head and just losing the plot? That was me. It took me almost a year to figure it all out."

"And how did you do that? I mean. Wow. That doesn't seem like you, at all."

"I think I just grew up, but it took me a while. A few months of waking up every morning thinking of Gabe and going to sleep every night thinking of Gabe. And not being so bloody angry."

"That kind of anger is hard to shift," Thomas said quietly.

"The worst," Bruno agreed. "And what kind of grand romantic gesture did I come up with to win my man back?" He had to laugh because now, almost twenty years later, it suddenly didn't feel like such a shameful secret anymore.

"I cornered him at school and told him to own up to the fact that he'd completely ruined my life, that he had to take some fucking responsibility because his life wasn't all about him anymore. I was part of his life, and he had to remember that. There were two of us to consider, and I didn't fucking care anymore. I just wanted to have a say in it. I made it seem like his fault. Again."

Thomas nodded knowingly. Whatever his and Frank's past held, he understood where Bruno was coming from.

"So, Gabe did the right thing," Bruno said. "He punched me in the face. First and last time ever, and I didn't blame him. We've been together since that day. Not always smooth sailing, but we figured it out. It took me a long time to get my head around that body parts and sexuality are two different things and that you just fall in love with people and have to go with the flow. You can't change things, just learn to figure things out. That sounds awful, but it's the truth. I love Gabriel. I love him with every fibre of my body, and even when things have been hard, I've always remembered that. That's what I'm trying to say here."

"I'm not following," Thomas admitted.

"You and Frank. What you have is worth fighting for. Don't let anger consume you. Take it for what it is. Don't make mountains when you can just talk yourself over those little hills. And don't be so bloody stubborn! I was, and if I hadn't gotten over myself, I would have lost the best thing I had going. That's what you need to remember. You have everything, right here in this shitty dump of a farm. Maybe your job will go. Maybe you'll have to make changes. But love that husband of yours because that is what really matters."

"And don't fuck it up." Thomas said the words quietly, like they were important. They were. Bruno knew that.

"Don't fuck it up," he whispered back. "We really like you guys. Sorry for going all deep, but I've regretted those months all my life. The things I said, what I did, what I didn't do. Regrets are horrible. I haven't always been a good person, and at times, I've caused Gabe a lot of stress. Sometimes I wonder if I caused more damage to him than I realise. I can't undo that, but I will spend the rest of my life trying to make him happy because that is all I can do. See what I mean?"

"I'm not always nice to Frank. I'm not always good for him." Thomas's voice was barely audible. "Is that what you're saying?"

"No, mate. No. I think what I'm saying is…sometimes we're not good for the people we love, and sometimes they're not good for us. I still haven't got it all figured out. I'm still making those goddamn awful mistakes. This trip? Perhaps I should have taken all the pressure off Gabe and just chilled. We could have stayed at home and he could have had a break from us all. I could have taken the kids to my dad's and given Gabe a chance to reset. But then, if we hadn't come here?" Bruno shrugged. "Things have changed, and now we have to go home, and I have no idea how to make these changes stick. How to go back to our lives and still hold on to what we've achieved here. I feel like I've made things better, but I have no idea how to not make them worse again. I've had too much time to think, sorry. This place does that to you, doesn't it? It makes you overthink shit and messes with your head."

He had to stop or he'd start to cry. Bawl his eyes out at the poor dude who looked ready to cry himself. What an arsehole he was. It was all about him. Him, him, him. The rest of the world could be out there burning, and Bruno Moretti was once again wallowing in self-pity.

"What I'm saying is…" He cleared his throat, pretended to cough. "Don't have regrets. Just grasp life. Roll with it. Love that man of yours because that… *that* is what will get you through all this. Don't sit here in a few years' time and have regrets. Life is for living. That's how I see it. Fuck your job. Fuck the world. Fuck everything else. Just live. Laugh. Be bloody happy. Oh, and go make that phone call."

"I'll throw that sentence right back in your face. *Mate*." Thomas smiled. "Stay. Just a few more days. Let's make this holiday worth it. Go out with a bang or whatever."

"I do want to," Bruno said, rubbing his face with his hands. "But I need to speak to Gabriel. And I've paid for the ferry tickets and all that."

"But you're going to talk to him, yeah?" Thomas said, standing up to leave. "If it makes any difference, I could do with a mate for a few more days. It's been good having you here."

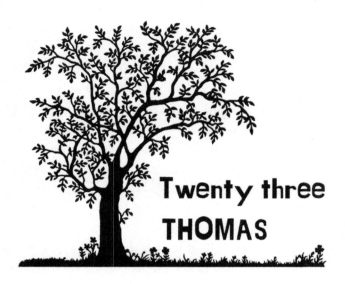

## Twenty three
## THOMAS

His arms were wedged against the headboard, his chest spread wide as he yawned loudly and stretched his toes as far as he could reach. Those satisfying creaks in his bones made him smile as he rolled his shoulders.

"You awake?"

Frank was staring up at the ceiling, not moving a muscle as Thomas nudged closer and slung an arm across his chest.

"What's wrong?" Thomas asked quietly. He could read his husband's face like an open book. The way his chest moved. Breaths too long and deep. Something wasn't right.

"Nothing," Frank huffed before drawing a breath and turning into Thomas's embrace. "Or..." His blue eyes were fixed on Thomas's as his fingers cupped Thomas's face, his thumb following the curve of his cheekbone up to the tender skin below his eye.

"What's up?" Thomas asked again. "You know you can tell me."

"Maybe you're right," Frank whispered shakily.

"Uh-huh?"

"About selling the farm."

Thomas didn't reply, just waited. Sometimes letting Frank speak was the best way to calm all those demons that seemed to constantly live in his head.

"Maybe it's for the best. To get rid of it. Maybe we can't do it. Or I can't," he corrected before clinging closer to Thomas.

"Or maybe it *is* worth it," Thomas muttered. "Maybe we're just now starting to discover that."

"I don't know. What's the value?"

Thomas shrugged. "I don't know. Things have been bad this year, same as always. But it's been different. I can't quite put my finger on why."

"Neither can I." Frank rose up on his elbow, a small spark of vigour back in his voice. "That's the problem. I don't know why I'm clinging to it. Except for the fact that this is *mine*, but that sounds selfish and childish somehow."

"Well, it *is*, yours," Thomas said. "And I don't think it's selfish or childish to relish that."

"Maybe not. But still, why is it good?"

Thomas had no answer for that. He knew most of Frank's demons were ghosts from his past, things that had happened way before Thomas had ever been part of his life. But there were still issues even Thomas struggled to get his head around, so he did what he always did and waited for Frank to explain. Or perhaps he was waiting to realise it was he who was unsure of how his husband's thoughts and plans would pan out.

"I'm trying to imagine life without the farm. It's surprisingly hard, despite the fact that we've only had it for a few years."

"It's a bit like having kids, I guess. They become a habit awfully fast."

"Mm. But still, even when I'm used to this, I'm not sure I really want it. It's nice to have this place, but it's kind of a restraint as well. It binds a lot of money and time. Like, will we want to spend our summers here forever?"

"Do you miss going elsewhere?" Thomas asked.

"No, not really. It's just...the possibilities, you know? If we don't have to go here, limiting ourselves with the precious little holiday time we have."

Thomas nodded. "But we don't *have* to come here, you know. We don't *have* to do anything," he added, knowing their budget would never stretch to the bloody Maldives or whatever Frank had in mind. "We could spend some of our holidays elsewhere."

"I know. Kind of. But still."

Thomas stroked a finger down Frank's neck. The skin was so familiar and smooth, and he gently massaged the muscles along the stiff tendons. "Maybe we should just clean out the barn anyway," he said. "It could be useful whether you build that film studio you're dreaming of or we sell up. Whatever you decide."

Frank nodded and rolled towards him, drowning him in desperate kisses while grinding against his hips.

"Are you trying to twist my arm here?" Thomas laughed into his mouth.

"Whatever do you mean?" Frank's voice was a mumble between wet, open-mouthed kisses that soaked Thomas's skin, his throat, his neck. His cheeks.

"You know I'll say yes to anything, do anything, say anything you want once you have me where you will in a minute or two."

"You mean when I have you all desperate and needy and begging for my cock?"

"Fuck off. I am totally in control here."

"I promise you, you will not be in control for much longer." Frank paused just long enough to press his nose against Thomas's, his breath deep and strong as he stared Thomas down, until Thomas was drowning in those eyes and barely registering the words Frank was whispering.

"I'm going to put my mouth where you want it. Trust me, you will lose control."

"Then make me," Thomas whispered back.

It was a strange feeling, being back to this. The Frank he adored, the one who'd always taken control. Once again, Thomas lay there while Frank arranged his limbs like an actor in one of his commercials, putting everything exactly where he wanted it. Thomas's skin prickled with every little touch, every naughty lick from his husband's wicked tongue, every little look and meaningful smile. He'd make him lose control all right, and there was no point arguing because Thomas's hips were already arching off the bed.

"The kids didn't go off until three. They'll be sleeping in, so don't worry. We could probably shout our heads off and they wouldn't even stir."

If Frank hadn't said it, Thomas would have because they knew each other, what would be going through the other's head, what would be done. The inevitable outcome.

"You ready?"

Thomas nodded. He didn't quite know for what, but he was. He'd take anything. Everything.

He got a warm wet tongue followed by a finger and couldn't help the groan that escaped his mouth and made his nipples stand to attention. Frank twisted his hand just far enough to elicit a gasp.

"You're going to kill me," Thomas said.

"Yup. Now be a good boy and do as you're told."

That made him laugh because he always did. Lifting his hips up to accommodate the firm pillow Frank pushed under his arse, he let his legs fall back as Frank really got to work. Fingers and mouth and then the unmistakeable snap of a lid before more lube than was necessary drizzled down his skin. He didn't care. He begged, whined, moaned, pleaded for more. More heat. More touch. More of those kisses that tasted of warmth and skin and him. And then Frank was there, inside him, where he'd always belonged from that very first kiss to now. Years and years of knowing that this would be it. It didn't matter that there'd never been anyone else, that he'd never had anything like this with another human on this planet.

Once Frank grabbed his wrists and held him down, fused their mouths together and jacked his cock into him with such vigour that the bed creaked and scraped against the floorboards threatening to demolish the entire house, the sounds coming out of his mouth didn't matter. The way his hands clawed, the ache in his hips, the lack of blood in his tingling legs—they were where they were always supposed to be, and as Thomas's world blackened out into nothing, Frank did what he always did. Whispered words in his ears that he would always comprehend. Life would be nothing without him, and as long as Thomas was there, things would always be good. Life would always be good.

\*\*\*

"You OK? You look kind of dead."

"No, I am OK," Thomas replied with a contented sigh.

He was barely alive after that little session Frank had pulled out of the hat. Even now, after a shower and two cups of coffee, he still felt wrecked. Long gone were the days when he could have sex for hours and still feel vibrant and alive afterwards. His legs ached, his head was kind of cloudy, and his hands shook as he drained his cup.

"I think I need to switch to decaf. I mean, two cups and I have the shakes."

"You just need to walk it off, babe." Frank barely looked up from his book, yet he was chuckling softly, that little thing he did when Thomas was being silly.

"I'm not joking. I've actually got the shakes."

"The power of my mouth. Amazing," Frank declared, with a dreamy expression on his face as Thomas threw the wrapper from the muffin at him, crumbs and all. And a stray chocolate chip.

"Just go, Thomas." Frank smiled at him. "Just go for a few hours. Smell the trees, feel the grass. You'll feel better afterwards." He reached out, massaging the top of Thomas's hand.

Thomas closed his eyes and leant into Frank's touch. "I don't really want to leave," he murmured. He wanted to curl up on the couch and not do anything useful or have to react to anything or decide or think or even have an opinion. Just listen to the silence and study the inside of his eyelids if anything at all.

As if Frank could read his mind, he moved around the back of the chair, and slid his hands effortlessly over Thomas's tense shoulders.

"Relax, darling."

"If I was any more relaxed, I would be horizontal," Thomas grumbled.

"Lies. All lies." Frank kissed the top of his head.

"What's on today then? Any more disastrous outings? Random shopping trips to obscure villages where everything is closed since being closed for the holidays seems to be the law of the land around here?"

"I could take everyone to the climbing park," Frank suggested. "The big one that opened last summer. It has Wi-Fi—the kids would love it—and it will force Gabriel and Bruno away from their ridiculous plan to leave. They're too wound up on organising everything. Or maybe we should go hiking instead." Frank laughed wickedly, and Thomas joined in.

"Don't be too hard on them. They're still city boys at heart."

"So are we."

"We might have grown up in the city, but you have two bad-ass outdoorsy parents, and while my own folks might have been crap at parenting, they did take me trekking when I was a kid. Andreas has taken these fancy survival classes. I heard Bruno brag about them the other day. They learned how to operate a gas cartridge stove by watching the instructors light one in the yard of the city school where the course was held. The kids weren't allowed to use open fire themselves since they could get burn wounds. He was completely flabbergasted when Maria and Fredrik gathered wood and lit a fire to grill the hotdogs. Fredrik said he almost freaked out when the smoke drifted towards them. He was worried they'd die from carbon monoxide poisoning or something."

Thomas could feel Frank's chest shaking against his back as he laughed behind him. "Did he have any idea about how to put up the tent?"

"Well, apparently..." Thomas winced. Frank was digging into his shoulders with more strength than was comfortable. "The kids managed to raise it, even without the pegs they left in the barn."

Frank chuckled. "Do you remember when we did that?" He changed the rhythm of his massage, rubbing small circles. "Your neck is really stiff."

"Yes, I clearly remember when *you* left them behind." Thomas shrugged against the twinge when Frank rubbed down his spine.

"*You* were in charge of packing the tent," Frank protested.

"But I told you to bring everything I had lined up on the kitchen table!"

"Was that the summer when the forecast said twenty degrees at night? Thomas, darling, how was I supposed to understand that you actually meant to bring the pile of rain gear and woollen undergarments from the table?" He was playing his spine like a piano—loudly.

"The tent pegs were there!" Thomas argued.

"Under the clothes."

"Yes, but I did tell you to bring everything—Ouch! Not too hard!"

"I need to soften your muscles. And we put up the tent anyway."

"Yeah, but be careful, please. You don't want me in bed with a pulled muscle either. And the tent fell down."

"Well, we still slept in the damn crooked tent. You're the grumpiest man ever when things aren't perfect," Frank joked. "And you bet I remember the tent falling down. It was kind of a mess." He chuckled again.

Thomas felt the butterflies in his belly when Frank spoke like that, like his love was contagious.

"You know I love you, don't you?" was all he could say.

"Of course I do," his husband replied.

\*\*\*

He listened to the cars leaving, the crunching of the wheels against the gravel gradually weakening through the forest until all was quiet, only the wind making its low sounds through the trees, the leaves rustling and the birds chirping.

The silence was stifling at first, surrounding him and choking him with the pressure against his eardrums and his skin. But in the end, it was a comfortable kind of pressure, safe, as if it was holding him down so he could relax. Not that he could truly relax. The rage in his chest was once again rising to the surface.

*Go for a walk*, Frank had said. *It will do you good.* Thomas didn't believe a word. It felt like a walk of doom as he set off along the lake, his phone in his hand like some kind of magic beacon, taunting him with its non-existent signal.

These past weeks had been much better than he could ever have anticipated. He'd been worried about coming here again; there was no use denying that. He'd feared the quarrelling, the fighting, grumpy kids, grumpy adults, dreaded strangers right on their doorstep, his head full of stories about nightmare holiday guests and nosy tourists. It would be another imperfect vacation that would taint the kids' childhood memories with pressured, tense interactions and late-night beers that would bring up those conversations none of them wanted to have. The rawness of them opening up, the pressure of sex and intimacy—Thomas had even feared the fear. He could admit to that uncomfortable truth.

It had been nothing like that. Stressful, sure, and humiliating and awkward, but mostly relaxing and...nice. They'd made friends, which was a surprise. Thomas couldn't remember the last time he'd made genuine friends. Of course, he knew a bunch of people around the schools and clubs and sports the kids did. He knew the names of most of the parents, had them all linked up on social media, chatted with them in the supermarket and over the garden fence. But they were hardly real friends; in fact, he couldn't remember making genuine friends since high school.

The lake was gorgeous in the summer sun, and he realised Frank had been right. The solitude was good for him. Calming, no pressure, just the gentle breeze in the shade from the trees.

He normally didn't like people. They drained all his energy. He preferred those in his small inner circle, people who were safe and not intimidating, but outsiders were rarely helpful, and while it was nice to not feel alone, he didn't expect anyone to be there *for him*. People had agendas, reasons for approaching you. There were always things they wanted or needed.

But Bruno—that guy might be a new friend, and the thought sat uncomfortably in Thomas's head. Bruno kind of understood him, and he felt like he understood Bruno. Yesterday, they'd lain in the grass for hours, watching the clouds and discussing the universe. Then they'd finally started clearing the barn. His mouth had felt dry like sandpaper after a while, not because of the dust and dirt, but because of the steady stream of words spilling out of him, questions and answers and laughter, reflected by Bruno, who'd worked tirelessly at his side, checking boxes, carrying furniture, piling junk onto the clearing between the barn and the lake. It had been really good to have somebody else to take over and make the bonfire at the beach, organise drinks and even carry the last of the junk down those gravelly slippery steps to the lake.

The silence was nevertheless welcome. Dark and soft and relaxing, it forced Thomas to listen to his heartbeat and concentrate on slowing his breathing; he resisted the urge to check his pulse on his watch. He stepped down onto a sandy patch of shore and sat on a fallen branch in the shade and stayed there a while, with his legs flat against the ground, birds chirping in the trees, cool seagrass tickling between his fingers, the greenery pushing against his back. The force of his body was equal to the counter-force from the earth, the thought of the opposite making him dizzy. Perhaps he would fall through the sphere, not even being forced up from the core as he would be if he dug through with the current gravity. The thoughts didn't even make sense in his head.

All he could do was sit there, listening and feeling and being in the moment, as a therapist might say. Breathing. Listening. Sensing. Feeling himself, the earth, the shade, the air, his body. Trying not to fall asleep or care about it at all.

His phone, still in his hand, suddenly sprang to life. It was a weak signal, but still, 4G, and the messages pouring in made his temper once again flare. He stabbed at the screen and held the phone up to his ear, his heart beating far too fast when the call connected.

\*\*\*

Thomas woke up a couple of hours later, dazed and confused, sweating from basking in the warm sun. He'd fallen asleep on the ground, his head leaning against the tree branch. The earth had spun another forty or fifty or sixty degrees, and the shadows had moved on to another spot, leaving his own place bright and hot under the blue sky. He sat up, scrunching his face against his sweaty palms. Everything was once again silent and calm, and for a moment he wondered where everyone was and where the hell he was. He slowly remembered, smiling to himself as he realised he would be alone for another couple of hours. Time to get his head on straight. He glanced down at his phone, looking through his work emails in disgust. Yes, it was all there in black and white. Numbers and contracts and dates and forms with deadlines and tick boxes of acceptance.

With some effort, he got up, stretching his stiff muscles and shaking his joints before starting the walk back. He didn't even have a car to escape this place. It didn't matter. He smiled, mentally crossing off the items of his imaginary list he couldn't do. Oh, well. He wasn't going to read any more emails or let the wankers at work destroy his future. He'd better get back and get something to drink as well as some lunch, unless the others had emptied the fridge before they left.

They hadn't, and Thomas grabbed a makeshift picnic on a plate, then sat in a stray plastic chair someone had left under the oak at the edge of the garden. The lake in the distance glittered in the mild breeze, tiny waves flittering on the surface of the water. It looked...light. Optimistic. Happy. Memories suddenly popped up in his head. Swimming with the kids. Walking on the beach. Working in the garden. Cooking.

Frank had been cooking every day recently, making his usual specialities for breakfast, lunch, dinner and snacks. They'd all stepped in to help, but Frank had been back to mixing, beating, whipping, flipping, doing all those things Thomas always loved watching him do, bringing back memories from when he had time to watch him, time to sit and laugh and do nothing while Frank worked. They'd had time lately. The realisation hit him like a hammer to the chest.

And the kids had seemed happy, too. Carefree, running, doing their things, not being angry or complaining about being bored. It wasn't only because of the other family being here either. Even Andreas had hung out with his dads doing whatever without Maria and Fredrik complaining.

It was like they'd finally grown into this place, found their space, like it was now shaping around them.

He banged his head back in frustration as the sudden influx of guilt took hold. Blowing air between his lips, he felt the wetness against his cheeks. He'd got this all wrong again because he'd gone into this with his eyes closed instead of seeing what he could so clearly see now.

He was exhausted. The academic life had been good; he loved research and science, but politics, and the pressure from others was sometimes unbearable. The head of department's constant demands for him to accept projects that were way over his budget, invitations to take up guest posts, and the constant cuts in funding were not for scientific reasons. Everything was part of a greater agenda there, and it was one he could never quite grasp.

Maybe he should just resign, jump off the cliff, metaphorically speaking. Ditch his career, stop publishing, no longer aim to be invited to the most prestigious conferences, no more contributing to international panels, clamouring to be one of a select handful of specially invited speakers. No more stressful travel that added to his worries, finding money for air fares even when they were short.

Step back. Chill out. Stress down. Get another job, one outside of academia, finally put his foot down, casually walk away saying that twenty-five years was enough. He could become a high school teacher, like Gabriel. He remembered his own teachers, how they shaped him—maybe he could ask around? Then he laughed out loud into the silence because he knew that teachers were the first profession to burn out, and he was right there on the edge of a massive burnout himself. The solution was not to try to cope with nerdy students who thought they were smarter than everyone else just because they got an A in physics. He knew shit about kids—he could barely parent his own. Being a gifted nerd like himself didn't make him some kind of expert on anything.

It would be good for Frank, too, and the kids. They could downsize, share the responsibility more evenly not only during the week, living a life that wasn't so busy, but all the time. Cooking meals, going out, movies and drinks. But there was no use in daydreaming about it all, even though the thought of doing fun things with Frank and the kids was tempting.

Reality sucked, and the thought of financial ruin, defaulting on what was left of their mortgage, the kids losing out...he suddenly yelled out into the still air, expelling his frustration. He screamed, wailed, waved his arms and stamped his feet on the deserted lawn. Birds nearby took flight, startled by his childish antics.

He needed to work. Frank needed to work. They needed to pay the bills and this? This goddamn place here? It was messing with his head. So, he shouted and cursed until his voice was hoarse and his legs folded underneath him. The tears ran down his cheeks as his hands shook in the warm caress from the sun. If he was losing his mind, he would lose it properly. He didn't know if he even cared anymore.

An hour later, he stood on the patio with the waffle maker plugged into an extension, and he was making a goddamn mess with batter dripping everywhere, but he couldn't have cared less. He could hear the cars approaching in the distance, and he smiled realising the smell was drifting towards the driveway. He was right, and before long the twins were running towards him, their faces a picture of anticipation, their mouths churning out stories in a language he would never master. He handed them waffles with jam and just shrugged when Frank asked if they shouldn't have dinner first, all while stuffing warm waffles with butter and cheese into his mouth.

"Waffles *is* dinner, dumb-ass," he half-whispered with a smile.

*\*\*\**

They all ate together, which had kind of become the norm, the double household. Cooking for nine wasn't that much more work than for four or five once you got the hang of the portion sizes, which were off anyway when both families were feeding teenagers. So, they usually tripled a normal family portion, and the amount of leftovers was usually nothing. Again, with teenagers.

Thomas shivered as Frank's leg slid along his during dinner, slowly up and down, keeping a steady pace. He waited for his hand and instead got Frank's cheeky smile and a gentle game of footsy. The anticipation was a feeling he hadn't experienced in a long time, the exhausted part of him usually won, over and over again. He sighed, looking at his husband. It was like he'd forgotten how gorgeous Frank was. How much he fancied him. Twenty years together and the butterflies were back, making Thomas giggle, excited for what lay ahead.

By the time it was almost nine in the evening, he was exhausted in a good way, his mind dulled by a few bottles of good beer and the kids' stories of climbing and the 'worst bruise of the day' competition.

Later still, his kisses consoled Frank and his bruised hip, where the skin had turned a deep shade of purple around the angry red scratches further down his leg.

"They made me do the zipline twice, and I crash-landed both times. I mean, the zipline had this curve at the end, where you swing sideways and you have to hit the ground running, otherwise you just kind of hip-flop onto your side. Bloody difficult to get right."

Frank was now stark naked on his side in bed, his hair wet from the shower and the towel flung carelessly on the floor.

"That was our last clean one," Thomas complained, picking up the sodden towel and trying to find a dry corner to wipe his face with.

"I'll do laundry tomorrow. I forgot yesterday, and today...well. Whatever."

"I'll go and hang this up then, shall I?" Thomas gruffed, stomping his way back into the bathroom, taking time—perhaps a little more than necessary—to spread it along the rail in the hope it would dry out by the morning. He laughed at himself, those stupid perfectionist traits always coming back to haunt him.

"Babe?" Frank called.

"What?" Thomas yawned as he shuffled back into the bedroom. Already wearing his boxers, he grabbed the shirt he usually slept in from the pile of clothes on the floor.

"You won't need that," Frank said, his voice low.

"Oh?" Thomas sat on the edge of the bed.

"I know you're probably not up for another fuck, but...I think I need to just...have another go at you." Frank crawled up behind his back. "I missed you today. I regretted offering to go on my own the minute I drove off. Everything's nicer when we're together." He sighed, his warm hand smoothing Thomas's back under his shirt and making him smile.

"I've been horny all day, just thinking about the things we did this morning."

"You managed to rest a little then?" Frank purred the words against Thomas's neck.

"I'm still tired." The reply was a well-oiled reflex. He wasn't, not really, but...

"Babe."

...he just knew Frank was smiling, confident this little display of affection would work its magic like always. Now the dirty talk was pouring freely out of his mouth, words that still made Thomas blush when he heard them, and his body squirmed under the assault of Frank's mouth. And his hands. He hadn't even noticed Frank fisting around his cock, his warm fingers coated with just enough lube to give that sweet slide, skin against skin, as Thomas's hole twitched with anticipation.

Yeah, hands were good. When Frank got all hot and horny and dirty-talked Thomas into letting him be all domineering and hard, he made Thomas hurt. Hurt so good, in the best way possible. He made Thomas squirm and beg and plead and, yeah. Thomas was a total slut when it came to this side of Frank, the one who suddenly had him face down on the bed, spreading his arse cheeks himself while his mouth ran off with pleas and demands to fuck him now, *please.*

*** 

Thomas fell asleep drooling into his pillow, his arse stinging with pleasure and sweat and that well-fucked feeling he would regret tomorrow. But for now? The light in the hallway was still on, and who knew if they'd locked the front door? None of that mattered. Frank had made good on his promises, and his arm was reassuringly heavy over Thomas's back.

And the rest of the world? They could truly go fuck themselves.

# Twenty four
## GABRIEL

Yesterday had been the hottest day yet, the sun burning bright in the sky, hour after hour of the children moaning inside the house then moaning even louder outside. The last couple of days had passed too fast, each blending effortlessly into the next. Lazy swimming in the lake, hosing the kids down on the lawn with ice-cold water that made them scream and laugh in the scorching sun. Then, of course, a film on the laptop and ice cream and finally hotdogs by the lake. Family dinners lounging on the veranda at Frank and Thomas's house and picnics in the garden. It had been pure bliss, a life so far from the usual mayhem because it had been too hot to do anything useful.

Today, though, the cool air was a blessing, and the children had once again disappeared with Thomas in search of the dreaded and hopefully fictional *bloodsucking wild boars*. Well, that, and the promise of seeing newborn kittens over by the farm, which would also give Thomas a chance to check out these mysterious neighbours. Watching his kids go off in Thomas's car, Gabriel realised he felt OK with that. It was like life had finally slowed down enough for him to catch up. The ground was more solid beneath his feet, and his mind was at peace. He even had a plan, admittedly a hastily scribbled-down plan, but he was impressed with himself for having one.

"I've made a plan," he told Frank, who appeared carrying another box of dusty books. They'd taken turns cleaning out the barn, sorting and stacking stuff. Even after getting rid of two entire bonfires' worth of rubbish down on the beach, they'd barely made a dent in the boxes piled at the back of the building.

"Plans are good," Frank said, dropping the box with a heavy thud. "As long as it's something small and achievable. Remember, we agreed not to overwhelm ourselves."

"It's achievable. I'm going to hand my notice in at the gym because it only brings negative energy, and it will give me the push I need to apply for teaching jobs. Even if it's just an assistant job or part time—a maternity-cover contract would be brilliant, just so I can get my head back in the game."

"Won't the time frame stress you out?" Frank's frown disappeared inside his shirt as he pulled it off and used it to wipe his forehead.

"It will, but in a good way. I won't have time to mope around feeling sorry for myself. I work better with a set time frame."

"Just as long as that's right for you."

"I think it is. Getting the gym job off my back will give me a break. I already feel happier knowing that soon I won't have to go back there, despite the workouts being good, and I'll miss free gym membership, but we have a good gym in the neighbourhood, which I can join once I'm back working. Not that I've seen a gym for weeks, and look at me. That's just from swimming and running around and...other stuff. But I'd be lying if I didn't look forward to getting back in there and doing some weights."

"Shame we don't have Wi-Fi. We could have gone over the ads, looked for openings."

"Nope. I'm still on holiday. No doing work stuff while we're here." Gabriel smiled and headed back into the barn.

There were hundreds of bags and boxes of folders and papers, stacks of heavily read romance books next to textbooks and encyclopaedias. This Auntie Bella had been a keen reader, that was for sure.

"I don't want to burn those," Frank said, sounding a little distraught. Gabriel felt the same. He loved books too, and the thought of burning this whole life of reading, the stories someone had loved too much to let go of, was devastating. But Frank was right.

"They are damp and there's mould all over them," Gabriel reasoned with a sigh.

"I know. The paperbacks are useless, and these big ones are all hopelessly out of date. We can't keep it all, and loading it all into the car would take hours of driving back and forth to the recycling centre, and the car would get filthy with all the dust."

"Just burn it, Frank. These are not your memories to preserve."

It sounded cold, but Gabriel knew they had to. His parents had kept everything, hoarding memories built into things that carried nothing but dust. He barely remembered half the things his mother had talked so fondly about, the precious items she stored on her shelves that meant nothing to him but carried her memories, things to treasure and share with her future grandchildren, she'd said, so they would always know what was important to her. Did she even remember who he was? Who he'd once been?

He had very little to share. Just himself, his love and his bond with the little family that kept him sane. He sometimes wondered what would have happened to him had he not met Bruno. The sheer thought filled him with a fear so strong he could barely breathe.

"You OK?" Frank asked, coming back for another box.

"Yeah. Just irrational fear. Parenting fear. Me not being enough fear. You know. Normal shit."

Frank nodded. They both knew all the normal shit. Normal shit that normal people shrugged off. Normal thoughts that became monsters in your head. Normal fears that grew into mountains. Normal. It was all normal.

He sat and mindlessly picked up a folder from the box nearest to him. The hardcover was splattered with dark growths of mould and a thick layer of dust that made him sneeze into the cool air.

"Frank? Did Bella write novels? '*Jag känner mig inte som mig själv,*'" he read out loud. "'*Jag förstår inte vem det är jag ska vara längre.*'" Gabriel didn't understand a single word, and his pronunciation was probably all wrong.

"I don't know." Frank planted himself on the ground next to him. "I think she wrote newspaper articles sometimes, the ones you send into the paper, you know like a reader's column?"

"This looks interesting despite the fact that I don't know what it says. It's like a novel, but there are no chapters." Gabriel flicked the pages back and forth. It was all handwritten in what must have been Bella's swirly script, but the sentences jumped back and forth, passages crossed out like she was arguing with herself.

"'Not being who I feel I should be,'" Frank read out loud. "'The expectations are unclear.'" He sighed, shaking his head. "It's in Swedish, but that's the basic translation."

"OK," Gabriel responded. "And this part?"

"There are mentions of an Erik. She adores him. Listen to this." Frank pointed at a passage and read out the words into the quiet space.

> Sometimes I wish I could be all alone in the garden, with the knowledge that nobody would disturb my peace. I would wander through the grass, my naked feet touching everything beneath me. The skin on my body free to the elements, my breasts no longer confined to the prisons that society pushes upon us.

"Go Bella!" Gabriel laughed. "So, she wanted to be naked and free. Good for her."

Frank flicked the pages forwards, looking for more, the tip of his tongue sticking out of his mouth as he scanned the pages.

> He was so gentle with me, his fingers caressing my skin like the softest feathers. Like he was afraid I would break under his touch. I told him I wouldn't break. I told him I was stronger than he thought I was, and that I was sure. And God help me, I was so sure. I still am. I am so pleased I carried this through because no woman should live a life afraid of the unknown. No woman should have to carry the guilt of knowing what her body can do, and that what is a beautiful and life-changing experience is pushed away like it's a sin. Because what Erik and I did was no sin. It was sweet and tender, and my arousal knew no limits once he removed his clothes. I knew I would find him attractive. I had seen his naked torso enough times working the land, his strong chest, the veins on his neck and the shape of his arms. I had known, oh, how I had known.

"How old do you think she was here? In her late teens? She sounds older."

"There's no date. Perhaps this is a diary? Maybe she wrote down the things she experienced. Is there more?"

Gabriel grabbed a few more folders out of the box, all the same type and filled with Bella's words. Frank took one and read again, his words piercing the silence.

> *He cried himself to sleep in my arms, his naked chest against mine. We had made love here before, but this time it was different. He loved me, I had no doubt about his feelings towards me, none whatsoever. His mouth bruised my skin, and the blanket beneath me felt like it was shredding my body into a million small shards of the person I used to be. His movements brutal, he tossed my legs over his shoulders and pushed inside of me. He ravaged my skin with his touch, like he was scared that he would never feel me again. I whispered words of comfort to him, trying to ground him in this place where we were just us, the two of us joined as one. Because, despite his despair and the dark place his head was in, I would always be there for him. I would hold him at night when his world was at its darkest. I would carry the weight of him when his body couldn't hold him up. I would love him through these times because without him, what would I do? You don't choose who your heart will love, and my heart is all for him. I will love this broken man until the day I die. I will carry him with me always because I am his and he is mine. I told him this as his body slumped over mine, as his lips took mine in the sweetest kiss. I love him, and that is all that matters. Then he cried, and oh, how he cried, this broken man of mine.*

"All I know is that she never married, but if this is her diary, then at least she loved someone."

"She was definitely in love with this Erik, whoever he was. He sounds like a horrible person, being all brutal with her."

"He might not have been. Maybe he was, you know, like me? She says his head was in a dark place. Maybe he thought he wasn't good enough for her—he could've been poor. She says he worked the farm. Perhaps he had someone else—Oh God, you know what we have to do, don't you?" Frank laughed nervously.

"Yes." Gabriel sighed. "We're going to have to read this now, find out what happened to this Erik dude and if he broke Bella's heart."

"God help him." Frank smiled. "My mum always referred to her as eccentric, even though they'd never met. I was surprised Bella even knew I existed, and I still don't know why she gave me this place. It just doesn't make sense. There are other cousins and lots of closer relatives, yet she chose me. It's weird. A few of Mum's brothers grumbled that it wasn't being sold off and the profits divided, but Bella was adamant in her will that the entire farm would go to me."

"Then there was a reason, and we owe it to Bella to find out. She wrote this, and perhaps it's all just made-up stories that she wrote for entertainment, but if it's true? At least you'll know something about her background. Who she was. Why you're the one sitting here now, on this piece of grass, reading her words."

Gabriel would be lying if he said he didn't feel a little bit excited. Bella's life was a mystery waiting to be solved. But it was also another little tie to this place, a place owned by strangers he'd probably never see again. The chances that they would come back here again were slim because no doubt next year Bruno would have come up with another of his masterplans and they would be holidaying in Iceland visiting hot springs and climbing volcanoes or something equally ridiculous. Gabriel should step away and leave this to Frank to figure out. It wasn't his Auntie Bella, and yet...

"You said she was never married, and it doesn't seem like she lived with a man here." Gabriel looked around as if the farm could give any answers.

"Erik died in the eighties," Frank said. "I found his death certificate." He started digging through one of the already sorted boxes in the *let's keep this crap* area. "And a note from Bella—just a few lines. I wonder what order these papers are in, if any. Damn, she didn't date them."

Gabriel patted Frank's shoulder. "OK, let's go through these and get them in order, and then we'll make a pot of coffee and see if we can make sense of this story. This is the first one, where she wonders who she is supposed to be, when the expectations are so unclear. I think. Or maybe it's the last? It was on the top, anyway."

"She talks about someone called Henrik here. Henrik Arvidsson..." Frank frowned, instantly absorbed.

"I'll go get the coffee." Gabriel laughed. "Because I can see you won't be moving from here for a while."

"Can you bring some deckchairs?" Frank called after him, and Gabriel just smiled.

They'd decided to stay a few more days, and now Gabriel never wanted this holiday to end. They could even stay a bit longer. They'd talked about it, and Thomas had apparently begged. Not that Gabriel could even picture Thomas begging for anything, but Bruno had sworn he had. Andreas was moping about saying he didn't want to leave yet, and the twins were truly having a ball. Alas, Bruno needed to get back to work, otherwise Gabriel would've been asking around about getting the kids into school here so he could keep hiding away in his own little piece of paradise forever. But life didn't work like that.

So, he loaded the coffeemaker and pulled off his shirt as the sun peeked out between the clouds. With the deckchairs lined up in front of the mountain of boxes piled on the grass, Frank clumsily climbed into one, letting the folder in his hands settle on his lap, his forehead scrunching up as he flicked through the pages.

"The bastard," he muttered. "The scheming fucking bastard."

# Twenty five
# FRANK

FRANK AND GABRIEL spent the entire afternoon reading through Bella's old diaries. What had started off as a chore had become an intimate journey through someone's past, but it felt *too* intimate, reading somebody else's personal words like that. Still, as Gabriel had said, Bella had plenty of time to get rid of the diaries if she didn't want anyone to find them in the barn. They hadn't been locked away or even hidden, unless you counted them being buried under boxes and boxes of books. It was also clear that Bella had been of sound mind and healthy until her heart had suddenly stopped. More importantly, she had willingly left this farm to Frank, with everything she knew it contained.

It had taken a while to get the books into some kind of order. Some had dates; some were clearly diaries; others had no indications of when they were written. Frank wasn't sure if they were all biographic, but piece by piece, they'd organised them all from the first, written in 1953 when Bella was ten years old, to the last in 1989.

"Wow, this is amazing," Gabriel said looking at their handiwork—the dusty pile of folders spread out on the grass in front of them. "If we've got this right, the diaries are complete. There are no gaps in the dates." That had been his job: since he didn't understand the words, he'd concentrated on the dates. "You can't burn these, Frank. At least donate them to a local archive. I bet they would be thrilled. It's like a memory capsule covering over thirty-five years. Almost an entire life."

Frank nodded, distracted. He'd been reading pages here and there, enthralled by the stories unfolding, enough that he'd hardly helped the sorting process. "Yeah, I won't burn these. Not unless we come across anything that really shouldn't be shared. But I agree. I doubt she'd have left them here if she didn't intend for me to have them. Or read them."

"It's like...her life story. Warts, sex and all," Gabriel said with a smile, yet Frank's mind was spinning.

An upper-class girl growing up in the Swedish countryside post-World War Two, a traditional upbringing on the family farm with farmhands and a couple of maids. She'd gone to school, finished high school in a nearby town, then taken correspondence classes in bookkeeping and secretary work. She'd wanted to leave, dreamed about Stockholm, but her family had kept her here. Her mother was anxious and, in Bella's words, *of delicate health, not wanting her only daughter out of her sight.*

Then there was Erik. Son of one of the farmhands, he had worked at another farm, the distant boy who got closer and closer, whom her parents wanted her to stay away from but who wanted to be a better man for her.

> *I want it so much, a future with him, a life with him. It doesn't matter that he has no money, that he can't give me the life my mother dreams of for me. All that would matter is to have him. But he has decided again and again that it can't be us, that he will be too much, that I deserve more. Why can't he let me decide for myself? Why do all men imagine women as fragile, as a thin straw that will break from a little resistance? I love him, and he loves me. Why can't he also give me the life I want?*

Her writing was angry, rushed and almost unreadable at the end of the paragraph. Those were the words of a frustrated teenager, written in 1962, when Bella was nineteen.

> *He left me. He just left. The past weeks have been horrible. Everyone has been so busy with the harvest; nobody seems to care for him. I talked briefly to his father. He didn't want to tell me anything and was furious when I asked if they had reported him missing to the police. Nobody wants the insane one, he said.*

*I tried to ask the police officer about him when I was in town the other day, but he just laughed at me and said they wouldn't take a report from a woman who wasn't even married to him. And if his father didn't want to report him missing, it was probably for the best. I have heard rumours about him being sent to Marieberg, to the ward for the utterly insane. But nobody will tell me anything. Everyone just stops talking when I get close.*

It wasn't until a week later she'd written again.

*I finally talked to Henrik. He said Erik has left. He has gone to Göteborg and has apparently taken up employment as a seaman.*

"So Henrik knew both Bella and Erik? Who is he, actually?" Gabriel asked. Frank hadn't even noticed that he'd been reading out loud, clumsily translating the words as he went along.

"She describes him as a friend to both herself and Erik. They seemed to hang out a lot as teenagers. He was into photography—she wrote about photo sessions they had."

"Maybe his photos are gathered in a box somewhere?" Gabriel suggested, looking over at the opened boxes they had discarded in front of the barn doors.

"I doubt it," Frank muttered, angry on Bella's behalf. "He was *not* a good man. I would have burned every memory of him if I was her. She had no feelings for him, and it doesn't look like he had any for her either, but her parents liked him—I bet he was from a good family." Frank tapped the page. "Here she calls him 'breeding stock'. Bella had a dark sense of humour at times."

*I finally got a letter from him. He thanked me for everything and said he loved me but that he can't let me live with the burden he is, so he is leaving so I can be free and so he can be free. But I don't want to be free, nor am I free without him! Now it's like I am tied to someone I can never have, so now I can never be free.*

For weeks after, she was sad and frustrated, and her moods seemed to vary a bit. While it was far from the unhealthy swings Frank experienced himself, he empathised.

> *I only sleep, work and eat. Every day is the same. What's the use in this?*

"She's skipped a few months here, where she must have been too sad to write. Then she's back and seems stronger. Listen to this." He shuffled in his seat, getting comfortable.

> *Henrik asked me to come to the autumn party tomorrow. I don't know, I don't really want to. But Mother is putting pressure on me. She doesn't want me moping around here. Maybe it'll get her off my back for a while if I just go. And she would be delighted if I went with Henrik. She clearly approves of him.*

"Blimey." Gabriel sighed. "I hope she didn't have sex with him."
"She did." Frank laughed. "See?" He pointed at a passage and kept on reading.

> *I had intercourse with Henrik yesterday. I don't know why I did it. I was drunk, but not that drunk, and he didn't force me, but it was far from good. Nothing like making love with Erik. It hurt, he was so fast. Not the slow movements of Erik, not the touches I still feel tingling on my skin when I think of it. I bathed in vinegar when I woke up. It hurts, but I've heard it's effective.*

"Then a few days after that, she wrote this." Gabriel was now hanging over Frank's shoulder, his hands gripping the edges of the seat.

> *Henrik came here late yesterday. He had clearly been at the drink. He told me he had received several letters from Erik, and that Erik doesn't love me anymore. I am full of regret over sleeping with him.*

Frank was struggling to sit still, despite Gabriel's hand resting on his arm, trying to calm him.

"Then this shit happens. It makes me boil just reading it, Gabriel. Just listen to this!"

> *I think I may be expecting. I haven't had that time of month for a while now. I am so tired and sick all the time. Can hardly smell anything without retching. Damned be everything.*

"Oh, shit," Gabriel said. "I can relate! So she has a kid then?" He paused, then added, "No, then you wouldn't have inherited the farm, would you? This makes no sense."

Frank read on for a few minutes, letting the words sink in before he spoke. "No, she didn't have a kid. She had an abortion. Sounds like it was pretty rough too."

> *I went to see the doctor today. He confirmed the pregnancy. His hands were so cold, inside me and outside me. I asked if he could terminate it, but he couldn't. He said I had to apply for it, to give a good reason, and that I should hurry up before I was too far along. But he doubts I will get an abortion because I don't fulfil the criteria. I am healthy, my parents have money, I could marry Henrik etc. etc. The doctor also knows someone, but that's another doctor in Stockholm, and I don't know how to find the money to get there. The train fare already ate most of my funds, and I don't know what excuses to use. I told my parents I had to see a doctor in Örebro for my weakening eyesight. If I say that again they may drive me. Maybe there is someone around here, but I don't know. If I just dared to confess to Kajsa or Maja...*

"Then there's this, two weeks later."

> *I went to the doctor in Stockholm today. Henrik drove me. He said almost nothing in the car, just smoked until I had to ask him to stop because I felt so weak and unwell.*

"She described it vividly, all the smells and the pain. I really don't want to read it..." Frank looked up at Gabriel, who shook his head.

"No, just skip it. Bruno studied it for one of his projects. He said there are so many sad stories about women undergoing unwanted pregnancies or trying to avoid them, and he's researched old journals to get an understanding of their practices and procedures. Many were completely unnecessary."

Frank turned the pages back again. "Here's something from the day before she went for the abortion. *'Today I talked to Henrik. I wanted to tell him about his child, hoping that he might help me find a solution.'* She's written a lot about her different options. She said she could cope with being a solo mum, but she needed money. There are a few pages discussing her future depending on what she chose—living in some mothers' home until birth, then adopting it or finding foster parents, or simply give birth and face the consequences. But listen to what she writes about Henrik. He really is a bastard!"

*He first asked if anybody else could be the father, but I denied that crazy allegation. Then he shook his head and said it was naïve of me to think he wanted anything to do with the baby. He was planning to go to college next year, he wants to be an engineer so he can get away from this godforsaken place. Then his eyes glistened. "Unless you love me and will marry me," he said. I cried and said he knows it's not him I love, that I still love Erik. "You have to write Erik a letter, too, saying you don't love him." He knows Erik's address! He just laughed when I begged him for it.*

Gabriel's sighs echoed in the silence.

*I'm still not sure, but Henrik is putting pressure on me. According to him, the only option is getting rid of it. Everything else will bring nothing but trouble. He's such a coward. He said he could give me money for the abortion and drive me to Stockholm. I know it's just to make sure I actually go through with it and spend the money for the abortion, but I don't care.*

*I hate Henrik so much now. I don't want his money either, but I don't have any other options.*

"The bastard practically forced her to get the abortion!" Gabriel shouted. "What a fucker!"

Frank nodded. "He didn't even accompany her. He just drove her to the residential area where the doctor practised from his own flat and set her down there, then picked her up again two hours later. She was in so much pain that she was about to collapse while she waited for him, and she was bleeding for a week afterwards, much heavier than her periods. On one of the days, she writes that she felt so weak and bled so much that she was afraid of dying."

"She didn't tell anyone?"

"Apparently not. Only herself, Henrik and the doctors are mentioned in the diary. She doesn't seem very close to her parents, and there are no siblings. A few female friends, but she doesn't confide in anyone."

"It must have been horrible. I can't imagine how afraid and lonely she must have been," Gabriel said, absently rubbing his belly as if he physically could relate to what Frank was reading. "I wouldn't have managed without Bruno. Not just for the practical stuff but all the emotions. And worries and questions, especially before Andreas was born."

"You married the right expert, then," Frank said. "But I bet he was worried too?"

Gabriel smiled a little. "He freaked out at first, then he was a wreck all through the pregnancy. I think sometimes I was more relaxed about it than he was. He was always thinking worst case, reading up on every possible complication, asking his colleagues at the hospital where he worked and people he barely knew for advice."

"Was the pregnancy not planned?" Frank wondered if he was being too intrusive. He remembered Thomas's worries, despite him not being a medical doctor or anything like that, just a worried scientific brain. "You said he freaked out. I assumed you had fertility treatment or something like that—if you don't mind me being blunt and asking. I know it's personal."

"Fuck no, it was a total fluke. I'd been on T for a while, and I kind of knew there was a tiny chance, but I had totally pushed that to the back of my mind. I was also a stupid kid back then, irresponsible and wild. I never did it properly, didn't always check my levels and forgot shit all the time. It didn't help that the two of us smoked more weed than was sensible. Anyway, we were always careful with condoms, and we talked about me having a hysterectomy because I had these annoying stray bleeds. Then I had an implant and I got really ill, so I had to have it taken out. A couple of months later, I was throwing up and feeling like death. I couldn't get up, and then I fainted in the shower and cracked my head open, and Bruno had me blue-lighted to hospital thinking I was dying. Little did we know. Then the doctor asked if I was pregnant, and I shouted, '*what the fuck?*' in his face. Bruno does a great impression of me getting told I had gotten myself impregnated by my boyfriend. Not one of those moments I thought I would ever have."

"And Bruno?"

"He didn't say a word for about an hour. I think I cried for most of that hour. It was hard to take in, and then...it was fine, you know? We freaked out together, and Bruno bought this stupid green dinosaur toy on the way home. We still have it, and he can't explain why he bought it. It was just the shock, kind of like, 'Hey! We're having a kid! We need toys!'"

"I would have freaked out too. Bruno must have been hysterical. I know I was when we were told we were having twins. I think I screamed, then drank about a litre of water and then felt like throwing up. I drank the water because my brain told me I had to stay hydrated to care for two babies. It's crazy the things you do when you're in shock."

"Yes! When we were expecting the twins, I had to constantly tell Bruno to chill. They were planned, by the way. A moment of total insanity if you ask me. I've no clue what we were thinking. If I'd known then what I know now... Yeah, I shouldn't even go there because the girls won't ever be something we regret. Twin pregnancies are high risk, and he was freaking me out with all his worries while I was trying to pretend it wasn't happening. I think I needed some more distance from it to keep afloat. I was in denial of Andreas being real until he actually came out, same with the girls. Then I had a planned C-section and suddenly two babies, and yeah. That's when I freaked."

"Tell me about it!" Frank laughed. "I sometimes look at Fredrik and Maria, and my mind kind of short circuits, thinking, *OMG, I have kids!*"

Gabriel laughed. "And you wonder why I'm fucked in the head, mate. All self-inflicted. But then, without all this madness, our lives would be incredibly dull. Don't you agree?"

"Madness and madness," Frank muttered. "Not sure I'd call it that."

"It's just life. Uncontrollably so."

"That I can agree with."

"What more do the diaries say?" Gabriel asked, clearly wanting to change the subject.

"It looks like she continued to write updates regularly." Frank swiped through a couple more of the books. "Some long and some short entries."

"Do you know how she got the farm?"

"I'm guessing, from her parents?" Frank shrugged.

"No other relatives?"

"Not as far as I know."

"So, she got it all then. Do you know when?"

"I'm not sure, but she owned it in 1970, as she writes a lot about the struggles of running the farm."

"She was young. Like...twenty-seven?"

"Maybe her parents were older when they had her?"

"It doesn't look like that." Gabriel pointed to the wooden-framed picture he'd found in the one of the boxes, which was on the table in front of them. There was a girl, about twelve or thirteen years old, with Bella's clear face, and a man and a woman, both perhaps in their mid-thirties, standing next to her. Bella had a huge white bow on top of her head. "It says 'mor, far och jag' on the backside—'mum, dad and I', I'm guessing?—and a year. 1955."

"Yes, she was twelve then, and they look like in their forties, maximum. No wrinkles and stuff."

Frank settled in with the diaries again, humming as he flicked through the pages, trying to find the right dates. The notes here were brief, just a couple of lines, descriptions of what Bella had done, large expenses, lists of what she had harvested. The farm life sounded tough. Long days harvesting in the rain with wet soil and mud, nobody to share it with. She seemed lonely, too, and her diary became disorganised, with dates in the wrong order, almost like she'd forgotten to write things down at the time and added them in later.

And suddenly there it was: 2 September 1969. The writing was more unruly than usual, with large, shaky letters. After weeks of page-long details about life and thoughts during summer, mostly Bella being frustrated about people gossiping in the village, she'd hoped to raise funds so she could afford a room somewhere instead of living with her parents, just a couple of lines.

"They died in a car crash," Frank said quietly. "They crashed into a tree outside the village at night. Someone found them the next day."

"Shit."

"Bella had to take over handling everything straight away, in the middle of the harvest season with hired help. No time for grief. They had a lot of livestock—cows and pigs—as well as fields full of ripe wheat. She pretty much says everyone and their cousin attended the funeral, but nobody offered to come stay with her and left her on her own. People all wanted in on the gossip and drama, yet suddenly nobody had time to help her run the farm."

He continued to read. "And fuck, that bastard had the nerve to come back again and ask for her hand!"

"What?!"

"Yep, Henrik asked her to marry him." He read on. "He promised her a lot of help from himself and his family...they were wealthy, but they wanted the land."

"I take it she declined his offer of marriage?"

"So it would seem. '*I will do this on my own, so help me God.*'"

"Shit, he really was a bastard!" Gabriel sighed. "I wonder where he is now. How old is he again? Around Bella's age?"

"I guess so. Born around 1940, by the looks of it. He seemed to be more Erik's friend than Bella's."

"So he might be dead by now. Did she get in touch with Erik again?"

"I'm not sure." Frank grabbed another diary from the pile, swiping his thumb along the edge of the pages and selecting one at random. He glanced down at the text. "Not yet," he muttered, then grabbed another one. "Not yet either."

"Are you fed up already?" Gabriel smiled.

"No. Just thinking."

"OK," Gabriel said sceptically.

"You know, this is like a movie. Everything happens for no apparent reason, and then everything changes. Thomas used to talk about parallel universes—what would happen if we'd chosen differently—and I can't stop thinking about what destiny they would have had if Erik hadn't insisted on protecting Bella from himself, or if he hadn't become sick, or if he'd kept in touch with Bella afterwards. What if her parents died because they went looking for her when she went to drown her sorrows?"

"They died on their way home from a church meeting," Gabriel pointed out.

"Yes, whatever. It doesn't really matter. What matters is the choices we make affect us!" Frank's face felt warm, and he couldn't sit still. He let out a couple of deep breaths, trying to calm down. "Sorry, I get excited easily," he excused, feeling dumb for getting so wired.

"No shit. I know you well enough by now to know that kind of thing is just Frank being Frank. Chill."

"I am chill!" Frank protested.

"You're hyped up like a sugar-fuelled kid. But you know, I had moments, just after I met Bruno..." Gabriel moved in the chair, waving his arms about too. "Moments, where I could have easily made the wrong choice. I was going to walk away from him because I didn't think he would understand. I didn't tell him at first, about who I was, and then I thought he hadn't understood because being me was a lot to take in, and it was all such a massive hurdle, you know. It didn't go well, and it took a long time for me to trust that he didn't care about anything apart from that he wanted to be with me, however and whatever that would look like.

"Once he came around, he was just so open and understanding, and I...I couldn't wrap my head around it all. When I was younger, everything was so easy, and then things became hard to explain, but I was me, you know? I would never be able to be all those things Bruno was dreaming about. I would never be his knight in shining armour. I would never be what I thought he needed, and it was stupid, because I kind of know now that I was exactly what he needed. Just like he's everything I ever dreamed of, this funny, crazy kid who made me smile and turned my world fucking upside down every time. And I bet it was the same for Bella. She would have chosen Erik, every time. He made her smile, and he made her happy, with all his flaws and his illness, and he made the wrong fucking choice.

Damn him. If he'd just hung on, if he had known Bella was alone on the farm, he could have come to her. She would have...she would have been fucking happy!"

"We should have a break," Frank advised with a grimace. "You're getting far too invested in this."

"It just makes me so angry! They would have found their happiness."

"Perhaps not. We never know what life has in store for us. Maybe Erik didn't love her. Maybe she was too clingy, too attached, and he needed his freedom. Maybe Henrik loved her and she hurt him by not loving him back. He could have been a good person with good intentions, and getting rejected made him cold. We'll never know. But regret... You know, we all regret things we've done. It's just life."

"I suppose so. Things I regret right now?" Gabriel chuckled. "The fact that I promised my daughters fish finger sandwiches for lunch, and I'm still sitting here and the damn fish fingers are still in the freezer."

"Dude. Get a grip. That's like a cardinal sin. Go make the bloody sandwiches." Frank's smile must've been catching, as Gabriel threw his head back in laughter.

"Keep reading," he insisted, wagging his finger in Frank's face, "and I will bring you an epic Gabriel Fischer Fish Finger Sandwich. They're the best. Fact."

"You do that." Frank grinned, turning another page in the diary. "And send my husband up here for a kiss if you see him?"

"Will do." Gabriel laughed as he walked off towards the house.

"Gabe?"

"Yeah?"

"Thanks, man."

"No worries."

"Joint dinner tonight?"

"Always."

# Twenty Six
## BRUNO

IT WAS FUNNY how this strange little house had become home. Bruno put his feet up on the rustic coffee table and pulled Lottie to his chest so he could sniff her hair, trying to get as many kisses as possible on her face in the process while she squirmed and squealed and punched her tiny fists into his stomach. So, yeah. He was overbearing on the cuddles. He never thought he would have been, but he loved it. Hugs. Kisses. Her sweet little breaths against his neck.

"Papi, read it again! Again!"

He'd read it to her a million times already, but this was the best of the three books they'd brought with them, and he'd read the damn thing a million times more as long as she was happy and laughing the way she was now as he carefully opened up the first page.

"Petronella Apfelhaus und Gurkenmus," he started, barely looking at the text.

"It's Petronella Apfelmus!" Lottie giggled. "You're reading it all wrong."

"Bloody Petronella Apfel whatever." Andreas huffed as he threw himself down in the armchair next to them.

"It's actually quite good," Bruno said and smiled at his son. "Perhaps you'd like to read it to her?"

"Never." Andreas cackled and patted Bruno on the arm. "You read it very well, and she likes you reading to her." He was being sarcastic, but Bruno still laughed.

"Have you seen Lilly?" he asked.

"She's with Frank cooking something up in the other house." Andreas sank further into the armchair, grabbing a stray cushion and hugging it. "They were being very secretive, and Vati's there still trying to organise those dusty old folders. He doesn't even speak Scandi, so I'm not sure what he's doing, but he keeps muttering out days and months in German. He was all stressed out, so I left him to it."

"At least it's fun stress. He's quite enjoying working on it. Frank was all excited last night, trying to tell us the stories. Anyway. You good, kiddo?"

"Papi." Andreas sighed. Sometimes he was full of words, needing Bruno's help and advice. Other times, like now, Bruno might as well have talked to a brick wall.

"I'm not asking you to talk about it. I just want to know you're OK."

"I'm OK." He sighed. "Dickhead won't even look me in the eye, and he certainly won't talk to me." Andreas hid his face in the cushion.

"Then you need to perhaps wait him out," Bruno suggested, which was totally the wrong way to go about it, but the right way was eluding him right now.

"Papi, read!!" Lottie shrieked.

"Why don't you go and find him and ask if he'll go for a walk with you. Totally safe. Down to the lake and back, and talk about normal things that won't make him uneasy. Then you can just throw in 'sorry if I upset you' and tell him you're an idiot and whatever."

"And whatever? Epic, Papi."

"I *am* epic. Admit it."

"*You* are an idiot. You say so yourself."

"Paaaapi, read the booooook!" Lottie whined in despair.

"See? Read the fucking book, Papi."

"Language, Andreas!"

His son haplessly slid out of the chair, lying flat on his back on the floor, still clutching the pillow. "I'm fucked. We might as well go home."

"I don't want to go home! Maria said she has a sofa bed in her house in Oslo, and Lilly and I can share it, so we're going home with Maria."

"You can't go home with Maria, Liebchen. You have to come back with Vati and me. Otherwise we'll miss you too much, and Katarzyna and Shajani and Kimmi and Otto and all your other schoolfriends will miss you too."

"I'm not going back to school."

"You can't just *not* go to school, Lottie."

"I can go to Maria's school. And anyway, Mrs Anita at the farm said I could have a kitten to take home."

"Good luck with that one, Papi." Andreas rolled over and got up. "We can bring all the kittens back to Berlin." He cackled evilly before kind of falling out the door, the way only Andreas could, with his trainers half on and half off, shoelaces trailing behind him. *He'll break his neck one day*, Bruno thought, watching Andreas through the window as he stumbled his way, shoulders hunched, through the long grass up towards the main house.

"Papi, we should bring three kittens home. One for me and one for Lilly and then one for Andreas too, because otherwise he will just cuddle our kittens. I don't want him to cuddle my kitten, and Lilly can't cuddle my kitten either."

"Sweetheart, we can't bring any cats home to Berlin. You can't take kittens away from their mummy when they're that small. They need cat milk, and then they need to learn how to be big cats and go to the vet and get immunised, and there are all sorts of permits you need for a cat to travel to a different country."

"But nobody will see the kitten. I'll hide it under my jumper all the way so nobody knows it's there. And I can make a little passport for it. I can put a picture of the kitten and everything."

Bruno couldn't help laughing at the way Lottie had it all planned out. Before he could restate his case, Lilly rounded the corner, and Lottie bounced off the sofa shrieking that Lilly had to come help her make cat passports and they were bringing all the kittens home, like she hadn't heard a single word he'd said.

"That's going to end in tears, babe," Gabriel said with a sigh as he flopped into the armchair, throwing the discarded cushion Bruno's way.

"I tried to explain," Bruno protested. "She just won't listen."

"She'll be obsessed with something else in a few days. She'll get over it."

"How is your organising thing going?"

"Almost done. We found a scrapbook full of newspaper clippings, I need Frank to look through them because I don't understand much. He'd already found Erik's death certificate, so we know when he passed away and who his parents were but none of his other relatives. Bella obviously knew he'd died, as she mourned him. There are just so many question marks over the whole story. Such a tragedy of wasted love. They would've been so good for each other."

"I like that you guys have something to do together. It's nice."

Gabriel smiled. "It's hard work but kind of relaxing."

"Did you see Andreas?"

"Yeah. Not sure what's going on, but he stomped upstairs and shouted that he wasn't moving until whoever was up there talked to him. Any idea?"

"Drama." Bruno laughed softly. "Just kids and their fucking drama."

***

Bruno wasn't wrong about the drama. Dinner turned out to be a tense affair, with Fredrik looking pale and withdrawn and Andreas staring at him from the other end of the table with a face like thunder. Frank caught Bruno's attention, side-eying the boys then nodding towards the kitchen. He wasn't even discreet about it, just got up and left. Bruno waited half a minute, then picked up a glass and carried it in to look helpful. When Frank saw it, he burst into laughter.

"So what's up with the boys?" he asked.

"Some argument over nothing, no doubt. I wouldn't worry about it." He wasn't going to give anything away here. The *Man-to-Man* talks were his badge of honour for fatherhood, something he'd worked hard to instil in his oldest son. Bruno wished he'd had his father's trust as a lost teen instead of hanging around until the internet turned up and taught him all the things his father should have, like putting oil in the frying pan instead of butter so the fish fingers didn't burn and that there was a difference between coffee cream and whipping cream, and that wanking was much better with lube. All things he'd learnt the hard way.

Frank just cocked his head. "You're a worse liar than my husband. Thomas can't lie for shit. His nose twitches and his eyes flicker, and he gets this nervous twitch in his top lip. It's so bloody obvious it's not even funny."

"And me? How can you tell I'm lying?" Bruno snapped, struggling to keep his cool. Who was he kidding? He had no cool. *Fuck.*

"You stand on one foot and alternate like you're tap-dancing. I bet you do that when you give patients bad news too, mincing your words to get around telling them their dicks are falling off or something."

"I've never had a dick fall off."

"See? That's the truth. You stood absolutely still as you said that."

"Bullshit."

"So what's up with your son?"

"Doesn't want to go home."

"Ah. Classic. But really, dude, what's up with your son?"

Bruno couldn't help it. He rolled his eyes and a nervous laugh escaped. Then he wiped his mouth with the back of his hand—another of his nervous tics, although that one he knew about. He had to fidget with something when he couldn't simply tell the truth.

"Look, Frank. I do know what the problem is, but I won't break that confidence. I will put your mind at ease, though, and say that the boys will probably be very, very important to each other for the rest of their lives. We just need to let them hash this out in their own time. It's nothing serious, and it only concerns the two of them—and they didn't take drugs, if that is what you're thinking."

Frank laughed incredulously. "Where the fuck would they get drugs out here?"

"The farm next door might grow weed in that barn for all I know. I have watched *Breaking Bad*, you know."

"You're worse than Thomas!" Frank said, still laughing. "Where did you buy weed when you were their age?"

"At their age, I didn't even know what weed was. I was a bloody altar boy at my parents' church and read comics at night. Innocent and naïve until my best friend offered me a bong on my sixteenth birthday, and then we met this guy Carlos who sold stuff and introduced me to his dealer. Before I knew it, I had a twenty-euro-a-week habit. It was so bloody idiotic."

"See? Just like Thomas. Stop overthinking shit."

"It's not overthinking to want to stop my son making the same stupid mistakes I did."

"Andreas isn't stupid. In fact, he's pretty cool. But can I ask you something? You don't have to answer. Just blink once for yes and twice for no. OK?"

"You do know this isn't actually an episode of *Breaking Bad*, right? And you'd better not be recording it on your phone either."

"Scout's honour!" Frank saluted him and grinned. "Seriously, though, level with me. What do you think the chances are that some of our children—there are several here, and we will not be naming names. But what, in your personal opinion, is the likelihood that one or more of our children might not be heterosexual? Again, you don't need to answer."

"Well, I would say, hypothetically, that first of all it's not an exact science, and that my gaydar has never been wired correctly. I didn't even spot that my boss was gay—he had to spell it out for me by showing me pictures of his, in my professional opinion, very built and handsome husband. But as far as the chances of one or more of the kids being queer? I don't have an opinion on that. As long as they're happy, I don't fucking care who they're with."

He said the last sentence a little louder than the rest, in case anyone was listening, as the dining area next door was suspiciously quiet.

Then he blinked. Once.

"Thought so," Frank whispered. "So you do know what is going on."

"Of course I know what's going on. Do *you* know what's going on?"

"Right now? Not a fucking clue, although I guess this was inevitable. My son has a massive crush on your son, and it's all somehow come out. If your son is giving him shit then I might have to have words with him—unless you've already had words. Fredrik is bloody crushed."

"No words needed," Bruno murmured. "Andreas is trying to make things right, and he's not giving him shit, I can promise you that. I think Andreas is dealing with this in a really good way, and I honestly think we need to just leave them to it."

"I know," Frank said with a sigh. "I just hate seeing Fredrik like this. He's only a kid and he's fucking heartbroken. He's been following that boy around like a lost sheep for weeks, and now he doesn't even want to leave his room."

"He'll be fine. I'll check in with Andreas later and make sure everything is good. OK? Would that make you feel better?"

"Yeah, it would, but don't tell Thomas, OK? I don't think he's aware of what's going on, and he might overreact. He blows a fuse if we're out of milk. That's kind of his level."

"Scout's honour." Bruno offered his fist, and Frank bumped it. "And by the way, where *do* you get drugs around here?"

Frank grinned. "Lady at the farm next door grows medicinal cannabis in the greenhouse. Don't tell Thomas that either."

"I bloody knew it!"

"Knew what?" Thomas interrupted. "We're sitting there like fools thinking you came in to get the salad and instead you're standing here gossiping like two old grannies."

"We are no grannies, and we're not gossiping. We're discussing serious shit." Frank made it sound like a joke and pulled Thomas in for a kiss. "What do you think about growing weed in the barn? Might be a good way to generate income in the future. We could have a lucrative little business here over the summer, maybe get a stall at the Henriksvik fair?"

"Fuck off, Frank and just bring out the salad," Thomas muttered with no venom. "And don't forget the ketchup."

## Twenty seven
## FRANK

"Hnnnnggfg."

Thomas dug his face deeper into the pillow as Frank opened the curtains and let in the bright morning sun before sitting on the edge of the mattress. He tickled the damp skin at Thomas's nape, making small twirls from the now longish hair. Based on his usual style, the man needed a haircut, but this new, wild, windswept look was a good one and very sexy.

"Wake up, babe." He peppered greedy kisses on Thomas's neck, the intoxicating scent filling his nose—soft sleep smells, sweat, spices, fruit, garlic from yesterday's dinner. It turned out salad and hotdogs hadn't been enough, and so they'd lit the barbecue. God only knew what freezer leftovers had become fire fodder as they feasted.

"I could eat you," Frank murmured and couldn't resist licking lightly at his skin, tasting the salty film on it.

"Frank..." Thomas turned around, his face suddenly right below Frank's. Frank bent down for a kiss, and Thomas scrunched his nose. "How much garlic dip did you put in those wraps yesterday?"

"Not that much! But there were three whole cloves in the tzatziki..."

"Ugh." Thomas looked away. "What time is it?"

"Uhm, you don't want to know." Frank chuckled. "But get up. I have a surprise for you."

"Surprise?" Thomas had that sceptical look.

"Yup. Get up!" He bounced heavily on the mattress, but then had second thoughts. Did Thomas get knots in his stomach every time Frank mentioned a surprise but then didn't say anything to protect Frank's feelings? He took a deep breath and looked closely at Thomas, trying to read his expression. Did he look worried? Annoyed?

With a sigh, Thomas sat up and rubbed his eyes, then reached for his phone. "Fuck. It's only seven thirty." He squinted at Frank. "I could have had three more hours of sleep."

"Well, I could have started repairing the rotten weatherboards around the windows, too. That was my plan for this morning, actually, but waking you up early seemed like more fun."

Thomas blew air through his lips in frustration as he rolled out of bed and set off towards the bathroom.

"So, do I need anything for this surprise of yours?" Thomas asked.

"Nope."

The toilet flushed, and Thomas returned, stepping into last night's clothes, which were spread around the bedroom floor. He looked cute with his ruffled hair, khakis and the old T-shirt that hugged his chest in all the right places. He would forever be that bewildered young twenty-something with the messy hair and gorgeous eyes that Frank had fallen in love with. Thomas had reeked of desperation back then, and Frank still felt that pang of need whenever Thomas looked like this. Needy, tired, desperate for something that Frank wanted more than anything to give him, even with the whiff of sweat from his armpits as he sat on the bed and downed the espresso Frank had left on his bedside table.

Frank nodded towards his stuffed backpack by the bedroom door. "Put on your trainers and let's go!"

Thomas groaned. "Trainers? There is no way I'm going running with you at seven fucking thirty in the morning when I am still on holiday!"

"Relax, babe. No running, unless you want to run for me," he joked hopefully. "You can wear whatever you want, but trainers are probably advisable."

They followed the path to the lake first, surrounded by chirping birds and thin sun rays through the leaves, the morning feeling calm and peaceful despite nature having been awake for hours already.

"So, we're swimming in the lake?" Thomas asked with a smile, grabbing Frank's hand as the path widened. He seemed more relaxed now, having come to terms with being woken too early and adjusted his head and mood from sleeping to awake.

"Maybe." Frank squeezed his hand lightly. It was nice to walk like this, hand in hand. It didn't happen too often anymore. They sometimes held hands, in bed, in the kitchen, or shared a quick touch between other things, like the last time they were at the cinema, which was only a couple of months ago. They should probably do that more often—hold hands and go out and catch some new movies back in Oslo instead of streaming them half asleep on the couch out of habit. He needed it, his husband's touch. It grounded him on days like this.

He turned right when they reached the beach. The lake was glittering to their left, small waves meeting the rays from the sun, the light-blue sky mirroring on the surface. It looked like it would be another warm day. The heat was somehow different here than the stifling city heat of Oslo, the lake providing a cooling sense of peace. It was no surprise that the kids had almost lived at the lake for the past few days.

Frank had bought a huge inflatable flamingo float from Amazon, and surprisingly it had even been delivered to their doorstep, even if it had taken a few weeks. He'd bought it on a whim, thinking it would be cute for the garden, but the thing had turned out to be three metres across, and it had taken the kids several hours to inflate with the old foot pump they'd found in the shed. Now the pink monstrosity was tethered to the sauna on the shore, and it seemed to magnetise the kids, who jumped off it, swam and returned to lie on it for a while before repeating over and over again. They'd even taken food and drink on board the giant, ludicrous floating bird that made Frank smile now, watching it gently bob on the water, tethered to the world by its long line.

The path turned into the forest again after the beach. Lush green nature surrounded them, still cool from the night. The tracks narrowed, but Thomas kept hold of his hand, following right behind him until Frank stopped.

"Shhh!" he said, pointing to where a young deer stood a few metres from them, munching on leaves. It hadn't seen them yet, and Frank wished he'd brought his camera, but all he had was his phone tucked into the side pocket of the backpack, and getting it out would disturb the animal. Instead, they watched in silence; with Thomas's fingers tight around his own, Frank wasn't sure he'd ever felt so content.

The moment was broken by a light but sudden breeze that startled them all. The deer saw them and froze for a second before jumping off in the opposite direction. Frank finally breathed out and felt his heart melt when Thomas smiled at him. Doing things like this didn't always end well. His impulsiveness wasn't always a good thing or appreciated, but for once, it seemed he'd got it right.

The small clearing brought them out of the forest, the path widening as a peak rose in front of them. It was neither big nor steep, and Frank knew they would run the last hundred metres; they always did. The kids too. He looked at Thomas with a grin.

"Race to the top?" he asked. For a minute, Thomas looked unsure, but as Frank set off, he followed suit.

Frank barely made it to the top before Thomas and was panting heavily, elbows resting on his thighs, when Thomas reached him.

"You cheated," Thomas laughed. "That was one *huge* head start."

"Did not." Frank shook his head. "You're just slow and old."

"And that's just rude."

"You've got more grey hair than me, and all those wrinkles," Frank teased. "But whatever, I still won."

The view was mesmerising reaching far in all directions, mostly forests, but also tracks through the green that Frank knew were roads. To the north, there were fields beyond the forest, a few farms visible in the distance. They could see the lake as well, the water glittering between the trees. Being up here always made Frank feel small and brought home how big the world was—bigger than anything he would ever comprehend—in which what they called a peak was nothing more than a gentle hill in the forest.

"Wow. It's a weird thing. Even though I know this view, the landscape looks different this year," Thomas said, scratching the stubble on his chin. He looked a little stunned, like a marble sculpture with his hand shielding his eyes from the sun. He might have been joking about Thomas being old, but he had aged well. A few years and Thomas would be a silver fox, a suave, handsome specimen. That he belonged to Frank was always something that shocked him back into reality, as it did now. He set down the backpack and opened it, laying out the contents on the ground.

"Breakfast is served," he said as he poured coffee from the flask into a mug and handed it to Thomas with a smile.

"So you did bring stuff." Thomas grinned and sat on a warm stone. Frank poured himself a coffee and sipped, relaxing for a moment before scooping up the cloth napkin.

"I made us food as well." He handed it to Thomas, whose grin turned greedy when he unwrapped the carefully made sandwich.

Frank settled on the ground and lay with his head in Thomas's lap, watching him break off small pieces of bread, the soft butter melting against his fingers, a piece of ham landing on Frank's forehead as Thomas took another big bite.

"I shouldn't have bothered making a sandwich for you. I should just have ripped the contents of the fridge into crumbs and shoved it straight down your throat. That's how you eat it anyway. What happened to your table manners?"

"It tastes better this way," Thomas mumbled through a mouthful. "Look, I'm even sharing my sandwich with you." He jammed a piece of cheese between Frank's lips.

"Is this how you eat your lunch at work, too? Nobody ever mention anything about your table manners there?"

Frank felt Thomas tense up. The hand that had been lightly rubbing his shoulder stilled, and his abs shook as he let out a breath.

"You OK?" he asked. Thomas took another deep breath and nodded. "You sure?" Frank reached up and touched Thomas's cheek. It was cold and clammy under his palm, his breath warm against his thumb.

Shuffling up, he sat on the stone beside Thomas, took the sandwich from his hand and wrapped his arms around him, pulling him close. "What's going on with work?" he asked against his neck, instinctively pinpointing the issue, or perhaps not instinctively. He'd noticed that any time someone had mentioned work recently, Thomas had become tense and quiet. He used to talk about his work all the time, but he'd spoken about it less and less over the past months, the strain of the workday seeping into their evenings at home.

Thomas took another deep breath and opened his mouth to say something, but it was like he couldn't get the words out.

"Not good," he mumbled eventually. "It's...too much. I've been wanting to talk to you about that."

Then it all poured out. Some of it Frank had heard before and tucked it away at the back of his mind, but he had to agree. It was too much.

Far too much. The responsibility. The new project. The cuts in funding. The redundancies and the threats of a move to Svalbard. He almost choked on his coffee hearing that. There was no way they were moving to Svalbard.

"You know you have options, don't you? I can pull it together and try to get more work. We wouldn't have the income we have now, but I will support you whatever you want to do."

"But I don't want to go!" Thomas stiffened against Frank. "The lab hadn't talked to me at all before writing the new proposal, and the new boss just threw me to the wolves. I didn't have a chance to prepare, and even if I'd had time, I would have said no, I don't want to do this! It's either take up this new post on Svalbard or take redundancy. I'm being pushed into a bloody corner with nowhere to go. I'm too young to retire, too antiquated to start over."

Frank pondered for a second, uncertain what to say. "Why don't you want to? Svalbard is a good opportunity, isn't it? You spent time there before and liked it, and you always talk so fondly about the people you cooperate with up there."

Thomas sighed, like this was a fight he'd already lost. "Yes, but..." He turned towards Frank. There was something in his eyes, something disillusioned, Frank thought. The anger from seconds ago was completely gone. "It feels like we aren't getting anywhere there. The research is stalled, or not the research, but the results. We add finding after finding, yet nobody is doing anything about it. They just talk." He sighed. "I feel like I would be sent up there as a scapegoat, to be the one in charge when everything crumbles. I couldn't cope with that. Not at this point in my career. I feel like...I'm done. Done with the rat race, done with the effort, and... and I don't want to leave you." Thomas stopped, and the pause that followed made him calmer. His voice no longer so strained.

"I've been thinking about it lately. Maria and Fredrik are off to uni next year, and maybe it's just me, but it terrifies me that we only have a year left. That they will be gone, living their own lives and...I want to be there for them, Frank. I want to be there for their homework and football practice and school events and pick them up from friends' and when they get too drunk at a party. I don't want all this to be your responsibility." He bit his lower lip. "I want to be there for you...and I don't want to turn into my father."

Frank slid his fingers through Thomas's hair. It was still as soft as when they met more than twenty years ago. Sometimes he couldn't believe it had been that long. Who would have thought, when they were on that dancefloor, that a stupid impulsive pull of a shirt, a random kiss, would lead them here and that they would still be an 'us' so many years later?

"You will never be your father," he said, giving Thomas a soft kiss. "And you know I will never try to stop you from reaching your career goals, don't you? No matter how much extra work that lands me, or how uneven you feel our workloads are."

Thomas nodded. "I know. But I don't think this is a good career move either. It's a plot to get me away." He sighed and shook his head. "I don't even think I want to be there anymore, but I have no idea what to do. It's the only life I know. Professionally, I mean."

"Then maybe you should, you know... Quit?" Frank felt the fear shoot through him as he said it. He understood as well as Thomas did what that meant.

"Take the redundancy and run?" Thomas looked equally terrified by the prospect.

"I think this holiday, the time here—it's been a wake-up call," Frank started, hoping the words were coming out right. "For me too. I mean, I know the uncertainty of your job has been on your mind for months now, but...this goddamn farm. There's something here that has kind of fallen into place, It's just been the last week or so, but I get it now, Thomas. We need this. Being here brings us some kind of...I don't know. Peace. It's where we belong. And I don't know if that will change next time we come here, when we're here on our own, or if there will be new people staying in the cabin because the thought of that already makes me nervous. I just know there is change in the air and that we have to do something about it. We need to stop what we're doing and change. I think we could turn this around, make it good for us. Make this place bring us an income, and I mean more than renting it out. There's something here I still haven't figured out, but I'm sure I will. And until I do? We'll cope. Wherever your career takes you."

Thomas shrugged. "I don't have another job. And I have no idea where to even look for a new career."

"You can still quit. Retire early perhaps. Take time off and write a book."

"I don't want you to stress about it. I don't want change."

"Now you're whining," Frank said with smile.

"Yeah, I know." Thomas huffed. "But I really don't want to look for a new job. Just the thought of it is exhausting, and then I have to explain why I left this job and why I want a new one and then maybe I'll get fired after the trial period—"

"Thomas, stop it. You're overthinking again."

He sighed. "The thought of staying where I am is worse than the thought of leaving to find something new."

Frank smiled because he knew exactly what Thomas meant. "I think you've got your answer there, haven't you?" He looked at Thomas again, serious this time. "Don't let the thought of us, of me and the kids, decide for you. Think of yourself for once. We'll manage. I can make more supermarket campaigns if I have to. Or take school photos. The ones I took at the kids' sports day turned out pretty cool, I think."

Thomas laughed. "You can't do supermarket campaigns, Frank. You'd flip from it. Imagine using your creativity for marketing yet another cheese brand or a low-budget sale on carrots. And shooting school photos would sink your career, not to mention that you'd run out of there screaming every time a kid wouldn't pose...in symmetry."

Frank chuckled. "OK, maybe not school photography, then."

For a moment, they just sat there smiling at each other. Frank felt Thomas's arm around his hips, all the points where their torsos touched. Thomas's deep-green eyes had almost disappeared in the liberating laugh. He looked freer than he had in a while, and right then, Frank knew they were completely together in this, that this was not just *Frank and Thomas* laughing, but *us*, the two of them, together.

"We're better here," Thomas whispered. "Things feel better. Calmer. We're talking again and not letting life make us so stressed. When I think back now, no wonder you had an episode when we got here because the last couple of months were insane. And I mean *insane*. I was stressed out of my head, and you were in a total funk, and we just screamed and shouted and fought."

"You screamed and shouted. I was perfectly calm."

That made Thomas burst into laughter. A laughter that blew away the last of Frank's nervousness from the morning.

Then Thomas got all serious again. "What about you?" he asked.

"Me?"

"Yes, all these plans for the farm."

"I've actually been thinking a lot about it. I..." He looked at Thomas, who watched him in anticipation. "I want to keep it," he said. "Gabriel and I, we've found so much about Bella, about her life and the people she crossed paths with, and the entire story is so interesting and touching, not necessarily because it is so unusual, but because she tells everything about it! Her diaries are extensive, Thomas! Raw and gritty and sexual and sensual and full of pain and grief." He felt all his newfound energy bubbling through his veins just talking about it.

"And last night I was thinking, it's no coincidence that I got the farm. My mum...when I was in hospital after...you know. They didn't think I'd make it, and at the time, I wasn't speaking to my family at all. They couldn't cope with my mood swings and illness, and episodes and that stupid, stupid suicide attempt kind of tipped them over the edge. It took you and our wedding and the kids to bring me back to actually having parents. You know all this, but...Bella must have somehow known about me and wanted me to have it, and now it feels like I can't let it go. And now I know what I know? I wonder if she thought, this guy—me—I had nothing, and I would become another Erik, so she wanted me to have something I could hold on to. Something that had given her happiness when there was nothing else in her life to smile about. She loved this place, and she gave it to me to love too. It sounds crazy, but in my head, it makes sense. I was meant to have this, and selling it... It would be wrong. So wrong.

"I don't really know what I want to do with it. Maybe turn it into some kind of holistic retreat. Or a studio. Can you imagine some huge rockstar making music here? Or perhaps a respite facility for people who need it. I guess I have to do some more research, but perhaps we could get some of the locals to handle some of it and get a charity involved, which wouldn't actually make us any money. But I thought, perhaps I can devote a few months to looking into things like that. The satisfaction of making it useful, I think I would enjoy that. But to be honest, I just want a huge win on the lottery to make all our financial worries just disappear."

Thomas hushed him. "Now you are just rambling," he said while giving his lips a soft peck. "Don't worry, Frank. If you want to keep the farm, just do it. You've been full of energy recently, and not in a worrying way. Your eyes are shining. You seem to have thought this through, and if it's something you believe in, then follow it."

Frank smiled at Thomas and stroked his cheek with his fingertips. His skin was soft and warm. Calming. "But what if it's a whim? What if it's just another of my hurried ideas that I lose interest in within a few months?"

Thomas shrugged. "Then you lose interest. If, and only if that happens, then we'll talk about selling it. We don't have to worry about that now."

Frank looked him in the eyes. "You didn't feel that way last year. Back then, you wanted nothing to do with this place."

"Sorry. I didn't realise how much the farm meant to you. I thought *you* thought it was a burden and you wanted to get rid of it, and that was OK with me. I didn't feel attached to it at all. But then you had all these plans, and I felt bad for not seeing it, for not understanding your feelings and dismissing that you had them in the first place." He smiled. "But it's strange. Now I understand. I think you never had anything that was truly yours. The house at home is ours. The kids are ours. This, I suppose, is ours too, but it belongs to you, and your passion for it, if this is what you want, will make it work. *We* will make it work."

Thomas leaned back, his gaze shifting to some distant point on the horizon. He looked...not troubled. Bewildered. "Things are different this year. I don't know how, or when, but this feels like home. Almost like I can't even imagine being back in Oslo. Back to the grind, the stress, a life I'm not even sure I want anymore. Promise me, *promise* that we won't go back to the way things were. We can't. I won't let us. I want this, what we have here, when we talk and laugh and sleep and go off and have breakfast on top of a bloody rock, and where I don't care about anything but you and the kids and—"

Frank silenced him with a kiss. Again. And again, and Thomas kissed him back, until a loud growl from his belly shattered the silence.

"Are you still hungry?" Frank asked, poking his finger into Thomas's stomach.

Thomas nodded. "Didn't get to finish my breakfast," he grumbled, picking up his sandwich again, "since someone said I was old and had bad table manners."

"Not old. Older. And you've aged gracefully, despite your disgusting eating habits."

\*\*\*

When they finally made their way back down from the hill towards the lake, Andreas and Maria were swimming around the flamingo while Bruno and Gabriel were watching the twins play by the shore. The teens cast them some curious glances and suggested they join them for a swim before lunch, which Frank declined.

"You sure?" Bruno said, laughing.

Frank felt the heat in his cheeks and looked at Thomas. He didn't want to break this newfound happiness bubble. The intimacy still felt a little brittle and raw. "Maybe a short swim would be nice," he said, receiving a soft squeeze from Thomas's hand in agreement.

"Where's Fredrik?" Thomas asked, looking up towards the house.

"He's in his room. Didn't want to come," Gabriel answered. "I tried to talk to him, but he's in a really strange mood."

"He was keen on the idea of coming to Berlin in October," Bruno said. "The kids all have a week off school. We'd have to check if it works, timewise, but you could send them on a flight down to us, and we would look after them. Andreas wants to show them around, and there's Oktoberfest and all the sights to see, of course. They said they've studied the Second World War—there are some amazing museums, and we can take them to the Wall and Checkpoint Charlie, do all the sightseeing so it would be educational too. Then we have to have lunch at the TV tower." Bruno was talking too fast, like he was trying to distract Thomas, who looked like a deer caught in headlights, other than that his head was clearly in turmoil, torn between wanting to run up to the house and check on Fredrik versus having a cool swim in the lake.

"I'll go check on Fredrik," Frank said calmly, catching Bruno's gaze. Bruno shook his head and shrugged his shoulders, which made zero sense, but Thomas looked visibly relieved at Bruno's suggestion.

"That sounds like a good plan," he said. "I have a shitload of work coming up, and Frank's schedule is always up in the air, so if you don't think it would be too much trouble...?" Thomas settled on the ground and took off his trainers.

"Shall I bring down some coffee?" Frank suggested.

"Coffee." Bruno sighed and lay back on the sandy beach with his hands behind his head. "Yeah."

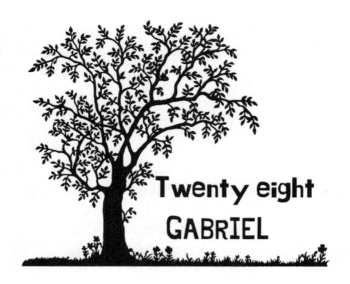

# Twenty eight

## GABRIEL

HAVING ANOTHER MASSIVE bonfire on the beach had seemed like a brilliant idea—at the time.

Now the kids were filthy and running around like feral puppies, jumping in the lake one moment, being cold the next. The twins were naked, then they were coming down from the house fully clothed and screaming about being eaten by giant killer mosquitoes.

"Come here, Liebchen!" Gabriel called to Lilly, who wasn't wearing socks in her trainers and probably no underwear either under the jeans that somehow had become far too small for her over the past weeks. Her buttocks were sticking up over the waistband, and the jumper she was wearing had ketchup stains all down the front.

"Nein!" she shouted back, expertly bypassing his outstretched arms.

He'd lost control, that was for sure. His darling babies were no longer the helpless children he'd brought here a few weeks back. They were independent adventurers who didn't even need him to get fed or go to sleep. Both the girls had spent the last two nights in Maria's bed, and Frank had fed them every meal.

Gabriel felt like a spare wheel, but not in a bad way, since he'd been absorbed in clearing out the barn and cataloguing Bella's diaries. There'd been moments of panic over missing books, but then they'd found more folders hiding in the main house, forgotten in the bottom of the storage area that had once been Bella's office. It was still an office, but where a few weeks ago it had housed a few hardback books and Thomas's reference textbooks from university, now it looked like some kind of mission control centre, with Post-it notes on the walls and organised piles of binders in straight lines on the desk. Frank had picked out a few of Bella's romance novels too, the ones that looked the most loved and were in good condition, to keep a little bit of Bella alive in the room she must have spent so many hours in, writing down her feelings for the world to keep.

It hadn't been how Gabriel had imagined spending this holiday, but he'd enjoyed the work. It had given him purpose and his head a kind of weird peace.

"Let the kids be," Bruno said softly, wrapping his arms around his waist from behind. "They're having fun, and we only have one more day, then we really have to go."

"That's what you said yesterday," Gabriel teased. Bruno kissed his cheek.

"I wish we could stay, but it's a great idea having the kids come to us in October—if it's Halloween, even better. Andreas could have a party and the girls could go stay with Mum, and you and I could go out for the night."

"Yeah, and come back to a trashed flat." Gabriel giggled.

"No, Maria would be there. I trust her completely to keep everything under control. I'm sure she would ring us if things were getting out of hand."

"Look." Gabriel turned around, covering Bruno's mouth with his hand because he didn't trust him not to make a noise, and right now, they needed to be quiet. Because Andreas and Fredrik were standing among the trees, and Gabriel was pretty sure there was a bit more than a friendly hug going on.

"What?"

"Just kiss me, you fool."

"Idiot." Bruno snickered and grabbed a handful of Gabriel's behind.

"I think Andreas and Fredrik are friends again."

"Thank God for that." Bruno pressed a wet kiss to Gabriel's mouth.

"I...think I need to throw a few more books on that bonfire," Gabriel said, laughing as he pushed Bruno away or tried to. He didn't try too hard, though, and ended up wedged against a tree with his husband's mouth sucking bruises into his neck.

"I want to have sex tonight," Bruno murmured. "I'm just throwing it out here, and you can say no, but baby, I really need you. One last time.

It's just better here. We're relaxed, and fuck. Baby. Just let me fuck you again. Please. You can fuck me too, and then—"

"Then we're going to be sitting in a car for two days straight with sore arses and you'll blame me."

Bruno's expression was priceless as he tried to put on full-on innocence but still looked guilty as hell.

"I can live with that," he said, plunging in for another kiss.

"Then I will happily fuck you later. Just help me get this last box on the bonfire, and then we can let the fire die down."

They worked through the box with ease, laughing at Thomas and Frank, who were play fighting in the water, and Maria and the girls running back up to the house to make popcorn. Fredrik was back to following Andreas around like a shadow, which was good. Comforting. Just the way things should be around here.

"Have you checked through all these?" Bruno asked, holding up a large envelope.

"Yes, why?" Gabriel sent a pile of newspaper clippings into the fire.

"Because these letters are unopened. Dated..." He stopped to read. "These are dated just a few years back. Perhaps they were forgotten about? They're addressed to Bella, and this one here has a book inside."

"What?" Gabriel grabbed the envelopes, calling for Frank to come up out of the water.

Bruno was right. It was a book—a brand-new paperback with a shiny cover and the spine intact. Gabriel's hand caught the paper that fell out of the envelope with it.

"Frank?" he shouted.

"Yeah?"

"Dry off, you oaf. We've found something."

"More dust," Thomas coughed, catching up with them.

"No. No, no, no, I think. Fuck. Frank. Fuck, fuck, fuck. Does this translate to what I think it does?"

"Let me see." Frank took the book from him, his breath hitching as took in the cover.

"*Breven till Bella,*" Gabriel read out in his broken attempt at Swedish. "That means 'The Letters for Bella', no?"

"*The Letters to Bella*," Frank corrected, his voice barely more than a whisper. "Look at the author. Erik N. Albrektson."

"Read it," Gabriel demanded, holding out the letter in his hand to Frank's face. "What does it say?"

*Dear Bella, I haven't had any response to any of my letters, but I hope they have reached you. My uncle's letters were finally approved by the publisher, and after a few small edits and changes, the book is complete. I hope that you will read it with kindness, because there are obviously private matters in his letters that I understand might be painful for you to relive, but I have given you the chance to read them before publishing. I sincerely hope that you agree with his words being shared with the world. As you must know, my uncle's love for you was lifelong, and he would have wanted you to know that, despite the unbelievable fact that he wrote you these wonderful letters and never had the bravery to send them to you.*

"Fuck!" Gabriel couldn't stop himself.

"What?" Bruno asked. "Is this something new? Was Bella published?"

"No, you dope. This...this here...is a published book of letters that Erik wrote to Bella that she never received, and bloody hell..."

"She never opened this. She didn't know."

Frank nodded. "So he says, or she says. The sender's name is Terje Blomkvist—Erik's nephew. I think? There's an address, and an email. Thank God for that. I'll email him, just hope he's our age, still alive and checks his email and all that. Is there more?"

Thomas held up two more envelopes. "These are unopened, too."

"You haven't thrown anything else into the fire?" Frank asked, the panic evident in his voice.

"Just a bunch of newspaper clippings," Gabriel said, his voice wobbling too. "Oh fuck. I hope not."

"What else is in that box?" Thomas asked, bending down and grabbing a newspaper article. "Oh my... Listen to this!"

*The Letters to Bella, the award-winning novel by poet Erik Albrektson, has been awarded the prestigious Nordic Council Literature Prize of 2020. The author, Erik N. Albrektson, who passed away at the age of forty-seven, has won several literary awards since his works were posthumously published in collaboration with Terje Blomkvist, Erik's nephew, himself an author.*

"Fucking hell. I'd heard about *The Letters to Bella*." Frank said. "I just never connected the dots. Ever. That Terje bloke was interviewed on TV. It never even occurred to me..."

"You are related, perhaps?" Gabriel said, then shook his head. "No, you are not. You're related to Bella, and Terje was related to Erik."

"We could have been if Erik hadn't been an arse and abandoned Bella. They could've married. There would've been kids, and those kids would have owned this place..."

"Instead, we are here," Gabriel said quietly. "And that's what fate decided. Bella left this place to you, hoping you would give it the love it deserved. She gave it to you so this place could have its happy ending with a family who were in love, and so you would have somewhere to raise your kids, and perhaps she hoped you would retire here, grow old among her apple trees and books and love this place as much as she did. She gave it to you, and you now know why."

"Perhaps you're right."

"It says here," Thomas interrupted, reading from another article, "*The Letters to Bella* has been translated into forty-five languages and that there were talks about a film."

"No way!" Frank said.

"We need to ring this Terje. We should go visit. Invite him over to see this place and maybe even show him Bella's diaries."

"Or perhaps you should negotiate with your own people?" Gabriel said. "Is this what Bella would have wanted? You're sitting on a potential goldmine here. The possibilities..."

"I don't know," Frank said weakly, clutching the book to his chest. "I don't...I don't know."

"Then let's just pack this box up and take it back up to the house. We don't have to make any decisions. We just take it up, and we can read through it."

They walked in silence, the box in Frank's arms rustling quietly as he stumbled through in the long grass.

"How did I not know?" he kept saying.

"Because nobody told you. Had we not found this box in time, we would never have known. Once we get on Wi-Fi again, I'll go online and order the book in German. I have to read it. I mean, we know all these things about Bella, and now we get Erik's side too. How amazing is that?"

"I want to meet this Terje. I'm not sure if I want to punch him or hug him. He had no right. That was Bella's life, and he's thrown it out there."

"He wrote her letters many times. There are quite a few in there, and she never opened them. Or perhaps she did, and then she stopped. We need to look through them and find out. But she knew about the book. If she wanted to stop it being published, she would have. Wouldn't she?"

"Maybe she'd had enough and didn't think it mattered anymore? I'd like to see the original letters, though. It feels like I have an obligation now, to Bella, to fight for her voice in this and bring those letters home. Maybe we should have them burned and the ashes scattered here among the trees, where Bella is scattered. I don't know. Am I being a sentimental fool again?"

"No, it's an interesting thought, but no. Too brutal. And I think, if this Terje is a reasonable human, he would agree. Or maybe we can just be less... dramatic. We could come back here next summer and read the book aloud under the trees for Bella. Let her have his words, read out to her in the sun."

"Gabriel?"

"Yeah?"

"Now you're being over-sentimental and dramatic."

They laughed, and it felt incredibly good. They were still at it as they stepped into the kitchen, which was brimming with smoke from the girls' attempt at making popcorn, the pan bellowing acrid fumes through the open windows where the mosquitoes were zipping in like there was an open invitation to feed.

"You know what?" Frank said, lifting Lottie up and giving her a hug. She squirmed, trying to escape his grip.

"What?" Gabriel coughed, as he let Lottie escape out the door, her footsteps echoing up the stairs to Maria's room.

"I think you need to come back next summer. Promise me that we'll do this again, and I will make plans to do something for Bella, remember her and all the things she did. And we should talk to Terje. Celebrate Bella and Erik together, remember the love they shared and do something with it. Make a documentary or something—something that shows the story behind the letters. The place where Bella lived."

"You sound like you have the blurb and the taglines already in your head." Gabriel laughed. "And we haven't even read the book yet."

"I know." Frank grabbed the book from the top of the box. "I'm going to read it first and then process it. Then I'm going to figure out how to put this show on the road. Bella's diaries need to be preserved, and I mean. There are so many possibilities. Books. Movies."

"Sounds like a good plan," Gabriel said. "Let the words sink in. No rash decisions. We have time."

Frank smiled. "We have all the time in the world."

*\*\**

Later that evening, Gabriel and Frank walked back down to the lake and sat quietly on the grass next to the narrow beach, resting their feet in the soft sand and watching the smoking remains of the bonfire. The sun was still up, but dusk was approaching, and the sounds from the children had disappeared. They'd stayed up too long, of course; the twins would be a mess when they got back home, and getting them back on track would be a nuisance, but it had all been worth it. Totally worth it.

"It was a good idea to put all the kids to sleep in the big house," Frank said. "The teens probably won't sleep until later, so the three of them can stay up watching the kiddos. Or maybe they'll all stay awake and yours will be exhausted for the drive back," he added as if he had some kind of mind-reading capability.

Gabriel swallowed and laughed. "I guess it will be mostly Maria, then. The boys may be...occupied," he said, feeling his stomach flip when he realised he might have given too much away.

Frank twitched, and Gabriel could hear his gulps through the silence before they were laughing again.

"Let's talk about something else," Frank suggested, and Gabriel agreed, not really wanting to delve further into the ideas of experimenting teenage boys. He was pretty sure Frank had been aware of the boys before their conversation. After all, Andreas and Fredrik had yet to learn the art of subtlety and discretion, instead being the typical brash teens who still had all life's hard lessons to learn.

They remained silent, listening to the tiny waves lapping at the beach in the calm summer night. The sun's orange glow glittering across the water, and a few stray seagulls were still flying high. Gabriel hadn't realised they came so far inland. He'd thought they were coastal birds.

"Are they seagulls?" he asked.

Frank looked up and shrugged. "I've no idea, but I think so."

"I thought you were bird enthusiasts?"

"Huh?" Frank frowned.

"The advertisement for the cabin says this area is perfect for bird watching, so we imagined some kind of bird nerds with green khakis and hugs binoculars."

Frank's laughter filled the silence. "Those were Thomas's words," he said.

"So, he's the bird man?" Gabriel teased. He couldn't really imagine Thomas trekking in the wilderness to spot birds before sunset.

"No, but he read somewhere that there were rare birds in these forests and that bird watchers were interested in them, so he just stuck it in the ad. Obviously driving a hard sell on the cabin."

"Maybe he thought these mosquitoes were small birds?" Gabriel joked as he whacked one with his hand flat against his leg, leaving behind a small black and red stain. "Got you," he muttered.

"Maybe," Frank said, still laughing. "Us city boys can barely tell the difference. I mean, Thomas is good with the lawnmower, but I can barely find my way around the garden."

"What am I not?" Thomas asked from behind them. He sat next to Frank and handed him a cold beer. A second later, Bruno slid down beside Gabriel. His breath smelled of fresh beer and his lips were cold against his own.

"Neither of us are very good at this outdoorsy country life," Frank said between the small kisses he planted on Thomas.

"Huh?" Thomas's attempt to look insulted was ripped apart by chuckles a few seconds later. "My hedge trimming is legendary. And I'm very good with the local wildlife."

"You really aren't! You can pretend all you want, but you have no idea how to trim hedges—or herd sheep."

Thomas shrugged. "There are other values to life. Other values and other skills."

"Renting this cabin was actually my idea," Gabriel blurted like he was trying to avert a brewing argument. Bruno chuckled and stroked his arm. "Usually Bruno does all the work, coming up with places to go and what to do and all that. But he was busy, and I was getting wound up over all his crazy plans. We needed to get away from the asphalt and smell and the city noise and find somewhere new—a fresh start.

"This place turned up incidentally when I was searching for something else. I wanted a house with a pool facing the sea, the Mediterranean or the Adriatic, and then Bruno started talking about going somewhere with museums and art and landmarks so we could take Andreas on some kind of 'cultural journey'. We were on the edge of getting into this huge argument about it. Gabriel shot a questioning glance at Bruno, who just shrugged, with his damned cute little smile stilling lingering on his lips.

"And then your cabin turned up, and I said, 'OK, let's go there. I don't want to fight anymore now. Fuck the Mediterranean and the museums, let's just go to the Finnish forests.'" Bruno laughed behind him. His fingers were tickling his neck. "And then Bruno said, 'OK, let's go to the Med and spend a month beside a pool.' He was obviously pissed off, and I was about to start a fight, frustrated because he gave in so easily, and I was being salty because I didn't get my own way, ever."

"And then Lottie started wailing from their bedroom," Bruno said, "and you just stood up and went to her room."

"Then you booked the cabin and the rest is history." Gabriel leant his head back and pursed his lips for a kiss from Bruno.

"We won't even mention the fact that this place wasn't in Finland, and that there were absolutely zero flights to bring us anywhere near here, and the cost of flying was astronomical, and Andreas kept going on about the environmental impact, so we tried trains. I'd just had enough by that point, so I decided we would drive and see something on the way, not just let the world whizz by." Bruno was smiling with every word.

"We missed the first ferry, and the motel turned out to be a pizzeria, so we panicked and drove for twenty-four hours straight. Fuck all the best-laid plans." Gabriel couldn't even remember the horrible drive to get here. It was funny how the human brain worked.

"And now we get to do that drive all over again," Bruno lamented. "Almost twenty-four hours of whining and whinging and vomiting and tears."

Gabriel looked across the lake. The sun had disappeared behind the hills opposite them now, the lake shimmering in darker shades. "The cabin reminded me of where I used to spend the summers when I was a kid." He'd hardly mentioned that cabin to Bruno. The memories had been hidden for so many years, memories from a past he hadn't wanted to bring with him, another life, another person.

"We had a small holiday lodge just north of Berlin," Gabriel continued, his eyes locked on the horizon. The darkness of the forest on the opposite side met the black water, quietly merging into one body of dark matter. "It was my grandmother's. My parents wouldn't have been able to afford anything like that, but we used it every year. It was small, but I had my own room. I didn't have to share with my siblings like I did at home." He had to stop and breathe, too many emotions flooding back. He hadn't meant to start talking, not about things like this, but the feelings were overwhelming and he couldn't help himself.

"My room was really tiny," he continued, trying to ignore Bruno's warm body against his back. "But it faced the forest and felt like a little cave. Nobody could look inside, and I could close the door and put a chair in front of it and then I could be alone and do whatever I wanted."

He let his breath move in and out, remembering the pain and the fear when he had used a narrow scarf as binder under his grey T-shirt and had to come up with an excuse when his father asked what the heck he had done to his T-shirt when he'd been forced to come out for dinner. The scarf had no elasticity and was tied too tight, and he'd almost fainted before he could get back to his room and finally untie the knot that had violently dug into his armpit. He remembered the panic when the knot slipped too far behind his back and he pulled a tendon in his arm trying to untie and release it.

Bruno calmly played with his fingers, breathing warm air at his neck. The closeness was calming, and Gabriel felt like he could breathe again, which was something he'd not felt in a long time. There was truth to his hunch that this place possessed a touch of magic. Well, there was something in the air here that made him happy.

"I used to say I moved the furniture to draw," he said. "Just so I could be truly alone. That cabin was the first sense of freedom I'd ever had. The drawing bit was true too. I had a roll of cheap, slippery brown paper that I used to pull out and draw these huge pictures on. I had to use markers to get any colour on the paper at all, often permanent markers, so the chemical smell lingered in my room for days after."

"Could explain a lot, baby," Bruno said with a chuckle.

Gabriel poked him with his elbow. "Idiot."

Bruno smiled and kissed him lightly on the cheek, encouraging him to continue.

"When I saw the pictures of your cabin, I wanted to recreate the feeling of those holidays for my own kids. Give them some kind of space to breathe. Grow perhaps. I don't know."

"Did you manage it?" Frank asked, looking at the open lake and the fields around them, probably thinking how un-cave-like this place was.

"No!" Gabriel laughed. "But this was better." He raised his eyebrows. "You know, I kind of think we not only found the dream holiday home, but also the dream hosts."

"What?" Bruno thwacked his head lightly. "I mean, I agree, they are handsome dudes, but..."

"Not like that, you moron." He elbowed him again with a smile. "It feels like coming home here, like finding you guys and this place was fate. All meant to be. We found a family, a new one or another one. I don't know. I just kind of feel...you know. That we belong here. With you guys. Weird, I know but...I guess it's the beer talking again."

Frank pulled Thomas closer, the two of them squashed together like they were conjoined. They weren't looking at Gabriel now, they were leaning towards each other, so similar, like brothers, it occurred to him, both of them tall and fair yet, as he had learned, so different.

He let his thoughts drift back to the start of the summer, not only the cabin and the family, but the experiences and adventures for all of them, the nature, fresh air, the kids' camping trip, that bloody moose safari, sheep, wild boar, all the coffee they'd been drinking, alone, together, swimming in the lake. He was still warm from the sunburn on his chest when he forgot to apply sunscreen, so used to keeping his T-shirt on, and then he found himself swimming naked in the lake with the kids for the first time ever.

"What happened to your grandmother's place?" Thomas asked.

Gabriel swallowed and shook his head. "I don't know. I haven't seen my birth family for many years. They've never met Bruno or the kids. I haven't seen them since...since I stopped being their daughter." He swallowed again, trying to stop the tears, but it was too late. His face was wet, and his body was shaking from the uncontrollable sobs. Bruno held him tight, his arm stretched around him, always there, always solid, always watching him. But there was something else, too. Other hands, other smells, soft hair, more arms engulfing him, holding him, keeping him here.

"You have us now, Gabriel. None of you are bloody alone."

"We are here for you. Always."

"Jetzt hast du ja uns und wir sind immer für dich da."

"You are not alone."

"Family. You said it yourself. If you choose us? We choose you right back."

# Epilogue
# Halloween
# BRUNO

"You CAN BE friends and still kiss each other," Andreas snarled from behind a crisp packet as Bruno threw another bag of snacks into the shopping trolley.

Maria and Fredrik were out of earshot, and Bruno had taken a rare moment to try to make some sense of Andreas's frankly erratic behaviour.

"I'm just worried about you," he said quietly.

"I'm fine. Freddie is fine. It's all good." Andreas smirked and stuck out his tongue.

The past week had been intense, he could admit that. He loved having Maria and Fredrik here; he could admit that, too. The two of them had run into his arms at the airport, clinging to him all the way out of the arrivals hall, down to the car that he'd parked miles away. Both of them chattered excitedly about their journey and flying on their own and were obviously high on sugar from buying their own breakfast. On top of that, they stank from spraying each other with perfume samples in the arrivals Duty Free shop.

It had been worth it, though, just to see the smile on Andreas's face as Fredrik had stumbled awkwardly over the threshold into the flat, falling exhaustedly into his son's outstretched arms.

"Freddie?" Bruno asked, raising a suspicious eyebrow. *When had it become Freddie? What happened to Fredrik?* He couldn't get a grip on these two boys and their messy friendship. He knew they talked every day, be it on chats or in gaming environments. He also knew that they fell out and made up on a daily basis that was easily read between the lines of Andreas's moods. Bruno saw the looks the two of them exchanged, the smiles and the laughter. Andreas couldn't shut up about Fredrik. They were clearly friends. Great friends. Definitely friends of the worrying kind, knowing what Bruno knew about heartbreak and figuring out who you were.

*Leaving the gym now*, the text from Gabriel said. His poor husband seemed to be permanently exhausted from working full time again, and he'd pulled a hamstring training for the Teachers' Association Christmas Marathon, which was nuts. Bruno kept telling him that. So now Bruno had to work over the autumn holiday, since Gabriel had the week off, being a jammy teacher again, and on top of that, he'd volunteered to organise this Halloween party for the five kids in his care while Gabriel conveniently popped off to the gym. This week had been...yeah. Intense.

"Papi, can we get more Hanuta? And we need at least two packets of Duplo to make that skeleton cake, and then, if we get some of these mixed sweets, we can use the googly eyes and marshmallows for the face. We got Maria some Milchschnitte—she's never had them. She doesn't even know what they are! We have to buy some so she can try them. We got two packets."

Lilly was jumping up and down, her hands bulging with sweet packets, and Lottie was still riding on Maria's back like some clingy baby.

"Mind Maria's back," Bruno lectured, getting a typical eye roll from Maria as she threw a packet of salad in the trolley.

"For dinner," she said, side-eyeing the frozen pizzas Bruno had loaded up. He had a clinic tomorrow morning, and he was too exhausted to cook anything that didn't slide effortlessly from the packet into the oven.

"We need breakfast foods too. The two of you finished the cereal this morning like there was a national shortage of food coming on." He snickered as Fredrik slung his arm over Andreas's shoulders and Andreas grinned like a fool.

"We are growing young men. You can't kind of survive on just *one* bowl of cereal in the morning," he declared, smiling like it was the funniest thing in the world.

"So you have five bowls each, emptying out every box in the cupboard."

"Cereal is nice!"

"You should be eating porridge," Bruno countered. "Fills you up for the day, and none of those nasty sugars."

"Eugh." Fredrik grimaced. "Thomas makes us porridge when he's forgotten to buy cereal. He even makes it before my early football practice, and it's like cardboard and water. Your cereals are much nicer."

"Can we buy some of this chocolate and orange muesli?" Andreas asked, picking up at box from the shelf. "Looks nice."

"It's like having dessert for breakfast." Bruno sighed, as Lottie grabbed a packet of some children's branded cereal off the shelf and threw it in the trolley shouting, "Wir sehen uns zum Frühstück!" mimicking the ads on TV.

"No more junk food!"

"We still need dip, and soft drinks," Maria reminded him, scanning the list in Bruno's hand.

"Do you really need biscuits?" he asked, and Maria nodded her head. *Ah. OK.*

"What about some soup?" he suggested. It was Halloween, after all, and that apparently meant soup and shit. He'd read that somewhere. "We could serve bread rolls and butter and soup."

"You are so grown up, Papi." Andreas laughed. "Nobody wants soup. A few pizzas for the oven, crisps and sweets and cakes. It'll be epic. You and Vati can have soup and eat it in your bedroom out of sight. Can you please at least leave the apartment for an hour or two?"

"Honestly? Again?" Bruno sighed. It had been an ongoing issue since the Norwegian kids had arrived. Gabriel would've preferred to stay, and Bruno couldn't say he blamed him. The three of them and their friends on their own partying in their flat with no parental supervision—well, technically they wouldn't be alone, and Andreas had so far been the perfect tour guide, dragging Fredrik and Maria around all his favourite places, while Lilly and Lottie sulked and whinged at home. Gabriel had even resorted to putting the twins into the school holiday club for a day to cheer them up, which had only meant they'd cried their eyes out at not being with Maria for a whole day.

"Lils and Lots are going to Grandma's overnight," Andreas tried, locking eyes with Bruno. "You could go to the cinema. Vati wants to see that new Alexander Fehling film. You could take him."

"I could watch a film at home. In bed. With Vati," Bruno countered, giving his son a firm stare.

"You could be a decent, trusting father and cut us some slack," Andreas returned.

"I trust you, and I know you'll be fine, but I can't just go out and leave all of you in the flat for a few hours with live candles and who knows how many other people that you've invited to this party."

"I met Ingo and Hans and Guzman yesterday," Maria cut in, always trying to be the diplomat among them. "They were really nice. I promise I will keep the guys under control."

"Guzman," Fredrik sung, with a wink. "*Guuuzman*."

"He flirted with Maria to the point that she threatened to kick him in the nuts." Andreas laughed. "She was hardcore. I bet you anything he is crushing hard on you now."

"See? I can't leave," Bruno said, flicking his fringe out of his eyes. "Someone has to be there to protect Maria's virtue."

"What does that word mean? What you just said? *Virtue*?" Lottie asked, skipping alongside the trolley. "I am learning so much English with Maria here."

"Never mind," Bruno dismissed quickly, sending the girls on a hunt for yoghurt and butter, while Andreas and Fredrik were looking at packs of cheese with far too much excitement for Bruno's liking. No way were they discussing dairy products. They were hatching a plan to get him and Gabriel out of the house. He would have to stand firm, not fall for any of their tricks.

He stopped and fished his phone out of his coat pocket, scanning the messages.

> *Gabriel: I'm home, and the place is trashed. Where are you and all those gorgeous kids of ours?*

> *Frank: I haven't heard from the kids all day. Are they still alive or have you had enough and finally thrown them all under a bus?*

*Frank: Or a tram. Forgot that you guys have trams too. Have they spent all their cash? Let me know if they need more, I can top up their cards if needed.*

*Frank: How are the party plans coming along? Get Fredrik to bake some bread rolls. He's good at baking.*

*Mama: Can't wait to see the girls tomorrow night. I've made stew for them and bought juice. Am I allowed to give them sweets? I just wanted to check. I don't want you to get upset at me if I feed them sweets.*

*Thomas: All good?*

It *was* all good. He was doing good, he thought, as he threw some bottles of red wine in the trolley. They were all on special offer, and to be honest he was too exhausted to even check what they were. He would be needing a glass or two tonight, once he'd successfully negotiated the tram home with a trolley full of shopping and five children and himself.

He threw another bottle of red in for good measure and took a deep breath before calling for the boys to keep up. The girls were nowhere to be seen, and the boys hadn't even noticed him pushing the trolley past them towards the checkouts.

He texted them all instead, pushing the words into his phone a little too vigorously. *CHECKOUTS, NOW!* he sent into the group chat and laughed at the boys, who simultaneously checked their phones. Of course, neither of them moved. He started unloading the wine onto the belt and nodded politely at the checkout lady.

It had been a long week. A long day.

Home. Wine. Sleep.

\*\*\*

Two days later, Bruno still hadn't slept, and living in a flat with five children who just wouldn't sleep at night was taking its toll on his sanity. At least Lilly and Lottie had been safely deposited with his mother, who'd looked ecstatic at the thought of some alone time with her granddaughters, while Bruno yawned and coughed and blew his nose, wishing that he could throw himself down on his old childhood bed and sleep for an hour or two.

Instead, he and Gabriel were sitting at the Indian restaurant down the road from their flat, picking at poppadoms and giggling like schoolboys at the complicated menu, hoping that whatever they ordered wouldn't make their taste buds explode.

"I want the lamb chops and a side of chilli paneer," Gabriel decided and slammed the menu down onto the table, while Bruno flicked a well-aimed piece of poppadom at him.

"I'm sticking with korma," he admitted, feeling defeated.

"You're such a child." Gabriel laughed. "Korma is like the Happy Meal of Indian cuisine. It's pretty much cream and sugar with some token chicken thrown in."

"But it's nice, and I won't have heartburn for the rest of the week," Bruno muttered and smothered another piece of poppadom in yoghourt raita. He spilled half of it down his chin, again, making Gabriel roll his eyes and dig out his phone.

"Maria says everything is under control," he said, his fingers working across the screen.

"Thank God for Maria. Those boys are still on a different planet, no clue what is going on around them."

"Babe," Gabriel said, putting his phone back down. "You do realise they're probably having sex?"

"What?" Bruno coughed, then laughed at Gabriel's blush. "Of course they're having...well, I don't think they're having actual sex. I don't really want to think about it. For all we know, Fredrik hasn't slept on that mattress on the floor. It's full of junk and bags."

"They *are* having sex. I changed the sheets this afternoon, trying to make the house presentable."

"Ah." Bruno laughed. "Shit, this is awkward. They're still kids."

"Yeah, but Andreas is responsible, and I know he has any supplies he might need. I bought him loads a while back, although..." Gabriel whispered, "I didn't find any evidence of wrappers or condoms."

"We're not supposed to go looking for shit like that," Bruno whispered back. "We're supposed to be cool and responsible. Andreas is almost eighteen. He will be having sex, at some point anyway, and I'd rather he did it safely at home than in some dirty back alley. Don't go and search his room. That's the kind of stuff he'll blow a fuse about."

"I know, I don't want to. But the bed was kind of...yeah."

"I don't want to know." Bruno squirmed. "We're having dinner. Can we talk about something that doesn't involve bodily fluids?"

Gabriel laughed. "How was work?"

Bruno sighed. "Full of bodily fluids. Dr Aziz and I removed an anal abscess before lunch, and then did a vaginoplasty after. It was a good day. Interesting."

"Babe, we're having dinner." Gabriel looked a little green.

"Then let's talk about something more palatable."

"Like sex?" Gabriel laughed, and Bruno threw another piece of poppadom at him.

"No, like Christmas. Do you think it's achievable, what Frank was saying?"

"Yes, I mean, it will be bloody expensive, but if we find decent flights..."

"And there're no hotel costs. We should offer to pay for half the food, and we can bring sleeping bags and stuff."

"We won't need five sleeping bags. Andreas won't need one."

"We said we wouldn't talk about sex."

"No sex."

"We need to think about Christmas presents. We need something for Fredrik and Maria, and then something nice for Frank and Thomas."

"Like what? I hate presents. Bloody glass bowls or vases or dust traps like that?"

"No, we can get them some Jägermeister and a couple of bottles of German Riesling perhaps. Something local."

"Nice and thoughtful." Bruno sighed. "Also boring."

"I can't think of anything else."

"We haven't even said yes yet."

"Well, that's something we can tick off the list then." Gabriel picked up his phone as the waiter approached to take their order.

Bruno ordered, probably pronouncing all the names wrong and hoping he'd got it all right, despite the waiter assuring him that nothing they'd ordered was too spicy. They'd eaten here before, and Bruno knew the drill. If you asked for non-spicy items, they'd throw a few chillies on there for fun. Gabriel loved it. Bruno's stomach not so much.

"Hey!" Frank's face was staring at him from the screen in Gabriel's outstretched hand. "You're coming for Christmas then?"

"Yeah?" Bruno grinned as Thomas's naked form whizzed past the screen behind Frank.

"What?" Frank said, looking behind him as Bruno exploded with laughter.

"You were shagging. Sorry to interrupt."

"Nah, we were pretty much done." Frank yawned like it was totally normal, while Thomas could be heard shouting something in the background.

"How are the boys?" Frank asked.

"Weird." Bruno shook his head. "We have no clue what's going on, but they're happy, and Maria assures me all is going well and they're having a ball. We haven't seen the police or the fire brigade approach the flat, and we have curry and naan bread coming our way in a few minutes, so I'm a happy man."

Gabriel turned his phone back. "How did your meeting with Terje go?" he asked, and Frank launched into a long explanation about publishing rights and proposals and a pilot and finding a scriptwriter—things that no doubt Gabriel would explain in fewer words so it would make sense. Frank had not only landed a major publishing contract but was also planning a documentary series. Things were going well, and a film contract to follow on from *The Letters to Bella* was something they were now actively pursuing, should the right offer be made. With Thomas still at home after accepting a redundancy payout, he'd slid effortlessly into project managing it all, leaving Frank to handle getting the diaries onto a hard drive, and the Norwegians were making the most of their sudden childless state.

"We would obviously contribute to the food and board," Gabriel continued on. Bruno grabbed the phone back as Thomas's face filled the screen.

"Are you sure you want this? It's a lot to deal with, having us all come for Christmas," he said seriously.

Thomas laughed and shook his head. "It will be mayhem. Total mayhem, but isn't that what Christmas is about? Family and fun and food and a big fuck-off Christmas tree? Frank is already making lists of what to cook, and you *know* Fredrik and Maria will be over the moon to have you all back.

You're family, after all. And anyway, why would you even want to be in Berlin over Christmas? We have snow. Sledding. Skiing. Beer. We have good beer."

"Bah." Bruno laughed. "Your beer is like coloured water. I'll be shipping over a crate of Weissbier and some Jägermeister so we can have proper Christmas drinks.

"Bah yourself." Thomas huffed in mock disgust. "Weissbier is like piss-coloured marsh water. We have IPA. Gløgg. Gingerbread biscuits. Proper shit."

"We will bring Lebkuchen. You guys don't even know what you're missing out on. And marzipan!"

"We have marzipan," Frank protested. "I make my own. It's kick-ass good."

"And anyway, that Gløgg thingy is like our Gluhwein. Same shit."

"It's not," Gabriel argued. "It's like sweet, warm juice."

"We put vodka in ours. Spirits. Make it hard."

"We are not getting drunk with the kids."

"We are *so* getting drunk without the kids. We'll let Frank's parents take the kids to their cottage for the day, and we can get pissed and go on a pub crawl." Thomas suddenly had a dreamy look in his eyes, and Frank's face appeared on the screen again.

"We would love to have you. We miss you. It's been ages, and I mean, *come on!* The kids will love it. We have proper snow, and we live in a proper house, so there's plenty of space. We have a guest room and an extra living room and all, and the office, and you know the kids will all bundle up in their rooms."

"Yeah." Bruno laughed and met Gabriel's eyes.

"And remember," Frank added, "we have Wi-Fi. Real, working Wi-Fi."

"We're coming!" Gabriel decided, grabbing the phone back. "We're a family and we're spending Christmas together."

"Yay!" Frank cheered from hundreds of miles away, and Bruno smiled.

*Family, eh?* Well, he supposed they were. He looked over at Gabriel, who was gabbling into the phone, his eyes wide open, full of sparkle and happiness. He smiled.

Because life was good. Life was really good, despite it sometimes being a total fuck-up. He was loved. He loved. He had a family and some really good people around him.

His phone lit up with a message, making his breath hitch as he read it.

*Maria: All is good, but we burnt the pizzas and the fire alarm is going off like crazy. Do you know how to switch it off? There's no button on the one in the kitchen, and it's driving us all mad. Help?*

Life was good. Sometimes it was better than other times. And sometimes the little lies were good too.

*No idea. Open the windows and stick some earplugs in your ears?*

He chuckled and nodded at the waiter delivering their food, then replied properly.

*Red button on the wall panel by the stove. Don't worry about it. Order some takeaway pizzas if they're inedible. Andreas has the app on his phone. Have fun!*

"We're going to Oslo!" Gabriel shrieked and put down the phone.
"And we are NOT driving this time."
"Hell no. Flights and drinks this time. I never want to see that ferry again. The car still reeks of vomit."
"Speaking of which, how's your food?"
"Nice and warming." Gabriel laughed, shoving in another mouthful.
"Extra spicy vindaloo." Bruno chuckled. "I'm not kissing you tonight."
"Indian Happy Meal for you then." Gabriel stuck his fork in Bruno's bowl and took a bite. "Yum. Sugared chicken."
"Fuck off."
Life...
Life was good.

*The end. But then....*

# Life is Right Here

"We're going to have a brilliant Christmas, Andreas. Just like it was ten years ago, all of us together," Vati said, placing steaming cups of coffee in front of us. "We're just pointing out that you and Fredrik always had something special, and you haven't seen each other for years. It will be lovely for you to reconnect."

"Reconnecting is fine. We can discuss college life versus German nursing schools, drink Jägerbombs and watch weird Norwegian shit on TV. Christmas will be thrilling."

"Andreas..." Vati warned as Lottie burst into giggles.

"You adore Fredrik. Still. I can see it in your eyes. You go all panic-stricken and weird when we even mention Freee—"

"Fredrik has a girlfriend in America. Maria hates my guts. Frank and Thomas will whip my butt for not visiting over summer, and anyway, I have to buy them a big present to bribe them to even talk to me."

Vati smiled. "Frank and Thomas love you like a son, and they will just hug the shit out of you as usual."

"Alongside Maria's boyfriend, and Fredrik's girlfriend. It will be a delightful group hug." I snarled.

"Fredrik's girlfriend isn't coming. I told you that," Vati said sternly. He was pissed off with me already, and we hadn't even had breakfast.

"Whatever." I huffed.

*Awkward* was the word I was looking for. This whole thing was going to be super awkward. Because they always were. And Fredrik? My world used to spin around the strange, blonde boy who was my best friend for a few years. He lit up my life. Then he fucked off. Well, he fucked off because I told him to. I was stupid and scared. I think he was too.

*Awkward.* That wasn't even the start of what this Christmas was going to be like.

***

*Life is Right Here* takes place ten years after the end of *Life is Good and Other Lies*. Everyone has lived a little better. Loved a little harder. Lost and found, over and over again. But how do you move on when you're supposed to have grown up, but you're still the same person you were ten years ago? How do you find someone to love when your heart will always belong to someone else?

But most of all, how do you keep living, when your world is slowly crumbling in front of your eyes, and there is nothing you can do to stop it.

Life is right here. And you just have to somehow live it.

*Life is Right Here* will be out in December 2022. Pre-order here. mybook.to/Lifeisrighthere

**Magdalena di Sotru**

**Magdalena di Sotru** is an information security and data protection enthusiast from Norway. She is a mother of two and wife of one as well as a long-established fanfic writer. Her favourite food is (actually) salads (without mayo), her favourite guilty pleasure is fresh bakery goods (and that explains why everyone would think the salad was a lie). She knows her way around knitting, lock picking and skydiving (all at about equal skill levels – go figure). *Life is Good* is her first novel.

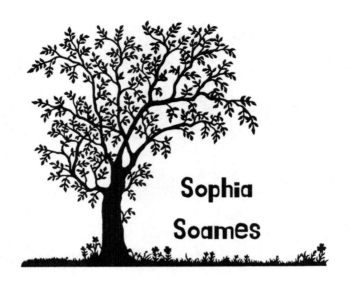

**Sophia Soames** should be old enough to know better but has barely grown up. She has been known to fangirl over TV shows, has fallen in and out of love with more pop stars than she dares to remember, and has a ridiculously high-flying (un-)glamourous real-life job.

Her long-suffering husband just laughs at her antics. Their children are feral. The dogs are too.

She lives in a creaky old house in rural London, although her heart is still in her native Scandinavia.

Discovering that the stories in her head make sense when written down has been part of the most hilarious midlife crisis ever, and she hopes it may long continue.

Linktr.ee/sophiasoames

**Life is Good and Other Lies**

## Magdalena:

Sophia and I started writing this story during spring 2019 and spent the following six months knee deep in Frank, Thomas, Bruno and Gabriel's world. It was a massive ball-throwing game of taking turns in writing chapters, with various plots and cliffhangers being hurled at the other, and four different POVs didn't help at all. Sophia still hadn't discovered offline mode in Google docs, so it was always a battle to make sure the shared text was actually up to date with Sophia's Word doc (since Sophia tended to write a lot when airplane mode should be on). Magdalena soon force-taught Sophia to use Google docs after a panicky episode of not having saved her work. Strangely, our co-writing became blissfully undramatic after that.

Magdalena stuck to writing Thomas and Frank throughout, and Sophia wrote Gabriel and Bruno. We continuously edited each other's chapters, making sure we saved important points and got the cliffhangers we needed. Most of all, we made sure the story *never* followed the circa ten-chapter plot line we'd started with.

We used Pinterest boards to get a feel for how we viewed the houses, landscapes and colours, and had many deep discussions about the correct use of commas and quotation marks. Luckily, we are just a Norwegian and a Swedish writer with no deeper skills in zum beispiel German typography!

In the end, we view the world in a pretty similar way: a forest is a forest and wouldn't a crazy moose safari be a nice experience?

Magdalena did, however, kill a lot of Sophia's *alots* during the process. *Alots* are evil. Magdalena also killed a car, but Sophia saved that wreck of an error and got us back on track.

We have written several stories together (so there may be more to come). Finally, the funniest thing about writing with Sophia is that she is completely unpredictable yet still coherent. (Sometimes the coherence needs a little push to be obvious.)

## Sophia:

That makes Sophia sound like a complete nightmare to write with. (Which is absolutely true. She is.)

Magdalena and I started fangirling over each other's fanfics a few years back, and I always loved her quirky stories. I mean, she's the writer who wrote a whole fic about GDPR...and Coffee. (That fic is awesome, by the way.)

We chatted, gifted each other ridiculous ramblings, and wrote fanfics for each other's fanfics. And then Magdalena insisted I join her in a multi-author experience on Ao3 writing in Swedish. That was probably the hardest thing I have ever done. Anyway, after that? There was no going back.

*Life is Good* started with a silly prompt, an overenthusiastic seemingly impossible venture. But then we are who we are, and it was actually quite an interesting idea. For me personally, I loved the intrigue of trying to figure out your marriage, your future and your past. It was also a massive learning curve involving some very interesting research, and parts of this story have changed and evolved from the early versions as we read up on and expanded our knowledge. Massive thank-you to Author Roe Horvat who let me ask him all kinds of questions to ensure our characters were more realistic and truer to themselves.

While Fredrik and Maria were already well-known original characters in Magdalena's fanfic world, they were still young kids, and it was brilliant fun to see them evolve into adults. Andreas, Lilly and Lottie were brand-new characters who took on more of a role than we had anticipated when we started writing. Frank, Gabriel, Thomas and Bruno were all original fresh takes on fanfic staples, but since this story was an alternative universe, there is barely more than a subtle hint of who they once were. The story is original work from start to finish. Because as you know, I can't stick to a plan to save my life. And as Magdalena said earlier, we started with a loose ten-chapter plan. That plan? Neither of us can even remember what it was. (But of course Google Docs could always dig it up. Because Google.) Instead we ended up with this.

The way we write is a constant game of challenging each other, with many futile attempts at throwing the story off track. Just as we think we know where the story is going, the other one throws in another curveball and shoots it off on a tangent. Often I would pick up Magdalena's chapters and swear loudly under my breath wondering how on earth I could get this back on track. And the same goes for Magdalena. Most of the time, she would rein me in, shouting in capitals and going no, no, NOOO! in the margins. We got there in the end.

In December 2019, Sophia texted Magdalena and said, *Hey! What about a Christmas epilogue? Since Gabe and Bruno are going to Oslo for Christmas?* Magdalena promptly replied (from being knee deep in work, kids and Christmas preparations), saying, *You want it? You write it.*

She should have known better than to challenge me, and before we knew it, we had ten chapters of something neither of us could have anticipated. So if you want more—more Fredrik, more Andreas and more of everyone— ten years later? Then sit tight.

**Life is Right Here** will follow shortly. mybook.to/Lifeisrighthere

Massive thank-you to Karen Meeus, who expertly sorted, organised and straightened out our glaring mistakes, to editor Debbie McGowan, who had her hands full with this manuscript and still waved her magic over our words, and to Suki Fleet for her eagle-eyed proofing. We both wish to extend a heartfelt thank-you to Mary Vitrano who was our Italian linguistic advisor, and Dieter Moitzi who supervised our German, making sure Lilly and Lottie made sense. Dieter should also be given credit for the *Sexchoklad* bit. Made me laugh, so of course, I had to put it in there for the amusement of anyone who has ever visited the Nordic countries.

Finally a huge thank you hug to Author Vin George who sensitivity read for us. Your input was invaluable.

Thank you for reading. We hope you loved these people as much as we do.

Magdalena di Sotru and Sophia Soames. October 2022

STORIES TO MAKE YOUR HEART FLY · Sophia Soames

717 Miles
717 Miles Christmas

*The Scandinavian Comfort Series*
Little Harbour
Open Water
Baking Battles

In this Bed of Snowflakes We Lie
The Naked Cleaner

*The Chistleworth series*
Custard and Kisses
Ship of Fools
This Thing with Charlie

*The London Love Series*
BREATHE
EXHALE
TASTE
SLEEP (coming soon)
SKIN and BONES (coming soon)

Force Majeure
Life is Good and Other Lies
Life is Right Here

*Short stories*
What If It All Goes Right
Viking Airlines
Honest

Printed in Great Britain
by Amazon

14496101R00180